Morning In The Land

Books by
JESSICA NELSON NORTH

Poetry
A PRAYER RUG
THE LONG LEASH
DINNER PARTY

Criticism
INTRODUCTION TO PAINTINGS

Novels
ARDEN ACRES
MORNING IN THE LAND

Morning In The Land

By

JESSICA NELSON NORTH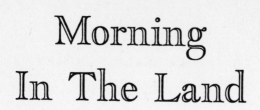

THE GREYSTONE PRESS
NEW YORK

PS3525
A1977M6

TO MY FATHER,
DAVID WILLARD NORTH,
WHOSE MEMORY HAS SUPPLIED MUCH
OF THE MATERIAL FOR THIS BOOK.

Morning In The Land

Part One

I

IN MAY of the year 1840, the schooner *Alice Rand* lay at anchor beside the yellow wharf of Milwaukee. The waves lapped against her stern as she nosed up into the quiet water between the piling to northward and the piers of the dock. Sailors and Indians had unloaded her mixed cargo and now lumber from the Pittsburgh sawmills lay piled with window glass from Buffalo, while codfish and herring from Maine mingled their smells with those of cinnamon, ginger and sassafras. The few passengers who had come on the schooner, and who stood with their luggage at the side of the wharf, seemed unwilling to break their last connections with the East and set their feet on Wisconsin soil.

Laurent Solomon Juneau came striding down the planks with the air of a first citizen. He walked up to the sailors, who were beginning to straggle toward shore.

"Whereabouts is the master of this vessel?" he asked.

He had adopted Milwaukee when it was little more than a mud-wallow, wild, unprepossessing, with a trader's shack and a few wigwams on the bank. The wharf, the road to the wharf, the village at the other end of the road were products of his hope and enthusiasm. He shook the graying curls from his high forehead and looked along the dock till he saw a short, red-faced man hurrying toward him.

"Captain Elijah Barnes, at your service, Mr. Juneau," the man said, bowing.

"A good afternoon to you. What are you loading for return cargo, Captain?"

"Mostly furs, Sir, but I'm not partial. Whatever offers."

"Could you find room for two cartloads of pig-lead?"

The captain looked at his craft, riding high, relieved of her freight, and made a momentary calculation.

"I'll ship it. How came the lead to Milwaky?"

"Out of Sugar River by way of Fort Atkinson, Mr. Barnes. The drivers blazed their own trace."

Excitement lay behind the calm words of the two men. If lead from the western diggings could be shipped from Milwaukee, their fortunes were made. Mr. Juneau would own an important port. Lake traffic would prosper. Heretofore the miners had shipped by Mississippi River packet to New Orleans, where the metal was reloaded for the Atlantic coast.

"I'll take it!" Captain Elijah said again, striking his hands together.

"Good. The drivers will be down from my trading-post directly."

6

Mr. Juneau turned to go, but was stopped by one of the passengers. The stranger made an odd appearance, even in this new country which seemed to attract oddities. He was so tall he towered above all the others. His hair, under an outlandish round hat, was a silvery blond and his eyes were a piercing blue. He wore a fringed shawl and loose trousers tucked into high cowhide boots.

"Didst mention Fort Atkinson?" he asked in a booming bass voice. His manner was stern.

"I did, Sir."

"Didst say the 'ighway were clear to westward?"

"Oh, there's no highway as yet. Only a trace through the forest. To my mind, the drivers will do well to get back again."

"Ah!" said the stranger, folding his arms under the shawl.

"Are you aiming to reach the Rock River country?" Solomon Juneau asked.

The blond man made no reply, being forestalled by his wife who came up and curtseyed.

"Please, is there a *hinn?* For my lads are fagged from the journey and we've a deal of plunder, chests and boxes and such-like to be conveyed."

"A what? Oh, an inn!" Solomon said, smiling. "Our taverns are overcrowded, Ma'am, but you can stay at my house till you have other accommodations."

Ann Wentworth was used to smiles and acts of kindness. They had come her way ever since she left Derby-

shire as a tribute to her rosy face and rounded curves.
Now she introduced herself to Mr. Juneau and told
him her husband's name was Thomas. She returned his
look of admiration with innocent interest, taking in the
good tailoring of his suit and the good silk of his cravat. Her two boys stared up at him steadily, the older
with blue eyes, the younger with brown. Mr. Juneau
winked at the little fellow, who carefully winked back
before hiding his face in his mother's skirt.

"If you'll come with me, Mr. Wentworth, we'll get
your goods to a wagon. Are all these boxes yours?"

"Aye. Nine there be."

Nine boxes of stout English manufacture, corded
and nailed for the long voyage from Holmesfield. They
contained all that could be brought along of the life
this family had known in Derbyshire. On each box
Thomas had tacked an inventory, written in flourishing
script. The smallest read:

> 8 chair cussions
> teapot and cosey
> 4 scirts
> 8 pair wollen hose

One chest held sixteen scythes of Wolstenholm make,
bought in Sheffield at a good price but likely to bring
still more in America, where prairie grass must be cut.
When one of Mr. Juneau's dock-hands began to raise
this box, Thomas glanced quickly at his wife. She
herded her boys before her and followed the scythes
closely along the wharf.

To north and south the shoreline of Lake Michigan stretched swampily away, dotted with hummocks of marsh-grass, wild-flag and rushes. The road to the village crossed the marsh on logs laid side by side in the muck. Over this corduroy the cart bumped heavily, carrying the Wentworth family and their luggage up to higher land. The smallest member of the group lay on his stomach across a box, looking down at his father and Mr. Juneau, who were walking. His red cheeks shook like molds of jelly. He stared solemnly at the spreading horns of the oxen, at the yellow cowslips which fringed the corduroy. His mother spoke to him gently.

"Do-ant let the box take thee in the stummick, Dick. 'Twill give thee hiccups."

"I like hiccups. They be jolly."

"Coom now. Sit oop fine and straight like thy brother 'Arry."

Harry Wentworth sat beside his mother with a serious, responsible air. His thoughts were of practical matters.

"Will there be beds, Mother?" he whispered.

For three months they had been sleeping on wooden shelves, first on the sailing ship which carried them across the Atlantic, then on the *Alice Rand*. On the ocean voyage every high sea had rolled someone out of bed. On the lakes the dining-salon had been flanked by curtained cupboards for berths, so that wakers and sleepers disturbed each other with inappropriate noises.

"Aye. Beds there'll be, I don't doot," Ann replied cheerfully.

She felt less sure when they drew up at the door of the Juneau house. From within, three dogs rushed out barking, followed by groups of children till she had counted twelve.

Twelve children, and the house smaller than her own cottage in Holmesfield. Two rooms and a loft, that was all. She could not know that Solomon's half-Menominee wife would bear him nineteen heirs, and that not until the birth of the sixteenth would he build a larger house. Where the man kept all his fine clothes and how he managed to entertain strangers, no one could understand. Ann saw his wife in the doorway and climbed down from the wagon. So did the boys, who were greeted by the twelve children and lured away.

When the luggage had been put down, Thomas took a wallet from beneath his shawl.

"How much is't?" he asked, fumbling with a bill.

"Nothing at all, Sir. The men are in my employ." Mr. Juneau waved a hand and oxen, cart and driver began to vanish toward the wharf. Thomas frowned.

"I can well afford to pay."

"Certainly, but I can't take money for what's to my own advantage. It's my business to encourage settlers here. Besides, the Indians are of my wife's tribe."

At this Thomas relaxed, and was about to put away his wallet when Solomon held out his hand.

"Let me see that money!" he said sharply, and then, "How much of this stuff have you?"

Plainly the Englishman thought it was none of Juneau's affair. He looked haughty and only replied after some hesitation:

"Two thousand pound it were in English gold. Likely 'tis worth more here, for they told me I'd profit in the exchange."

"Who told you that?"

"The bankers as met the boat."

"Scoundrels!" Mr. Juneau muttered. "They should have been pushed off the dock."

Ann clasped her hands together.

"Is aught wrong with the notes, then? For we meant to buy 'ouse and land with it and all. 'Tis every bit we 'ave in the world."

"My poor woman, it wouldn't buy you a sack of flour. Printed paper. That's all it is! Madam, your husband has been taken in by Yankee sharpers like many another honest man. It's the curse of this free country that such rogues go unhung."

He spoke bitterly and turned his eyes away from the dismay he had planted in her pretty face. There had been too many penniless newcomers, and here was one who would have been a substantial citizen, brought to poverty by the Yankees, for whom Mr. Juneau had no love. Thomas Wentworth could have bought a county with his gold. Two thousand pounds! Now he must be a poor squatter like the rest.

The Englishman was looking unconvinced.

"Be there a bank in this village?" he asked.

"I'm chief bank here and chief banker, Mr. Wentworth. The currency is in my pockets and in my strong box at the Milwaukee House. What I tell you is the truth, man! If you gave me a thousand of those bills I could only use them to light my fire. And you'll find no more bankers betwixt here and Galena."

Thomas Wentworth stood for several minutes in meditation. Then he turned slightly toward Ann, who came to him and put her small hand through the unyielding crook of his elbow. Mr. Juneau had expected outcries or tears, but he was mistaken. The man's eyes grew more brilliantly blue. The woman gazed steadfastly toward the west. When they had come inside the house, Thomas walked to the hearth and slowly opened his wallet above the glowing coals.

2

FIVE MONTHS LATER, little Dick Wentworth was
sitting in the doorway of a one-room log cabin not
far from the Milwaukee River. His arms were about the
neck of a collie dog. It was Sunday and he was ready
for church; his curls had been brushed around his
mother's index finger, his white collar was clean and his
nails trimmed. In the room behind him he could hear
his mother humming a tune. It hovered half out of
reach, growing thinner and louder at intervals as she
moved back and forth. Dick stroked his dog's neck and
stared out at the marshy wilderness on the other side
of the road. The marsh was a bad place, his mother
said. A little boy could get drowned there, dragged
down in the black water and tangled in the roots of
tamarack trees. Mosquitoes were thicker there too.
The cabin was high and dry, a house to thank God for,
not forgetting Mr. Juneau, who owned it.

Dick had heard his father speak harshly about Milwaukee, saying he would be glad to "get shed of sooch
a muck-hole," but he knew also that the name meant
"good land" in the Indian tongue. He tried to recon-

cile these facts. Perhaps the Indians liked to play in the white sand along the beach. He and Harry seldom were allowed to stray so far from home, but he remembered the sand as being very pleasant. His father's discontent made itself felt vaguely in his childish mind as a sense of impermanence. Nothing was sure. Nothing lasted. Soon this cabin would be left behind and lost, like the cottage in England, the ship where he and Harry had played on tilting decks, the barge on the Erie Canal, the lake schooner. He tightened his arms about the collie. No one should take Bije away.

"Do-ant let Bije lick thy face, Dick," his mother said, coming out. "He'll spot thy collar." She pulled the dog aside and took him into the cabin.

Ann was dressed for Sunday too. Her flaring bonnet showed two inches of dark hair at the front, parted in the middle and brushed to a gloss. Her best dress of blue merino was sprigged with white flowers, and billowed out over three petticoats. Dick looked down at her feet, which were buttoned into thin leather shoes.

"Be-ent thee wearing thy clogs, Mother?"

"Nay, lad. The going's dry." She mocked his big eyes by making her own large and round, and then stooping impulsively, buried her nose in his soft neck.

"Oh!" she said. "Mother's going to bite her lamb."

Dick laughed and wriggled, but he felt that he was getting too old for this baby game of theirs in which the wolf pursued and the sheep tried to get away.

Harry had gone on ahead with his father, who was

so afraid of being late to church that he was always too early. Dick and his mother took their time on the way, strolling along the trail toward the main part of the town. Soon they could see all of Milwaukee at once, including the wharf and the harbor. Nondescript houses were scattered about as if they were dice someone had thrown out. Houses of square-hewn beams, of peeled logs and logs with the bark still on them. Stone houses, chinked with mud. Thatched roofs, roofs of bark, every sort of makeshift architecture could be seen. There were even a few more costly buildings of pine planks from Pittsburgh, like the chapel to which Dick and his mother were going. The Wesleyan chapel was plain and square, clapboarded, surrounded by a picket fence.

"Mother," Dick asked, "what be a Catholic?"

"Why, lad, thou can see the Catholic church now. Yonder it be, with its gold cross on the steeple."

"Is't a wicked thing?"

"Nay, Dicky. Mr. Juneau's a Catholic, thou knows."

Dick sighed. He had heard his father call the Catholic church a place of sin, but now, since his mother said it was no such thing, why couldn't they go there? The gilt cross was so beautiful! Why must they go to a plain little church?

"A great many folk go in and oot there, Mother."

" 'Tis not for the glory of the world we go to church, lad. Where a few are gathered in his name the Lord will come."

At any rate it was too late now, Dicky thought. They were coming into the chapel yard. Now they were in the entranceway, passing the wash-basin and bucket, the Franklin stove. He saw Harry, sitting by his father on the men's side. Usually Dick had to sit with his mother, but he tugged away from her and she reluctantly let him go. He tiptoed down the aisle and climbed up by Harry, where he sat swinging his plump legs with an air of importance. His big brother gave him a look of surprise and displeasure, but this did not affect Dick's spirits in the least. By a familiar smell he realized that Harry was sucking a peppermint. With nudges and ingratiating smiles he got one for himself.

In front of them was the hymnal rack, and in front of that a row of men's backs with coats on them. Some of the coats were long ones with button-tails, some hung clumsily and were patched with cloth or leather. One man wore a shawl, another an old army overcoat of faded blue, with buff lapels and cuffs. Peering between the backs, the boys could see hats, resting on their owners' knees. There were one or two beavers, coonskin caps with tails, round felt hats from Germany and the knitted and tasseled caps of backwoodsmen. They grinned at this array, quite unconscious that some small Yankees at the end of the row were being amused by the hand-plaited straw on the knees of Thomas Wentworth.

The pastor was late. To fill in the time an elder

16

struck a pitch on his tuning fork while all stood to sing.
Dick recognized his father's favorite hymn:

> How tedious and tasteless the hours
> When Jesus no longer I see . . .

Thomas threw back his head with its mantle of ash-
blond hair, tapped the floor with his cowhide boot and
let his bass ring out:

> Sweet prospects, sweet birds and sweet flowers
> Have all lost their sweetness to me.

Dicky, looking up at his father, was keenly conscious of
his pleasure. No wonder he liked the song, the little
boy thought. It was all about sweet birds and flowers.
Glancing across the aisle he saw that his mother too
was watching Thomas. As he stood there, Dick felt a
new period of his life beginning, a time when he could
sit on the men's side. He was six years old.

The minister came hurrying in, wide-legged from
riding his Indian pony through twenty miles of forest.
He had been preaching in the Waukesha woods.
Mounting the platform he blew his nose loudly, and
then for several seconds busily cleared his throat. With
no other preamble he began:

*For God giveth to a man that is good in His sight,
wisdom and knowledge and joy but to the wicked He
giveth travail. Let us bow in prayer.*

Dick leaned his forehead against the hymnal rack
and felt the sharp edge of the wood. He pressed for-

ward more heavily so the mark would show after he sat up again. During the prayer he frequently took the hard peppermint out of his mouth, looked at it earnestly and put it back.

And lastly, O Lord, we beseech Thee, let the light of Thy countenance shine upon our President, Martin Van Buren, upon his goings out and his comings in, upon his risings up and his lyings down.

Dick's father stirred impatiently. He did not approve of President Van Buren, who was known to be a worldly man.

The sermon was a long one and the bench very hard. Harry turned the pages of a hymn-book, spelling out the simpler words with silent lips. Dick tied knots in his cotton handkerchief to make a rabbit with long ears. Over their heads the pastor's voice droned on:

Because thy rage against Me and thy tumult is come up into Mine ears, therefore will I put a hook in thy nose and a bridle in thy mouth and lead thee up in the way whence thou camest.

"Amen, Brother, Halleluiah!"

The voice of him crying in the wilderness, prepare ye the way of the Lord. Make straight in the desert a pathway for our God.

At any rate he understood that, Dick thought. The pathway was the trail, leading right past their cabin. He knew all about the wilderness too, and the voices crying in it. They cried all night long. Panthers, wolves, screech-owls and bob-cats. Sometimes they sounded like

angry children. His conviction was strengthened that
the Wentworths were the chosen people of God. Why,
His highway went almost through their front yard!
But—a hook in thy nose? He would have to ask
mother about that one.

He smelled the balmy breeze through the open window, the tallow on his father's boots, the peppermint
he had just finished eating. His curls fell over his face,
his head sank against Harry's arm. When they woke
him the sermon was done.

The Milwaukee cabin was made of split oak-rails,
caulked with mud and banked with rubbish on the outside to keep out the wind. Oiled paper made the three
small windows, and the one room was never very light.
In warm weather when the frames with the paper were
taken out, enough sunshine came in so Dick could see
the letters on the nine boxes—big black letters from
which he was learning to read.

> John Webb, Shipping Agent, Mersey Docks,
>   Liverpool.
> Quotations furnished.

The whole alphabet was there, with the exceptions
of x and z, which his mother supplied.

One of the boxes was their table now and four
smaller ones were chairs. One had been opened to take
out clothing, bedding and dishes. They used as few
articles as possible, because any day now they would be

going farther west. At first Dick's father and mother
had been stunned by the loss of their money. They had
not even the price of a pony on which Thomas could
ride to Hampstead Prairie, the English settlement in
the Rock River valley. The letter they had sent to Will
Beeson, their good friend at Hampstead, had never
been answered. Perhaps the returning lead-drivers had
forgotten to deliver it. Any reply would have gone the
long way around, by New Orleans and the Gulf, and
that took a long time and involved many chances of
accident. They themselves would have entered the
country by way of the gulf port, if Will had not written
them that yellow fever was very bad there. He thought
the Milwaukee road might be open by the time they
arrived in America, so they had taken a chance and
come to Milwaukee. It was not Will's fault that they
were stranded, but no more teams had come through
from the west.

Hampstead Prairie was ninety miles inland, and
seventy of that was unbroken forest and swamp.
Twenty miles west of Milwaukee the military road
from Fort Dearborn to Green Bay was a landmark,
and sometimes soldiers or circuit-riders from that road
passed the Wentworth cabin. For twenty miles there
was a faint trail with marks of pony's hooves and the
ashes of camp-fires.

Thomas had found plenty of work in Milwaukee.
His size and strength made him a valuable helper in a
country where much depended on muscle. Other immi-

grants were paid one dollar a day. Thomas demanded two and was worth it. He split logs, hauled water and helped in raising houses. By fall he had saved one hundred dollars and was ready to leave for Hampstead at once, but was delayed by a letter from his sister in England.

Jane Wentworth had a friend near Hampstead too, a young miller named Sam Weymouth. He had sent passage-money to Jane to come and be his wife. She had replied that she must wait until a sick cousin died, because she was to fall heir to a good lot of linen and china. The cousin lingered on, but Jane wrote Tommy that she could not last longer than December. Would they wait for her in Milwaukee? She said she would sail on an ocean steam-ship. Ann shook her head at this. It was just like Jenny to ignore all the stories of boilers blowing up and propellers fouled in mid-sea. It was like her too, to want the newest and best. A sailing-ship had been good enough for the rest of them. At any rate the cabin seemed the safest place to spend their first winter, warmer than any house they could quickly throw together in the western settlement. They decided to wait.

"Willy Beeson could be finding us a tract of land, for I'm told the Yankees are buying it all oop to sell for a profit," Thomas said.

"Aye, there's little Willy wouldn't do for us if he but knew," Ann replied. "Ah me! 'Tis a queer country. Here be we, and yonder be Will, and never a post-road between us."

"If God's willing I'll be my own post," Thomas resolved. "For I'll set out on foot so soon as ever 'tis spring."

"Tommy, I think thou'd best get thyself a guide."

"Nay, nay! I'll go it alone."

Well, he was stubborn, was Tommy. He would have nothing to do with the foreigners, and to him every man was a foreigner who was not English and a Wesleyan Methodist. Ann knew it would be no use to argue, so she set herself the task of finding out everything she could about the western settlement from the conversation of others. Once a week she went to the nearest trading-post for supplies, and there she deliberately eavesdropped while the trader measured out sugar, salt, flour and tea. Rough men eyed her from head to foot, enjoying her fresh color and pretty figure. Ann looked them over too, and sometimes they had to turn away from her honest gaze. Years afterward her sons met men who remembered her, as she leaned on the counter in scoop-brim bonnet and shawl. She had no time to think of the picture she might be making, being too busy putting together what she overheard.

"I hear tell Don Upham crossed through the forest to the prairies and reached Elk Grove in four days' time."

"So I believe."

"He seed a great fire in the Hampstead country.

Some squatter threw out a bucket of hot ashes into the prairie grass and burned ten mile of trees. Had to jump into Rock River to save his life, he said."

Then the talk would turn on the subject of ferries, so that Ann soon learned that Rock River could be crossed in two places below Lake Koshkonong by ferry, but that where the lead-trail from Galena ended at Fort Atkinson, above the lake, it had to be forded. She judged rightly that no more teams had come through because the water was too deep. Someone said, however, that Milo Jones intended to build a ferry above the lake. She tried writing down all these bits of information in a copy-book, but gave up the task. Ann's spelling and penmanship were not equal to more than the simplest of letters to her mother in England.

In March the first lake schooner to struggle through the floes brought further news from Jane:

"I have reached Buffalo, and am taking passage on the *A. C. Baldwin,* Ben Sweet captain. I have good hopes of seeing you soon."

"Hurray!" Dicky shouted. "Aunt Jane!" He danced around the little clearing with Bije at his heels. Dick hardly remembered his aunt, but the excitement infected him. Harry soberly reminded him that this meant they would be leaving Milwaukee for a new home in the west.

A few mornings later their mother woke them by candle-light. It was almost five o'clock and their father

23

was starting, she said. They got up sleepily and stood huddled under a shawl, while Thomas, in the doorway, shrugged experimentally and tightened the strap that held his pack across his shoulders.

"God be with thee," said their mother.

"And with thee," he replied.

"Happen thou'll meet up with a woodsman as knows the way."

"And welcome, if he can keep step with me." Thomas had a mighty stride.

"Thou'rt a proud man, I fear," his wife said, fondly.

Their father turned toward them the happiest face he had worn since landing in Milwaukee. Then he was off, and as they watched him from the door they saw his shadow preceding him down the trail toward the West, gigantic in the rising dawn. It appeared and disappeared for a time between the trees, then it was gone. Ann turned back into the cabin, sat down on a box and put her apron to her eyes. Both boys came to her at once.

"Don't fret now, Mother." Harry said in a deep voice.

"God will take care of him," added Dicky. "He is making in the wilderness a pathway for our God."

His mother stared at him with such delight that he was embarrassed and knew he had said more than he meant. She jumped up and began briskly shredding some salt beef for their breakfast, chattering all the while.

"Oh, he's safe as a church, is thy father. The red men hereabouts be mostly friendly, and the Potawotami be shy creatures."

"Potawotami, Potawotami!" both boys cried, laughing.

"Aye, there's a name for you! My word on it!" their mother answered gaily.

3

Dick's mother said that she could never forget Mr. Juneau's kindness. If she thought of him often, with a flutter of the heart which was not all gratitude, that could be explained by his interesting clothes and the way he had of bowing, holding his top hat against his breast, a gesture which always raised Ann's opinion of America. She never went out on the trail without thinking that perhaps she might meet the great man of the town. Her hair must be smooth and her bonnet in exactly the right position.

As for her sons, they remembered the night in the Juneau house, chiefly because they had not slept. They had shared a small loft with twelve other children and three dogs. During those uncomfortable hours, Bije had attached himself to Dick and would not be separated when the time came to go. The little boy had an uneasy feeling that the Juneaus wanted Bije, that they would come to take him back. He was always relieved when the children passed by without stopping, but he felt somewhat indignant that they ignored him. It never occurred to Dick that he and Harry were only two of hundreds of immigrants Mr. Juneau had helped.

The town of Milwaukee was divided by its river into Kilbournetown and Juneautown. A new bridge connected the older half, where the Wentworths lived, with the rival division. Dick's mother had heard that fish were cheaper on Mr. Kilbourne's side, where they could be bought right off the hook. But what if she were to go there, buy a fish, and then meet Solomon Juneau on her way back? After some time her thrift got the upper hand of her conscience and she decided to see if the other housewife had told the truth. While Tommy was gone, she would take the boys and go across the river. It would be an adventure and help to pass the time. One morning she bundled them into warm clothing, greased their shoes, and sighed as she fastened Dick's.

"They're too small for thee, poor lad. What wouldn't I give for a sight of Cobbler John!"

"Dost remember John?" his brother asked.

"Aye," he said doubtfully. As with so much in England, he remembered only the name.

"What else dost remember in Holmesfield?" his mother pressed him. He knew by her tight voice that she was feeling homesick and tried hard to recapture the fading images.

"I 'member my puss. Her were gray-like and had a ribbon."

"Aught else?"

27

"And a walk with cobbles and a garden with flowers."

"Aught else, Dicky?"

"Auntie Jane, with a pink dress."

"Ah! Sprigged muslin it were!"

"And Cobbler John."

"Dost remember Granny?"

"Nay."

"Dick, Dick! Granny would weep to hear that!"

He hung his head with a sense of failure and shame.

"Well, it cannot be 'elped, and this will buy no fish," said his mother, putting on his mittens. They started out. Frost was still in the ground, but the air was sweet with the promise of spring. They trudged along by the river, the children so well wrapped they looked stout and clumsy, their mother in several shawls and wooden clogs. The boys stamped the dirt, kicking up frozen oak-leaves from the ruts.

" 'Tis a stern country," Ann said. "Stern, but oh, 'tis beautiful too!"

The Milwaukee River was almost free of ice. They crossed it on the narrow foot-bridge and saw on the far bank a number of fishermen. One of these they knew by sight. He was Leander Shotwell, called "Lem," a New York State Yankee, whose leathery face was permanently creased with laughter.

"Whatever's yon great fellow?" Ann asked, pointing to a flopping fish in Lem's catch.

"Thet's a catfish, Ma'am. They're running jest beautiful today."

Ann looked at it curiously. "How dost cook a catfish?"

"Why, roll it in cornmeal and fry it in lard like any other fish."

"I fear 'twould 'ave a rank flavor."

"It tastes beautiful. Ye'll lick yer chops, Ma'am. Sartainly ye will."

She counted out fifteen pennies and bought the fish, which Lem strung on a willow-withe for carrying, after he had rubbed each penny on the seat of his breeches and put them in his pocket-book. He clucked at Harry.

"How's my fine little feller? Goin' ter be a fisherman when ye grows up?"

"Nay," the nine-year-old said scornfully. " 'Tis a poor occupation."

Lem roared with laughter. "I got my answer. By Gum, I did! How d'ye make it out to be so poor?"

"Fishes has blood and they stink when they be dead. I'll find me a job where there be no killing."

"Ye've got sense boy, but yer facts is mixed. Fishes has blood, but they aint got souls, so it aint rightly killing to do away with them. Them red deers has souls. I'd as lief shoot a human as one of them. But fishes. They're different."

Ann's catfish made a last desperate lunge in protest at this libel. She held it firmly, knotting the withe more tightly through its gills.

29

"My 'usband has taken the trail to the west," she said, out of her desire to talk about Tommy. "He's gone to Hampstead Prairie."

"I aint acquainted inland," Lem told her. "I never heard of the place." He pinched Dick, who was looking up at him with bottomless eyes. "Bad Daddy, to leave such a nice little boy."

Dick had the impulse to repeat his surprisingly successful remark about God's highway through the wilderness, but he desisted from a vague fear that it might not go so well a second time.

"I've a good mind to start west myself," Leander Shotwell said. "A good mind. In Rock River, they say there's an abundance of fish. Tell ye what! I'll get a map and ye can look for yerself and find Hampstead Prairie on it. Mr. Kilbourne's platted all thet country for a canal."

" 'Tis a kind thought, surely," said Ann. She gathered the boys and started homeward, trailing the fish on its handle.

"Hold it clear of thy skirts, Mother," Harry said, pulling a face. " 'Tis slimy."

"And thou'rt e'en finicky to notice slime when a good dinner's on hand."

Halfway home, as she had feared, she met Solomon Juneau. As she had hoped, he bowed from the waist, one hand holding his top hat against his breast, the other sweeping back his long coat from his trousers of

cream-colored gabardine. Ann was so embarrassed by
her fish that she could hardly bow. She passed on
hurriedly.

As they drew near the cabin they heard Bije howling
because they had shut him inside.

"Poor Bije!" Dick exclaimed with puckering face.

"Do-ant be such a great baby," Harry said. "He only
smells the fish."

"He'll have 'ead and tail of it soon," their mother
prophesied.

On the next day at noon, Thomas arrived just as he
had planned before he left. He was walking proudly
beside a yoke of oxen, who pulled a creaking wagon,
with wooden wheels, hickory pole, and iron chains.
Thomas strode properly at the left side of the oxen,
holding to the bow. He wore a broad smile.

"Oh, Tommy!" his wife said. "Thou'rt as good as
thy word. Didst walk all night?"

"Mostly. How dost like the beasts?"

"Thou's not bought them?"

"Aye. Fifty dollar they were."

"They're great beauties, sure enough."

Dick shivered with excitement as he watched his
father unharness the animals, lean the ox-bow against
the house and turn them out to graze.

"Will they run off?" he asked.

"Not they. Wilt thou, Buck?" Thomas gave the

nigh ox a blow on its hairy flank. " 'Tother's Bright,"
he said. "Buck and Bright their names be, and they
know them well."

No one asked him questions about his trip. If he
wanted to tell he would do it, but they all knew there
was no use quizzing him. At dinner Ann tried very
cautiously to draw him out.

"Be it a great town, Hampstead?"

"Nay, not so great."

"How dost like Will Beeson's new wife?"

"Her be well enough."

4

A FEW WEEKS LATER, the *A. C. Baldwin* came gliding up to the Milwaukee dock, her rail lined by tired faces, for it had been a rough trip since they came through the Sault. Jane Wentworth's sharp little face could be seen among the others, and her white handkerchief waving, but it was another half hour before the ship was properly moored and the passengers put off. Jane came running down the planking and Dick was shocked to see that he had not remembered her at all. It was only her name and the pink dress. They went around to the benches at the side of the wharf to wait till her box was unloaded.

Jane had been a servant in the mansion of the Duke of Rutland, where her honesty and common sense had earned her the post of housekeeper. She had carried the keys to all the cupboards, including the ones to the library. There she had become self-educated and nearly read her eyes out. Now, as she began to tell them the news from home, her speech sounded strange to Dick. Jane talked like the quality, his mother said.

33

"Polly Huntington had her ninth child in the week I was leaving," she told them. "Her husband's still poorly, and they've taken that worthless Arthur in to stay. I'm sure I don't see why. The house is like to burst with them all."

Dick listened to this in astonishment, seeing a house literally bursting at its corners and all sorts of people popping out.

" 'Tis a wonder 'Untington wouldn't fix the floors and be rid of his rheumatics," said Ann. "A river of water run through that 'ouse with every shower."

"Ah well, they're slack folk and always were. I doot they'd get along in a new country." Thomas was still feeling triumphant over his Hampstead trip.

"There's my box coming down!" cried Jane. Over the ship's side a wooden chest was slowly descending, revolving in a swing of rope from the hook of the derrick.

"What sort of box is that?" Ann laughed. " 'Tis all over nubs." The oak was stained a dark brown and heavily carved with grapes, leaves and the heads of cherubs.

" 'Tis a communion chest from the old church," Jane said proudly. "His Grace gave it me for a bit of home."

" 'Tis a stout one," Tommy admitted. His voice conveyed the feeling he had about the church at Belvoir Castle, which had always been too high for his Wesleyan beliefs. Jane glanced at him and made her next remark an appeasing one.

"There be a lot of the old things given away. He'd have the stained glass window-panes out if her Ladyship weren't so fond of them."

Thomas smiled and went to fetch Buck and Bright alongside the dock. When they were all in the cart and creaking homeward, Dick sat down on his aunt's box. One little cherub was leaning out farther than the rest. Dick looked at this one intently and made an exciting discovery. The cherub was sticking out its tongue.

That evening, Lem Shotwell brought his plat of the proposed Rock River Canal, and they spread it out on the table-box. Milo Jones would have his ferry ready, Lem thought, before they reached the river. Lem had been making inquiries everywhere. He told them much that they wanted to know, and even Thomas seemed interested. As man to man, they discussed matters. Thomas told Lem he had forded Rock River on his trip west and had driven his oxen back by way of the Goodrich ferry south of the lake.

"Did ye hear that Dan'l Webster was buying land out there?" Lem asked.

"Aye. Thousands of acres. He'll make a good profit on them."

"But ye intend to pay only the government price? Ye'll pay no more?"

"Not I."

"Have ye picked yer farm, then, Mr. Wentworth?"

"I've done so."

It was the first Ann knew about that.

Before they could leave Milwaukee, the spring rains began to fall. The river flooded. Fog rolled above the water, white as wool, and streamers of mist blew out across the trail. One load of oxen had been enough to bring the empty cart to Milwaukee over half-frozen ground, but now the wagon was heavily loaded and the wheels had to labor hub-deep in mud. Buck and Bright were barely equal to the task and stopped often to rest. Thomas, knee-deep in the mire, plodded beside them, encouraging and scolding. In the first long day they covered twenty miles and came out at sunset on the Fort Dearborn Road. Slashed through the forest as if with a knife, the military turnpike connected Chicagau on the south with La Baie Verte at Fort Howard. The oxen pulled up, lathered and drooping. Dick and Harry stood in the cart, gazing up and down the road. They were glad of the chance to see any distance through the woods, but they had hoped to meet soldiers, or perhaps a stage-coach. No travelers were in sight.

Their mother and aunt sat in the rear of the wagon on a canvas-covered box, too tired from the jolting ride to do anything but sit. As for the boys, they had wanted to talk all day, but could not make themselves heard above the creaking and their father's shouts. Now there was nothing to say. A fine drizzle of rain fell on their heads and shoulders. Bije shook off the drops from his coat, transferring most of them to Dick. Wheels, oxen, chains, and wagon-boards were plastered with reddish mud.

The silence and loneliness about them were so deep it seemed wrong to speak. Dick began to wonder whether he would ever see a house again. Trees choked each other, battling for sunlight. Saplings crowded up between the giants, dwarfed for lack of room, and dead oaks lay across the roots of living ones. The road under their wheels was made of rotted logs, broken and scattered by hooves. In the heart of Thomas Wentworth that day, was born a hatred of the forest that never let him rest until he had grubbed his last stump. He felt God had called him to root out the trees and rid good land of a worthless growth.

Dick, standing in the wagon, had no such thoughts. The woods might be rank and desolate, but they were full of interest to him. He saw the few birds flitting in the boughs and several last year's nests. He picked and examined some sticky buds, lacquered with red and just breaking into pale green leaf. He noticed the wet moss and peeling bark, and then, turning his face up to the mottled sky, studied the dark clouds scurrying over a gray background.

"There be rain in Heaven, Mother."

"Not in Heaven, child. There the sun always shines."

He was disappointed. Where was Heaven then? Not

37

in the sky, but farther away. At that moment the clouds parted and he saw a red light shining through, pointing like a finger to the middle of the sky.

"Oh!" he said to himself, enlightened. Someone was back there, sitting behind the clouds.

Dick's Aunt Jane looked pale and disheartened.

"Dost repent of coming, Jenny?" his mother said.

" 'Tis too late for repenting."

This was obvious, and Ann's only answer was to lift the hamper of food and take off the clean towel that covered it. They had ridden all day without eating. No wonder their spirits were low, she said. She took out a loaf of bread and a great chunk of ham and began making thick sandwiches. Soon they were all munching and for a while there was no conversation.

"Look yon!" Harry exclaimed suddenly with his mouth full, while Bije, feet on the front-board, began a furious barking. A man was coming, but he looked more like an animal in his shaggy buffalo-coat and fur cap. Ann turned toward her husband, startled. He showed no surprise. As the man came nearer he laid down his sandwich and lowered himself into the road.

"Here we be, McNaughton," he said.

"Could ye no have waited yer sooper-r-r? Ah've tea boilin'," the stranger said in a profound Scottish brogue.

"We could do with a dish of tea, but as for vittels, thou'll 'ave us for brekkus."

He included the women and children in this remark

by a wave of his hand. Probably Thomas reasoned that Ann had heard all about this Yorkshire-born Scot who had preached for twelve years in the Waukesha woods. Probably too, he knew that McNaughton could tell his sister from his wife by general appearances. At any rate, he preferred not to waste good breath on an introduction. He was right about Ann. She remembered all she had been told of the relationship between the Scotsman and the Indians; how he fed them, converted them, and then managed to get their services and furs for almost nothing. She realized that Thomas must have stayed with McNaughton on his other trip, that this meeting had been arranged, probably to the very hour, and that their apparent slowness in getting away from Milwaukee was merely Tommy's effort to keep his plans intact.

The oxen were slapped and urged forward. The wagon came down off the turnpike with a bump and settled into the mud again. Soon, however, they reached McNaughton's own corduroy road and turned off toward his clearing and three-room house. Dick was first out, springing down on a soft carpet of tan-bark which kept the clearing dry. Bije jumped after him, then Harry, who ran away with the men to stable the oxen and cover the wagon. Firelight was shining through the windows as Dick and the two women approached the house. When they came inside they saw the table laid with a red cloth and lighted candles. The main room was neatly whitewashed.

"Only look!" Jane said, "how clean and decent he keeps house."

"Aye, Jenny. Many a lone man learns such ways in the new country. See the bread he's baked, too." A loaf lay on the table with a sharp knife beside it.

"There's a smell of hides, though," Jane protested. The floor was covered with skins, some of them freshly cured; a bear, two timber-wolves, a lynx and a pony had supplied McNaughton with rugs. The pelts of two bob-cats with the heads still on them, hung from the wall, gazing down with glass eyes. Dick shrank from these.

"Mother, Bije willn't come in."

The collie stood bristling in the door. Dick ran to him and tried to drag him over the sill.

"Leave him be, lad. He be squeamish of the hides."

The men came in, trailed by Harry. McNaughton brought out hand-basin and towel, and after they had all taken turns at washing he poured out the strong tea.

"Wad the bairns tak a bit of sweetnin'?" he wanted to know.

Dick and his brother had never been allowed sugar in their tea at home. Now they were delighted to get a spoonful in each cup. Dick stirred his with one finger, sucked the finger, drank the tea ravenously and turned the cup upside down over his nose to get the last drop of syrup.

"Greedy pig!" his aunt said, hugging him.

After tea they all had to kneel in prayer. Dick was

sure Mr. McNaughton would never stop praying. Even his parents admitted afterward that their knees had suffered.

"Aye, he were over long in the wind, but he put a power and a grace into it, nevertheless," Dick's father said.

"Now," their host explained. "We'll give the ladies the ane bed. The laddies we'll hap up in skins by the hearth, and you and I, Brother Wentworth, will make shift beside them."

So they spent the night. Bije refused to sleep at Dick's side. He made it known in a doleful voice that if his master chose to wrap up in a bear-skin he could take the consequences.

In the morning, the Scotsman called Dick's father aside.

" 'Tis a rough land," he said, "and an uncertain life, and a mon does well to make his deceesions promptly."

The gist of the remainder was that McNaughton had made his. He wanted to know how Miss Jane might regard him as a husband. Thomas had difficulty to keep from smiling.

"Thou'rt a bit late, I fear," he answered. "She's e'en taken passage-money from Mr. Weymouth at Hampstead, and be in honor bound to go through with the bargain."

The truth was that Jane had been hot and cold about the whole affair. She had changed her mind so often that

Sam Weymouth must have thought her hardly worth what he paid. She had even tried out other young men, but not from Totley, Holmesfield or Dromfield Wodehouse had she found Sam's equal. So here she was, far from home, the passage-money all spent, and half inclined to bolt even now. It had been seven long years since she had fallen in love with the young miller. She had grown up since then, earned her own living and lost the emotion of her first love. Something of this Thomas conveyed to McNaughton, though it never occurred to him to tell Jane of the Scotsman's offer.

"Ah weel," said the latter, rubbing his chin. "I needna be ower hasty. If the lassie seems inclined to slip the noose, however, ye might juist tell her of my proposeetion. A part of her passage-money I might e'en . . ." he broke off, cautiously.

They were lucky to have watered the oxen well at McNaughton's spring before leaving. The whole of that day passed with no sign of stream or pool. The forest floor had soaked up the rain and the trail was following a watershed, with streams flowing away in either direction, but nothing near at hand. A mile south through unbroken forest, the Scuppernong rolled along, but the mile might have been ten, for even if he had known of the river, Tommy was in no mind to get off the trail and hunt a drink for man or beast. He was having a hard enough time following the faint trace of the lead-drivers. The marks of his own last trip were lost, but an occasional blaze on a tree-trunk, a log rolled aside, broken twigs and abraded stumps showed where the ox-teams of the year before had gone through. Once he saw an Indian camp-site, turned off toward it and found the way impassable. With great difficulty he got the oxen back again. By late afternoon the beasts were tortured with thirst, rolling their heads from side to side and bellowing. He continued to shout and threaten, urging them forward.

The oxen were as stubborn as Tommy. When at last they smelled a rivulet in the bottom of a gully, it made no difference to them that it was off the trail and over a gravelly bank. Downhill they went, crashing through underbrush, racking the wheels against boulders.

"Jump, lads, jump!" Dick's mother called as the cart was heaved over the brink of the gully. The nine boxes came up against the front-board with a bang that should have staved them in. Buck and Bright took the full impact on their great rumps, standing in the freshet-water. They were drinking their fill at last, while Tommy threw his weight furiously against the ox-bow, shouting:

"Gee, Buck, I tells thee! Haw, Bright, thou great fool!"

Even after they had drunk their last, they saw no reason to pull the wagon out again. Thomas had never used whip or prod in his life, but now he took out his clasp-knife and began to sharpen a stick. Meanwhile Dick, kneeling on the ground above, had folded his hands in prayer:

43

"Halmighty God. Please to make they oxen behave. Please to make them come up out of there. Put a hook in their noses and a bridle in their mouthies and lead them up in the way whence they camest."

"Lord save us!" his aunt giggled. "I do believe he's had a call to the pulpit."

At this moment the beasts, who had changed their minds, crashed out through the undergrowth onto the trail again.

"Now mind, Jenny," Dick's mother said proudly, "'Twas wisdom in the mouth of a babe, and 'twas not for thee to mock him."

Thomas, who was a man of few words, said nothing about the prod, so Dick went down in family history as a deliverer.

For three days more they creaked along, seeing no human being. At night they slept in the wagon with a fire to guard against wolves. The boys lay looking up at the stars, warm and comfortable under sheep-pelts, but listening uneasily to the screams of coyote and lynx. They slept through the visit of the Potawotami, who circled their camp in friendly curiosity, leaving telltale footprints in the wet moss. They ate all the ham and were obliged to stop at last, while Tommy did a bit of hunting. Their dinner that night was of partridge and squirrel.

At the end of their fifth day they saw ahead of them the stockade of Joshua Feather, surrounding the best house in that part of the wilderness. In the large clearing were sheep, cattle, and a number of white hens. At the well, Mrs. Joshua stood, drawing a bucket of water. She was a bent, gray-faced woman. Her mouth, permanently turned down at the corners, interested Dick.

"Poor little feller," she kept saying each time she noticed him. He wondered why he was being pitied.

She took them into her clean, warm house with its well-sanded floor and iron stove. A supper of chicken and wild rice was cooking on the griddle. She said her husband had bought the rice from some wandering Winnebagos.

"You're welcome to share with me," she invited them. "Josh give them Winnebagos one good side of pork for the rice, and the rest he's toted to Janes Ferry, ten miles down the Rock River. He'll trade the hogs for wheat flour. I dunno. It's a hard life here, when you can't sell your pork, but got to trade it for flour. Why did we come so far west, I ask Josh, when our children are all buried in Ohio except George who aint dead yet, and we never thought to raise him he was that puny? Four graves and nobody to tend 'em. It's a hard life."

Her weary guests twisted in their chairs. All except Dick. Dick was sitting unnaturally still. He faced the window, and he had seen an Indian in a red blanket approaching the stockade. From without, a brown hand reached between the pickets, seized a white hen by the throat and smothered its squawking. Dick watched,

45

fascinated, while another brown hand appeared, neatly twisting off the chicken's head. The body, pouring blood, disappeared through the fence. Darkness deepened. Soon Dick could see nothing in the window except his own round face, distorted in the flawed glass.

The next morning they were up early and on the trail again. More hours of creaking and rattling went past. They crossed the Bark River, the oxen, belly-deep in water, pulling the cart over a hard shale bottom. The trees grew larger and more graciously spaced. They were coming into the famous forest of the Rock River valley, called "oak-glades" by the English settlers, a region unusual for its ancient and spreading trees. Here the road grew more distinct, with real wagon-ruts and the plainly marked hoof-prints of oxen. Buck and Bright seemed to know their way now. They pulled along steadily with no urging.

"Aye," said Dick's father, "the end's nearing. No doot they've traveled this road many a time."

In another half hour they came out on a height of land above the river. The beautiful Rock flowed below them in broad curves, its water shining in the sun. On the river bank were a scattering of houses and a de-serted fort with a broken stockade. Harry and Dick rose and yelled, swinging their arms. Their mother and father exchanged a long look.

"Thou sees, my lass?"

"I see, Tommy."

This was the Paradise for which they had set forth, about which they had heard so much in Derbyshire. The rich Wisconsin prairie, land of flowers. Who would believe such a place existed beyond all those miles of swamp and forest?

Milo Jones' dairy, beyond the fort, had been operating since "thirty-eight" when the officers and their wives needed cream and butter. Mr. Jones brought them a pail of milk from which the boys drank heartily, coming away with moustaches of white foam. He said he had finished his ferry, but was waiting for rope from Galena. He meant to run it by pulleys between trees on either bank.

"Hast no poles?" boomed Thomas.

"I can cut some. Current's pretty strong this time of year, though. We'd need six men. Have to take the raft upstream to allow for the down-drift."

Four men were rounded up, and six poles. The raft was towed up river and securely fastened to the shore. Buck and Bright were led down to the water, but when they had taken one look at the ferry, they stood firm. Fording was one thing. This teetering raft was quite another. Thomas unhitched them and turned them around. He backed them onto the raft and pushed the wagon down the bank after them. For a few minutes it appeared that everything would go overboard. The raftsmen thrust their poles in the river-bottom and steadied the ferry. The passengers went on board.

Three men on either side now began thrusting their

poles in at the front and running to the back of the raft. Dick stood at the rear, watching the whirling wake. In mid-stream the current caught the ferry and the sweating men fought in silence to keep it from being carried down into the lake. Toward the other shore the water grew still again and they landed at the foot of the Galena trail where it ended in the ford.

Above the bank, the road was deeply cut into the prairie loam. A wide, wasteful thoroughfare, it scarred the landscape in a ten-rod swathe, where the oxen had been driven out around mudholes.

As the character of the road altered, the country-side changed too. The forest hung back, lying blackly along the horizon. Near at hand were only bare, rolling hills with lakes in the hollows. Bright streams flowed across the trail. Fording these they saw glacial gravel in the beds. In one valley a cluster of wigwams stood, not pointed, like the Milwaukee tepees, but bowl-shaped, roofed with bark. Squaws, busily pounding rice, did not look up as they passed.

Two lead-wagons were coming, announced before-hand by the terrific thunder of their wheels and the oaths of the drivers, who lashed out at six yoke of oxen with long leather goads. Ann put her hands over Dick's ears, and Thomas drove far out of the trail to let the huge "toad-crushers" pass. He smiled afterward, thinking of the teetering raft at Fort Atkinson and the job of getting such outfits aboard it.

Emerging from a grove of maple trees, they came unexpectedly upon a creek, in which a groaning mill-wheel turned. Above the door of the mill-house, in letters a foot high, they read:

Sam'l Weymouth. Flour and Feed.

"Hold a bit, Tommy! My word, you might have told me!" his sister said, with fiery cheeks. No one in the world but Thomas Wentworth would have let a girl meet her lover unwarned after seven years.

"Get down be'ind the wagon, poor Jenny. Here's a towel and a bit of water," Ann comforted her. As she struggled to put her long hair back in its net, Jane found that she was facing the young miller, who had laid his gun and a brace of rabbits on the ground and was coming toward the wagon.

He looked at the girl he had sent for, quite as if he had gotten the wrong parcel in the mail. Jane's family rallied about her, the boys leaning over the side of the cart, Ann and Thomas at either elbow. Ann began to chatter.

"Why, Sammy Weymouth, I do-ant believe 'tis thee. What a great man thou'rt grown! Here be my two lads, Sam. 'Arry was the baby when thou left Holmesfield."

"Did we take thee by surprise?" Thomas asked, and by the way he said it, Ann knew that this meeting too had been arranged.

"Nay, hardly, that is, I don't know," Sam said, stammering. "I were getting rabbits for thy supper, if fortune so favored me."

5

BEYOND THE MILL at intervals of a mile or two, log-
houses punctuated the road to Galena. Will Beeson's home was the third of these, a cabin with one
room and a loft, in which Dick and his brother slept
on their first night in Hampstead and for more than a
month afterward. A ladder of peeled saplings led to
the loft, swaying dangerously as one climbed. Above
the opening the low room looked cosy to Dick, with its
single candle lit, showing the two beds covered by
patchwork quilts. It was warm up there, with the heat
from the room below and from the great chimney that
formed most of one side of the loft. Dick said his
prayer in bed, curling his cold toes in the palm of his
hand. He was tired and the feather-bed seemed too
good to be real. He looked across the closed trap-door
at Harry, who appeared to be settling down to sleep.

"Be-ent thou going to say thy prayer?"

"Not tonight."

"Why not?"

"Because I do-ant choose."

"God will be angry."

"Nonsense, Dick. What good be all they prayers and preachings? He's too far off to 'ear them."

Dick would have been more deeply shocked at this if he had not remembered the red finger in the clouds. Harry hadn't seen it then. It was for him alone. He went to sleep nursing his splendid secret.

In the room below, the others were still talking. Will Beeson, at the table, showed Thomas his account-books, the cost of labor and seed, of tools and rope and wagon-grease. The women by the fire were deep in discussion of an even more fundamental problem.

"Hast found a physician to tend thee when thy time comes?" Ann questioned Molly Beeson, "For 'tis far from any town, and reckonings are like to be wrong. I mind me when my 'Arry were born, it were two weeks ahead of our count. Tommy 'ad to run a mile in no time."

"I've thought little of it yet," Molly replied, her greenish eyes roving toward the men. "Martha Hall 'ull likely be midwife to me."

She was a puzzle to Ann. Her red hair, always falling out of its knot, her dress, open at the throat with no collar or brooch, her sullen mouth. She had lived in Liverpool, and how she happened to marry a farmer, God alone knew. Perhaps because he was going to a new country. She let her bread run over the sides of the pan, boiled her tea once and threw out the leaves, instead of drying them for another using. Her plates were all stacked on the dresser in uneven piles, when they should have been standing behind the rail. As for the way she looked at Thomas . . .

"May God forgive me for my sinful thoughts," Ann said to herself. And she made herself think of something else. After all, what woman wouldn't look at Tommy after living a year with homely Willy Beeson? She remembered the bolt of longcloth in one of her boxes and began to plan little dresses and petticoats for Molly's child. In the dreary days that followed she got out the cloth, cut into it liberally, and with Jane to help her, began basting, scalloping and running miles of tiny tucks. Molly looked on, but never offered to lend a hand.

The rains held these people together and forced them to be patient. There was no escape till some sort of shelter could be built on Tommy's new land. The trail was such a sea of mud that no one went out on it except in deep necessity. Will Beeson's yard was not much better. The boys could run to barn, "hen-peak" or "backus" on the slippery log walks, or to the well on the chips and bark at the back door. They were often allowed to draw water, a task that required both of them. One hung on the sweep, set through the crotch of a tree, one leaned over the curb to grasp the bale of the bucket when it came in reach. A peg in the curb was strong enough to hold the bucket until a grown-up could come and lift it out.

When Dick had used up every excuse for getting out of doors, he had to stay inside. He ran up and down the ladder to the loft twenty times or so until his mother told him to sit still with his hands folded. Then he was obliged to amuse himself by using his eyes, and before long he knew by heart every inch of the Beeson living-room, the big hearth, where the three-legged spider had coals under it and in its hollow cover, cooking the next meal, the pots and pans, hung in rows beside the hearth, the water-bucket and gourd. A candle-stand held the open Bible. Beside this document of peace, stood rifle and shotgun, with ox-horns of powder and pouches for bird-shot and bullets. In a corner, the men's heavy coats and the women's shawls hung on pegs, with hats and bonnets above them on a shelf. On either side of the large room were four-poster beds, whose hangings gave only a semblance of privacy at night. Jane's pallet in another corner was sheltered by a screen of quilts.

Jane was to leave them as soon as the circuit-rider came, but the rains had kept him away. She was not sorry. Sam and she were still dreadfully shy of each other, and unless they took to the barn they could never be alone.

For three weeks it rained, sometimes in downpours so heavy Dick could not see through the windows, sometimes in a gentle dripping, monotonous on roof and sill. When the weather relented and a watery sunlight began to shine, the passenger pigeons came through, and the sky was darkened again. They filled the air with the sound of their wings and their mournful crying. Will and Thomas took their guns to the barn, where they stood in the doorway, firing into the sky. A lucky shot would bring down forty birds. They piled up enough for a day's meat in a short time, but sometimes went on shooting for pleasure.

Dick was allowed to watch his father cleaning the birds. There was something brutal about the sight—the huge man seizing the limp little bodies, snatching off the feathers and slitting open the pale bellies. Holding his axe close to its blade, Thomas chopped off legs and heads and threw the birds into a tub of cold well-water. Later there would be pigeon pie, which Dick loved, but the preliminaries filled him with disapproval.

The pigeons came north for the wild rice that grew in Lake Koshkonong. Sometimes a crop would burst and shower the ground with rice kernels.

"Do the baby pigeons eat rice too?" Dick asked his mother. "Do-ant they 'ave worrums like other little birds?"

"They 'ave milk to drink, Dick. From their mother's bills. Thy father opened a mother's crop yesterday and 'twere full of milk."

He stared at her, his eyes slowly filling with tears. But when the meat pie came on at dinner-time his hunger was greater than his compunction.

On the first sunny day they all rode in the ox-cart to visit their new farm. As farms went about Hampstead, Tommy's was a very small one, only eighty acres bought with his own savings and with a loan from Will Beeson.

Most of the eighty was in timber and would have to be cleared by gruelling labor, but Thomas had sworn to pay no more than the government's dollar and a quarter, and all the clear land had been bought up by speculators. Timber was almost worthless. It could be floated down the river to Illinois, but after it got there it would hardly sell for the lumbermen's wages. Thomas knew this, but he felt triumphant because he had outwitted the Yankees. At least they had made no profit out of *him*.

For a small tract the land had great variety as the boys discovered on their first day. On the west forty a spring bubbled up and flowed away in a clear brook. Near the spring was an oak tree, so tall it could be seen for miles above the forest, while at the opposite boundary a linden had drooping branches on which one could swing. A limestone outcropping had been opened for building-stone by earlier settlers, leaving a deep fissure in the earth. Dick climbed down in this hole and tore his breeches and stockings. He ran around the oak-tree till he was dizzy, swung on the linden till his arms ached, and after his father had driven a barrel into the spring, and the water was flowing from the bung-hole, he drank until his stomach hurt him.

Harry soon grew tired of playing with Dick and went over to help his father begin their new house. It was to be a mere shelter of saplings and sod, with a bark roof, a fireplace of stones and mud, and a floor covered with straw. Anything more ambitious was impossible, with

55

spring plowing demanding to be done. Harry ran back and forth carrying stones and bark.

The sunshine lasted. For a week men, women and children worked together on the house, so that when it was finally completed they all felt proud and no one could complain. Their home had one real luxury, a glass window they had brought from Milwaukee. Ann was proud of the window, and said she thought Willy must have been blind to overlook such splendid land. The Beeson farm was not half so nice, she thought.

In the bed at Willy's, on the last night before they moved in, she leaned on her plump arm and whispered to Thomas: "Oh when my curtains are all oop, and the cups on the dresser, 'twill be a lovely parlor. We'll 'ave Molly coom over with her young un, and Jenny from the mill, and that Mrs. Hall, as I 'aven't met yet. . . ."

"What parlor art talking aboot?"

"Why our own, for we'll be living in the sod 'ouse only so long as it takes to put oop another one. . . ."

"And who's to put oop another while I'm plowing and chopping?"

"Oh Tommy! We'll never spend next winter in yon!"

He did not answer, and Ann realized that they would have to live through a bitter Wisconsin winter in their sod shelter.

"Tommy," she whispered again, just as he was going to sleep.

"What now?"

"Why didst say Hampstead were a town? The 'ouses are a mile apart."

"I never. I said 'twere not a *great* town, and so it weren't."

In their first home the beds had been made by sawing off trees and nailing frames around four of the trunks for each bed. Dick thought it very queer that his new bed was rooted in the ground, but he rather liked it too. The table was made the same way. It could not be shoved back against the wall, but at least it was better than a box. One's knees would go under it. Along one wall the nine boxes stood as they had in Milwaukee. Dick began to learn his alphabet once more.

They were no sooner settled than a new excitement was in the air. Dick thought it must be because the pastor was coming and they were going to meeting in John Hall's house down the trail. When Sunday arrived he was washed and brushed and squeezed into the blue suit he had not worn since leaving Milwaukee. His arms stuck out too far from the sleeves and the trousers were too tight.

"Mother," he said, "summat's 'appened to my clothes."

His mother paid him no attention. She was fussing with his aunt's dress, pinning ribbon on her bodice and smoothing her skirts. His aunt looked small, young, and rather frightened.

57

"Pinch thy cheeks, Jenny," Dick's mother said. "Else thou'll be but a pale bride."

"Pale or not," his aunt sighed, "Sam'll have to put up with me."

This meant nothing to Dick, so he went back to mournful contemplation of the blue suit. It never occurred to him that he had grown larger. He decided that the suit was fading away and would disappear altogether like the little copper-toed shoes he had brought from England. Those shoes had gotten too small, and then one day they were gone. He made up his mind he would keep his eyes on the suit. His mother must not pack it in the box again.

John Hall's place was three miles west. His big room, with its sanded puncheon floor, was full of benches, made by laying planks on saw-horses. The men in the rear were roasting their coat-tails before a fire on which beef and Yorkshire pudding cooked. At the front, the minister literally had his back against the wall. The "amen row" sat directly beneath his chin.

This was the first chance Dick's mother had of seeing her new neighbors. She made the most of it. At length she decided with pleasure that their own clothes were as nice as any, and better than most. Just as she was enjoying this discovery, three more people arrived. The lady had a bonnet of black lace with curling feathers. She carried a fan. The little girl wore her hair in a snood and had a shirred "pocket" of taffeta. As for the man, he was every bit a gentleman, spare, baldish and

58

with gold-rimmed eye-glasses. Ann's heart leaped as they came quietly in and sat down on the bench with the Wentworths. The little girl was next to Dick. She laid her taffeta "pocket" on the rough bench, smoothed her long skirt and folded her hands. Dick turned to her with a wide smile. He liked, especially, the scent she wore.

From time to time, during the sermon that followed, Martha Hall rose to stir the pot of boiling beef. She wore her big white apron right through the meeting. A coach-dog ambled across the room to the hearth, and flopped bonily down beside a cat, who swelled up and spat at him. This Dick noticed, turning his head first to one side, then the other. The clock struck twelve, and a Swiss bell-ringer came out above the dial and shook his little bell. Birds were carrying straw to build a nest outside the window. Dick heard not one word of the sermon.

Unexpectedly, his Aunt Jane stood up and walked to the front of the room. The circuit-rider took her hand and gave it to Sam Weymouth, who rose from the front row.

"What's her doing?" Dick whispered to Harry. "What's it all aboot?"

"Hush! Her's getting wedded."

"What's wedded?"

"Hush!"

That night as he lay in bed he put out one hand and found something small and soft growing from his bed-

post. He picked it and felt of it in the dark. It was a
new leaf. Poor little bed-post tree! Outside it was
spring and things were growing. There would be no
sunlight for the bed-post tree.

The wind blew an occasional gust down the chimney,
scattering ashes on the hearth. Far off in the forest a
wolf howled, and Bije, on the straw by Dick's bed,
whined and stirred. Somewhere down the trail a night-
rider was coming. Dick could hear his pony nickering.

He could not hear all the sounds in that wild country,
the sheep-bells tinkling at Beeson's, the drumming of
the milk in the pails, the groaning of his new uncle's
mill-wheel. He lay and thought about them, and about
what he had learned from the little girl who sat beside
him in church. After the meeting she had told him her
name was Eliza Morton. She was ten years old. She had
books to read and a harpsichord, and she lived in the
next house to theirs. Her house was set far back in the
woods. You couldn't see it from the trail, she said. It
had been built of stone from Dick's quarry, before anyone had claimed it. He wondered about the harpsichord, trying to believe he heard Eliza playing.

There were other sounds. Westward along the trail,
the first big shipment of lead to Milwaukee was passing
Exeter, toiling through the dark. South, at Indian Ford,
lumbermen had tied their rafts up for the night and
were getting noisily drunk in the tavern. East, on Thebault Point, the fur-trader Thebault belabored his

Indian wife with a canoe paddle. North, the village of
Four Lakes blew out its candles and settled to rest. At
Fort Winnebago, farmers brought in their pails from
evening milking, at Fort Howard dancers cut pigeon-
wings in the torchlight. And everywhere, unseen, the
Indians of the woods kept their peace, still frightened
by the massacre of Black Hawk's people.

It was two hundred years now since the four thousand braves feasted on beavers with Nicollet at Green
Bay, since he fired his blunderbuss into the air and was
proclaimed the "thunder-bearer." It was just a century
since Marin slaughtered the Outagamies at Butte des
Morts because they charged toll on his boatload of furs.
It was fifty years since little Black-Bird, the twelve-year-
old chief, killed the captain of the Fort Howard garrison to avenge his father's murder. Through all those
years fur-traders had claimed Wisconsin, and when the
first farmers came in they were hated and destroyed.
Farmers drove away the fur-bearers, spoiled the Indian's hunting, cut the trees. Until the Black Hawk War
was over they were not allowed to farm in peace.

Now Dicky Wentworth could sleep safely. Black
Hawk, brought out of his Virginia prison was being
made to entertain audiences with his broken speech.

"I loved the Rock River country," he usually said. "I
loved the good land, the home of my fathers. I fought
for it. That is all."

Spring plowing had been one thing in Derbyshire, where Percheron horses pulled plows through the fine loam. It was quite another here. In Wisconsin the trees had to be chopped down and dragged away with chains, the stumps pulled, the grubbing hoe wielded on the last stubborn roots. Boulders must be moved. Then the great breaking plow with its sixteen-foot beam and razor-sharp blade was hitched to four or five yoke of oxen and the forest sod was upheaved in ragged furrows, still full of sticks and brush. Tommy, who had taken first prize at the Sheffield County Fair for the cleanest furrow plowed without reins, groaned inwardly when he saw the condition of his new land.

"I doot I'll ever sow wheat on yon," he said.

Will Beeson convinced him that the first planting should be to sod-corn. Corn would grow with no cultivating in the ragged furrows, and as each year leveled them down, wheat could gradually replace the other grain. Dick's mother was dubious about corn-meal. At first none of them liked the coarse bread it made, but they decided to get used to it.

Harry Wentworth was ten that year. A tall, fair-haired boy, he was always at work, running errands, splitting firewood, helping to clear the land. He could get to Beesons' and back in no time, when his mother wanted a live coal to start her fire or fresh "balm" for the baking. He sometimes walked three miles to the mill with a message for Aunt Jane. He milked the cows. They had two of these in a sod stable near the house.

When his mother began to make butter he peddled the extra pats to Aunt Jane at the mill, or wherever else he could sell them, bringing home ten or fifteen cents to put in the old ginger jar that was their bank.

One day he came back with a message from Mrs. Morton. She would like his mother to do her churning for a wage. His mother's black eyes flashed at this. She had been cherishing hurt feelings for some time because the lady in the stone house nearest theirs had never come near her or welcomed her as a neighbor.

"I did wrong to curtsey to her that day at church," Ann said. "Likely it gave 'er false notions. I'll do the churning and welcome, however. She be but a poor sickly creature."

"I want to go," Dick begged. "Let me go too." He had not lost his first interest in Eliza. His mother sent him to wash his face and hands.

Roger and Margaret Morton had left Nottingham and come to America because of a family quarrel. It had to do with religion. They had become Wesleyans, so it was natural they should follow the trail other Wesleyans had beaten to Hampstead Prairie, but their disappointment in the new country was great. Most of their money had been spent on passage, on the farm of four hundred acres and the house. They had fine land, but like Thomas, they would have to clear away the timber, and Roger Morton was not by nature a farmer or woodsman. He tried to hire men, but in that

63

country where exchange was made mostly in labor, he found it hard to get steady help. His wife had offended the women on the prairie by offering them money as she had done with Ann. The rude settlers laughed at them because their ways were strange, and enjoyed their mistakes and struggles. Meanwhile Eliza would have to grow up in this wilderness with no chance for a suitable marriage.

Ann Wentworth had no sooner come inside, than she saw how it was with Mrs. Morton. The poor lady was still in her wrapper and curlers at ten o'clock. Dishes and linen were soiled and spread over the table and stove.

"I'll take a bit of soft soap and a tea towel," Dick's mother said. "We'll e'en have to tidy oop before I can churn."

"You won't find any clean towels," Mrs. Morton answered listlessly.

"Then we'll do withoot." Ann found a rag and set to work. It was a pleasure to handle the fine cups and plates, to wipe off the shelves of the hand-rubbed cupboards. She noticed the small brass hinges, set back into the wood, the polished plate-rail and cherry-wood table. If envy had been in her nature, she would have coveted this kitchen.

When the tidying was finished she found the churn in the cellarway. It was half full of soured cream.

" 'Tis a bit far gone, I fear," she told Mrs. Morton, experimentally working the dasher up and down.

"I know. I can't churn. My arms get too tired."

"Aye, surely. 'Twill tire thee at first. The next time 'twill be easier and so on. The Lord favors people who fend for themselves. I mind me when I learned to spin, how weary I grew with the walking to and fro. Now 'tis a child's play."

Her round arms were briskly moving up and down, plying the dasher. Ann's own churn turned with a crank and she was so preoccupied with the new method that she did not see the expression on Mrs. Morton's face, gradually melting, growing happier.

"You have a rarely pretty child, my dear," she said, nodding toward the parlor where Dick was playing with Eliza.

"Aye, he's well enough . . . coom butter!"

"Why did you say that?"

" 'Tis forming-like on the top. A body must say 'coom' before 'tis done."

"What if a body doesn't?" Mrs. Morton laughed.

"Ah, then it cooms anyway, but it be-ent so yellow."

Dick had grown tired of looking at Eliza's scrapbook. He was on the stool at the harpsichord, longing to touch the keys. He tried one carefully and started back from the husky note. Eliza put away her scrapbook and sat near him.

"Do you like it?" she asked. "It was my grandmother's long ago."

"I have a Granny."

"Everyone has."

"Where are they all, then?"

"Some of them are in Heaven, and some are in white houses with roses around the door."

"Oh!" shouted Dick.

"Whatever's the matter?"

"Oh! I remember my Granny. Her's like that."

A picture, brief as a flash of light, had appeared on his retina. The face of his grandmother, the door, the roses. He rushed into the kitchen and threw his arms about his mother so vigorously she dropped her ladle.

"What ails thee, Dick? Be more careful," she scolded him.

"I remember her now."

"Who, lad?"

"My Granny. I remember."

"Of course, Dick. Whoever said thou didn't?"

6

ON A MONDAY MORNING in mid-September, 1842,
Dick was swinging back and forth from the
bough of the linden tree. Harry had gone off on an
errand and his mother had told him to keep away from
the linen she was washing and spreading on the grass.
He was lonely and the woods seemed too still. He hung
at arm's length, and let himself drop on the carpet of
soft yellow linden leaves, already fallen from the tree.
They were like newly-tanned leather. He began to
make himself a pair of shoes to put on his bare feet,
pinning the leaves together with twigs.

Somewhere in his brain a bell semed to be ringing. At
first he hardly noticed it, but at last it forced itself upon
his attention, became real and insistent. It was the
dinner-bell at Roger Morton's house. Most of the
settlers used ox-horns to call the men-folk for a meal,
but the Mortons had a bell, hung on a bough outside the
back door. Two things troubled Dick. In the first place
the Morton family had no hired men to call, and in the
second place it was not dinner-time. He decided to ig-

nore the bell and went on with his play. The bell went on, too. At last he could stand it no longer.

"Stop it, bell!" he shouted, but the bell went on ringing. He took off his linden-leaf shoes and started toward home, running across a pasture-slope and a plowed field and then into the yard where his mother was still washing.

"Mother," he shouted. "Eliza's ringing the bell."

"Well," she answered impatiently, "What's a bell to fash thyself aboot? Look at thy face and 'ands, Dick. They be all over dirt."

He looked into a tub of clear water and saw his round, grimy face.

" 'Tis ringing and ringing. It do-ant stop."

His mother took her arms out of the suds and rolled them in her apron to dry them. "I cannot 'ear it, lad."

"By the old linden tree I 'eard it."

"Coom along. We'll go there, then."

When they got to the linden the bell was still ringing. Ann took him by the hand and set out through the woods toward the stone house. His bare feet stumbled over sharp twigs and bits of stone, but she walked rapidly ahead. When they came into the clearing they saw Mr. Morton sitting on the ground with the bell-rope in his hand, pulling at the rope in a slow, dazed way as if he hardly knew what he was doing. He looked up at Dick's mother and put his hand to his head.

"Be aught amiss? We 'eard the bell and came," she said.

He tried to rise and fell back, and when Ann took his arm to help, she found he was burning with fever. She could not lift him, so she let him lie on the ground and turned to go inside.

"God has taken them both," he called out in a hoarse voice.

"Do thou stay here, Dick," his mother told the boy, "Do-ant coom in." She went in and up the stairs, and there, decently laid out, her hands folded and her eyes closed was poor Margaret Morton. Beside her on a trundle-bed Eliza was dead too, but still warm, her slender body twisted in a spasm. Ann had dealt with death before. She straightened the child and covered her with a sheet, then turning about saw Dicky, just behind her. His teeth were chattering.

"Get thee 'ome, thou naughty boy!" she said. "Send thy father to me."

He tried to go, but his feet stuck fast. He felt frozen.

"Lad, I need help now," his mother implored. "Be my big man, Dick. Send me someone to help me."

He turned and ran. On the way home he met Harry and began to sob out the story of what he had seen. Dick hardly understood that a little girl could die. He had observed death only in the form of animals killed for meat. Once, however, the wolves had taken a sheep and being shot at, had left it limp and warm, but somehow not living any more. So he told Harry between sobbing,

"The wolves 'ave got 'Liza."

69

The tragedy at the Morton farm was not an unusual one, nor any more terrible than the fate of other families on the frontier. A trader from New Orleans had come along the trail with kegs of molasses. Feeling sick, he had turned off up the lane to the stone house, and spent the night in their kitchen. In the morning he seemed better and went on his way, only to die in the woods halfway to Milwaukee. The trader had yellow fever.

When his wife and daughter sickened a week or so later, Mr. Morton thought they had caught cold, and at first he nursed them, dosing them with the home-made medicines from the pantry. Nothing seemed to help, so he sent a neighbor to call the doctor from Exeter, forty miles away. The doctor came, but he had never seen the "black vomit" and did not recognize the disease. He left pills and plasters and went home. By the time they died, Mr. Morton was far gone with the fever.

Every person on Hampstead Prairie knew about the epidemic, how it had taken a third of the population in New Orleans, how fathers turned their dying daughters away from the door and children refused to attend the burial of their mothers. No one would come near the stone house, either to help make coffins or to pray at graves. Thomas sawed and hammered for the best of two days and on the third day dug two holes in the hillside in the pasture. Between times he milked the Morton cows and his own, fed the chickens and sheep and pigs, and implored someone to find the circuit-rider and send him to say a prayer at the burial. Dick and Harry went to their Aunt Jane's.

Meanwhile Ann was nursing Mr. Morton. It seemed to her he was getting better. The fever had gone down, and though he was terribly weak, he had stopped vomiting. He had not asked about his wife's grave, or Eliza's, and it was just as well, she thought, for the circuit-rider could not be found and Tommy would have to say a prayer himself after he slid the boxes into the hill. Ann's own love of life did not blind her to the fact that poor Mr. Morton had nothing left to live for. She had to save him if she could, but it would have been kinder to let him go.

On the third day he suddenly stirred and spoke, asking her for pen, ink and paper. She brought them from his desk, propped him against a pillow and spread the sheet of foolscap on a writing-board in front of him. He wrote a sentence or two in a trembling hand, folded the paper and laid it on the window-sill by his bed. She waited for some time, then saw he was sleeping and took the materials away. Before morning he woke in a spasm and died.

Ann forgot all about the folded paper where it lay behind the window-curtain. She had to wash the dead and lay out the body. Tommy must make another coffin and dig another grave. Will Beeson had gone for the minister, and this time there would be someone to pray over all three graves when Roger Morton was buried.

She looked across the clearing and saw people standing there. Martha Hall by the look of her, and probably Sarah Goldthorpe and one of her boys. Ann came out on the back "stoop" and hailed them:

"Who'll come and sit watch for one night while we get a bit of sleep?"

"Be he dead then?"

"Aye. All three of them, poor souls."

"Coom away, then, Ann Wentworth. The dead need no watchers. Lock the 'ouse and coom away," Martha Hall shouted back.

"Nay. I cannot do it," she said. She and Tommy spelled one another for two more nights, sitting by the coffin.

When it was all over, they were so tired they could hardly get into their own bed at home. They fell into profound and dreamless sleep. At two o'clock a wind came up and blew rain and dead leaves against the bark roof. Ann woke.

"Tommy, I left a window open over yon."

"Who's to care, lass? Go to sleep again."

"Tommy."

"Aye. What?"

" 'Twill spot the blue wallpaper with the roses."

He sighed and got up, put a candle in his horn lantern and dressed. When he had come back to the empty stone house and unlocked the door, he was glad Ann had waked him. The house smelled sweet with the cleaning they had given it, and dampness would soon spoil everything. On his way upstairs he heard a rustling noise and picked up a piece of paper, blowing down. He put it inside his waistcoat. It might tell him whom to notify.

In the morning he spread the sheet of paper on the breakfast table and began to read it. His wife recognized the foolscap she had given Roger Morton. She knew better than to look over Tommy's shoulder or ask questions before he was through, but her curiosity grew harder to conceal when she saw the expression on his face. He passed the paper to her without a word. Ann gave it back.

"I cannot read it, Tommy. It be-ent plainly written."

"'To whom it may concern'," her husband began solemnly, "(that be legal writing, lass.) 'To whom it may concern, I, Roger Morton, being of sound mind and without living heirs, do bequeath all I now possess to Thomas Wentworth to enter into and enjoy said property upon the hour of my death.'"

"Ah, poor body! With his last bit of life he wrote that, and 'twere all for us." Ann burst into tears.

"I doot 'tis lawful, with no witness," Thomas reassured her.

They had lost one fortune and gained another, and it was doubtful which event most distressed them. Surely they could never live in the stone house with its atmosphere of death! The three graves on the hill would always be there. The place would seem haunted. So Ann said, with a vague feeling of guilt because she had once wanted to keep house in that kitchen and even now had a sense of ownership born of scrubbing and polishing every inch of it after its real owners were dead.

" 'Withoot living heirs,' " Thomas quoted, "He meant the child, but I'll e'en go through his desk for letters from England. Likely he's a brother or some next of kin."

But, though the mahogany highboy was packed with letters and accounts, nothing from Nottingham indicated that relatives were living there. Roger Morton and his wife had made a clean break with the old life.

Harry and Dick were much grieved at the thought of moving from the little house they had just helped to build. During the warm months they had forgotten the feeling of cold, but their parents had not. The strongest argument in favor of accepting the will was the tight stone house with its stove and good fireplace. Then too, if Tommy had to milk the cows in the stone barn both morning and night, he might almost as well own them. It would be worse, Ann thought, if poor Mrs. Morton had ever loved that kitchen or taken a bit of care how it looked. Then it wouldn't have seemed possible to have it for her own. As it was, she found herself growing discontented with the puncheon table in the sod house, with the sooty pot in the hearth and all the other hardships.

"John Hall be a justice of the peace, Tommy," she suggested.

"Aye, so he be."

"He might know."

They took the sheet of foolscap to Mr. Hall, who gave his solemn opinion that in the case of yellow fever no witness could be required. Outside his legal capacity, he assured them that no one else wanted the place. It was a pest-house, he said, and they would be foolish to move in before time had cleansed it. Ann thought of the soap and water she had used and felt certain they were more potent than time.

"Oh, Tommy!" she said, seized by a dreadful thought, "Happen the folk will shy away from us always. Dost think we'll 'ave no visitors there?"

"Not they. We'll 'ave them soon enough. Never fear."

"If I could only take my bed. My poor little bed!" Dick mourned.

"Do-ant be such a baby, Dick," his brother told him.

A week of early cold drove them into their new home. They felt very strange on that first evening, with the fires lit and all the unaccustomed furniture around them. They slept poorly too. Ann woke in the night and missed her boys, reached out one hand toward Dicky's bed and realized that he was in another room. She moved closer to her sleeping husband.

"I cannot sleep. I be thinking aboot them, yonder on the hill. 'Tis snowing now," she whispered.

"Spare thy pity, lass. They sleep sounder nor we," he answered.

75

In the morning the boxes had to be opened and the new life began with a cheerful bustle of activity. Dicky watched his mother taking things out of the boxes, exclaiming over mildew, shaking and sorting more stuff than he had ever seen. There were bed-curtains, table-cloths, shawls, petticoats, and bonnets. According to the inventories there were also nine aprons, fourteen pairs of hose, window linen, Orleans coats, waistcoats, umbrellas, muslin gowns, bed-caps, counterpanes, blankets and quilts. The last box was full of Cornish luster-ware, cups, plates, pitchers, teapots and trays.

"Who did all they things belong to?" Dick asked.

"Why to us, lad. Do-ant thou remember the curtains?"

"Nay."

"Nor the little quilt from thy crib?"

"Who 'ad the skirts and bonnets, Mother?"

"They were part of my wedding-clothes. In the old country thy mother were a fine lady," she said, laughing to keep from crying, because the clothes reminded her of England.

Upstairs in the new home there were two bedrooms, one large and long, with blue roses on the wall, the other small and square with pink roses. Dick and Harry shared the small room, the four-poster, wash-stand and highboy. Their casement windows looked out on a flag-stone walk which, though it led only to the outhouse and garbage dump, was beautiful with lilac trees. Their floor had a rag carpet, comforting to little bare feet on cold mornings.

Downstairs was a parlor and kitchen and another bedroom. Roger Morton had used that room for a study and the walls were lined with bookcases full of leather-bound books.

Outside the house, beyond the small clearing, the woods were dense and full of wild animals. The boys heard close at hand those forest noises for which they now knew the names—screech-owl, great snowy owl, bob-cat, lynx, timber-wolf. They heard the raccoons washing their crawfish in the little stream near-by, mourning over them in heart-breaking tones because they were about to be eaten. Once a doe crossed the clearing in panicky haste, followed by a spotted fawn.

They explored the four hundred acres thoroughly before winter was over, always excepting that hillside where three stone markers stood. There they never would go, though Dick had almost forgotten Eliza and could not realize that she lay under the ground. His father would not let him open her harpsichord. That, it seemed, was still hers. All her little frocks and shoes had been given to Cissy Goldthorpe, who lived a few miles west. Out of doors they found traces of her, the houses she had built of pebbles and twigs, the small bridge across the stream. Even these vanished in the storms of the winter. Gradually the place became their own.

As for their mother, she found so many reminders of

Margaret Morton that she had to learn a way of ignoring them. Either she pressed them into common use
until they became hers or she put them out of sight on
one high shelf of the cupboard. For a long time, Ann
Wentworth felt that she was working under supervision.

7

EIGHTEEN HUNDRED AND FORTY-FIVE. Harry lay sprawled on a low bed in the kitchen. His left leg hung over the side of the bed, moving back and forth in unconscious rhythm. His flaxen hair fell over his forehead, his too-short trousers wrinkled up below his knees, exposing coarse red underwear and ungartered socks. From time to time he scratched his ear or shook back the falling locks. Harry was not in Wisconsin at all but in Ancient Rome. Gibbon's *Decline and Fall* lay before him, its tooled-leather binding hidden under a slip-cover of unbleached muslin. As he read, he steadily pronounced the words with silent lips.

Dick was curled at the opposite end of the cot, but his attitude was one of relaxation. He was reading Goldsmith's *Deserted Village,* a poem he hardly understood, but which he knew almost by heart. The sound of his mother's spinning-wheel and her regular motion in the next room blended with the lines. Nothing disturbed his pleasure, not even his brother's impatient twitching.

Immortality is achieved in many ways. Roger Morton's unfinished book, *A History of Religious Wars,* had gathered four years' dust in the attic above the blue bedroom, but his library of other men's works kept his influence alive. In the fertile minds of Harry and Dick Wentworth his interests bore fruit. The boys had read, or tried to read, every book on those shelves with the exception of Voltaire, whom a visiting minister had branded as sinful. Voltaire was under lock and key.

Twice a week for four years, their Aunt Jane had heard them recite their lessons. Forced vacations had occurred when her Sammy and Lisbeth were born. Now Harry was graduated. His aunt admitted that her scholar had gone beyond her.

Harry, having no more prospect of schooling, felt keenly his responsibility to educate himself. He had even undertaken to change his way of speaking from the familiar Derbyshire to something he hoped was more American. Gradually he was pressing these same changes upon Dick, with the result that both of them were continually confused in their word-forms.

"Fetch the candle, Dick," he said, without raising his eyes from the Roman Empire.

"Nay, I'll not, then. Get it yourself."

Harry was too deep in the past to notice this defiance. After five more minutes of reading in the half-dark, he raised his head again and keeping one finger on a line, repeated,

"Fetch the candle, I say."

Dick got up. He disliked the feeling of rebellion. It

drove out other sensations, warm and pleasant, like the memory of beautiful words. He took a piece of bark, twisted it soft and fibrous, and held it in the hearth of the cookstove until he had a taper. Then he lit the tallow-dip and set it on the stone window-sill. Harry read obliviously on.

Outside the window, in the failing light, Dick could see the church his father had built for the people of Hampstead. Since they had come to live in the stone house, Thomas had cleared the trees between house and church, a distance of nearly one hundred rods along the trail. Now it was possible to see the five tombstones in the churchyard, the austere double doors, the limestone steps.

Thomas Wentworth would have been angry if anyone had suggested that the church was an offering of thanks for his unexpected inheritance. He had built it in love, not in gratitude, with limestone from his quarry, oak from his trees, and the labor of his hands. He had traded wheat for the windows, including the little fantail of colored glass, the church's only ornament. Dick was thinking of that window now, and how, with the sun in the west, it would be shedding red and green and blue light through the empty aisles. Often, when the sermons were too long, he was saved from boredom by those colors, transforming drab clothes and dull faces into something worth his attention.

Over there in the church, Eliza's harpsichord was

closed. The table held Methodist tracts, smelling of printer's ink. The bookcase was half full of volumes no-one ever read, the commentaries of Josephus, the life of John Wesley, the Book of Martyrs. They belonged to Dick's father who was prouder of them than of all his inherited library. On Saturday evenings, Thomas swept his church and laid the fire. On Sunday mornings he was there an hour early, opening the doors, opening the Bible on the altar, making ready for the circuit-rider's arrival. At such times the fan-tail window never showed its beauty. Only at noon, when the meeting was in full swing and the sun began to move down the sky from the zenith, the colored light would enlarge, lengthen, leave the pulpit-rail and steal into the aisles.

> "Heaven like a dome of many-colored glass
>   Stains the white radiance of eternity. . . ."

Dick said, repeating aloud the lines he had seen on a mourning card in Roger Morton's desk. Harry put down his book.

"You'd best leave off reading poems and such truck, Dick. They teach you naught. Improve your mind, lad. Read facts. Tell me now, what were the causes of the Punic Wars?"

This was a part of Dick's latest history lesson, which he would have to recite to Aunt Jane soon. He was saved the humiliation of confessing he had forgotten by the entrance of his father, followed at a respectful distance by Hugh Henderson, the hired man. Dick

knew what to expect if Hugh found him sitting on the
cot in the window. He jumped up quickly and stood by
the stove, holding *The Deserted Village* under one arm.

The cot was Hugh's only fortress. He had made it
himself, filled it with straw and covered it with the
blankets he had carried on his back when he first arrived
at Thomas Wentworth's door, hungry and destitute,
but rich in self-respect. For two years he had lived with
them, and though the best afternoon light came from
his window, though the kitchen was always warm when
the other rooms were chilly, no one questioned his right
to eject trespassers. Now he advanced upon Harry,
dragged him off onto the floor, and set Gibbon's *Rome*
firmly beside him. Then he established himself on his
own bed and began yanking at his wet leather boots.

"Get me the jack, son," he said, with a humorous
twinkle in his eyes.

Dick rather enjoyed this spectacle of his older
brother's subjection. He, himself, was too light to be
much good at the jack. When Hugh began to jerk his
leg with the boot held firmly in the vise, it needed someone heavier even than Harry to hold things down. The
wet leather clung like armor. While they pulled, the
older boy and the hired man kept up a conversation
punctuated by jerks.

"You throw down the hay, yet, Hugh?"

"Left it for you. Been chopping."

"Been in the cow-house at all?"

"Just now."

"How be Sukey?"

"Won't eat her corn. She'll calve tonight."

The boot surrendered too suddenly, and Harry went over backward, the stool on top of him. He got up, still intent on the conversation, and continued as if nothing had happened.

"I'll sit up with Sukey. The moment ever she begins, I'll call you."

"That's for your father to say."

Thomas had finished washing his face in the basin and was running a comb through his wet mane of hair. He turned to his eldest:

"'Arry, thou'll not sit oop. Say no more aboot it."

"I have to know some time."

"I tell thee, nay!"

Though the boom of his father's voice shook the kitchen, Harry seemed to be quite unconscious of its tone. Dick, however, felt acutely uncomfortable. He was not afraid of anger, but it embarrassed him. It seemed to make Thomas smaller instead of puffing him up. He was glad when the spinning-wheel in the next room came to a stop. The door opened and his mother emerged with an anxious glance first at her husband, then at Harry. She began to lay the cloth for supper. Harry brought the dishes.

"I told father," he said casually, "that I'll sit up tonight and call someone when Sukey begins to calve."

Ann fell into his trap. "I'll leave a bit of hot broth

on the stove for thee then," she said. "Happen thou'll
want a sup at bedtime."

The look Thomas Wentworth gave Harry might
easily have felled one of his own oxen, but Dick knew
the trick had worked again as it always did. Harry
could never be punished without one parent turning
against the other. He carefully planned it that way.
Dick, on the other hand, usually ran full tilt into both,
and though he disobeyed much less often than his
brother it was always more disastrous for him.

"What's so grand about seeing Sukey get her calf?"
he asked later. " 'Twill be bloody, I don't doubt."

"I'll tell you, Dick. 'Tis because I'm going to be a
doctor. I have to know all such things."

If Harry said he was to be a doctor, it was certain
to happen. Dick was convinced of that. Harry never
announced a fact until he was sure of it; he never under-
took a task he could not finish. Dick knew Harry would
make a better doctor than those he had seen, but he
felt his brother's life would be wasted in such a calling.
Doctors wore rusty black clothes and carried rusty black
bags. They had pills and plasters and powders which
they left on a saucer, and sometimes they measured out
"paddegorick" and quinine. They asked for hot water
and made bitter tea out of tansy or boneset, or they
helped rub a child's chest with hot lard-and-turpentine.
It seemed a dreadfully dull occupation to Dick, but he
soon found himself an apprentice in the trade.

"Go out and get me some sweet flag, some penny-royal and smart-weed and dogfennel," his brother would say, arranging the row of bottles he kept in the woodshed. Dick would go. He knew much better than Harry where to find the herbs because of his camera-like memory on which every clump of vegetation imprinted itself. A cluster of sweet-flag in the marsh—how could anyone confuse it with the blue iris? They were as different as two people. He had only to shut his eyes and he could see the exact location of those sword-like leaves and knobby, aromatic roots. In the same way he knew just where to go for spiderwort along the bank of the stream, or for horse-mint or wild lettuce. With his help Harry made some weird medicines, sweetened them with honey and tried them out on Dick, or on poor Bije, who was getting old and rheumatic.

Dick's mother was sometimes heard to say, "Aye, he's a one to notice things, my Dicky." His dark eyes were always busy. He knew the geography of their four hundred acres in minute detail, the long lane from the barn to the pasture, the two gates, the forest on either side, now falling away before his father's relentless axe. Beyond the pasture, the marsh, covering not more than an acre. Beyond the marsh, the hillside, where spring flowers grew in profusion. In the yard around the house he could have walked blindfolded to any object, the chopping-block and saw-buck, the lye-leach, the rain-barrel, the smoke-house and soap-kettle.

Beyond these was a rail-fence, and in the farthest corner of the fence a boulder with a vein of shining mica. He knew the markings of the boulder by heart.

The little stream which flowed across the floor of the stone "buttery" and kept the crocks of milk cool—he knew that by touch as well as by sight. His bare feet had explored every foot of its bottom, locating crawfish, clams, soft sand, slippery shale and mud. Schools of small fish and minnows had made themselves known to his ankles as he passed.

There were other things, not so pleasant, which he had to remember against his will. The time when he found a sheep, long dead, its ribs bare to the sunlight. The queer swelling that overtook the animals at certain times of the year, and seemed usually to end in their having small ones of their own kind to feed and care for. Harry and he had discussed this, but it was still mysterious to Dick. Sheep had their lambs in the far pasture sometimes. A ewe would fail to show up at dark when they brought in the others. They would think the wolves had taken her, only to have her come out of the bushes the next day followed by a wobbly-legged lamb. And once Dick had leaned on the pig-yard fence, glued by horrified curiosity, while a sow farrowed. It was a grisly business and he had no use for it, but the result was six squirming pink babies. Remembering these things, he was very much upset one day, when Harry told him:

"Don't say aught, and I'll tell you a secret. Mother be having a baby."

"Oh Harry!" he said in distress. "Are you sure?"

"Of course I'm sure, or I wouldn't say it."

"Who told you, then?"

"I heard mother tell father as how we'd be going to the mill-house when it came."

Well, that was one comfort. Dick loved to sleep at the mill. But he began to remember all the babies he had ever seen—Christine Beeson, with her birthmark and red hair, his own cousins, who had cried with colic.

"Why do we want a baby?" he said. "We've got Lisbeth."

"She's Aunt Jane's."

"Well, I do-ant want another."

"Mother does, or she wouldn't be having one, so 'old your tongue."

They did not go to the mill-house that day or the next. Meanwhile, Dick began to study his mother's appearance. Of all the familiar sights, the most familiar should have been this gentle person who fed and cared for him, but he had never really seen her as a whole. He had memorized his mother piecemeal, her round arms, dimpled at the elbow, whirling the washing-peggy in the tub of boiling suds, her gaitered foot on the treadle of the loom, her hair, rippling under the brush, shining in its coil. Now he set himself to seeing her all at once, and soon knew that Harry was right. She was swollen and clumsy, just like the cows before calving. He began to feel sick.

"Don't stare at me, lad," she said, blushing.

"I won't then." He turned away. Her eyes followed him, brooding. All at once, from being unhappy that he knew a secret she would not tell, he began to be sorry for his mother. He stood behind her chair for a moment, and then leaned his cheek against her hair. She put her arms around him.

"Ah, Dicky!" she sighed, but would not tell him the truth. That evening the boys went to their Aunt Jane's, and with his entrance into the mill, Dick dropped his cares and plunged headlong into a new world of sights, smells and sounds.

Sam Weymouth had built his own mill of the materials at hand. Wheels, cogs, shafts and levers were of hickory wood. The building itself was of limestone from a near-by hill, the floors of native oak. Only the stones that ground the grain came from far-off Pennsylvania. When the water-wheel was running, the whole mill shook and shrieked with the labor of the wooden machinery. Every night, Sam carried a bucket of lard down the ladder and greased the shafts, but the groaning continued.

Dick liked the process of milling wheat-flour best, from the time the sacks were dumped into the hopper until the grist was divided, and flour, bran and shorts

89

went home in the farmer's cart. His eyelashes and hair were full of white dust as he stood on the platform, helping with the sacks. He looked prematurely old. He would have been perfectly happy to stay in the mill, but Harry was larger and stronger than he and better help with the heavy flour. Soon Dick would hear his aunt calling him to mind his two small cousins. Reluctantly he went.

Jane Weymouth lived in constant dread that her children would be drowned in the mill-pond. Her husband had fenced off the yard, but Sammy, who was five, climbed over the rails, and Lisbeth, who was three, crawled through. Whenever Dick came to the mill, he was asked to mind the children. Sometimes he took them into the safe woods to build a house of branches. Sometimes he drew pictures for them in the dust by the loading platform. Sammy and Lisbeth loved him and in a tempered fashion he returned their love.

After five days at the mill-house the memory of their reason for coming had grown much less hard to bear. He was quite reconciled to having a baby and had told Harry so, when their Aunt Jane called them in and said they could soon go home. She waited a moment and added rapidly, averting her eyes,

"You have had a little sister, but she died."

The death of her daughter saddened Ann Wentworth's spirits for more than a year. Dick, who was used to seeing his mother's knitting needles fly, whenever she had time to sit, now was troubled by her folded hands. Often she took out the letters from England, already worn by constant handling, and read them again with tearful eyes. To Dick, these letters were puzzling. His mother sometimes gave them to him to read, saying as she did so,

" 'Tis from Granny, lad. What wouldn't I give for the sight of her sweet face!"

And then Dick would decipher the crabbed handwriting, running both ways on the same page to save paper, and it would be nothing but an account of griping pains, violent deaths and other catastrophes, with occasional grim references to the Lord, who brought these trials to test his children. He could not connect such thoughts with the person his Granny was supposed to be.

That year brought the first Norwegians to the prairie, a kindly, independent race. They straggled by on the trail, stopping wherever they could find work, for most of them were without money. Lars and Ole Rud, brothers from Bergen, lived in the sod-house for a year, helping Dick's father and carving furniture for his mother when farm-work was slack. Two boxes by the fireplace occupied their spare time for a while, and were finally complete with elaborate scroll-work and wrought-iron hinges and locks. These men bore good-naturedly the practical jokes of Hugh Henderson and his laughter at their mistakes, knowing, perhaps, that jealousy for his position was at the bottom of it.

In the spring, the three hired hands sowed wheat while Thomas followed them with the A-drag. Dick followed too. It was his task to keep the birds away until the drag could cover the seeds. Rushing back and forth across the plowing he flapped a white towel wildly in the air. The birds, hungrily swooping, barely missed getting tangled in his curls. Always just ahead of the oxen, just behind the three sowers, Dick's movements had to be rapid.

Whether in sowing or harvest, Hugh Henderson and Thomas made a famous pair. They could sow grain as fast as they could walk, spraying it evenly first from the right hand, then from the left. At reaping, Thomas walked ahead, swinging his scythe with its cradle, laying down the grain in swathes as smooth as a well-brushed head of yellow hair. Hugh, moving rhythmically behind him, caught up the swathes into bundles, tying them with a twisted band of wheat-straw. Lars and Ole Rud came in for some quiet teasing as they helped in the harvest.

"Shall I drop my rake while I tie the bundles?" Hugh would ask.

"Aye, drop it. Lars will show thee."

"It's a good way to waste the time if you're in no hurry."

Ole swung his scythe too low, and Hugh would frequently comment on it, suggesting that he was hunting field-mice for dinner. The good-natured newcomers took all this as a part of the game, laughing heartily at their own blunders.

Halfway to his uncle's mill, Dick sometimes stopped at the log cabin of Snor Bergstrom. Snor had been the first Norwegian in that community, and seemed to have little in common with the rest. He was not so easygoing, nor so ruggedly built, and his manner was sometimes aloof. He made the same mistakes in his English, however, so at first the people of Hampstead Prairie thought him fair prey for their ridicule. They called him "that crazy bug-man." He was always out at night with a lantern, collecting insects. He gathered plants, too, and pasted them on the brown pages of a great book, writing names under them in Norwegian script. He stuffed birds. This last accomplishment was what finally won him the respect of his English neighbors. A farmer could get an owl stuffed by Snor and pay for it with pork or cornmeal.

Sometimes letters were seen on the table in the log house, bearing the seal of the University of Uppsala. The visitor, waiting for his stuffed owl, would handle the letters rudely and curiously, scornful of any language he could not read. Dick was first to inquire about the queer postmark.

"Where is Uppsala, Snor?" he asked, as he leaned against the curb of the Bergstrom well and drank from the tilted wooden bucket.

"Vad? You don'd know Uppsala? Don'd you know the master, Linnaeus?"

"No, Snor. Who was Linnaeus?"

The Norwegian sat down on the well-platform and made Dick sit beside him. Clasping his thin fingers about his knee, he began the story of Carl von Linn, who had first described and classified the plants of Lapland. Dick listened, entranced, missing much of the tale because of Snor's dialect and more because of his own childish ignorance, but drinking in the glamor of the Lapp country, the tents, which Snor assured him were like the Indian wigwams of Wisconsin, the reindeer herds, the snowy plains and frozen rivers. Dick's eyes grew large and deep, his cheeks burned.

"And did you know him?" he said, when the tale was finished.

"Ja, I know him. He die before I was born, but I know him. In Uppsala he is everywhere. When they sent me to America, they say to me: 'Do for that new country vad Linnaeus did for the Northland.' So I find all the plants. I give them their names. I name the birds and the beetles. Do you see, Dick?"

"Are you a master too, Snor?"

The Norwegian shook his head, but his blue eyes shone, and Dick went away with the impression that his friend was a great man in disguise. Harry was inclined to agree, mainly because of Snor's knowledge of medicine, a knowledge which later led to Dick's undoing.

He had been sent by his mother to borrow some

laudanum from Helga Bergstrom. Helga was typically
the wife of a genius. She rocked her baby in a home-
made cradle on a dirt floor like other pioneer women,
but the cradle was overhung with wasp-nests, rattlesnake skins, cocoons, and the beaks and claws of various
hawk-species. Her bed in the loft was festooned with
the same sort of trophy. In her chest of drawers no
room was left for her linen because of her husband's
herbarium. Sometimes she must have wondered whether
Snor knew about the baby, oblivious as he was of everything outside his work. The story went that she had
saved her child's life once by pouring boiling water on
a rattlesnake that was about to strike, and that Snor
had scolded her for spoiling the skin. No wonder
she had frequent headaches which she soothed with
laudanum.

Dick had no way of knowing the serious nature of
his errand. An immigrant family in the sod house were
down with cholera; he knew his mother was nursing
them, but not that they were in danger, so he loitered
on the way. A butterfly crossed Beesons' cornfield. Dick
followed it, trailed a zooming bee back to the road
again, picked three wild orchids and stuffed them into
his pocket and sat down on a stump to watch a butcher-
bird impaling a dead mole on a black-thorn. He wandered on for a while and then stalked a covey of quail
into the outskirts of the forest. Soon he found himself
in a part of the woods he did not know.

"I'd best be getting back," he said. He set out toward

95

the trail again, but it seemed to be a long way off. After some time he reluctantly realized that he was lost.

"Ho!" Dick said aloud, to down the rising panic in his heart, "that's easy. The moss is on the north of the trees." But the trees in this forest were very odd. The moss was all the way around the boles, perhaps because no sunlight came through. Dick stooped low and tried to follow his own tracks back again, but there were few broken twigs and the ground was too dry for footprints. He swallowed hard, and attempted to think of all the woodman's wisdom he had ever heard.

"I'll climb a tree and look for the sun," he said. " 'Twould be summat to eastward still, for 'tisn't noon yet."

He hunted about until he found a tree that looked taller than the rest. Its branches were too high on the trunk for climbing, but he scrambled up another tree beside it and then swung himself over into the giant white oak. With great difficulty he got to the uppermost crotch and lay there resting for a few minutes before he looked at the sun. To his disappointment the time had slipped away and it was now high noon. He could see beyond the edge of the forest, however, and could make out what seemed to be the trail, a cleft in the waving foliage. He took his bearings carefully and climbed down again.

When he had walked for some time in the proper direction, he came out on a trail, indeed, but none he had ever seen before. The wheel-marks were green with moss, the road itself was narrow and strange, more like the tracks he remembered in the dense forest when they first left Milwaukee. Dick stood still, no longer in a panic, because a road is a road and always leads somewhere, but stunned by the discovery that he had unwittingly disobeyed his father's strictest command.

He was on the Barribault road. It was little more than a provisions trail, used in times of emergency to get food from the settlement called Adams or Barribault where the Fort Snelling garrison kept their supplies. Because the farmers were able to reach Milwaukee now, the road northward had been neglected, was overgrown with moss, infested by wolves and used more by Indians than by whites. Dick and Harry had been forbidden to explore it.

"Ah, but I didn't do it a-purpose," Dick thought. And as if the devil were prompting him, the temptation came to set out in the wrong direction instead of turning toward home. The right-hand way would lead south to the familiar Galena trail; the left went glamorously into the unknown. Dick drew a long breath and began running northward. The road grew even more narrow, overhung by trees, dark and oppressively still. Dick realized he was now in the midst of that forest which fringed the prairie, land still unclaimed, and unmarked anywhere by fences or private lanes. Though the silence was profound, he had a queer feeling that there were living creatures near him. The woods were full of an uneasy breathing; behind the trees which shut off the road like a wall, other boys seemed to be running, keeping pace with him. He slowed down; the unseen boys slackened their pace too. He turned his head sharply to one side or the other and they stopped breathing as if they held their breath for fear of being discovered. It was the echo of his own panting, the sound of his own laboring heart, thrown back on his ears by the wall of forest.

At last he could bear it no longer and was about to turn, when he heard a splashing noise and saw he was coming to a stream. It flowed across the mossy road. He would have to wade it if he went ahead, and in spite of his nervous tension he wanted to put his bare feet in the water. He took off his shoes—he never wore stockings in the summer, and was soon sounding the depth of the creek.

"What stream can this be?" he thought. It was flowing toward his uncle's mill. Probably it was Koshkonong Creek, only much smaller, much farther upstream than he had ever known it. It would be a rare adventure to follow the stream to his Uncle Sam's.

By this time, Dick had completely forgotten the laudanum. He turned off the road and began wading downstream, sometimes on the bank, when he had to go around deep holes or fallen logs, sometimes in the water. The woods seemed less oppressive now. They fell away in small clearings and grassy slopes. He was enjoying the springy turf and its sweet smell under the noonday heat, when he came to a footpath, leading down to the bank of the creek.

Dick was acquainted with the difference between Indian paths and those made by white men. The paths of white men had heel-prints here and there, destroying the grass roots or driving them down into the clay. Indians wore moccasins with no heels; they scuffed the grass off evenly so the path had a fuzzy look. Usually, too, the Indians followed a deer-track and hoof-prints of deer could be seen. Dick knew that this was an Indian path, even before he smelled the pile of over-ripe muskrats and mingled grease and smoke of their fires. He drew back, sheltered by low-growing osiers, and stood as still as a doe. Above him on the slope were five round hunting lodges, roofed with mats of rushes. In the circle made by these huts, several squaws were hulling rice, pounding the kernels with sticks in a square of deerskin, pegged to the ground at the corners. A young girl was building up the fire under the iron soup-kettle.

One of the squaws made a movement with her hand and spoke, her voice sounding mellow and musical. The girl straightened from the fire and turned around. Dick peered through the osiers in astonishment. She could not be an Indian girl because she had yellow hair!

She wore a woolen skirt, tucked through a beaded belt. Her blouse was of white deerskin, tasseled with fur. Her legs were bare, her beaded moccasins laced about the ankles. She came toward the women and bent low, talking to the squaw who had called her. A rosary swung forward from her neck and the cross glittered. Apparently the Indian woman gave her a new task, handing her a sharpened stick for digging. The girl came down to the stream, and without seeing Dick in the willows, began to dig tubers of wild potatoes, tying them together by the rootlets.

She came so near to Dick's hiding-place he could have reached through the osier screen and touched her yellow hair. After watching her for a while he forgot to be quiet, rustled the branches and drew his breath audibly. She startled like a wild animal, whirled around and saw him.

"Hullo," he said softly.

She put down her digging stick and drew nearer but did not answer. Dick was surprised. He thought she would have run away. He grinned at her, holding back the branches.

"What's your name?" he asked.

"Nom Marie. Ah, pauvre Marie!"

Of this he understood only the name. He began to wonder whether she were not one of those kidnapped children everyone told about, who were held up to more fortunate ones as reasons why they should be grateful and good-natured. The Indians were always taking white children from their parents, though why they should want them, Dick couldn't see. According to such stories the unfortunate lost ones were beaten and starved. This little girl looked well-treated and unusually well-dressed. She was plump and pretty; her hair shone as if it had been carefully brushed and her skin had a fair, clean look. Still it seemed to Dick that he must rescue her. That was what boys always did in the stories.

"Come here," he said.

She moved cautiously around the end of the hedge and did not resist when he took her hand. They stood staring at each other. They were exactly the same height.

"I'll take you home," Dick whispered. She shook her head. She did not understand him. He began pulling her by the hand and she followed him for a few yards in the direction from which he had come. Suddenly she stopped and stood as if frozen. Six Indian braves were coming down the path to the stream.

They were directly in front of the children. Dick dropped like a gopher into a gravelly washout and Marie followed him. They lay side by side against the loose stones of the bank, and she began to whisper to him volubly in a language he could not understand. Then, reaching in her deerskin blouse she took out a little package and pressed it into his palm. He was too much frightened to open it at once. He put it in his pocket. The girl set her hand against his shoulder, pushing him back. She made it plain that he was to stay there, that she would go. She climbed over the edge of the gully and the next moment he heard her talking to the Indian men, moving farther and farther away.

He lay still for some time. He had begun to feel weak and wondered how long it would take him to get home. The Indian soup was cooking in the kettle up on the slope. It smelled good to Dick, even though he knew it would be made of muskrats, berries and wild onions. His mouth watered. He slipped out of the gully into the stream and moved silently along, sheltered by the bank. When he had gone some distance he began to run, and ran until he was out of breath. A paddling noise around a bend of the creek made him cautious again.

"No doubt 'tis only an otter," he said to himself. But it was a man who came around the sand-spit, wading in high boots. It was, in fact, Leander Shotwell, though Dick had forgotten him. He was holding a snapping-turtle upside down and helpless.

"Snap away, my fine feller," Lem said to the turtle. "Ye won't be so peart in the pot."

"Oh do-ant boil 'im," Dick exclaimed. "Give 'im to me. I need a turtle."

"Ye need him, hey? What fer?"

"To put in my turtle-pond. My last one got away."

"Well, here's yer little pet, then. Look out how ye take holt."

Dick took the turtle carefully by the shell. He looked Leander over thoroughly, feeling that he was familiar.

"I've been lost," he said.

"Yer in wild country, sure enough. How'd ye get here?"

"By the Barribault trail and the creek."

"Where ye headed fer?"

"My Uncle Sammy's mill."

"That's pretty far downstream, boy. Better go back the way ye came."

"'Tis too dangerous. There's a camp of Injuns yonder."

"You're the Wentworth boy, ain't ye? I thought so. There ain't two cut by that pattern."

"There's Injuns up the creek. They've got a lass there with yellow hair."

"Now yer romancing, sonny, to use a perlite word."

"'Tisn't a story. Lookee what she gave me." He took out the package. Lem opened it and found it to be a small prayer-book, bound in sheepskin. On the flyleaf someone had written

Marie Gagnier, Belle Fontaine, Ouiskonsin

Lem began turning the pages.

"It's Latin, or some such heathen tongue," he said. "Belle Fontaine. Thet's up in the Fox country. These fellers can't be Fox, though. Must be Winnebagos. Wonder if they ain't Whirling Thunder's people."

"I want to go home. I'm hungry," Dick said. Lem gave him the book.

"We'll strike straight back through the woods now. Pretty soon ye'll know yer way." And sure enough in half an hour they were on the Galena trail.

"Hold on to yer turtle an' pike for home. In the morning we'll see what to do about yer Marie." Leander Shotwell gave Dick a westward shove and began walking east. Soon he was out of sight.

As he passed Snor Bergstrom's cabin Dick remembered the laudanum. But when he knocked no one answered and he decided they had gone on one of their flower-hunts. He went on, empty-handed and suddenly overcome with guilt. He was desperately hungry by now and saw with misgivings that the sun was far down the sky. Dick was afraid to come home, but there was nothing else he could do. He stopped only to put the turtle in its pool.

When he came into the kitchen he found the family and three hired men at supper. Harry gave him a long, warning look, but no one spoke. Dick sat down by the door. The smell of fried potatoes and fresh applesauce was too much. His head whirled, but he was afraid to go to the table, and no place had been set for him. He clasped his arms over his clamoring stomach. It seemed an age before the chairs were pushed back noisily on the oak floor and the men went out, Harry with them. He was left alone with his parents.

"Where hast been?" his father asked him.

"I lost myself. I followed a covey of quail into the woods."

"Where hast been, I say?"

"By the Barribault trail and down the creek."

A rawhide whip hung beside the door. Dick had felt the flick of its lash on his bare legs more than once, but always lightly, just enough to sting. Now his father took it down with a deliberate movement that was terrifying.

"Take off thy shirt."

Dick obeyed, hanging his shirt and undershirt on a chair. Stripped, his slender body looked white and childish. His father winced.

"Dick, I have prayed to God to mend thy ways. Thou'rt become a vagabond. I have prayed that thy heart be made 'umble. It be disobedient and proud. 'Ephraim feedeth on the wind and followeth after the east wind, saith the Lord. He daily increaseth lies and desolation.' Thou carest naught for God's word, but thou'rt filled with poetry and worthless tales."

As he finished speaking, Thomas brought down the rawhide with a force that cut through the skin. Dick screamed once and then set his teeth. He had been taken unaware. He told himself that he would die before he made another sound.

"Dicky," his father said in a trembling voice, "tell me thou'rt sorry."

He thought of his adventure, of Marie and the turtle. "I be-ent sorry," he said. The lash came down again. Twice. Three times.

"Dick, Dick, say thou'rt sorry. Ask God's pardon for telling a lie."

So that was it! He was being whipped for saying he was lost.

"I didn't lie, Father. I lost myself."

His father slowly raised the whip again. Dick, looking up, was able to see, even in his pain, that his father's stern lips were blue, that he moved with an effort.

"Tommy!" his mother cried. She was sitting huddled together like an old woman. His father threw down the rawhide and stumbled outdoors.

"Put on thy clothes, lad," his mother said, gently. He got into his shirt, flinching as it touched the welts. She took his hand and drew him toward the door. Scarcely knowing what he did, dizzy with pain and hunger, he followed her. They walked along the darkening lane and down the trail to the sod house. Inside, men were sitting around his old bed in candlelight, and on the bed was a form draped in a sheet. His mother drew back the sheet, revealing a boy of his own age, dead.

"Look well, Dick," she said. " 'Twere for him I wanted the laudanum."

"Mother, mother," he cried. "I didn't know."

"We never know, lad. 'Tis for us to obey."

8

MEN WHO LIVED on Hampstead Prairie were likely to welcome any excitement. Once shooting at Indians had been a dangerous sport, but now the clans were frightened and in hiding and settlers could harass them with complete safety. Thomas Wentworth was not cruel as were some of the other Englishmen. In church he deplored the desire to torment the red men and said a great deal about one's duty to all God's creatures. When begging squaws came to his door they frequently had borrowed other women's papooses. Their pleas for food were based on fertility.

"Ugh, ugh, flour for this papoose, milk for number two, pork for number three."

As nearly as she could, Ann supplied their wants. Before they were outside the property they would have lit a fire, dipped their chickens or ham in mud, and put them to bake. Naturally the neighbors were surprised when Thomas joined the armed posse to look for the kidnapped Marie. Lem Shotwell had told Dick's story far and wide, and from every house a man with a gun had been sent out to find the white girl with yellow hair.

After his father left, Dick discussed the rescue with his brother. He was lying in that almost pleasant state of sickness which accompanies a fever and the privilege of staying in bed when everyone else is up. Harry had bored a hole in his turtle's shell and tied it to the leg of the washstand where it stood phlegmatically, its front feet in a pan of shallow water. Bije was there too, and whenever the turtle moved its ugly head the collie growled and bristled. This was amusing to the sick boy, and so were the yellow chicks who peeped continually from their box on the chair by the bed. The day appeared to be a great success, though Dick regretted he had not told the posse about the gully where he had been able to hide. Suppose some Indian should put an arrow right through his father's heart! As he thought of this, he lost his last resentment at the whipping.

He was not told that his parents had spent half the night in prayer for his sake. Thomas considered it unlikely that a whipping, justly given, could cause fever and nausea. He thought Dick had taken the cholera. His wife had been putting ointment on her child's back and knew the real trouble. There was silence between the two, and for the first time a slight lack of sympathy. Thomas was glad to go with the other men.

"What if they do find 'er," said Harry. "She'll be no better off than before. Nobody knows who she belongs to, anyhow."

"Belle Fontaine," Dick muttered, groping under his pillow for the prayer-book. It was gone.

"Father took it while you were asleep," his brother explained. "He's sure 'tis sinful and a papist book, and he means to show it to Brother Shrewsbury." Harry spoke with a slightly sneering inflection, just enough to let Dick know what he thought of the whole affair.

"He can't do that. 'Tis mine. Marie gave it to me!" Dick rose up angrily.

"Now, now. Lie down and do-ant shout so. Likely he'll give it back soon," Harry soothed him, and then quickly went on to say how lucky Dick was to have ventured on the Barribault road. He, himself, had only been waiting for an afternoon off to try the forbidden trail, but now Dick had got in first. In the pleasure of making his brother envious, Dick forgot the prayer-book.

"But you shouldn't 'ave got so near the Injun camp. That was dangerous."

"It was wonderful, Harry. Like Sir Francis Drake on the Spanish Seas."

"Aye, and the bottom is strewn with their bones," Harry replied, quoting a poem they both could recite.

Shortly after noon the posse came back, dropping its members along the trail as each came to his home. They had found the camp easily enough, but the Indians had gone. Only the stripped poles, ashes and broken pots had been left. There was the path, leading to the stream, just as Dick had described it, there were the muskrats, too far gone to be removed. There was the screen of willows behind which the boy said he had stood. Thomas came upstairs and laid a peace-offering on his son's bed, a bone bow, broken at the middle where it had been wound with sinews. The Indians had thrown it away, but to Dick it was a valuable thing. He repaid his father with a melting smile and Thomas laid his huge hand over Dick's.

"Likely the Injuns caught sight of thee, lad."

"They might have 'eard me running away."

"Well, gone they be, and where the lass is, God only knows."

Indians hampered by a fair-haired white child would always be in trouble, Dick's father explained. They would have to stay in the deep woods. Sometimes white children had been sacrificed to get rid of the nuisance. Dick had no fear of such a fate for Marie. He recalled her beautiful moccasins and white deerskin blouse. Someone had loved her to make her those clothes. What wouldn't he give for a shirt like that! Because of his interest in them, the Indian clothes had left a vivid picture in his mind. He could not forget the pattern of beads on the shoes, or the white fur tassels.

What he did forget was the face of the little girl, its expression of wary stillness, the shape of her dark eyes, her passionate pleading as she lay beside him in the gravel of the ravine. He dreamed about her for years, but always in some romantic guise quite different from her own. She might be Cora in *The Last of the*

Mohicans, swooning and lamenting while he fought off her assailants with his father's gun. Or again she became Pocahontas, dressed in robes strangely like the lithograph of the young Victoria, but always Dick was the rescuer, braving perfect torrents of arrows, tomahawks and flint knives for her sake. These were the dreams he never told. They buried themselves deeply in his emotions until they were a part of himself. After a while no one would have identified their heroine with the hardy little girl who carried a digging-stick and a bunch of wild-potato tubers.

The whipping, too, had its symbolism. It merged into all the tortures and trials of endurance Dick had ever heard of, the walking-on-coals, the piercing of lips and flagellations. He felt community of experience with the young braves just come to manhood, and also with the boys of the Prairie, who were whipped every Saturday night to make them humble for the Sabbath. Now he knew the real meaning of those welts on Ethan Hodge's back. And Dick could rest assured his own were as bad as any.

Soon the whole settlement was in fear of the cholera. It swept mysteriously through one family after another, leaving death and sorrow behind. Every day for more than a month, coffins went by on the trail and new graves were dug in the churchyard. When little Sammy Weymouth died, his mother was in childbirth. Dick could hardly forgive his Aunt Jane because she named her third child Sammy too. He vowed he would call the baby something else.

"Jenny knows what she's aboot," his mother said. "We cannot die with the dead, so we must e'en live with the living."

Harry had read an old document about the London Plague. Some doctor had been wise enough to suggest that the foul water might be a cause. Plague was not cholera, but Harry set to work to boil the drinking water. He filled the big soap-kettle, built an outdoor fire under it and left it to boil. Then he hung it down the well to cool. The result was a tasteless, slightly soapy drink, a little cooler than lukewarm. No one liked this water. Hugh Henderson affirmed that it gagged him, that he preferred cholera any day. But, such was the force of Harry's character, they obeyed. Whether prayers or boiled water saved them, the Wentworths escaped the epidemic.

One day, in the year Harry was fifteen, he and Dick were strolling along the lane. They meant to bring in the cows for an early milking, but were making the most of the walk. There had been a summer rain. Everything about them was drenched and steaming, and Harry remarked that he hoped the cows had done their grazing before the shower and not filled up on wet clover, a good way to get colic.

Both boys were in homespun and jeans. Their mother sometimes said she could not believe they were the same children she had brought from England, so well-clad, with their nice little suits and blouses. She mourned the primitive life that made good clothes suitable only for church. The boys laughed at her and said they liked to go barefoot, to dress in jeans. They were comfortable and content. Dick had a new pocket-knife. He whistled as he walked, stabbed the knife into tree-trunks, or flipped it into the ground from the back of his hand in a running game of mumbledy-peg. Harry was deep in thought as usual; he strolled with his head thrown back, his hands in his pockets.

"I told father," he said, "that I'd be going to school next year, and he said as how he couldn't spare me from the farm. That's a warning to you, lad. Do-ant work so hard as I if you want to get away. Keep on being lazy, then he'll spare you and send you to school."

"What school do you mean? Milton won't give you much doctoring. All they learn there is Greek and Latin—and the lads wash their own dishes."

"I mean Milwaukee."

"So far away? What if father won't give you the money?"

"I'll beg a ride from one of the lead-drivers. When I get there I'll find work. He can't keep me, Dick. I'm bound to go."

"What did mother say?"

"She thought maybe I'd like to be apprentice to Charley Stafford and learn the drug business."

Dick wrinkled his nose. Neither of them had their parents' respect for Mr. Stafford. He had been chemist with the Earl of Chesterfield, had been sent to America to cure his whiskey habit, and now owned a store in Fort Atkinson. Dick thought his connection with nobility poor compensation for the fact that he smelled of liquor, suffered from catarrh, and had a perennial drift of dandruff on his shoulders.

"Mother thinks," Harry said, "that poor Mr. Stafford's failing fast and I might step into 'is shoes. Now Dick, you know I can't be a village apothecary, or a country doctor on pony-back. Aim low and you'll land low. I'll be the best doctor in the northwest or none."

"I'm sure of it," Dick agreed. His spirits were dashed by the thought of his brother's ambitions. Harry would leave home and then the old round of chores would go on with Dick doing them all. Hog-feeding, egg-gathering, milking, hoeing, wood-splitting, they were only bearable with companionship.

"Wonder what's ahead of me," he said. "Wonder what I'll do when I'm grown."

"That's easy. You'll do whatever they ask, because you don't like trouble."

" 'Tisn't that I'm afraid, though."

"No. You're not afraid, so I can't understand you. Why don't you stand up to father? He roars, but he thinks the more of me when I get my own way."

Dick had begun to answer this when they reached the pasture gate.

"Hullo!" Harry exclaimed. "Summat's wrong with the cows."

Three of Thomas Wentworth's pure-bred Jerseys were on their backs, legs thrust rigidly upward. Six others lay on their sides, kicking feebly. Harry leaped the fence. Dick took time to open the heavy gate. As he dragged it back, he saw his brother run from one cow to another, thumping their sides with his fist, passing his hands down their bellies. Harry came running back.

"Give me your knife, Dick."

"What'll you do?"

"Lance them. They're full of wet clover. Bloated."

"No, Harry! You'll kill them, sure enough."

"Three dead already. Give me that knife."

He wrenched the knife from Dick's hand, opened the larger blade and running back again, plunged it into the flank of a dead cow. An explosion resulted, blowing the hole wider open. Dick turned away, sickened. Harry studied the mess.

"Don't you go running for father now. I know what to do," he said. He closed the big blade, opened the little one and went to another carcass. This time he slowly pressed the small blade in, the gas slowly whistled through the opening, the cow's sides gradually collapsed.

"Keep your back turned if you don't like it," Harry said as he took the sick cows in turn, puncturing their taut bellies. One after another they grunted, kicked, sank back to normal size. Harry wiped the blade, closed the knife and stood back to survey his work, half-shutting his steady blue eyes.

"Will they live?" Dick asked with twitching lips. These cows had names, mostly of his own choosing. He knew their ways, as different as those of men. Crumple and Sukey were still standing with ten others. Baby and Tillie and Bess were dead. Only last night he had leaned his head against Tillie as he milked her.

"Can't tell yet. Got to watch. Take the others home, Dick, and keep them moving. Let them walk it off and they'll be well enough."

Dick started the standing cattle down the lane. They tried to stop every now and then, but he pulled switches from the poplars and struck their legs. At last they were in the barnyard and his father still in the field. He sat down to wait. After a half-hour had passed, Harry came, driving what might have been a procession of the risen dead. His six patients walked vaguely as if they had expected never to see the barnyard again. But they walked. Harry had a definite swagger.

Life on the Prairie centered in the trail. Women worked near the front windows in order to see life flowing along that artery, men spent their loafing hours looking at the road. Even when it was deserted the trail represented a world outside the encircling wilderness. If one followed the wheel-tracks long enough there would be towns and people, harbors and ships.

Every morning a knot of pony-riders passed at a

gallop—mail-carriers who would soon divide to different posts, Outlet Koshkonong, Catfish Mills, Hampstead or Indian Ford. Some went on to the west and met carriers from Galena. Circuit-riders in flapping black coats rode by, keeping their pacts with the Methodist "Plan." An itinerant shoemaker with lasts, rolls of leather, hammer, clout-nails and wooden pegs sought lodgings from which he could go out every day and make boots for the settlers. Great wagons, canvas covered, took weather-beaten families on their way to new claims farther west. And always the lead-teams passed, laden with pig-lead from Shullsburg, New Diggings, Mineral Point, Sugar River or Exeter. Returning they carried cloth, foodstuffs, dishes, cutlery, wall-paper, patent medicines, Bibles, window-glass, whiskey. Without the lead-drivers, the pioneers could have had no unbroken contact with the Milwaukee stores.

The drivers were an uncouth lot of men, hairy, gruff-voiced, given to oaths that rasped on the ear long after they were gone. They drank whiskey like water, left unwelcome insects on the clean English sheets. They told stories so raw or so terrifying that women often went early to bed, but wherever they asked for lodging they got it free. They were the newspapers of that wilderness, the conveyors of gossip and public opinion. The Oregon boundary dispute, "Fifty-four forty or fight," Texas and the Rio Grande,—the terms of the outside world rolled easily from their tongues. They discoursed in picturesque language on the state of the nation. Hampstead was like a colony of Old England, content to make money on foreign soil. But in the corners and shadows of those log houses were children, seen-and-not-heard as good children should be. From the lead-drivers they learned that America was their country. Dick Wentworth was one of these. Nodding at ten o'clock he would waken to hear a tale of conquest going forward, the story of some Welshman who had brought his family to Galena:

"So there we was, by golly, pitch dark in the woods and no town nearer than Apple River, twenty miles east. Children all asleep under the wagon, oxen turned loose, wife and me just kicking off our shoes, and by God, right then the big wind hit us. Say, it tore a strip out of that woods just like a razor-cut through a ten-months beard. Wife and I grab three young-uns apiece and down we flop into the stream just as the first trees smash over the wagon. Didn't last five minutes, by Jesus. Where be you, Maria? I yells. Right here, Jackson, she says, with Hannah and Mary and John. I says, all right, I've got the other three, but where's the baby? I thought you had the baby, she howls. No, I says, I give him to Hannah to give to you. No, Paw, says Hannah, that was the cat you gave me, all rolled in a gol-darn blanket. Well, sir, we climbed out over the damndest mess of trees you ever see and there was the wagon smashed like a cardboard box and a smoke coming up where our fire had been, and right between them lay the baby in her gol-darn basket sound asleep."

"What happened then, Mr. Jackson?" one of the listeners would ask.

"Why we ate the dead ox, by golly, and we built us a house out of the fallen trees. T'other ox I drove in to Apple River and traded for food. Took up our claim right there, with the land all cleared for us."

Most absorbing to Dick were the Indian tales that every driver knew. How the Winnebagos, besieged on Doty's Island in Lake Winnebago, ate even their dogs but would not give up to their ancient enemies, the Fox. How the Fox sent fifty chiefs in canoes with food and offers of peace, and were received and feasted and a treaty made. How that night as they slept in the guest-lodge, the treacherous Winnebagos poured boiling water through holes in the roof and parboiled their guests, whom they ate for breakfast.

"Ate fifty chiefs?" Dick asked, incredulously.

"Yep, every man jack. Go ask Four Legs on Doty Island if you don't believe me."

Rudolph, toughest of all the drivers, liked to tell tales of massacres. Red Bird, the Beautiful, was his favorite hero. Red Bird, who came into a house at Fort Crawford, scared away the rest of the family and scalped the baby as it lay in the cradle. The mother came back, said Rudolph, and found the child still alive. She sat down and nursed her, for the last time, she thought.

"But it warn't, by Cracky. She's alive and growed up, only she aint got no hair."

"What's her name?" Dick asked.

"Sophie Gagnier."

"Was there a girl named Marie?"

"Nope. Not that I ever heard of."

9

THE WORD *Koshkonong* means "lake-we-live-on." The Winnebagos named it in the days when they first came there, driven from the Green Bay country by their deadly foes, the Fox. Lake of wild rice, deer, mallards, blue-gills and berries. Along the heights the clan effigies of the Winnebago stand, the man-mounds, turtle-mounds, beaver and birds. Rock River idles through in a slow current, coming in at the northeast and leaving by the southeast corner. At the lake's head, General Atkinson built his stockaded fort, at its foot Mr. Taylor kept a tavern on a limestone cliff honeycombed with caves. Along the western side were several landmarks, known to the Indians, fur-traders, bateaumen and later to the English farmers. Five mineral springs used for medicine; a giant oak; Crabapple Point, the home of White Crow, the Blind, and his people. And north of Crabapple, the delta of Koshkonong Creek, making a half-submerged peninsula.

Through the tall marsh-grass and reeds at the creek's mouth, thousands of mallards were flying. It was spring, in the year 1848. Green herons stood, hidden by last year's flag-leaves, striking at passing sun-fish with their dagger-like bills. Mallards floated on open spaces of water. Snipe circled above their breeding-grounds, falling through the air in a series of brief plunges. Their wings, flapping against the wet atmosphere gave forth a bleating sound. From nests on higher ground, green-winged teal shot out over the slough. Bitterns boomed. A rail, safely concealed, made a continuous noise like an old hinge. Sandpipers darted by, trailing their legs in slanting flight.

In the midst of this teeming bird-life, two larger bipeds moved. Dick and Harry Wentworth, long-legged as herons, were wading up to their knees, hunting for a mallard's nest. Every year they tried and failed to hatch a flock of tame mallards under one of their father's hens.

Harry, at seventeen, was more than six feet tall, powerful of build like the men of the Wentworth family. Dick resembled his mother's relatives, the Blands. He was shorter than his brother, more graceful and agile. His complexion was of the glowing brunette type, like the coloring his mother had brought from England and lost, somehow, in the Wisconsin woods. At fourteen, Dick had a faint line of hair on his upper lip. His arms and cheeks were covered with dark down.

As they stood in the swamp, Dick looked very much at home, like a marsh animal in its familiar haunts. Harry was too tall, too conspicuously fair. He seemed a blond god, entangled against his will.

"Here's a full nest," Dick said, in a husky, changing voice. "Shall we take them all or leave some for the mother?"

"Take all," Harry answered in a profound bass. "She'll not come back, now we've meddled with 'em."

They lifted the nine pale-green eggs into a basket of hay which hung on Harry's arm. The empty mallard's nest looked so forlorn that Dick put his foot on it and trod it under water.

They came out of the marsh. The ground under the water grew more boggy as they approached the lake. Besides the creek, willow trees had made an island with their roots, catching bushels of debris as it floated downstream. On this island the boys stopped to rest, warming their soaked boots in the hot sun of April.

"Put the eggs in the shade or they'll be well on the way to hatch," Harry said. Dick took the basket and set it under a low bough.

" 'Tis a real bit of luck for us that the land's too wet for plowing today," he remarked. "Else we'd both be in the furrows on the west eighty."

"We'll be there anyhow, soon enough. No bird-nesting after that," his brother muttered.

"And I'll have the oxen to drive, I suppose, while you take the new team."

"Duke and Dan? Not likely. Father'll have the horses himself. Thomas Wentworth of Sheffield, you know. Prize-winner and all that."

Harry's voice was so bitter that Dick could think of

nothing to say. He knew what was troubling his brother, of course. Three years gone by—and Harry was still a farm-boy! His ambitions festered within him. By one means or another he had been thwarted, kept on the farm, or traded out to the neighbors for payment of various debts.

"First he offers to pay me for a year's work," he burst out, again. "I work like a fool. Does he pay me? Not father! He might be short of cash as he said, but he pays his other debts. Then the government opens more lands and all the Norwegians get farms of their own. No help to be had at any price. How fortunate for Mr. Wentworth he's got two strong sons!"

"Why don't you go like you once said, get a ride to Milwaukee with a lead-driver?"

"Maybe I will, but he'll have to pay me first. I've lost three years."

"You could find a job there, Harry. It'd take longer to get your doctor's license, or whatever they call it . . ."

" 'Tisn't only that . . . what's to become of you and mother when I'm not here."

"Become of us?" Dick asked, surprised, "Why, we'll be taken care of like always."

"And worked to skin and bone. Look at mother. Never a day's rest nor a penny of 'er own. Father can hire ten men at harvest and such, but no help for mother, and she has to feed them and make their beds and wash their clothes. Then, on top of it all, this business with Molly Beeson. . . ."

"What about Mrs. Beeson?" Dick was now thoroughly bewildered.

"Oh, Dick! You're such a great baby." Harry sighed and rolled over on his back.

"There's no sense in what you say. We've got a good father. He's not a mean man, and he gives us the best home for miles around. 'Tis the truth he's short of cash, because he can't sell the wheat. You know very well that Ben Weymouth dumped a load in the Milwaukee River rather than bring it home again."

Harry closed one eye. With the other he studied the grass-stalk he was chewing.

"As for Mrs. Beeson, folk should be kind to 'er. She stays away from church but so would we, if we could. She's very lonesome, and told me so 'erself."

Harry laughed so loudly that a striped bittern near by changed himself into a clump of dead rushes.

"What's wrong with you today?" Dick asked impatiently.

"Well, as you insist, I'll tell you. Molly's been after father since first we came here. It took 'er nine years to get 'im, but maybe she thinks he's worth it."

"You're crazy as a loon."

"Maybe so. And as for father's money, 'tis gone, right enough—into gambling stocks."

"Gambling!"

"*The Great Ocean to Ocean Tea Company*. Bah!" Dick was shocked, but unconvinced.

"Why father's the head of the church!" he said.

"Everybody respects him. Anyhow, Harry, if what you tell me is true, he should be glad to send you away. He'd be afraid to have you around."

"By golly, Dick!"

"By golly, what?"

"Nothing. I just had an idea. Don't remember what I said, lad. I was wrong. I get foolish notions sometimes."

"You certainly do," Dick said, his heart rebounding with relief. " 'Twill all come right, though, Harry. I'm sure it will. As for me, I don't mind the work. Get along to Milwaukee if you can."

Harry sat up, clasped his long fingers around one knee, and stared with narrowed eyes at the water. He might have seen a great many interesting things going on, but he saw only his thoughts. He was in the grip of some new scheme. As for Dick, looking in the same direction he saw four fires, sending up smoke on the far shore, and decided the settlement of Mormons had moved their camp again, probably because the English suspected them of horse-stealing. He saw two long boats moving slowly toward Taylor's tavern loaded with supplies from the Milwaukee trail. A raft of logs drifted with the river current, and he could make out the lumbermen's red shirts as they directed its course. From Crabapple Point a wedge of Indian canoes had set out toward the delta in wild-goose formation.

"Hullo!" Dick said. "White Crow's back again."

He had made out the style of head-dress on the Indian in the first canoe. Soon he noticed that one of the rear dugouts was rolling dangerously, paddled by a novice. It fell out of line, and while the other canoes shot around the creek's mouth, the unsteady one came straight to shore.

"Hi, Eth!" Dick exclaimed as his friend Ethan Hodge got out of the boat.

"Seed you from the Point," Eth said, coming over to the willows. "Been out all morning in the dugouts. Talk about fun!"

"What's White Crow doing back, Eth? 'Tisn't corn-planting yet."

"Ho, 'tis 'unting time, though! Should see the deer they've got over yonder. Half in the pot and t'other half 'ung up to dry. Now they be off after fish."

"They ought to let 'im alone this time," Dick said. "Why can't the government leave 'im the Point to live on? White Crow's a good Injun."

"Mr. Bissell's got the land."

"Paid the government, but White Crow didn't get a penny and he's lived there fifty years."

Ethan shrugged. Dick's interest in the Indians left him cold, though he was always happy to play in the camp of the kind old chief.

"Lookee 'ere!" he said, plunging his hand into a pocket. He brought out a blue cotton handkerchief, a handful of gun-wadding, apple-core, corks and fish-hooks. "Pshaw! Summat's in 'ere if I could get to it."

Summat proved to be a dainty rosary of snail-shells, strung on deer sinew. From the center a pipestone crucifix dangled. The Indians had made it; it was quite unlike a white man's rosary.

"Seed this 'anging on a stump," Ethan explained, "and thinks I, 'Finders keepers, losers weepers,' so I took it along to give to Cissy Goldthorpe."

"Give it here a minute," Dick said, and took it in trembling hands. An image, brief and vivid had crossed his brain: Marie Gagnier bending to speak to a squaw, her crucifix shining and swinging forward.

"D'you fancy the cross, Dick?" Eth said, looking at him curiously. "Take it, then. I couldn't give Cissy the crucifix anyhow. She wouldn't 'ave it." He detached the pipestone ornament and gave it to Dick, who put it in his pocket. He thanked Ethan casually enough, but he was still excited. Plenty of Indians wore rosaries, but Dick had never seen one among the Winnebagos. The dainty necklace seemed to suggest a fair young girl.

"Bet anything you like, you can't paddle that dugout," Ethan boasted.

"Bet I can."

"Bet you'll be in the water afore five strokes."

"Bet I won't." Dick stood up. "I'll show you."

"You'll do nothing of the kind, Dick," Harry said, coming out of his trance. He had no more than spoken to Ethan when he landed, but now he threw the weight of his authority against them both. "A wind's rising,"

he said, reasonably. "You're a new hand at the paddle
and the water's too cold for swimming."

Dick looked at his brother with amused rebellion.
Harry was so sure of himself he had not bothered to
rise. He simply leaned back against the willow-trunk
and rested his steady eyes on Dick like a restraining
hand. The younger boy stood undecided for a moment
and then with a movement as quick as a wild animal's,
leaped the strip of marsh, shoved the canoe off with
three running steps in the shallow water and clambered
perilously in. The log boat rolled wildly, dipping to the
water on first one side, then the other. Dick dropped so
low that only the top of his black head could be seen.

He could hear the other two shouting directions from
the land. In his mind's eye he saw them there behind
him, but he dared not look for fear of tipping his
treacherous craft. After some time he wormed himself
to a sitting position and saw that he was already a good
way from shore. Choppy waves darkened the water
just ahead. He would have to get the paddle to work
or the canoe would turn broadside in the wind. Holding
his body carefully rigid, he slowly lifted the short-
bladed Indian paddle. The whole trick was to move in
perfect rhythm. A jerky motion would throw him into
the lake.

The bay was shallow, with wild rice just sprouting in
the bottom. A month later it would be a tangle of lily-
stems. Dick smiled as he imagined trying to steer the

dugout through the maze of lilies. He dared not even turn around in open water. He was steadily coming closer to White Crow's camp.

"Harry and Eth will have to take the mallard eggs home," he thought, as at last he prepared to land his canoe in a cove on the shore of Crabapple Point. A few minutes later he had climbed the gravel of the bank and discovered the village hidden behind a thicket of black crab branches. Dick approached quietly, not because he was afraid, but in order to get a look around before he was interrupted. Two squaws came out of the nearest wigwam, carrying baskets of refuse. Dick raised the flap and looked in. Nothing there but an evil smell. He went along to the next lodge. That was deserted too. He carefully observed the wooden dishes half-full of food, the mortar with its pounded maize, the clothes and skins rolled behind the ribs of the roof. Then he dropped the door-flap and examined a scaffold on which meat was drying. The half-deer Ethan had mentioned was easily identified. There were also muskrats.

"Coon too," Dick said, sniffing.

He raised the flap of another wigwam. A gust of acrid smoke set him coughing. Hearing a low chuckle behind him, he turned around and saw an old Indian chief in elaborately beaded shirt and buckskin trousers. By the blind eyes, blue-white and opaque, surrounded with countless wrinkles, Dick knew this must be White Crow. The chief's white hair was long and adorned with three eagle-feathers.

"Smoke no good," White Crow said, laughing.

Dick was embarrassed because he had been caught peeping. Though the blind man could not have seen him, he evidently knew. Dick had heard that White Crow knew more by means of his four senses than most men learn with five.

"I brought back your boat," he said, to justify himself.

"Good, good," White Crow said. "Sit down." He walked forward without hesitation and took his place on a platform of branches that seemed to have been built for his use. Dick obeyed a dignified wave of the chief's hand and sat beside him. He was too much in awe of this old Indian to begin a conversation, and as White Crow seemed content to puff at the pipe he was smoking, there was silence for several minutes.

"You Wentworth," the chief said at length, "You Engliss."

"Yes," said the boy in astonishment. He could not imagine how the blind man knew his name, unless Ethan had mentioned it when he first saw them from the Point.

"Good, good. Tell Engliss, White Crow come back for deer, for fish."

"I'll tell them." Dick felt sad. The Indians were hungry. Lake-we-live-on had always furnished them food in abundance. Now it was no longer theirs.

"Some day come back for corn-in-the-dirt. Some day for rice."

"Yes. I'll tell them that."

"Good. Engliss buy place. Some day White Crow be in ground long time. No trouble to Engliss."

Dick sat crumbling a dried sweet-flag root between his fingers. He felt very much like crying. White Crow smelled the herb.

"Mananga kereli" he said, "fine for belly-ache."

"Mananga kereli," Dick repeated, intending to remember the name for Harry. "I'm sorry they bought your land," he added.

The Indian sat, impassive, smoking his pipe. The blue vapor threaded through his nostrils, and as he inhaled, the porcupine quills in his ear-lobes trembled against his corded neck. The eagle-feathers in his coarse white hair drooped as though they shared his fallen state. Dick took the pipestone cross from his pocket and put it in the chief's open palm.

"She go," White Crow said, immediately. "In the time when deer whistle, she go."

"Where?"

"With the one called Dog Head."

"What was her name?"

"Mah-ree."

IO

HARRY'S OUTBURST was not easily dismissed from Dick's mind, even though he thought it ridiculous to connect his father's visits to the Beesons with Molly's good looks. Why, everyone knew that Thomas labored to bring women as well as men into the sheepfold of the Lord, and Molly had been mentioned often in family prayers as someone God coveted but had not quite obtained. Perhaps not so often in the last year. No, now Dick came to think of it, he had hardly heard her mentioned since the previous summer. His father still walked down the trail to the Beeson home, but his mother seldom went along. Willy seemed as much his father's slave as ever, and that in itself disproved Harry's crazy suspicions. In fact Dick was not quite sure what Harry had implied. He understood much better the reference to speculating in tea company stocks.

He was sitting in the study one day, deep in his fourth reading of *The Merchant of Venice,* when his mother and aunt came into the sitting-room. Dick's door was ajar, but he had no intention of eavesdropping. He sat quietly in the next room because he should have been hoeing potatoes. He had come into the house for a drink of water, found the rooms empty, and lost himself in Shakespeare. "A bit of selfishness is what you need, my dear," his aunt was saying. Through the narrow opening, Dick could see her, sitting primly upright and knitting as fast as her fingers would fly. "Surprise your Tommy with a taste of neglect," she added. " 'Tis an experience I'll warrant he's never had."

"Jenny, I cannot change."

"I doubt he's so much as touched her arm, my dear. He's mistaking his feeling for summat else. He's strayed only in his heart."

"His heart is what I care aboot," Dick's mother said, weeping.

"Aye, but 'tis a comfort to think it has gone no farther, and I believe it hasn't."

"Thou needn't keep saying that, Jane. I know my own 'usband."

"Not so well as I do, for I grew up with Tommy, and I've smacked his face more than once for his high and mighty ways. I don't think him so wonderful and wise, and as for Molly Beeson I'd like to go over right now and drag her about the house by her carrot-top."

Dick kept quiet until they were in the kitchen, and then slipped out of the front door. For the rest of the afternoon he plied his hoe vigorously and wished he had not overheard the conversation. If he repeated it to

Harry, his brother would simply say "I told you so."
He was terribly upset. At the dinner table he could
hardly look at his parents; for the first time he seemed
to feel a queerness between them. Alternate waves of
love and revulsion swept him when he met his father's
eyes. Love conquered, and he decided there must be
something he could not understand. He went early to
bed.

Harry, too, was behaving strangely. Will Beeson had
lent Thomas a man in plowing time, now he asked for
Harry during late sowing. The customary thing was for
Harry to protest. He disliked the whole Beeson family
and especially Molly's cooking. Both boys referred to
Christine as the "red-haired wildcat." Naturally, Dick
was surprised when his brother accepted the arrange-
ment with a suspicious eagerness.

"He's up to another trick," Dick thought. He was
sure of it when Harry came home the first night looking like an arch conspirator, now deep in thought, now
smiling broadly to himself.

While Harry was gone, Dick tried to comfort his
mother without letting her know it. He hated house-
work and she seldom asked for help. Perhaps if he
wiped dishes voluntarily it would please her. He tried
it for several days, but she thanked him vaguely, out of
a sad preoccupation. She hardly knew he was there.

"You were right about Mrs. Beeson," his brother
said one night while they were undressing for bed.

"She's lonesome." He laughed disagreeably. "Dick, you've no idea how lonesome she is."

Dick had no wish to talk about Molly. It was a subject he could hardly endure. He quickly switched to something more bearable.

"How's the wildcat?" he asked. He and Harry could always agree on Christine's behavior.

"She's an unusual child. She's learned to stay out of the house when her mother has company."

"Have the Beesons got company?"

"Oh Lord, Dick!"

"What's the matter?"

"I wish you weren't such a baby. I can't even talk to you."

"Don't then!" Dick said, angrily, getting into bed and covering his head with the sheet. Harry sat perfectly still, one shoe in his hand. After several minutes Dick pushed back the sheet. In the late summer twilight, his older brother looked stern and unhappy.

"Is it about father?"

"No. Go to sleep."

Harry had yielded in nine days to the pressure his father had resisted for nine years. When he first realized this, when he knew that Thomas, however bewitched, was still able to call himself a man of God, Harry was sadly shaken in his opinions and conceit. He had been wrong in his whole concept of his father's character, but he had also been wrong about himself, and that was what hurt. It was not like Harry Wentworth to lose sight of his main purpose for very long, however, and after a week of drifting he had another inspiration. He had meant to blackmail his father. Now he reversed his tactics.

"If he won't send me to school for his own sake," Harry thought, "no doubt he'll do it for mine."

It was not by accident that Thomas Wentworth found his son in Molly Beeson's arms, nor was it unplanned that he should walk the woods groaning and mentioning the name Jezebel in his prayers. Harry was a good actor. He gave every indication of shame and humility, and showed only gratitude when his father discovered enough ready money to buy him a new suit and pay for his board and room in Milwaukee.

What neither of them foresaw was the end of their antagonism. They had a common bond now, however unacknowledged, and a common secret, however painful.

II

STAND UP for yourself, Dick. When you know what you want to do, don't let anything stop you. I can't help you any more. Don't let father hold you too long. He means well, but he doesn't realize. If you want to be a farmer, all right, but 'tisn't what I'd choose for you. Do some thinking, lad, and make some sort of decision."

Harry's portmanteau was packed in the chilly bedroom. He was wearing a new suit, strangely elegant. Dick was in his ordinary plain clothing. It was not the only thing which divided them, nor the first. They had been set apart all autumn by the fact that Harry was going away as soon as frost began.

Now the grain was winnowed, the wood cut for winter, the ears of corn husked and cribbed. On a high scaffold many carcasses of hogs and sheep were piled, ready to be taken to Milwaukee. It was early December, but cold enough so the meat was safe. In the darkness of morning, a horn lantern flickered on the scaffold. Hugh Henderson was up there, loosening the meat from the planks with a crowbar.

The trip to Milwaukee was about to be made by a caravan of four ox-carts, each with three yoke of oxen. Thomas drove the first cart, and after him were John Hall, Joel Sharp, and Amos Hodge. Harry and Dick came downstairs and began putting on their warm outdoor clothing beside the kitchen stove. Through the windows they could see the bobbing lanterns of the caravan, moving about in the clearing.

"Keep up your schooling, Dick. Whitford Rush will read Latin with you. I had father ask him yesterday."

"Don't go on like that, Harry. It sounds as if you were dying."

"And you'll likely pay just as much attention afterward as if I were dead."

Out in the yard, a trial of strength was about to begin between the caravan drivers. The boys hurried out, not to miss it. Harry walked stiffly. He was in constant fear of splitting his tight trousers or breaking the edge of his starched collar.

"Heave away, Hugh!" Thomas Wentworth boomed. He had drawn his cart up beneath the scaffold and was standing beside it.

Hugh Henderson had pried loose a frozen three-hundred pounds of pork and fastened the hook of the windlass into the meat. Now he raised it, swung it clear of the scaffold and waited for the signal.

"Let 'er coom!" roared Thomas. Hugh dropped the three hundred pounds on his shoulders. Thomas took the hog's front legs in his hands. The rope slackened. He was bearing the whole weight.

There was a breathless hush. The other men held their lanterns high, flooding him with light. He took three steady steps forward and unloaded his burden on the ox-cart.

"Next!" he said.

John Hall was sixty years old. He asked for no quarter and got none. When he reached the wagon he tried twice, but could not get his pig over the side. Thomas helped him load it.

Joel Sharp fell flat under the first impact. Amos Hodge staggered to the cart and fell as the carcass went over the side. The rest of the meat was lowered by windlass directly into the cart.

Dick's mother had planned to go with the caravan. She had not been outside Hampstead Prairie in ten years and in that time, she heard, Milwaukee had grown to be a great town. Feverishly, Ann went through her array of bonnets and dresses. She feared they were out of style, she pressed and basted and trimmed. Every day she thought of some new reason why she could not leave home. The chicks would die, the fires would go out, Dick would take lung fever. When the day arrived she had talked herself out of the trip. Dick could go in her place and ride as far as Fort Atkinson, coming back with Ben Weymouth, who was hauling flour to the Fort. He kissed his mother good-bye.

"Ah, Dick, I'm glad thou'rt coming home! I couldn't 'ave let my little boy go."

He laughed at that, because as he stood beside her, his mother came barely to his shoulder.

"Dost recall how I used to play wolf with thee?" she said.

"Aye. The sheep could eat the wolf in one bite now."

At Weymouth Crossing, day was beginning to break. Jane came running out to her brother's wagon.

"Tommy, the slough's been all laid over with fresh corduroy. The logs aren't down in the mud yet. I doubt you'll get across."

When he saw the marsh, Thomas and the others doubted too. After much discussion they decided to hitch a "snatch team" to the rear of each cart to pull back when the wheels were going down. This would have worked if the logs and wagon wheels had been in the right ratio, but they were not. When all oxen were pulling and the front wheels were going up, the back wheels were going down with a frightful bump. The reverberation shook the prairie. The great pole swayed from side to side, slapping the oxen's flanks. They shrank away, bellowing. Harry jumped down, forgetting his tight breeches.

"Cut poles, men. Lay them between the logs."

The older men were inclined to be scornful of advice from a stripling, but something had to be done, and

Harry's scheme seemed as good as any. They cut poles and made a sort of moving platform, laying them parallel with the logs. As a cart passed over, they picked up the poles and laid them down again in front of the wheels. In an hour all four carts were over the marsh.

At Rock River, Dick saw with great excitement the new ferry, worked by a system of pulleys and run by the current of the river. He rode across with each wagon and back again. Before he returned from the final trip his father bade him good-bye.

"Say thy prayers, lad. Read thy Bible daily. Spare the corn with the laying hens."

"I will, Father."

"Look to Crumple's teats when thou milks 'er. Rub them with tallow. They be cracked since frost."

"I will."

"Remember what I spoke of this morning, and don't forget me, Dick," said his brother.

"Oh, Harry!"

"And don't be such a great baby," Harry said, for the last time.

Part Two

I

LUCY HAMMOND was sitting in a small rocking chair, but she was not rocking. She sat with her narrow feet parallel, her full skirt spread decorously around her. Her hands were folded in her lap, but her mother's hands were gesticulating rather freely. Her mother was in the midst of one of those arguments which flushed her plain face and brought out a burning red color on the bridge of her hawk-like nose. The shriller and more rasping Mrs. Hammond's voice became, the more gently modulated was Lucy's.

"This Richard Wentworth, then, unless he is using an alibi . . ."

"I think *alias* is the word, Mother."

"Unless, I say, the name is fictitious and designed to deceive an innocent girl, for I hope, my love, we may still call you innocent, though others might consider you bold and experienced in view of your rash behavior . . . where was I?"

"You were speaking of Mr. Wentworth, Mother."

"Yes. I cannot imagine how any daughter of mine,

145

though of course I have only one, but to speak figuratively . . . could have been attracted by a young man who behaves in so unconventional a fashion. To begin with, he scraped acquaintance with you in a public building, for a library, though it is supposed to protect the young people who frequent it, can hardly be said to be other than a public . . . where was I?"

"He scraped acquaintance."

"Yes. A young man who behaves in this fashion must be ashamed to approach you in the ordinary manner."

"I feel sure you won't find him ashamed, Mother. He should be here any minute now."

"And consider the fact that he calls on you without my consent!"

"He could hardly get your consent without calling."

Mrs. Hammond's emotions had left her somewhat breathless. She rocked back and forth vigorously and wielded her black fan.

"I insist Lucy, I really insist that you retire while I interview this brash young man."

"I wish you wouldn't call it an interview, Mother."

"Very well. I shall just inquire as to his social and financial situation. I'll confine myself to a few pointed questions."

Lucy's delicate eyebrows elevated themselves into a pained arch.

"You must not forget, Lucy, that such things are important. Your father, as you know, is a self-made man, but your mother was a Cornell from Philadelphia."

"Well, as you and Aunt Kate are the only Cornells I know, I'm not overwhelmed."

Mrs. Hammond started at the impact of this barbed shaft and was about to return the shot when the knocker outside the door was raised and brought down vigorously in a series of raps.

"Here he is now! Retire, my love, retire!" She pushed Lucy out of her chair and toward the staircase, and bustled to the front door, forestalling a servant-girl who peered uncertainly from the dining-room portières. Alpaca bosom crackling over a starched foundation, Mrs. Hammond reared back to confront the caller, who stood on the door-mat, holding in his right hand a cornucopia filled with garden roses. Dick put the flowers in her hands.

"Please give these to Miss Lucy and tell her I've arrived."

Mrs. Hammond's nose came down several inches and she struggled with a hurt expression.

"I am Lucy's mother, Mr. Wentworth, though you've evidently mistaken me for a servant."

Dick had won this first skirmish by accident, but he was too naïve to see his advantage. He knew only that this was to be his mother-in-law if he could possibly manage the miracle, and that he must somehow correct an error.

"Do forgive me," he said, with a disarming smile. "I'm entirely blind from the sunlight and can hardly see you."

Mrs. Hammond backed silently away from the door and motioned him to enter. He came into a severely formal room, the drawing-room of Colonel Hammond's mansion. He could see, through the open door, the sitting-room where Lucy and her mother had been arguing, the two rockers close together and the cheerful colors of the rugs, but in the drawing-room all the chairs were arranged stiffly along the wall and the fireplace and center table were of cold white marble . . . "tumstun marble" the inhabitants of Hampstead Prairie would have called it. He put his beaver and gloves on a console by the door and sat down on one of the straight chairs, pulling up his tight trousers a little at the knees. Mrs. Hammond laid his roses on the console by his hat as if they were too inconsequential to be put in water immediately.

"I shall give these to my daughter shortly," she said. "Lucy is making her toilet, Mr. Wentworth, and I must take this occasion to become acquainted with you, an event which you have carefully avoided."

"I haven't chosen to avoid you," Dick hurriedly assured her. "I never choose to avoid people. I grew up in the forest, Mrs. Hammond, and had occasion to observe plenty of wild animals, but very few human beings. People are immensely interesting to me."

"Well!" Lucy's mother exclaimed, letting her breath out suddenly so that the edifice of starch and alpaca collapsed. "Well, indeed! I'm glad you find me more interesting than the wild animals. Was it this passion for observation that made you pursue my daughter?"

"Yes, at first."

"And you later found other reasons. What brought you out of your wilderness, Mr. Wentworth?"

Dick drew his breath like a diver about to plunge.

"I was sent here as a lay delegate to the Methodist Conference."

"As a lay . . . you are very young to be a delegate, surely."

"Yes, but it was not to my credit at all, since my father owns the church that sent me."

"The church, my good young man, belongs to God."

"At any rate my father built it and keeps the key."

Mrs. Hammond found herself weakening. The boy was probably lying, but he was not afraid of her and she hated young men who were afraid. Dick kept his eyes on her face as if he thought her worth looking at, and it was most unusual for a man to pay her this compliment. Even her husband, the Colonel, when he was at home, was inclined to glance away frequently. As for Dick's own looks, they were good and she could not deny it. His hair, glossy and black as a cocker-spaniel's, curled crisply away from his pleasant, ruddy face. She thought his clothes somewhat countrified, but not bad. She would have been astonished if she could have seen them cut out on Sven Gunderson's kitchen table. Ann Wentworth's flair for material and style had triumphed again.

"Perhaps you will tell me," she said almost absently, as she dragged her attention from Dick's appearance, "Perhaps you will enlighten me as to the circumstances of your very casual meeting with my daughter."

"Why, why it was about a copy of Pliny in which she couldn't find the reference she wanted."

"What did the reference concern?"

"The early church fathers in Asia Minor."

"Hm! And so you were able to help her in this very *unaccustomed* interest. Really, I am beginning to think you the flower of wisdom and chivalry. Did you come to the conclusion that she wanted further assistance?"

"I—I thought she might not object." Dick was beginning to look hard-pressed.

"And why did you think that?"

"Well, Mrs. Hammond, in the wilderness I come from, we have a simple way of finding out. It's all a matter of the look in the eye of the lass."

At this, Lucy came in. She had been eavesdropping and was crimson with suppressed laughter.

"Oh, Dick! You're a wretch. Mother, I've made you acquainted with an accomplished liar and taught myself a good lesson. Never give a downward push to a man who's headed in that direction by nature. I told Dick to impress you in any way he could and you see what happened."

"So you aren't a lay delegate, Mr. Wentworth?"

"No, Ma'am. I was sent by my father to haul a load

of wheat to Madison and find out from our assembly-man when the new road will be through."

"And as for Pliny?"

"It might have been Pliny. I didn't look at the book."

"It was *Love and Lightning* by Mrs. Barr," said Lucy.

"Which I forbade you to read," her mother added grimly.

The truth about their meeting was simple. Fate had managed it, perhaps, but Lucy had lent Fate a helping hand. She had dropped her glove, mixed up her books with Dick's on the librarian's desk and finally taken an armful so heavy that she had to be helped as a matter of Christian charity. Thereafter they had met a great many times as her mother had deduced from her use of Dick's first name.

He had come to the Wisconsin capital in early fall, driving up along the Barribault trail. His father had sent him to Madison on a venture, having heard that wheat brought a good price there.

"Mind thee, lad," his father had said, "if thou finds a ready market, 'alf the profit's thine from then on. And see Mr. Haskins aboot the road too, for I cannot break the new field till I know where the line will lie."

As he sat on the sheepskin-covered wagon-seat beside his friend Ethan Hodge, Dick had no premonition of the romance awaiting him in the capital. He listened to

Eth's enlightened comments about women, shouted above the rattling chains and creaking wheels, and was somewhat envious of such superior knowledge. He could add little to the conversation, though he had not escaped the girls of Hampstead without occasional "bussings" in haylofts. He wondered vaguely what adventures were ahead of him.

They took lodgings with Whitford Rush, the circuit-rider with whom Dick had studied for five years after Harry went to school. Mr. Rush had a church in Madison and had settled down since his riding days. His house and stable were always at the disposal of his old friends who had generously given him room and board in other years. Dick stabled the oxen and sold the wheat. He had not been in Madison three days before he met Lucy.

She was coming out of a house on State Street which bore on one of its double doors the words *P. Barrett, Bookbinder,* and on the other *Free Library.* The house was a forbidding edifice, box-like and gray, with that unloved look of old homes deserted by their owners. In the center of its wide front steps, however, Lucy stood. Her blue taffeta mantilla was crossed on her breast and belted in to a slim waistline. From beneath the mantilla, undersleeves of creamy muslin emerged and were caught at the wrist with circlets of rosebuds. Frivolous curls, pulled forward under a wide bonnet-brim, belied her serious face.

"My word!" Dick said to himself. "What is a girl

like that doing in a library?" Excepting his Aunt Jane
he knew no women who liked to read. He started impulsively up the steps. Lucy passed him, going down,
her chin in the air. Nevertheless, he believed she had
noticed him, and even formed some sort of decision
about him.

He had made an appointment with Congressman
Haskins for the next day, and with some difficulty, for
Mr. Haskins disliked being questioned on the subject
of new roads by his constituents. Dick broke the engagement without a second thought. It seemed imperative
that he should go to the library again. Three o'clock
found him reading *The Life of Napoleon* with one eye
on the door. He sat in the hard wooden chair for several
hours and was disappointed but not discouraged when
Lucy failed to appear. The next day he was there as
soon as the doors opened. He had not gone far with
Napoleon before Lucy came in, exchanged a demure
greeting with the black-bombazined dragon at the desk,
and passed so close to Dick that he heard the rustle of
her petticoat. She barely flicked his face with her blue
eyes but he felt bathed in their color. He could not drop
his own gaze to his book again but quite frankly and
devouringly stared. She turned her back to him and sat
down at a table.

He tried to read but the type swam under his eyes
and the words had no meaning. He beat his brain for
some ruse by which he could make Lucy notice him
again. Then he saw that she was only pretending to

read. She had not turned a page in ten minutes. Their awareness of one another flared like a rocket in the library's dim air.

That night, in his room at the minister's house, he wrote a letter to his father:

"So, as it seems Mr. Haskins is a very busy man and requires coaxing besides, and as I know you want the road hastened, I will wait a little longer until I see results. Ethan will bring home the beasts and Waggon and your share of the Wheat money. I am keeping my own half against necessity."

The "little longer" had become six months.

"Did my mother frighten you?" Lucy asked, when she had finally left them. "Did you find her terrifying?"

"Not at all. I liked her very much."

"What did you find to admire?" Lucy said, looking surprised. "I suppose I've lived with her too long to see her virtues."

"Well, her vocabulary is very impressive. She could give points to Mr. Webster."

"Oh yes. I've never thought she lacked eloquence," Lucy murmured, pulling her pretty mouth to one side. "Of course it's one of your charms, Dick, that you like almost everyone. You even like me . . . a little bit. Don't you?"

He answered this as she had hoped and she escaped breathless.

"I'm surprised at you. I didn't hear you ask my mother's permission to pay me any addresses."

"Oh dear! I forgot to, Lucy. Call her back, won't you?"

"Do you really want me to? Don't you think she needs rest?" Lucy leaned toward him.

"God loves filial piety," he said as he kissed her again.

"Neither of us deserves his love then. Your poor father must be wondering about you."

"They all know what has happened to me. I've dropped more than one hint."

"I must write my father, Dick. I know you'll like him because men always do. He'll be here from Washington in July."

"I ought to like him," Dick said, glancing again at the Colonel's portrait which hung above the marble mantel. "He looks like you. And then too, he was kind enough to leave you behind when he went East."

As a matter of fact, the portrait, with its air of uniformed authority, made Dick somewhat uneasy. Lucy's father was the sort of man he had never understood, the impregnable, self-assured, worldly type. At least, so he appeared in the picture. His eyes, like his daughter's in form and color, had a wholly different expression, as a shallow pool resembles the serene, blue lake.

Dick was somewhat troubled, moreover, by his first view of Lucy's home. Its formal elegance was strange to him, but it was Lucy's background and she might find his own very crude by comparison. He said to himself, loyally, that he preferred his mother's rag rugs, spinning-wheel and dresser filled with copper and blue luster-ware, but he realized that his taste and Lucy's might be far apart. These doubts barely ruffled the surface of his new happiness. He could not look forward or back while he had the beautiful and enormous present to consider.

He went out of the house with the imprint of cool lips on his cheek and walked down the street without feeling the movement of his feet. He had forgotten to put on his hat and it was still in his hand. As he blindly rounded the corner, the beaver collided with a lady's skirt and was knocked to the ground and Dick with a murmured apology stooped to retrieve it. To his astonishment the lady stooped too and got there first. She restored his property with a free, athletic movement of her body. He was startled into forgetting Lucy; his vision cleared and he saw a pretty face, a vivacious smile.

"That was clumsy of me," he said, contritely.

"It was my fault. The crinolines take up half the walk this year."

"And the men's hats are twice too tall," he countered laughing.

At the corners of her mouth he saw dark accents of down. Her lips were very red, her teeth flashingly white. She wore a small straw cap like a saucer, perched carelessly on the back of her head. Her features were stronger than Lucy's and her figure taller. Dick hesitated a moment as he looked at her and was bowing to turn away when she stopped him.

"Haven't I seen you somewhere? Don't you attend Mr. Rush's church?"

"Why yes, but mostly because I'm living at his house. He was my tutor."

"Then we're as good as introduced. I think him such a saintly man."

He knew these words for an invitation, but he wanted to go on dreaming about Lucy. Automatically he found himself saying,

"May I walk with you?"

She accepted his suggestion almost eagerly. They turned the corner and for a moment he was afraid he would have to walk past Lucy's house again in the company of the stranger. He was looking for escape when she stopped, half a block short of the Hammond house.

"This is where I live and my name's Josephine Wills. We haven't much of a place, but it's something to live in the same block with the Colonel. If you want to walk past his house you might catch a glimpse of Miss Lucy through the window."

"Miss Lucy?" Dick asked innocently.

"The Colonel's daughter. She's a lovely little snob."

The railroad from Milwaukee to Madison had been finished for almost six months. The one train left Madison at eight in the morning and made the hundred-mile trip in six hours, including stops for passengers, wood and water. Returning the same day it reached Madison at late supper-time and the engine was allowed to cool off all night. Dick had never known anyone who traveled by rail. Ordinary people could not spend a week's wages to get to Milwaukee; besides, they thought it courting death to travel at such a rate of speed, to make in six hours a journey the Lord had intended to be made in six days. Capital society was more sophisticated and laughed at these fears. Senators and representatives went to Washington on the trains, but they were a minority hardly to be considered in any survey of public opinion. Most citizens, like Dick and his friend Whitford Rush, went down to the depot at eight o'clock to see the puffing engine depart, and stood curiously but without envy while the passengers climbed aboard, the last wood was thrown into the cab, the throttle opened, the bell-rope pulled, the track cleared ahead by running men who leaped off the track as the engine picked up speed.

"I don't like it, Richard," Whitford Rush often said. "I don't approve of it at all. The train seems like a Behemoth of haste which man has made, but which will probably destroy him. A great invention of course. Ah yes. I salute it. But I also distrust it. Give me my pony and saddle-bags and you may have the railroad."

Dick's opinions were still unformed. He resented the train, partly because he feared he could never afford to use it and partly because he still remembered the first adventure of his life in the New World, the trip to Hampstead Prairie. The railroad seemed to make light of that trip, the six days in uncharted wilderness, the wolves, the Indians, and the sense of thanksgiving when Rock River finally was reached. Now the same distance could be covered in one afternoon!

On the morning after his interview with Lucy's mother he came to an important decision. He had been earning a small wage all winter by working in a drug-store, writing labels for bottles and keeping the ledger. Some of his money was still in his possession. Why not spend it on a private celebration? Why not take a ride on the train? At first he intended to ride only as far as the first fuel-stop and walk back. Then he changed his mind as he read a letter which Mrs. Amos shoved under his door. It was from his father.

"Thy brother Harry is bringing home his wife. We are ancsious about thee and wish to have thee here."

He decided to spend all his money except the price of Lucy's ring, to go home on the cars. Harry would have to share the attention this time! He would come home like a city man and announce his betrothal to his family. He went down the stairs, two at a time, full of excite-ment and happiness. Mrs. Amos, the housekeeper, was rolling pie-crust in the kitchen.

"I'll thank you, Mr. Dick," she said, "not to come down them there stairs in that there fashion no more. They aint made of iron, nor yet my nerves aint."

"Oh, come on now, Mrs. Amos. You can't know what nerves are, a fine, healthy person like you. You're only trying to be cruel, along with locking up the cookies and so forth."

"Did you want a cookie, then? Why didn't you say so? I only locked them up for convenience and account of the last batch disappearing so fast."

"Speaking of nerves," Dick said, munching his cookie, "how'd you like to take a trip on the cars, with the engine knocking your ear-drums out and the whistle tooting every three minutes?"

"Heaven save us! Don't mention the railroad to me. Folk must be mad to get aboard as they do with never a thought for the consequences. You don't know anyone who's taking a trip on the cars, do you?"

"Yes. *I* am."

"Now that you aint! Not while Mr. Rush is alive to stop you."

"Yes, Mrs. Amos, I *am*. What's more, I'm going to be married."

"Lord preserve us! To who?"

"What sort of pie is that?"

"Gooseberry tart."

"That settles it. I'm marrying you."

"Oh, get along! You'd tease the heart right out of a dead heathen mummy."

Dick went out, slamming the front door. He strode down the street in the sunshine and felt that the boards of the sidewalk were springing up and down under his feet. Beautiful world! Madison, with its green lawns and white houses was like Paradise. Hammers were ringing from the hill, where a new hotel was being finished. Everything looked bright, hopeful and young.

On Gorham Street he met the Reverend Mr. Rush, who walked slowly, tapping the pickets with his cane. Whitford Rush at forty was graying, scholarly and precise. Dick looked down at him as from a height and pitied him with all his heart.

"Good morning, Richard. You look very fine."

"I've just decided to go home tomorrow."

"Ah, too bad! For us, I mean. Of course it had to come. Is the . . . suit not progressing?"

"Very well. In fact," Dick blushed, "it's finished."

"Splendid! So the young lady accepted! Well, well, well!"

"And I thought, to celebrate, I'd ride on the cars."

"Oh, hadn't you better think that over? I know how you must be feeling, but life is precious, my dear boy. More so than ever, eh?"

There was much more argument, but Dick was determined, so his friend promised to see him off the next day.

He spent his last evening with Lucy. They wasted a good part of it talking about the future of the railroad, since her mother sat near them with her needlepoint and an unmovable expression. Lucy delivered a creditable lecture on transportation with sidewise looks that implied much she could not say.

"It's very important, I think, that we should learn to use the trains. The West cannot develop properly unless we do. At least my father says so. Of course it's dangerous, but so are stage-coaches, and we never think twice about a coach-ride. Please be careful, Dick, not to look out of the window. It makes one dizzy and my father had real nausea when he came back from Washington last summer, all because he was too much interested in the landscape. It's better to keep your eyes on the center aisle."

The hour arrived. Dick climbed into the rear car just as orders were given to clear the track. The wheels began to revolve. Whitford waved an anxious white handkerchief from the depot platform and the train gathered momentum. For some time the track ran on a level but as it passed the outskirts of Madison it sloped sharply downhill and picked up speed so fast that the brakeman jumped to his levers and applied the brakes with a terrific screeching noise. Dick almost clapped his hands over his ears, but remembered the other passengers. No use looking like a greenhorn. The engine plunged into dense woods and the trees began whizzing past the windows. Dick followed Lucy's advice and fixed his eyes on the center aisle.

"How fast is it going?" he asked the old gentleman beside him.

"Don't know, but almighty fast."

The quavering voice told him that this man, despite his good clothes, was a novice too. Sunlight, shining through the trees, kept up a shifting pattern on the floor. Dick felt dizzy. How awful if he should be sick! There were ladies in the car.

Slowly his qualms subsided and he adjusted himself to the new way of traveling. The brakeman had announced proudly that they were now going thirty miles an hour, but it seemed impossible. In fact, a rocking stage-coach gave the impression of more dangerous speed. As for the other people in the car, they were not the gilded creatures Dick had imagined. They were ordinary citizens like himself and no doubt they were discovering the same thing about him. Certainly the mere matter of traveling by rail made no difference in a man. Changes, Dick decided, are made from within. Falling in love with Lucy had altered him far more than riding on the train. And he began to think about her so intently that he forgot where he was.

That odd black-haired girl. What had she meant by saying Lucy was a snob? The word was fairly new to Dick, but he thought it meant a person who was proud of having money. Nothing could be less true of Colonel Hammond's daughter, who treated her mother's servants like equals, who had been willing to love and marry a country boy. Perhaps her reserve and dignity seemed like pride to Josephine Wills. Perhaps it was only that Lucy was so sure of her opinions. Under her soft ex-

terior lay a firm foundation of conviction and sometimes, when Dick encountered that firmness, he felt pro-
voked almost to the point of trying to break it down.
He wanted to crush her with love and then re-mold her,
but he knew the wish for selfishness, even if it could
have been done. Lucy was right as she was. He had
fallen in love with her sureness. Why should he resent it
now?

Before he realized it, the train had reached Fort
Atkinson. His first trip, including four stops for wood
and water and a flag-stop where a farmer got on with
a basket of chickens, was ended. He climbed down at
the depot and made his way across the tracks to the
river-front and the grain-market. There he found Jane
Weymouth's grays, hitched to a rail with twenty other
teams. Dick got into the wagon with his portmanteau
and sat down to wait. Sooner or later a driver must appear. He began to wonder if there were any news of his
Uncle Sam.

Six years had passed since Sam Weymouth left home.
The gold fever had swept Hampstead Prairie like
cholera, taking one grown man out of five. Jane's husband had been like a madman until she let him go, until
she saw it was no use to tie him to the mill when his
whole heart was on the Pacific coast. Her face had
grown pinched and hard while she fought the losing
battle and now she neither wept nor smiled, but went
grimly on with life. Since the day when he crossed the
Colorado River, Sam Weymouth had never been heard

from again. Neither had Hugh Henderson, who went at his side. The desert had swallowed them, or perhaps they had won through, only to discard their old ties and settle down to the newer life. At any rate, Jane was mistress of the mill now and a hard task-setter for anyone who helped her. She was bringing up her boy with one idea. When he grew old enough he must find his father or his father's grave.

Six years had so dimmed Dick's memory that when Ben Weymouth, his uncle's brother, came around the corner of the grain block, he thought for a moment he was seeing the lost one. The family resemblance was very strong.

"Looking for company, Ben?" he laughed.

"On my soul! Where didst come from, Dick?"

"Off yon cars," Dick said, relapsing into his native speech. "I've been a step above thee, Ben. Two hour since, I were in Madison."

Ben's astonishment was gratifying. He could not hear enough of the details and Dick talked all the way home. It occurred to him, with the impact of a discovery, that adventure is of value chiefly in the telling.

2

HARRY HAD MARRIED Agnes Tredway, of the Milwaukee Tredways. Her father had wealth, and her mother something more impressive, an ancient French line. Agnes was the product of careful breeding. She had been taught to smile only when it served a purpose; for the rest of the time her colorless face and large eyes remained quite frozen. Usually her features lit up for men, and especially for her husband. She was convinced that Harry had a great career and fame before him.

Ann Wentworth longed to chat about her son. She was proud of him too, but Agnes had put him on such a pedestal that he could not be discussed. His childhood, with all those early evidences of genius which his mother loved to relate, was a closed book to his wife and she did not want it opened. She had not known Harry then. He had not been hers, and what was not hers was somehow less valuable. If he must be talked about, Agnes preferred to do the talking and tell his mother what he was like.

"Thou'll have thy cross to bear, my dear," Ann said.

"A doctor puts his work first, and thou'll likely be lonely. But Harry was ever like that. His ambition was wonderful to see."

"Thank you, Mother Wentworth, the doctor and I understand each other perfectly. Will you give me my handkerchief? These country floors are so draughty. I may be taking cold."

Ann brought a footstool and fluttered about closing windows. She was concerned because her new daughter-in-law seemed unhappy. If only she would talk, she could be comforted, but her manner made it impossible to ask what was wrong. Perhaps, Harry's mother thought, Agnes was already in that condition one expected in a young married woman. No wonder the poor dear was downhearted! She redoubled her attentions. The bride accepted them all without smiling.

Naturally Agnes could not confide her real reason for distress, which was the dreadful coarseness of Harry's family, the commonness of his home, and the fact that he fell back into his old ways so easily and happily. When she first saw her husband put on a ragged sheepskin coat and go out to help with the milking, Agnes was inexpressibly shocked. She had seen him always in a good suit or a surgeon's jacket. When his mother gave him three pairs of hand-knitted socks, he praised them heartily and put on a pair at once, though he never wore wool at home. And though the food seemed carelessly cooked and served, Harry praised that too. It was almost more than she could bear.

This awful brogue! It simply could not be understood, so she seldom listened. Her husband should have warned her. She had no idea his background was so low. When the table was full, with the Weymouths and hired men present, it was like living in a foreign country. Everyone gabbled at once.

"Do-ant sit there saying naught and understanding naught, my dear. Do a bit of asking and we'll make ourselves plain," Ann told her.

Jane Weymouth was less charitable. She did not like Harry's wife, so she waited her chance to bring the mighty to earth. Agnes could understand the conversation if she wished to, Jane thought.

"Thou's a morsel of gravy on thy chin," she said, and chuckled inwardly at the instant attention she got.

When Dick walked in, carrying his satchel, even Jane might have pitied the bride. The brothers had not seen each other for three years, and they tried to make up for it all at once. Harry had been in Boston and New York, studying medicine. He told Dick more about his experiences there than he had ever told his wife. At intervals they reverted to childhood and played a silly game they had once called "apostrophe."

"Glorious Apollo, far-darting, god of the silver bow, where gottest thou the skin-tight breeches. Do you put them on with a shoe-horn, Dick?"

"Nay, not so, O Hector of the glancing helm."

Agnes felt completely at sea. Dick was quick to notice

her pallor and remoteness. He spoke of it to Harry as they left for a tour of the farm.

"Jealous as a cat, lad. That's her trouble," said Harry. "She's not content to go her own way and be happy. She has to go mine."

"No doubt she's in love with you," Dick reproached him.

"Well, no doubt," Harry admitted, grinning.

"You're a queer fish, you know. You don't care a nickel's worth about people, but you spend your life trying to save them. You look right through them with that surgeon's look and miss everything important on the way."

"I look through Aunt Jane at any rate. Did you ever see a body so thin?"

"She's like a weed after a grass fire," Dick said. "Still standing, but a breath would blow her down."

"You're wrong there. The old girl has iron in her. She's just heard, you know."

"Heard?"

"They found Hugh Henderson."

"Oh, Harry! Good old Hugh! I'm glad."

"They found his bones, Dick."

A cloud crossed the summer zenith, trailing its shadow rapidly over the cropped pasture below. Dick shivered. He saw the desert, the man lying there, as he had once seen a sheep, ribs bare to the sunlight.

"Poor fellow. He was a long way from the road, and he hadn't a canteen, so they think Uncle Sammy went on with the water. Hugh was holding father's Bible when he died. That's how they knew where to write us, from the address on the fly-leaf."

"So they think Uncle Sam's alive?"

"He might be, Dick. Or he might be dead a little farther on."

"Queer his brother wouldn't mention it today."

"Ben Weymouth wants to marry Aunt Jane and own the mill."

"Oh, I can't believe that of him," Dick insisted. He had heard the rumor before but thought it malicious gossip.

"It seems reasonable to me. He's put in years of hard labor there. Uncle Sam deserted, you know, and he had to stay. He puts ambition first."

Supper that night was at the mill. Though Dick had made no announcement, he knew the reunion was in his honor by the way everyone looked as he came in. His senses, sharpened by absence, took in the homely details of the meal, the pots and pans stacked on the stove, the great platters of food, his cousin Lisbeth, grown all at once to a young woman, serving the long table. The platter of spare-ribs, stacked high, was going the rounds. To Dick's undoing, it resembled a skeleton.

"Come here with the ribs, Liss," his aunt said. "Dick'll want another."

He drew back as Lisbeth set the platter before him. His mother looked at him anxiously.

"Thou's not queasy, Dick? Happen city life's to blame."

Harry gave him a keen glance and changed the subject.

"I see you've cut the trees this side of the stream, Father. Isn't that a mistake? The soil will wash in and muddy the cattle's water farther down."

"'Tis a good bit of lo-am."

"What can you do with it? You've two hundred acres of plowing now and no market for the wheat. And you can't get enough hands since they're all going west."

"Thou knows naught aboot it. I must clear my land."

"But you've left the buttery with no shade."

Dick had noticed that while he was away his father had rooted out a long row of beautiful maples. The water which had once flowed clear and cool over the buttery's stone floor, was now luke-warm and full of silt. He would not have taken his father to task for this, but he was glad Harry had the courage to do it.

"It's a short-sighted way to make money," Harry said. "One day that lumber will bring you twice what it does now. The rivers are choked with logs. Everyone's at it, cutting down the forests. Half of it goes into bonfires."

"I'll not see good farm-land littered with timber and such worthless truck."

"You mean to clear the whole four hundred?"

"If God spares me."

"Oh, Tommy! Leave me a bit of woods to walk in," his wife begged him.

"When did you ever walk in the woods?" Jane asked, laughing.

"Why, once a biddy strayed with her chicks and I went to bring 'er back. 'Twere April and the spring beauties were out. Then when my little Jenny were born and died, I sat under a tree in the east eighty for nigh an hour. It made me think of the dale near Totley where we went maying with cousin Charley Bland."

"The wild-flowers are out now. After supper you come with me. I've something to tell you," Dick said to his mother. At once all eyes were turned on him with deep interest.

"Go along, Aunt Ann. Mother and I'll red up," Lisbeth insisted.

Half-guiltily, she tucked her hand through Dick's elbow and went. Ann's shapely fingers were flattened and worn by scrubbing, her nails blackened and rough. Dick took up her hand as if to kiss it.

"Go on with thee, lad," she protested, embarrassed. "Thou'rt learning fancy ways."

Once he had walked to church beside her through the Milwaukee woods. He remembered that time. She had worn a pale blue dress, sprigged with white flowers. He had hurried to keep step with her, had reached up to take her hand. Her fingers had been perfumed and smooth. Dick thought bitterly that his mother had never been protected. Not as he would protect Lucy. And then he smiled at himself, because he had nothing to give Lucy but his love and four dollars.

"Tell me all aboot 'er, now," Ann said. " 'Tis fair popping out by itself."

"Not yet," Dick answered. He thought he must choose a beautiful spot to tell her—some place that would be worthy of Lucy. They took a path into the woods toward a hillside he knew, where once he had tended his young cousins and his uncle's sheep.

"I suppose father knows what he's about, cutting off all the timber," he said.

"Oh, aye. Thy father's a thoughtful man. And the woods harbored animals as preyed on the chickens and lambs."

"I'd like to see him stop for a while. It would give you a rest in the winter if you'd no hands to feed. He must have had six men at work last winter to cut away so much of the woods."

"Well, the sod house was full most of the time."

They still called the shelter by its old name, though it was no longer built of sod and saplings. Like a garment that has been patched so often nothing of the original remains, the sod house had been replaced, a wall at a time, with lumber. One after another the tree-beds had broken down. Cots had taken their places. The mud fireplace had crumbled and fallen. Thomas had put in a stove.

"I suppose you did their washing and mended their socks," Dick grumbled.

"Aye. The poor lads be out at the toes, ever and anon."

"Nothing will change you. You'll work yourself into your grave."

" 'Tis a habit now. I be happiest at work, Dick. Doant fret aboot me."

"Well, then. Let's sit down among the violets."

"And now tell me, lad."

"I don't know how to begin."

"Begin with 'er name."

"Lucy Hammond." The words seemed to make a ripple in the stillness of the woods.

"Lucy is a fine name. I had a cousin Lucy. Is she nice to look at?"

"Beautiful!"

"I'll be bound."

The subject should have been inexhaustible, but Dick could think of no more to say. His mother made an effort.

"What's her mother like, Dick? Will her and I be friends? For any young couple's 'appier if their folk agree. Dost think Mrs. 'Ammond will like me?"

"You won't love her, Mother."

"Why not, then?" Ann Wentworth looked distressed. Dick laughed.

"I've never seen anyone like Lucy's mother. She's like a granite cliff or a bald eagle, and she talks like a lawyer."

"Oh, aye!" said Ann, bewildered.

"Mrs. Hammond thinks Lucy's too young to marry."

"To my mind that's nonsense, Dick. To my mind life's all too short and when we get the right one, then's the time to settle doon."

"I'll have to find work. I don't know what I want to do."

"That's all taken care of. Thy father has set aside enough land for a farm and will 'elp thee build a house on any forty thou wants. Lucy 'll be quick to learn, and I can show her how with the 'eavy tasks like rendering and soap-boiling."

"Oh, Mother!" Dick protested. Those rosebud-circled wrists plying a lard-spoon! That willowy waist, bent above a soap-kettle!

"I see. She's too fine." Ann bowed her head over a handful of flowers and Dick guessed that her eyes were full of tears.

"I'm behaving poorly," his mother said. "Likely I'm a bit jealous, Dicky, and then Agnes is no daughter to me, thou knows. I'd dearly love a daughter."

"You'll love Lucy."

"Be that as it may. Thou's thy own life to lead, and the sooner the better, I say. In the winter thy Granny died. I didn't tell thee, because I said: 'the lad's courting. Why sadden him now?' But she died, Dick, and I remembered what she said when last I saw her. 'Daughter,' she said, 'I'll never see thee again on earth.' I laughed at her. I said, 'Oh, Mother! Never's a long time.' Ah, Dick, 'twas true. There be no truer word

than 'never.' Days pass and never come again. Marry
thy Lucy now.''

Harry and Agnes slept in Dick's bed. Dick took the
pallet in the kitchen which had once belonged to Hugh
Henderson. On the wide stone sill was the same candle-
stick, at the end of the cot was Hugh's bootjack. As
he lay down, Dick was thinking of Hugh. He drifted
later into thoughts of Harry. Very decidedly, he did
not envy his brother. The idea of being married to
Agnes set Dick's teeth on edge. It must have been a
marriage for money—or for position. That would be
just like Harry! Perhaps he wanted wealthy people
for clients and took Agnes as the first step in the
scheme, or perhaps he wanted to buy a hospital. At
any rate, Dick thought, Harry could sleep upstairs with
his cold-faced wife. Dick would rather be alone on the
pallet. Some day he would be lying in Lucy's arms. As
he realized this, he was filled first with emotion and
then with peace. He turned his face to the moonlight
and slept.

When the first roosters were crowing, he stirred in
a deep slumber. A hand was tugging at the covers above
his throat. Someone seemed to be bending over him.

"Hugh!" he said, fighting back the coverlet, and was
not surprised to hear the well-known voice:

"Get out of my bed, you lazy sluggard. Get up,
Dicky, and give me what's my own. I've no other place
on earth to rest my bones."

Dick sprang to his bare feet. The bone-white arm across his pillow was only a shaft of moonlight. The breeze was sighing like a man stretching himself out to rest. He found a cushion and quilt and spent the rest of the night on the sitting-room floor.

3

OXEN WERE DISAPPEARING from the Wisconsin farms. Heavy horses of part-Percheron breed had come into favor for hauling, and light trotting nags for driving. Dick liked handling the reins. He sometimes drove his father's light horses rather too fast for the roads, which were still deeply rutted in places. The state was gradually abandoning the old trails or covering them with gravel to make them safer for the horses' slender ankles, but the Galena trail was unchanged. The new road was to pass through the Wentworth property a mile from the old and Thomas impatiently waited for the surveyors. Meanwhile the trail was pocked as always with the holes where three decades of oxen had sunk their hooves in mud.

Now the prairie began to take on the look of farming country, squared off with fences to hold in the herds of horses. The sheep no longer grazed at random, watched by boy and dog. Fences did the collie's work. Dick, who had learned the whole cycle of wool and mutton-raising and knew it by heart, saw that the day was coming when his mother would no longer card, spin and weave, when the lengths of homespun, the harsh red underwear and thick carpet-wool would be a part of the past. For the time being, however, he still went through the routine, the "tupping" season, when the ram's breast was rubbed with red paint and the lambing week reckoned from the first red mark on the ewe's rump, the lambing, often by lantern-light, with its attendant birth-bleating and weak new-born harvest, the shearing of ewes and lambs while the weather was still warm, and then the final shearing—of old rams and ewes. Before the shearing the sheep must be washed, and since the stream was too shallow, Thomas had gouged out a pool for sheep-washing opposite the fold.

Dick went into the pool again that summer with a sense of elation. The smell of wet wool and the grass-sweet breath of the floundering sheep filled his nostrils while he stood in the strong current. Bits of wool matted with burs kept floating away; the whole contents of the pool were momently changing and he felt the warm body of the sheep he was holding pressed tightly against the wet cotton of his undershirt. It struggled and gasped. He held it firmly, lathering it from a pan of soft soap which floated beside him. Gunnar Larson, who worked with him, fought with his own ewe a few feet away.

"Dis one been in cockle-bur, Dick. I took out a tousand-hundred cockles already."

Gunnar's speech had a rhythm of its own, unlike most Norwegian brogue. He was from Hardanger and used the Norwegian language almost as badly as the English, or so his friends from Christiania insisted. He turned all his sentences up at the end with a lilt which gave an expression of gaiety to everything he said, a gaiety supported by the light in his gray eyes. Gunnar was Dick's age, but he had never been protected. He had crossed the ocean alone, lured by the extravagant descriptions of Oleana, the American colony founded by Ole Bull. When he saw that the colony was not yet established, that the great violinist's title was not even clear, he did not despair. He walked to Chicago from Pennsylvania and on to Waukesha from Chicago, pausing to work when he ran out of money. Dick knew that Gunnar would move farther west as soon as he saved one hundred dollars. He meant to buy government land in the hills along the Mississippi. Meanwhile he lived in the sod house, cooked his own breakfasts and darned his own socks. He would have done his washings too, but Thomas never gave him enough leisure. Ann Wentworth washed the heavy shirts and trousers and exclaimed admiringly over the neat patches Gunnar made.

"Why you tink sheep hunt for cockle-bur, Dick? That yearling I wash yesterday run off in hassel-brush like it's hunting more cockles."

"Maybe it likes to have you pull them out," Dick suggested. He had noticed this peculiar behavior in sheep, especially the young ones. They were "prone to wander" as the hymns said. Instead of taking a short and certain cut for the fold at dusk they went this way and that, making circles around the hazel-brush and wasting the shepherd's time. They could not be driven or led in a straight line. And, as Gunnar complained, they came back with their wool full of burs. The saving circumstance was that they always came out a little farther ahead in the lane. In the end they got home.

"Sheep are pretty much like men," he said, as his ewe, released, scrambled sullenly out onto the bank and went back to grazing. "Don't you ever hunt burs, Gunnar?"

"Naa, Dick, I tell you I got to hunt money for a while yet. When I could buy me some land, then I stop and take a look around. I send for you, then. We could hunt some burs together, ei?"

The milk and cream could be marketed now, since horses could get them to town before they soured. Leeds, seven miles away, had built a creamery above the creek with churns run by water wheel. Farmers for miles around lined up in the early morning at the high platform and unloaded their cans of milk. Caspar Fletcher, the dairyman, was town crier, news-vender and political demagogue, all in one.

Dick had not been at home long before he found himself sucked back into the old routine, working long hours every day without a suggestion of wages. Once this would have seemed natural enough, but now, with Lucy's future to consider, he was anxious. Could it be possible that his father still thought him a child? Must the suggestion of some financial settlement come from Dick? In all his life the only money he had received from Thomas had been the wheat money he had purposely kept. Yet he had seen the hired hands punctiliously paid each week with ten dollar bills peeled from the roll in Thomas' pocket.

So, as he delivered the milk each morning at Caspar's creamery, Dick spent his driving time trying to think of some way to make his father realize the facts. If he were to stay on the farm he must share the profits or be otherwise paid. Nothing else would be fair to Lucy. Yet he winced as he recalled Harry's warnings, and the pathetic little hoard of pennies his mother gathered from selling eggs and cheese. He doubted if his mother ever handled a dollar herself. Bills for food and clothing were presented to Thomas, who paid them scrupulously.

If he left the farm, what then? Should he take up some dull task like the job at the apothecary's, sitting all day between shelves of bottles, or dry-goods or tobacco? What future was there in that? To be shut away from the outdoor world summer, autumn, winter, and spring, doing silly tricks with money, when all the while fields were being planted and harvested and the great spectacle of fertility was going on! It seemed too great a price to pay for having wanted to marry. He tried to imagine Lucy as a farmer's wife and failed. But would she be any more happy as the wife of a clerk? Or could they be content to wait while he read for the law or made himself into a physician? Whichever way he turned he confronted a wall.

Here on the prairie everyone knew him. He had standing. He was not a nobody aspiring to marry the Colonel's daughter.

"Great day, Dick!" Ethan would sing out as Dick's faster team flew by, or perhaps Christie Beeson in her father's cap and coat would turn her plain freckled face toward him with a smile. Even Caspar, busy with his line-up, would take extra time for Dick.

"Well," he would say, "what did you think of Mr. Buchanan's speech?"

Dick never saw a newspaper unless it was given him by some more public-minded man.

"Pshaw, boy. You're an American, aint you? And haven't heard what Buchanan has to say! Well I think little enough of it, myself. I don't cater to Whig or Democrat. But read it anyway, Dick. Be a patriot."

Usually he brought out a week's collection of State Journals, tied together with twine and threw them in the back of Dick's cart.

Leaving the creamery one day in late June, Dick drove to the village store and postoffice. Lucy's square blue envelope was in the mail for him, sealed as usual with pink wax, and bearing his name in her feminine, but firm handwriting. He felt unable to open the envelope in a public square. He slipped it inside his waistcoat, jumped back in the cart and drove to a small park by the bank of the creek, where he loosened the reins to let his horses drink from the watering trough. A fine rain had begun to fall and he opened his coat and made a tent for the letter while he read it. Lucy spent three of the four pages on the subject of abolition:

"I should never be able to respect a man who did not think the slavery custom horrible. I do hope we shall agree on this, Dick, because it is one subject on which I feel strongly. My father has been talking today about the stubborn attitude of the South. He will not be going back till late November, and I wish you could be here in Madison before he goes. He wants to meet you, and you will find his views very interesting."

Dick had to read a great deal between these lines in order to satisfy his longing. He was thinking how little slavery meant to him, how far away and unimportant those planters and plantations seemed. Carolina, Virginia! They hardly existed for Dick, but to Lucy big issues were always real and vital. Dick had once offended her by saying that such things as slavery should be settled by experts, not by uninformed outsiders.

"Probably it's a fault in me," he thought, "but I can't feel a responsibility in politics or any other far-away matter. Yonder little wag-tail's more interesting than all the slaves in the cotton-fields." He turned his eyes, following the flashing movements of the small bird.

On the creek's bank, something moved. At first it looked like a pile of rubbish, but it soon took on the semblance of a man, very sick or very drunk. He had been there all the while, but his clothing was so sodden

and dingy it could hardly be distinguished from the wet
clay. Dick got down and went toward the ragged heap.
He was met halfway by an odor of cheap whiskey.

The rain was falling faster. What had been soaked
in alcohol was getting soaked in rainwater. He took
the fellow's sleeve and tried to roll him over, but succeeded only in rolling his head against the wet bank.
It was a head of coarse black hair, cut clumsily short.
The red neck suggested an Indian's. Dick went back
to his cart and drove to the creamery again. His thir-
teen-year-old cousin, Sammy Weymouth, had just finished unloading.

"What's amiss, Dick? They said you'd been and
gone an hour since."

"There's a man in the mud over there."

Caspar Fletcher laughed. "That's Joe Sobish. Injun
Joe. Leave him to soak."

"If Sam'll lend a hand we can get him to higher
ground. He's like to roll into the creek and drown."

"Good riddance, then. One more bad Indian dead.
Joe's a grandson of White Crow, the old fellow who
lived on Crabapple Point. They drove the old man out
with bullets and it wouldn't hurt if they did his grandson the same way."

(He was blind. He led his people as well as he could,
to the rice-beds in season, to the muskrat houses, the
deer-tracks, the prairie-hens. He bade them plant corn
and pick berries for pemmican. The land was his and
we took it.)

185

This passed through Dick's mind, but being an amiable young man, he smiled and said:

"Come along, Sam."

When they were out of hearing, he turned to his cousin: "You'd think a man so bent on freeing the Negroes as Caspar ud be a lot more merciful to the Indians."

"He don't have to live with the Negroes," Sammy replied wisely. "He probably never seed one in his life."

" 'Tis wonderful how easy it is to mind other folks' business."

"Joe Sobish is a sot, though, Dick. He lives over in Thebault's cabin and he's got him a white wife from somewhere. They came in while you were gone last winter. Lisbeth and I were out on the ice and we saw them." They had drawn closer to the subject of their discussion and Sammy wrinkled a fair, freckled nose as the fumes rose to greet him.

The Indian was slippery and heavy. Sam took his arms and Dick his legs, but his limp body buckled in the middle. It was more of a struggle than they expected to haul him up the bank to a drier place. Even then he seemed about to roll right back down.

"If I could get him in the cart, I'd take him home," Dick said impulsively.

"My word, Dick! Would you drive ten miles for a drunk fool?"

"I'd be doing it for his grandfather. I knew White Crow, Sam."

"But 'tis fixing to storm."

Dick let the tail-gate of his wagon down and slid out several planks that had formed a double bottom under the milk cans. The boards made a ramp with a projecting end at the top. Sammy grinned at the idea of trying to get Joe Sobish up the ramp.

"What do you want me to do, Dick?"

"Get up and sit on the ends of the boards."

"All right. Sitting's easy," said Sammy.

As a matter of fact Dick had no idea how to proceed, but at that moment fate came to his aid. Joe Sobish stood up with the unexpectedness of drunken men, began weaving toward the wagon and, urged by Dick's hand, fell across the boards. Dick raised the lower end of the seesaw and slid planks and Indian into the cart. He slammed shut the tail-gate.

"Tell father I'll be back by noon," he said as he dropped his cousin at the creamery again.

He was regretting his charity before he had been long on the road. He was soaked with rain and so were his father's horses. He would be having to stable them and rub them down. He must drive a mile down river to the only bridge, and then back up river to the lake. Joe was rising in the back of the cart and muttering what sounded like threats. Dick kept a wary backward watch. The barricade of milk cans between them protected the driver, but Joe might throw himself out into the road. By the time Dick reached the bridge he felt strongly like dumping his passenger into the river. He drove on, however, chiefly because he was already half-way to Thebault's Point and it seemed the easiest thing to do.

The lane that led to the Point was little traveled and as the wagon jolted over roots and stones the loose boards gave the poor Indian a continual spanking. His mutterings grew louder and more reproachful. Dick was greatly relieved when they emerged from the woods and came out into the clearing by the old fur-trader's cabin.

Children considered this log house haunted. Dick remembered when the Frenchman had been murdered, supposedly by his squaw, who wanted to go back to her tribe. Thebault had been a symbol of Wisconsin's history, a first settler whose trade had been ruined by the farmers and whose squalid life, once universal in the wilderness, had come to be a disgrace.

A trickle of smoke issued from the chimney of the cabin. Along one side, pots and pans, rusty and patched, lay drying. A young woman was washing others, bending over a puncheon bench. Dick tied his horses to a tree and came toward her.

She wore a man's torn shirt. It stretched tautly over her full bosom and was tucked into a skirt that looked like a scrap of woollen blanket. Her bare white ankles tapered into the tops of a man's cowhide shoes. Her hair was heavy, the color of wheat straw, with greenish shadows. It came down over her shoulders in thick braids.

"What do you want?" she said, and though her words were abruptly English, they had the sing-song, effortless music of all the Indian voices he had ever heard.

"I brought Joe back. He's over in the wagon."

This must be the white wife Sammy had mentioned, though Dick had not expected anyone so young and fair-skinned. He tried not to stare at her. How incredible that she should be married to the wreck he had just hauled in!

"I'm afraid he's drunk," he added as a warning.

"Yes," she said, simply, and walking toward the wagon, called, "Joe. Get out now."

The drunk man rose obediently, peered out at her with his eyes almost crossed, and then dropped back to his hands and knees in the wagon-box.

"Get out, now," the woman repeated. He clambered over the side and fell on the ground. She made no effort to help him, but stood beside him, arms folded, face opaque and uncommunicative.

"Shall I stay?" Dick asked uncertainly. The rain had stopped and the sun was shining. She would probably leave Joe out in the sun until he sobered up. She must be used to his ways by now—must know what to do.

"No. You can go." As before, the abrupt words were belied by the slurred softness with which she pronounced them. Dick bowed and turned away. With his hand on the side of the wagon he looked back.

She was standing in the same position, her face immobile, but the look in her eyes had changed to one of loneliness and despair. He came hurriedly to her.

"What shall I do? Let me help you."

She shook her head silently and veiled her eyes against him. He walked slowly back to his cart again, jumped in and drove away. Before the forest hid her from view he turned once. She had not moved.

Lucy's letters came with punctual regularity all summer. Dick carried the square envelopes next to his heart and often took them out of his shirt stained with sweat. Sometimes his mother found them under his pillow and laid them away in his wash-stand drawer. At the end of the summer he had quite a pile, but in all of them there was scarcely a word of love. He explained this to himself as womanly shyness, but was often impatient with the paragraphs about Washington affairs, gleaned second-hand from her father's conversations, with the small lectures on abolition, free-soilers, and other national questions. Lucy wrote well; she had a natural gift for expression and it was right that she should use it, but he longed for some sign of emotion.

When October had come and the harvest was in he planned to go to Madison, perhaps to get a small job there for the winter, for he still thought of himself as a farmer. Now was the time to approach his father about money. Now or never. But he hesitated; the habits of years wound him in strong tentacles and he could not begin. Should he stop his father as he left the barn after morning chores? Should he wait until bedtime? Finally the time was growing so short that he rushed pell-mell into the situation. Thomas was thrusting his great arms into the sleeves of a woolen smock, preparatory to shelling corn to take to mill.

"I'm going back to Madison, Father. Tomorrow."

"Ah!"

"Can you let me have some money? Wages for my summer's work?"

His father pierced him with a blue gaze.

" 'Ow much were the wheat money?"

"The wheat money! That's a year ago!"

" 'Ow much, I say."

"Twenty dollars."

"How much didst make at the apothecary's?"

"Four dollars a week."

"A good sum. What didst do with it?"

"I bought a coat and hat and there were other things . . ." Dick stopped himself, biting his lower lip. From force of habit he had been about to account for every cent.

"What didst pay Mr. Rush?"

"Never mind that. The money's spent. If you can't treat me as well as your farm hands it's quite all right with me."

"I have set aside for thee eighty good acres of land.

191

'Twill be thine when thou'rt married. I will build thee a house. I have paid thy bills for food and clothing."

Dick was silent. Harry had been through all this and had somehow won the battle though the method was still a mystery.

"I have done my part by thee, Dick."

"And I by you."

He was very angry, but in spite of himself his voice was mild. His father looked at him strangely as if he wondered just what Dick meant, but the young man turned and walked away. What he had really meant was that he would never work on his father's farm again.

Even in the placid atmosphere of the Rush household there was much talk about abolition. Whitford Rush could work himself into a rage on the subject, a scholarly rage that left his scalp showing pink through his thin hair.

"I tell you, Richard, there is no middle course. Young men like you must choose and choose now. Slavery is a cancer. It must be cut from the body of our nation, even though we lose the limb."

"How can I choose sides on a subject I know nothing about? And if I chose, what influence could I have?"

"Young men have a great influence. I am afraid they may soon be exercising it."

"Where?"

"At the cannon's mouth."

192

Dick thought this statement overdramatic and the whole subject of slavery somewhat dulled by emphasis. Injustice in the cotton fields of the South could hardly be righted by sending young northerners to death, he said.

"I don't like to hear you talk in that fashion, Richard. To die for one's faith is a glorious thing."

"To kill for one's faith seems less glorious, though."

"God tells us to make war on evil."

Dick had ridden horseback to Madison. On the morning after his father's refusal to pay summer wages, he had been about to start out on foot. Thomas had stopped him.

"Gunnar, bring oop the filly," he said, and when Betsey, a black three-year-old, was at the door, he had asked Dick,

"Dost think thy lass can ride 'er?"

At once, just as he had melted so many times in childhood, Dick softened his heart again. How generous of his father! What a fine gift for Lucy! All the same, he wished he were not going back penniless. He was glad he had been able to buy Lucy a ring before he left Madison, though it was a cheap and rather pathetic ring, set only with a small sapphire. Still, she had worn it proudly, though not on her wedding finger. Her mother had suggested that for the present the engagement should be a secret. The sting of this was softened now by the magnificence of being able to give Lucy a saddle-horse, something she had never owned.

As he was looping Betsey's bridle-rein through the ring of the hitching-post the next day, he saw Colonel Hammond coming down the walk. Dick liked the man better than the portrait, while finding his resemblance to Lucy less marked. Perhaps the absence of his uniform had something to do with the effect of jovial good fellowship the Colonel radiated as he shook Dick's hand warmly and clapped his left palm down over the handshake. It was a politician's gesture but a pleasant one.

"Well, my boy! The women saw you coming and they're all agog. Thought I'd take a look at you myself while they catch their breath."

"I'm glad to meet you, Sir."

"I needn't inquire about your health at least. What a color! That's a neat little nag you have."

Dick remembered the bridle-rein and finished tying it.

"I ride, myself, but I take a heavier mount. One hundred and ninety pounds! And once I was slim like you."

Lucy's father did not look heavy, Dick thought. His military bearing, combined with his graying hair and good features, made him a handsome man. It was easy to see why Lucy adored him.

"I brought the mare to give Miss Lucy if she'll accept her," Dick said.

"A splendid gift, my boy. Well, well, it remains to be seen." The Colonel shifted his gaze and seemed embarrassed.

Lucy came out on the veranda with her mother. She looked like a late rose, standing in the frosty air between the withered vines. She wore a morning costume of shepherd's check, and as it demanded a cap, Lucy's curls of which Dick had often dreamed, were tucked out of sight. She seemed remote and somehow different. A faint smile hovered about her lips as she greeted him. Her mother did most of the talking:

"Have you had your breakfast, Richard, for I must use your Christian name now that so much has passed between us, or rather between you and dearest Lucy, though of course nothing formal has actually taken place—I mean nothing irrevocable, providing circumstances, unfortunate though they might seem, should cause us to reconsider by mutual consent our, or rather *your* plans for the future, my dear boy," Mrs. Hammond said.

"I have eaten, thank you." Dick felt puzzled and alarmed, but he had been lost in the verbiage and had not quite grasped the meaning of the sentence. Really, he thought, she *is* like that! Several times during the summer he had remembered Mrs. Hammond's syntax with wonder.

"Then let us sit down for a minute or two." The Colonel forestalled his wife, who was drawing breath for another barrage. Dick was holding Lucy's hand;

he had forgotten to let go, and she was gently trying to disengage it. Behind her parents' backs he pressed her fingers to his lips before releasing them. She flushed and did not meet his eyes.

The atmosphere of the Hammond drawing-room was stiff and chilly, though a bright fire was burning under the marble mantel. The four sat down, formally.

"We have been holding a conclave, Dick," Lucy said, "and we have come to a rather important decision. Shall I tell him, Father, or will you?"

"It is possible," her mother interposed, "that another opportunity might be more propitious, or that under other circumstances what now might appear disastrous may in the light of pure reason resolve itself. . . ."

"In short, my boy, Lucy's mother has decided to come back with me to Washington, and naturally we must take our child with us. Lucy wants to make the journey. She has a keen interest in politics—too keen for a female, but I won't quarrel with it. If your plans go through—and I hope they may, Dick. I liked you from the first—I say, if you and Lucy still want to marry when we return, there's little chance she'll ever get to the capital again. Now you see why I couldn't say more about the riding horse you brought her."

"Oh, Dick! Is that lovely little horse for me? Oh, I should dearly love to ride her!"

"My father sent her," Dick said, shortly. He was beginning to feel angry and desolate.

"Perhaps you'd like to ride her all the way to Washington, Lucy," her father teased her. "I'm afraid you'll have to choose between the two. Of course animals have been shipped by rail, but it seems cruel to me."

"I should not wish to suspect," Mrs. Hammond looked severe, "that the gift of a horse should cause us to hesitate in the course of an action so carefully arrived at, after so much fevered, though I will not say bitter discussion. I should wish to think that your year in Washington. . . ."

"Mother! You promised it should be only six months."

"Pshaw! The fat's in the fire again!" said the Colonel. "Milly, I am about to take a walk, but just outside." He had bitten off the end of a Havana cigar, and finding no way to get rid of it, was still holding it in his mouth and talking around it. "My dear, we should leave these young people alone for a while. You must have household duties."

"Certainly," Lucy's mother replied with an injured air, "woman's work, though sometimes neither manual nor menial, is never done."

When Dick and Lucy were alone they looked troubled. The months of separation had marred their close understanding of one another, at least temporarily.

"Lucy," he said, "don't go away. Don't leave me."

"You left me. You haven't been near me all summer."

"I was working."

"You were doing what your father wanted. You didn't think of me."

"I thought of you every minute and longed for this time to come."

"Going to Washington was mother's idea. She thinks you have no ambition, Dick. Sometimes I think so too, but it makes no difference. I'll always love you."

"Then don't go."

"I couldn't live here by myself. Besides, I really long to see Washington—to ride all that way on the railroad, meet those famous people. I might be able to help the cause of abolition in some humble way."

"Lucy, if three months does this to us, what will a year do? Don't leave me. Marry me now."

"You should be more foresighted, Dick. What could we do for money? No, I must go, but I promise not to forget you. When we come back . . . and meanwhile, I'll be helping my father fight slavery. I wish you were one of us, Dick."

"You choose a poor way to convert me."

His nerves were raw with emotion. He could hardly tell whether he was feeling anger or love. Lucy was so close he could have crushed her in his arms, but she was not his. She belonged to herself. As for her family, he supposed they were being friendly, but it meant nothing. They were taking her away from him as if he had no right to her at all. He had hoped for a beautiful winter.

Now he saw the cold months stretching drearily ahead of him. Without Lucy the city would be a desert.

"At least we have two weeks before I go."

The Colonel was pacing up and down the walk. As Dick came out he threw away his cigar.

"Well, are you resigned?"

"No, Sir."

"As a matter of fact," the older man said, lowering his voice, "I'd like to get you to Washington. My wife has an idea that Lucy should meet young men of fashion. Now, Dick, I know the sort. They wouldn't suit my girl. Have you any experience in business?"

"None at all."

"That's very bad. It costs money to live in the East. Have you read any law?"

"No, Sir."

"And I suppose you don't know any foreign languages."

"Latin and a little Greek."

"No value at all. You might get a secretary's job, but even those are scarce as hen's teeth."

"To tell the truth, I've stayed too long on my father's farm. I'll have to begin at the bottom, and Lucy seems to think I lack ambition."

"Better too little ambition than too much, Dick. It's like the straw-bread men eat in a famine. Fills your stomach but doesn't nourish you. You always crave something more. I had ambition and nothing else. I grew up in Beetown in a log cabin with my drunken father. One cow, two hens and a potato patch. I came to Madison ragged and dirty, plowed gardens, watered horses, sold papers and bought myself my first pair of shoes. I married money, got into the army and politics, and here I stand. What have I got that I wanted? I don't care a hoot for anything but Lucy's happiness. I want her to be happy."

"And so do I."

"Well, as between her happiness and yours there's something of a pull just now, eh?"

"A year's a long time," Dick muttered.

"I know. I know all about it. I've suffered the agonies of separation. Oh not from . . ." he nodded his head respectfully in the probable direction of Mrs. Hammond. "I spoke of another."

A great deal can happen in two weeks. Lucy learned to ride the three-year-old or at least to stay in the saddle with Dick's help. She clung to the pommel with faint shrieks while he held the bridle-rein and kept Betsey's pace to a minimum. Lucy's helplessness on horseback was easier for his wounded pride than her usual confidence. His good spirits began to return. Together they planned that he should find a secretary's position in the new State House and progress from there to Washington.

One day Lucy's riding lesson took them as far as the

shore of Lake Mendota. The beach there was still something of a wilderness with grape vines and woodbine tumbling over the bank above, red with frost. The day was warm and Lucy wore a light cape and a small plastron of braid upon her curls. Dick lifted her down and tied Betsey to a tree. They sat together on the bank of the lake, talking, as always of their separation.

"I'm afraid of one thing, Dick. It may not seem important, but truly it would break my heart if it happened."

"Well, I've made so many vows one more won't matter. What is it?"

"Don't grow a beard. It would cover up your nice chin."

"I'm going to grow a long one that will tuck inside my belt. I won't shave till you come home, so you'll do better to hurry."

"Oh, Dick! Any beard you grow will be black and curly and you'll look like a pirate."

"My brother has some side-whiskers. Would you like that better?"

"Heavens! That would hide your nice cheeks."

"Well, will you promise not to come home with skirts like a circus-tent?"

"I'll promise nothing. My mother has already ordered my hoops."

"Oh, Lucy! Why do we talk about fashions? If your love doesn't change you can wear anything you please."

"I'll never see another man. It's you I love."

He kissed her passionately and her hand, encountering his watch chain, pulled it forward. The pipestone crucifix which he wore as a balance, came out of his pocket.

"What a queer fob, Dick! Where did you get it?"

"The Indians made it."

"It's a cross. Did it hang on a rosary?"

"Yes. On a rosary of snail-shells."

"Who could have worn it?"

Dick said nothing and she looked at him intently.

"You know who wore it, don't you?"

"Yes."

"It was a girl, wasn't it? Oh how can you treat me so badly?"

"Silly Lucy. She was ten years old and I never saw her twice."

"Only once. But you remembered her. Throw the cross out in the lake. I don't like it."

"I can't do that," he said slowly. "It really isn't mine."

"Oh! You're keeping it for her. You think some day you'll see her again?"

"No. It's more like a charm. I can't throw it away; I've worn it too long."

Lucy shivered. "The sun's getting low. Don't you think we should go home?"

4

IN THE NOVEMBER ELECTIONS Frémont carried Wisconsin. Nineteen states of the Union had voted for
Buchanan, however, so abolition suffered a setback.
Buchanan would be the new President—a Democrat
and a compromise man. Colonel Hammond went back
to Washington under a cloud, and Lucy's square blue
letters began drifting westward:

"The capital is very crowded and we are happy to
get a modest little house. Every public building, every
eating place is overflowing with visitors. They think
because they have helped elect the government, they
should attend the first meetings of Congress. Men
stand in line at the barbers' for hours, and one can get
a newspaper only by speaking for it the night before.
Theaters sell standing room until the aisles are packed.
My father has forbidden me to attend a single per-
formance.

"I am sorry for the common people in the streets.
They think themselves in a democracy, but they soon
find out the truth. They are pushed around and handled
roughly while politicians and wealthy men get all the

consideration. Ruffians go about making chance acquaintances and introducing themselves as 'Senator
This' or 'Representative That.' The country man is delighted to have met someone of importance at last and
does not learn better until his pockets are picked.

"One sees so many beautiful costumes, but of ridiculous proportions. My father says a common excuse
when a clerk is late, is this: 'Beg pardon, but I met a
skirt and was unable to pass.' And you would laugh,
Dick, to see a hansom cab, its top turretted with hoops
which could not be gotten through the door. Of course
the wearers are inside the cab.

"In contrast to these gay ladies, who seem to be
everywhere, we see sad and discouraging sights. Washington has too many beggars, men, women, and children. No one pays the least attention to them and I
think a child could starve in the street without attracting
notice, though in Wisconsin we fed every Indian who
came to the door. Food is too costly here; it is seldom
given away.

"We have had visits from several of my father's
associates and their wives. I sit with my mother and
feel quite at ease, though so much younger. Mr.
Chandler, the senator from Michigan, spoke at some
length on the subject of women who use their influence
to change their husbands' votes on measures in Congress. He was very stern, and all the while his wife had
an insincere, pussy-cat sort of smile. I'll wager she has
him wrapped around her little finger.

"Mr. Harlan, of Iowa, is a nice, simple gentleman, but his wife was too elegant for a morning call. Mr. Polk of Missouri is still governor of that state, but has been sent on to Washington as senator. I don't know what they will do about it.

"You would not begrudge me this year, dearest, if you knew how much I am enjoying it. . . ."

Dick had twice interviewed Assemblyman Haskins about his father's road. When he went to the squat yellow sandstone State House for the third time, he still had only vague promises, though the money had long been appropriated. This time, however, he was offered a secretary's job and found himself installed in Mr. Haskins' office at ten dollars a week. He was asked to iron out the assemblyman's speeches for the newspapers, straighten the mixed tenses and tone down extravagant statements made in the heat of debate. Dick found plenty to do, but soon learned how to imitate the politician's grandiose style while changing the grammar of his sentences. Sometimes he grew bolder and changed the implications. His employer was always pleased.

"Did I say that? Well, that's very nice. I told you the newspapers made a monkey of me."

Dick had a desk with quill pens, ink-powder and a quire of writing paper adorned with the seal of the new State of Wisconsin. The office was usually empty except for the half hour when Mr. Haskins was dictating letters in the morning. Dick was lonely and soon tired of the sight of the green walls, homely black stove and cupboards full of law-books. He knew the almanacs and State Journals on the table from cover to cover. The State House was supposed to be the most eventful place in an eventful capital, but to Dick it was not half so interesting as his father's wooded pasture, where even now the chickadees would be darting from stump to chip-pile and the flickers drumming on tree-trunks.

For the first time in his life he was able to save and handle money. Whitford Rush had suggested that he earn board and room by doing tasks about the stable and house and this offered a welcome relief from desk-work, but gave him no reason to spend what he earned. A tin box on his closet shelf began to fill with bills. He wrote to Lucy:

"The money, though I work for it, seems of no more value than wrapping-paper. I twist a bill between my fingers, hold it to the light, try in every way to get pleasure from it because I want to think I am not working for nothing. These greenbacks will be worth nothing to me until you come home and help me spend them."

A season's work on the farm would have produced something solid and fundamental—a granary full of wheat, corn or oats, a dozen new lambs, a row of cheeses in the cellar. Yet men worked all their lives for nothing but meaningless coins and banknotes. In London and New York, men were garrotted for ten dollars. He went back each morning to his office with the determination to change his viewpoint. Otherwise he would never be a success in business, and that was what Lucy wanted.

Across the hall from Mr. Haskins' office, in the suite assigned to the governor, a number of young men were employed as clerks. Dick met them every day in the corridor, but they seemed stiff and unfriendly, forming a clique from which he remained excluded. Actually, he thought them stupid, but he was lonely enough to try to break down the barrier and make friends, and to invent excuses for going into the governor's rooms after fresh ink, paper or quills. The clerks were always aloof; sometimes as he left he thought he heard a murmur of amusement or comment. Dick felt snubbed. Could something be wrong with his clothes?

As he was putting away his work one day, preparatory to his solitary walk home for dinner, he was surprised by a visitor, whom he was glad to recognize as his favorite among the other clerks, though he did not know the young man's name.

"I'll introduce myself," the caller said. "I'm Freeman Wills."

He was built like a bronze statuette, with just enough flesh adequately to hide his bones, and his dark, aquiline features carried out this impression of power, though his manners were curiously debonair.

"I was hoping someone would come in. It's been a

207

dull day," said Dick. He was making an effort to conceal the real extent of his pleasure.

"Days in the State House are all alike." Freeman Wills smiled wryly. "Nothing ever happens here, yet we're seeing government from the inside."

"You ought to see more of it than I. My boss isn't very important."

"Ah, you don't know the governor! A great bore. All talk and no action. He has a perfect *furor loquendi*. After you hear him once you know all his thoughts."

"People never bore me," Dick said. "It's a failing and it gets me into no end of trouble."

"In that case you might not mind having a chop with me at the little place by the post office."

"I'm expected at my rooming-house . . ." Dick was still pretending that his life had been bearable, but now he knew how much he had been hating those lonely noon-hours.

"Oh, come along! I'm the very *crème de la crème* of eating companions."

This trick of using foreign phrases was typical of Freeman Wills, as Dick soon discovered over his chops and coffee. Some of the Latin ones were incorrect, and he supposed the same was true of the French and Italian, but evidently Freeman thought anything better than the midwestern dead level. It flattered Dick that this new friend should treat him like a man of the world. Glib references to Kant and Schopenhauer rolled from Freeman's tongue. Whenever Dick spoke, he gave him the most serious attention, and this was not displeasing to one who had been so thoroughly ignored. Dick was chagrined later to discover the cause.

"What are you?" Freeman asked him suddenly, "Irish?"

"Of course not. Why?"

"I'm trying to make out your accent."

"I haven't an accent," Dick exclaimed indignantly.

"Oh, not of any consequence. A slight roll on the r's and so forth. And you move your voice up and down so charmingly. Americans keep the pitch on a monotone and talk through their noses."

Dick laughed. "I suppose it's Derbyshire, then. I thought I was rid of it."

"Oh, English! Well, if you've wondered at the coolness in our office, I'll explain. They thought you were Irish, and they're all Methodist as hell."

"Good Lord, they ought to meet my father! He'd set their Wesleyan souls at rest. I was brought up on Coke and Asbury and the sins of the high church. We boarded every circuit-rider in southern Wisconsin."

"And damn sanctimonious hypocrites they were!"

"Well, I don't know about that. Their chief sin was gluttony."

"Saints and sinners are all cut from the same bolt. The truly good are the in-between like you and me."

Freeman apparently told his fellow-clerks that Dick was a safe companion. They began dropping into his office at all hours, but none of them was as interesting as his first acquaintance. The stimulating flavor of Freeman's talk whetted Dick's appetite, yet he was afraid of pushing the affair too far and boring his new friend. He was elated when he found himself included in a skating party, planned by the other clerks.

Dick had never owned a real pair of skates. He had learned to cut figures with a pair of smithy-forged runners on the rough ice of Lake Koshkonong, and when he found himself skating on fine steel racers on smooth ice, he felt as if he had wings. He set out from the shore of Lake Mendota in the moonlight with Freeman and ten others.

"The ladies are at our house now," his friend said, gliding easily beside him. "My sister will come down with them a little later."

"Why didn't you tell me it was a mixed party?" Dick protested, thinking ruefully that he should have worn better clothes.

"Jo and her crowd always go with us. We don't make much fuss over them."

From the ice, the city of Madison spread out like a crescent-shaped panorama drawn in charcoal. Gray and white, punctuated by red-yellow lights where the kerosene street-lamps glowed, or the pale gold windows of the buildings burned along the shore, the capital looked like an enchanted place, full of adventure. A year before it had been so to Dick. Now, with Lucy away, the town was a hollow sham, beautiful and empty. But he could not deny its beauty, nor could he help recording with camera-like clearness every detail of the sight, the moving lanterns of the carriages, clustering slowly around State-House square—the governor must be giving a party, Dick thought—the wood-smoke, pluming softly out from the chimneys to melt away in the moonlight, the banner of flame above the kiln at the brickyards.

Some distance down the shore he saw a dark knot of figures, which dissolved itself, as he drew closer, into a group of chattering, laughing girls. They wore fur-lined bonnets and carried muffs. One of them glided out to Freeman and took his arm. He turned to Dick.

"This is my sister, Josephine," he said carelessly.

Dick was startled to recognize the strong features and flashing white teeth of the girl who had once rescued his hat. Her bonnet made him a little uncertain, and at any rate he was not sure he ought to claim her acquaintance, remembering how casually they had met. He bowed, and Josephine settled the matter by saying,

"I've met Mr. Wentworth, but he doesn't remember me."

"You are accusing me of great age or blindness," Dick responded gallantly. "A year's a long time, however."

Freeman was obviously surprised. "Since you're such old acquaintances," he said, with a slightly malicious emphasis, "I'll leave you to yourselves."

Even in the darkness, Dick thought he saw a scornful look on her face as her brother skated off. She crossed her mittened hands and took his naturally, and they began skating together. She was an expert. He had to exert himself to equal her.

"Don't tell him how we met," she said. "He'll raise heaven and earth to find out, but let him wonder."

"Why should he be curious?"

"Because that's the way he's made. Freeman's like a woman, you know. He has to pry and peep."

"Oh, come!" Dick said, feeling uncomfortable.

"Yes, really. He's mean, too, in small ways. Once he found out we weren't properly introduced, he'd hold it over me. I wouldn't hear the last of it."

Dick reflected that Josephine might be right, but that he felt no more inclined to believe her than when she had once called Lucy a snob. Perhaps it was an unfortunate accident that he had heard only criticism from her lips. He skated silently, and his mood appeared to reach her. She apologized.

"I suppose you like my brother. Men often do."

"I like him very much. He was the first person to be kind to me at the State House."

"In that case I won't unsettle you. Oh, look! They've made a fire."

Ahead of them on the lake-shore the leaping flames of a bonfire lit the night and sent out a sharp smell of burning pine. Skates clanged against the ice as the men removed the girls' skate-harnesses from their shoes. Dick knelt at Jo's feet and fumbled at the straps, feeling acutely the warmth of her ankles and the intimate touch of her hand on his shoulder.

As the party sat down around the fire, their faces became visible and Dick realized that they were well chaperoned. Two of the ladies had gray hair. The men had been carrying rugs on which the women were now sitting, their skirts spread decorously about them. He had no rug for Josephine. He took off his square muffler and she sat on it, cross-legged he thought, from her easy posture.

"I wish we had some apples to roast. Did anyone bring apples?" Freeman asked. Someone had remembered apples and brought out a paper sack of Tolman Sweets. Someone else had sharpened sticks and hidden them in the bushes that morning. Soon all the men had sticks and were roasting apples for themselves and their ladies. Jo seemed to have been generally accepted as Dick's girl for the evening. He knelt in the snow and began to roast her apple.

Oh, to have Lucy beside him in the moonlight! Not Lucy, the abolitionist, nor the Washington belle she had now become, but his own sweetheart, soft in his arms as he had held her once or twice. What was he doing beside this other woman, who watched him so intently with her black eyes?

The apple sizzled and dripped. He took it off the stick and gave it to Josephine, who rolled it in the snow.

"Don't do that. You'll wash off the honey," he said.

She stopped obediently and sank her white teeth into
the fruit. Dick was momentarily pleased at her manner.
Perhaps she was not always so headstrong and out-
spoken. It was very evident that she liked him and
wanted his admiration. Another man might have made
love to Josephine to pass the time, but Dick was not
tempted. His heart ached with emptiness, but he refused
to fill it with husks.

"I can't do it," he said to himself and involuntarily
struck out with one hand and hit Josephine's shoulder.
"Oh, do forgive me," he apologized.

"It's quite all right. You'd merely forgotten my existence," she said rather tartly, but he had felt for a
moment that she wanted to seize his hand in hers, that
she would like to have him jostle her again. The conversation was going on around them, leaving them on
their island of emotion.

"When I was small we lived near the old capital at
Belmont. . . ."

"I know. It looked just like a district schoolhouse."

"Well, the legislature used to come in French
sleds. . . ."

"Why *French?*"

"I don't know. They were just boxes, drawn by
tandem horses. A six-foot box held ten assemblymen."

"Don't pack them in like herrings!"

"Well, six, then. One politician per foot. . . ."

Someone started *Sweet Evalina.* Josephine joined

the singing. She had a beautiful deep contralto. The moonlight fell on her animated face and gave it softness and glamour.

Political gossip was unrestrained in Madison. Freeman enjoyed retailing the latest scandal to Dick, especially when it concerned some statesman for whom Dick still had admiring moments. The governor was planning to retire at the end of his term. Everyone knew that his salary was not large and wondered what he expected to live on. Mr. Bashford had not been wealthy before his election.

"Bet you anything, Old Bashy feathered his nest from the University Fund," Freeman said, sitting on one corner of Dick's desk.

"You suspect everyone. What do you think my share's been?"

"Pooh! You wouldn't bother to pick up greenbacks if they were flying around like snowflakes. You never think about money. Why, Dick, you don't even suspect that boss of yours, who's so crooked he sleeps in a worm-hole."

"Haskins crooked! Why, he's open as daylight."

"Open to bribes."

"Don't sit on my desk and abuse my employer. Back up your statements, at least."

"You back them down. Tell me what he's done with the Road Fund."

"How do I know? I don't keep his books."

"Why don't you? Every secretary keeps his set of books but you."

"I never thought about that. Mr. Haskins likes to do it himself."

"I'll bet he does."

"Get out, will you, Freem? I've got work to do."

"*Tout de suite*," said his guest, unruffled. At the door he looked back with mock pity. "Wonderful, wonderful! That such faith still lives!"

Dick was so much irritated by these insinuations that he could not write letters. He remembered the big ledgers marked *State Roads, Receipts and Disbursements* which Mr. Haskins sometimes took out of the green iron safe. He had never been curious about them before, though he knew that new roads were not being built and that the money had been appropriated. If the ledgers were being juggled in some fashion, the procedure would be just as it actually was now. Mr. Haskins would keep the safe locked. He would never give his secretary the key. He would take out the books at closing time and work over them after Dick was gone. All these things he did, yet Dick had never suspected him.

Freeman followed up his first attack by tiptoeing around the office, peering behind cupboards, and otherwise pretending to do detective work.

"What in the world are you looking for?" Dick asked.

"A key."

"Have you lost a key?"

"Lost one? Why, no."

"Well, if you're looking for the key to that infernal safe, let me tell you where it is. It's in Mr. Haskins' weskit pocket, and you'll do me a favor by forgetting to be a nuisance."

Freeman laughed. *"Bon soir,* and remember the oysters tonight."

Oyster suppers were the latest innovation in Madison. People of means served them and so did most of the hotels, but poor families could not have them because they were sold only in large amounts. Freeman had made a bargain with the Belmont cook and brought home enough for a stew. Like many men who have temperament but no talent, he preferred to think himself a connoisseur of foods. He put on as many airs over obtaining the oysters as an artist at the opening of his first show. Dick had never been interested in exotic flavors. He was always hungry, but with a farmboy's appetite. He humored Freeman by pretending the oysters would be a rare treat.

It was not the first time he had been at the Wills home, and not the second time he had spent an evening with Josephine. The skating party had been only the beginning of an ambiguous friendship. He was being impelled steadily farther in her direction, partly because avoidance might offend Freeman, and partly by his own

217

amiable nature. When the time came, he intended to
call a halt, but he had no idea how to do it. Josephine
seemed simple and forthright; she was actually neither.
Dick had found her as full of wiles as Circe, but he was
still unenchanted.

Mother and Father Wills were a mild couple who
must have thought their children changelings. They had
long ago been coerced by the sharp tongues and strong
minds of their offspring into leaving the house, or staying upstairs when company came. Dick had barely met
them. They were always at prayer-meeting or in bed.
The room which had been their parlor, Freeman now
called the "study"; he had moved the mahogany and
horsehair to an upstairs room and refurnished with
maple and chintz, while the table which had held immortelle and the family Bible now supported Harper's
Weekly and a portfolio of etchings. The younger generation had further frightened away the old by putting
a pair of semi-nude statuettes on the mantel.

Dick liked this "study" very much, but he did not
tell Freeman why. It looked like his mother's kitchen,
in which even better books than Freeman's had been
spread about on window-sill and table, though without
that self-conscious attention which made the Wills room
artistic. Until he knew Freeman, Dick had always
thought reading pure pleasure. Now he saw it could be
a fashion as well. He wandered about, picking up one
new volume after another, wondering how Freeman
could afford so much literature on his salary.

"Come out, Dick. The feast is spread! Don't delay or you'll miss the first flavor." Freeman was walking around importantly in the kitchen, though Jo had done the cooking. The table was covered with a red cloth and a large china bowl of oyster crackers was set in the middle.

Josephine brought on a plate of cheese sandwiches. She sat down and began to eat without ceremony, raising a dripping spoon. As always, her youth and vivacity excused her manners. Dick watched her covertly.

"Mm! It's really good!" she said, with a mouth full of crackers.

"They'll do. I've tasted better," added Freeman, who had eaten oysters once before.

Dick's most sincere compliment was the fact that he finished a second bowl. He offered to dry the dishes for Jo while Freeman built up the fire at the front of the house. Almost at once he wished he could change tasks with Freeman, as Jo became possessive and domestic. He must tie her apron . . . her hands were in the water, would he please put back the net on her hair?

Her fingers grew bright pink in the hot water. Her heavy rings slipped about loosely. Finally she stopped, dried her hands on the towel Dick was holding, and took off the rings.

"Take care of them for me till I'm done," she said, putting them into his hands with a prolonged clasp. Her mouth was almost on a level with his and very near. He drew back.

"Have I offended you, Dick?" she asked, her vivid face sobering as if he had doused it with cold water.

"Not at all . . . how can you think so?" he muttered, taking her in his arms. She returned his kiss with hungry intensity. Simultaneously they saw Freeman watching them from the doorway.

Jo's brother was trying to look amused and worldly, but it was evident that he was both shocked and irritated. Dick was deeply embarrassed. He tried to face his friend down.

"You should knock before entering," he said.

"Obviously."

Freeman spoke coldly and Dick's embarrassment turned to defiance. Jo was old enough to answer for herself, and she had almost demanded the kiss. He could still feel the pressure of her lips; his blood was still racing. It seemed to him Freeman was acting very badly, rather like an outraged husband. Jo had begun calmly putting away the dishes as if nothing were wrong.

"It's discouraging," Freeman said, trying to return to his usual teasing manner. "I was playing some very elevated music, but it seems you weren't listening. You didn't rise far, at any rate."

"Well, you left us in the dishwater, you know."

"Leaving you anywhere was my mistake."

Jo whirled around angrily from the shelves, dropping a cup, which broke on the floor. Her face was contorted like a child's who is going to cry.

"Freeman never does dishes. Oh no! He likes to keep his hands pretty . . . so he can play airs from the opera. You think you're so superior, don't you, dear? Other people can drudge. They haven't such wonderful minds. What are you, anyhow? A five-dollar a week clerk and it's all you'll ever be."

Her breast heaved, her hands opened and clenched. Her bitterness was entirely out of proportion to its cause. Freeman interrupted with an effort at control which left him pale.

"So now I know your opinion of me. Let's go in, shall we, Dick?"

Dick followed him to the library in an uncomfortable frame of mind. He wished he were well out of this emotional mess. Half a block away, the empty Hammond mansion stood, and almost in its shadow, he had been unfaithful to Lucy's memory. Well, he would go no farther. He looked out of the window and saw the snow falling. In a little while he would be walking home, feeling the cool flakes gratefully on his hot face.

Freeman adroitly drew him out of his mood, talking easily and well as if nothing had happened, but Dick was surprised and puzzled to see that his friend was still pale, that he looked like a man who has received a severe shock. As for Jo, she stayed on in the kitchen, her smouldering wrath perceptible through three walls.

Winter passed slowly. Spring warmth was felt outside long before it penetrated the barn-like rooms of the

State House, but at last the janitor stopped carrying in wood for Dick's fire. His stove stood cold and empty. There had been a companionship about the crackling fire. Alone with the cold stove, Dick found his days hard to bear. Outside in sunlit King Street, robins hopped and tugged at worms, squirrels raced and chattered. A year ago he had sat with Lucy on the bench he could see from his window. Not a board of the sidewalk out there had escaped the imprint of her little feet beside his own. He felt desolately that their ghosts still sat there on the bench like lovers from an old story. He could hardly believe he would ever see Lucy again. She was so far away, and her letters seemed cold. His own nature demanded nearness, something immediate, tangible, warm. The ideal of faithfulness in absence was not enough.

It was not Dick's fault that he was still in Madison. His tin box held bills enough to take him to Washington, but Lucy's letters forestalled him. She had been planning to come home in six months, and though the time had extended itself to a year, she still wrote that she would soon be near him, that young men in the capital could not find work, that it did not seem advisable for Dick to come. He had made up his mind to go anyway, the minute the weather was warm enough. He had reached the end of his endurance.

The affair with Josephine made him all the more determined to get away from Madison. He had thought of Freeman as a possible ally, but his friend seemed to take a perverted delight in pushing Dick farther into trouble. He invented all sorts of excuses to leave the two alone together, and seemed to be viewing their progress with a queer, tortured fascination. Josephine was thoroughly in love. Dick thought of her kisses with extreme distaste, but was wretchedly aware that he enjoyed them too.

As he leaned on the window-sill, looking out at the new green leaves in the square, he saw a glimmer of steel in the casing. Something had been wedged into a joint of the woodwork. He took out his knife and began prying idly at the object. It was a small key. He thought of Freeman's suspicions about the safe. Perhaps this key would fit the green iron box. It looked like the one Mr. Haskins used. Dick slipped it into his pocket just as his employer entered.

"Well, boy! Sit down. Take a letter," the assemblyman said. "Yours of the 16th instant received and hasten to inform you that to all intents and purposes ... Are you getting this, Dick?"

"No, Sir. I'm sorry." The key in his pocket was on his conscience. It seemed that Mr. Haskins should be able to see through the cloth.

"Mind's wandering, eh? Ha, ha! Spring fever, Dick!"

"I'm sorry," Dick murmured again.

"Well, at your age I had it too. Oh, dear! I wish I

was twenty again. You can cut all the capers you like. Don't have to answer to God or nobody else, but don't go too far, boy."

"No, Sir."

"You're sure Miss Josephine isn't setting her cap for you, Richard?" his clergyman friend said that night at supper.

"I don't see why you think that," Dick countered. He was somewhat taken aback, because he had thought his friendship with Jo quite a secret.

"Ah well, I passed you on the square last night and the—— pose was—— ah—a trifle intimate, Richard." Mr. Rush bent his head to adjust his spectacles and the ministerial bald spot was very pink.

"Oh, laws! What if it was?" Mrs. Amos interrupted. "A kiss or two don't count between young folk. Time to settle down when the blood cools, I say."

"Did I mention a kiss, Mrs. Amos? No, I did not, and you are simply jumping at conclusions as usual."

"Beg pardon, I'm sure," his housekeeper said, haughtily.

"As a matter of fact, Richard, I have quite an interest in Miss Wills, ah, a spiritual interest purely, of course. I should not like to see her peace of mind disturbed."

As to Jo's mind, Dick felt somewhat ignorant. He could have testified more fully about her body, since she was one of those advanced young women who wore no stays. He sat with noncommittal face and downcast eyes, while thoughts went through his head which would have astonished Mr. Rush.

"Her father and mother are among my most respected parishioners, I—ah—wondered if she has been informed about your betrothal, Richard."

"Lucy wanted it kept a secret for the present." The fact was still painful, though he had forced himself to admit its wisdom.

"Don't you think that's a danger? An announcement might have been an—ah—anchor, you know."

"Yes, sir." (An anchor. A rock. A refuge.)

"Well, I may have upset you. I'll say no more. Perhaps a slight hint to Mr. Wills."

As Whitford Rush left the table he took Dick's hand in a surprisingly warm grasp.

The key lay forgotten until the next morning. How did one go about finding work in Washington? Dick had decided to leave at once whether or not Lucy approved. He meant to ask Mr. Haskins for a recommendation and letter of introduction to some political friend, though it seemed doubtful that the assemblyman would have much standing in the eastern city. Dick put his hand in his pocket and encountered the key. Curious, he tried to fit it in the lock of the safe; it went in easily enough but stuck and would not come out. He dropped to his knees and began to work it loose.

The janitor came in, but he paid no attention. If he went on with what he was doing the man would think it natural, while to rise suddenly would look suspicious.

When the key yielded, he turned and saw that it had not been the janitor at all, but his employer.

"What did you want in the safe, Dick?"

"Nothing . . . just to see if the key would fit."

"Where did you get the key?" Mr. Haskins sounded plaintive. "That's to my storeroom, Dick. And there's no cash in the safe anyway."

"You ought to know I wouldn't take money. I'm telling the truth, Mr. Haskins. I was just curious."

"I know who's been talking to you. That damn Wiesendonck! That rapscallion whose pockets are lined with public funds! He don't dare pull that trick on me. I know too much about him, and if he can talk, so can I!"

"You're mistaken."

"Sneaking in behind my back, talking to my secretary. He'll try blackmail, will he?"

"I tell you, it wasn't Mr. Wiesendonck or anyone else. I just wanted to see if the key would fit."

"Get out of here, and don't you come back. I trusted you. I looked on you as a son."

Dick began collecting his belongings from the desk. He was thoroughly convinced of his employer's guilt by this time, though a few minutes before he would have defended him against any accuser.

"Oh dear!" Mr. Haskins said, his fat face crinkling as if he were about to weep. "I don't know what I'll do without you." Then as Dick hesitated, he waved a violent hand. "Get out, anyway. You aint worth a nickel if I can't trust you."

"You were perfectly right, Freem," he said, a few hours later. "The man's a crook, but I wish I hadn't found out. I need an honorable discharge, and instead I got the sack."

"The State House is a dirty hole," his friend agreed. "If I don't move soon I'll have a touch of the tar-stick myself."

They were sitting in the chop-house at a table they had come to claim as their own. Dick looked at the alert, dark face opposite his and admitted rather reluctantly that he could not leave Freeman without a pang. What a queer fellow this was! He had no scruples, no great generosity; he was not above taking a mean advantage. His charm consisted in the fact that he made no pretensions of uprightness. In his devious way he was honest.

"Why don't you come with me, then?" Dick asked. "Toss up your job and get yourself a pony and come along."

"I might. But where?"

"Washington." As soon as he pronounced the word, Dick realized that his clergyman host had made good his promise about a hint to Freeman's father. The gleam in Freeman's eyes was disconcerting. "Or California," Dick added hastily.

"Washington would be best. Think of the social advantages!"

This remark implied a great deal, none of which was lost on Dick. It meant that Jo was a girl without background, that he had used her for entertainment while looking forward to a better alliance. He found the inference unbearable. Leaning toward Freeman, he tried to capture his eyes. Freeman looked away, pretending an interest in the none-too-clean decorations above the plate-rail. Dick did not move and after a few minutes he had his way. Freeman's eyes came back, flickering.

"You're thinking what isn't true," Dick said simply. *"Absolvo te."*

5

WITH THAT UNEXPECTEDNESS which Dick had begun to expect, he found himself riding westward toward Blue Mounds on a bright morning in middle May. Freeman rode beside him, astride a horse called Duke, but addressed alternately as Wales or Wellington. Before them lay the monotonous Dane County prairie, broken only by the purple dome of Mount Horeb on the horizon.

In spite of sunshine and piercingly sweet air, Dick's heart was dogged by painful memories. He had been in a mood of black despair from which he was slowly emerging. Lucy's letter, coming just as he was ready to go east, had so broken through his usually mild temper that he had thrown it into the cold ashes of his bedroom stove and with it the roll of bills he had been counting when he opened the envelope. He had retrieved the money, kneeling desolately by the empty hearth. The letter still lay in the grate, torn and crushed, its phrases, in Lucy's strong quill-strokes, running uphill and down among the crumpled folds of blue paper:

"My mother is in a state of the greatest excitement over an invitation from Mr. Simeon Drake to visit the Bermudas in his yacht. . . . I am being dangled as bait, for my poor parents are asked only because Mr. Charley Drake wants me aboard and his father can refuse him nothing. . . . If it were not so much to my father's advantage I promise you I should not be going. Mr. Buchanan's compromise attitude has made it very hard for the friends of abolition and we must snatch at all straws. I am afraid we shall not be coming back until August."

Dick had walked the streets most of the night, almost ready to throw his life away as he had thrown away the letter. In the morning the world seemed desirable again, but only if he could leave this ghost city, Madison, where everything was haunted by a lost happiness. Well, he could not go east, so he would go west! Quite wildly he had talked Freeman into going along.

"But no farther than Galena," Freeman said. "Beyond that all is sage-brush and Choctaws."

"Why stop in Galena? It's a dying town."

"So are Rome and Paris."

Lecturers and writers had been predicting for years that the Galena boom would die with the lead veins, and now their predictions had begun to come true. Great fortunes had been made from the striated folds along the Fever River, but now the Moses Meeker claims were for sale and the Bonner interests were being withdrawn. Old names like Peck and Heath, Parker and

Tilton, Bales, Lockwood, Harcourt were becoming forgotten. The romantic Sir Charles Augustus Murray had
long since gone back to Scotland, leaving behind him a
whole volume of tales of his daring adventures and
his name on more than half the deeds of Grant County,
Wisconsin. As if it were not enough that the lead veins
were running out, the gold rush had begun. In the mad
dash for California, miners had left pick and shovel
underground. At Potosi, Missouri, the galena was still
productive and the Wisconsin smelters still poured out
their molten harvests, but the Fever River colonies
seemed doomed.

"If we must go west," Freeman said, "let's stay
within the bounds of reason. Culture and society will
cling to Galena long after the miners are gone. As for
frontier life, Madison was crude enough for me."

Dick was not in a mood for argument. As if he had
eyes in the rear of his head, he continued to see visions
of the town he was leaving behind. Jo's pallor and
husky voice; Whitford Rush, his mask of cheerfulness
barely concealing pity and curiosity; the house on the
hill where Lucy's shuttered window looked down on
the rose-garden. What dresses and little shoes had
she left behind that blind window? Perhaps the frock
with the rosebud-trimmed wrist-bands in which he had
first seen her. No doubt it was hanging there, unwanted,
out of style, not good enough for Washington—like
her first love affair.

The capital had been so full of hope! Now he

brushed the thought of it from his face as if it were a cobweb. Was there something in him he could never escape? Some weakness or trouble he must take with him wherever he went?

At about the eleventh mile he felt the burden growing lighter. Black Betsey jogged along comfortably beneath him; he had begun to love her and was almost glad Lucy had not taken her. The blue sky was incredibly clear, the clouds china-white, and the two were doubled by their reflection in pools of water by the road. Meadowlarks spiraled up, singing. Now and then a partridge whirred before the horses' feet. Gophers sat upright at their kitchen doors. Little streams, cut deep into the black prairie loam, streaked off eastward to the Yahara or westward to Sugar River. Wild barley fringed the highway with its misty green and everywhere were patches of spring flowers.

Freeman rode ahead where the trail was narrow. Dick's lips twisted in an involuntary smile whenever this happened. His companion's costume and mincing seat in the saddle were very funny to a man who had grown up with horses. A brown twill coat with a self-conscious look of vagabondia and a velvet tam-o-shanter had struck Freeman as just the outfit for riding across country. He must have been studying some book on the English hunt, Dick thought, or he would never be sitting like that. Once in a while a rough stretch brought him to reality and then he forgot to be a country squire and became a Wisconsin traveler.

"From all I hear of Exeter's tavern, we might need firearms," Freeman said, looking back jauntily. "Those Badgers from the Million Dollar Field are a quarrelsome lot. Worse than Pokerville, they say."

"Oh, we'll just mind our own business."

"That's not enough. They might murder us because we look different . . . like young aristocrats, you know."

"You'll die first, then."

"Anyhow, Dick, don't hang your breeches over a chair-back with that roll in your pocket."

"How do you know so much?" Dick transferred his wallet to his waistcoat.

"I know you, where money's concerned."

"Oh, I tend this money like a sick child, and it gives me just as little pleasure."

Blue Mound rose ahead of them, beyond Mount Horeb, a dim barrier on the sky-line. On its summit was the fort, half-way station between Forts Crawford at Prairie du Chien and Winnebago at Portage. There, too, the circular race-track of territorial days showed like a white crescent on the hillside as they came nearer. Soon they must branch off to Exeter, where after a dubious night's rest they would take the Galena road.

The new trail cleft the plain, dipping to cross Sugar River and angling away again after the beguiling manner of unknown roads. Splashing through shallow water, they found themselves in the profitless "strip-mine" area at the edge of the mineral counties.

"Are you bent on staying at Exeter tonight?" Freeman asked suddenly.

"Not especially."

"Would you sacrifice adventure and the ubiquitous bedbug to stop twenty miles nearer with a friend of mine?"

"Male or female?"

"Neither. Disembodied. A Greek professor."

"Doesn't sound tempting at all. What's a Greek professor doing out here?"

"Teaching the sons of miners to scorn their parents. Didn't you know Bradford Academy is close by?"

"Never heard of the place."

"Doctor Busch went out there five years ago. From what I hear it's a pariah among academies. The boys sucked whiskey from their nursing bottles and learned their god-damn-its at mother's knee. Teachers get uncommonly good pay there."

"I should think they might."

"The boys' dads insist on refinement, even to Plato. Those old codgers are rolling in money and can't buy themselves a thing but a roaring spree, so they look around and the wistful eye lights on son and heir. He is snatched up by the seat of the trousers and cast screaming into Minerva's lap."

"Probably Minerva throws plenty of them out again."

"Not many. She's paid too well."

234

"And who'll go on with the mining?"

"New immigrants of course. The others will have made their pile. They won't care any more. Why should they?"

"And their sons will go east and the new immigrants' sons will go to Bradford and so forth."

"Well, Dick, if you're bent on maintaining the status quo, why didn't you stay on the farm?"

Dick shrugged his shoulders. The secret of his discontent with society lay in one word: Drake. The first Simeon Drake had been a ferryman on the East River, content with his monthly bath. The second Simeon had made his fortune in furs. Because he had a million dollars he lived in another world, America's new upper class. What chance had a farmer's son beside the son of Simeon Drake? Lucy was not choosing between men at all, but between two ways of living.

Even while he resented the division of the new country into classes, Dick realized a certain snobbishness in his resentment. If any of the Englishmen at whose mention his mother was still inclined to curtsey had come to Wisconsin, he might have granted them the right to hold up their heads. The Duke of Rutland, the Earl of Chesterfield—these names carried with them the prestige of generations. The American aristocrats were money-made and he had not learned to worship money.

"Maybe I ought to go back to the farm," he said.

"Society's like a boiling pot. Up, up, up. Some day there won't be room at the top and then it's going to boil over."

"Oh no. Not in America. There's plenty of room. What's more likely is that we'll have no servant class. Everyone will be prosperous."

"Look out!" Dick exclaimed. Freeman had almost ridden the Duke into the shallow pot-hole of a surface mine.

As they rode down the eastern border of Iowa County, they saw on all sides the pox-like pittings of the hardscrabble miners who neglected their mines to farm and neglected their farms to dig for lead. Groups of men, women and children could be seen, scratching in the earth on every hillside. To the east was a great walnut forest that stretched almost to New Glarus, to the west the country changed its character and seemed to be almost another climate. The undulating slopes looked worn and old. They had come into Wisconsin's pre-glacial area.

"We must be just west of Mineral Point," Freeman guessed. "Let's turn off and sleep at the Academy, Dick. Seriously, I'd prefer clean sheets. Perhaps the students aren't on a rampage just now."

"Lead on. I follow. Someone told me the Exeter landlord accomodates fifty guests to one bed by taking each man out as he falls asleep."

They turned off on the Mineral Point Road and had traveled for an hour when they met their first team.

Two great Clydesdales were drawing a wagon loaded with boxes from the Rountree mines. Next an ox-wagon brought freight marked W. S. Hamilton, Wiota.

Billy Hamilton's name had been known to Dick since early childhood, not because of his famous father, Alexander, but because Billy himself had driven the first great herd of horses into Wisconsin—seven hundred of them, dropping them off wherever he could sell them at points along the military road from Fort Crawford to Fort Winnebago. Some of these horses had been sold near Barribault and had then been peddled all the way to Hampstead where Tommy Wentworth had turned them down after a cold inspection.

"Little scion of a great family," Wisconsin men called Billy Hamilton, but he had made his name great too, in the lead country. Now he had been lying for several years in an unmarked grave in California while his sons went on smelting lead at Wiota, lead for the shot-towers, the paint-factories at Buffalo, the plumbers all over America. The huge cart rumbled by, while Dick and Freeman drew their horses out of danger.

"Beetown, Hardscrabble, Platteville, Swindler's Ridge," the signs said, as more teams came past them. Soon they met an old-fashioned "toad-crusher" drawn by eight oxen. It was loaded with pig-lead from Shullsburg. The rack carried a white sign with black lettering: "Gentry's Diggings." Freeman waved his velvet cap at the driver.

"How far to the Academy?"

"Eh, what?" the man said, cocking an ear.

"To the school—Bradford."

"Oh, aye. Ye'll cross Moscow Creek and the East Pecatonica, thou knows. On t' far side, turn right toward Military Ridge. Go straight on. T' school's on a hill-like."

"Derbyshire, by golly!" Dick exclaimed. "We're grateful to thee, lad," he called after the driver.

The gentle south slope from Military Ridge cast all its waters southwest to the Mississippi. The two riders looked across it into the setting sun and saw a broad plain, modeled smoothly into curves of valley and crest. The creeks and rivers flowed quietly here—the two branches of the spreading Pecatonica, Moscow Creek near at hand and far off the Platte with its adjoining mounds.

The deep silt of the prairie had produced a tall, wild grass. It stood almost to the stirrups, but everywhere it was treacherous with surface mines, concealed by the growth. The road wound among these diggings, sometimes coming out between fields of grain, luxuriant or sparse according to whether the land was weathered limestone or broken-down sandstone. The two kinds of soil adjoined each other in a series of stripes—the edges of the upturned strata beneath.

Where the thirty-foot chimneys of Morrison's blast furnaces punctured the skyline, the road to Bradford turned off and ran northward into a hickory grove. Dick saw, without comment, the trail-trees of the Indians, the branches, bent while young and trained to point the way. Hickory boughs, once trained, would hold their position for a century or more, accurate as an index finger. Freeman, riding ahead, passed under the guiding fingers without knowing what they were. He came back at a gallop, pale and frightened.

"There's been a hanging," he said.

"Where?"

"Around the bend."

A few minutes later they saw a trampled place in the road-bed and a figure among the trees, swinging from a rope.

"I haven't much stomach for this," Freeman gulped. "Let's go back."

"And sleep at Exeter? Look, Freem, it's a dummy."

The face, just turning toward them, was drawn with charcoal on a stuffed pillow-case; the shoes held an angle impossible for human feet. Freeman lifted reluctant eyes and drew a deep breath of relief. A sign, nailed to the tree proclaimed "sic semper tyrannis" and the label on the dummy's breast read:

"Frederick Jonas, D. D."

"Schoolboys on a picnic. See their shoe-prints. No other age varies that much." Dick examined the ground where very small and very large feet had walked side by side.

"The second generation must be in rebellion," Freeman managed to smile though he was still pale.

Cornish men had built Bradford, and the houses were as like their old homes as memory could make them, squat cottages of stone blocks with tiny windows and thatched roofs. The private walks were cobbled, the little dooryards primly set with bright flowers. The main streets of the town were paved only with ash and slag from the furnaces which belched smoke all day. From summit to base of the cliff on which the city rested, a fast current of water swirled, the creek that turned water-wheels for mills and furnace-bellows.

Bradford village had a look of complete solidity, but in actual fact it was a honeycomb. Under the streets, under the houses, even under the churchyard were the holes and passageways of the "badgers." Wherever a vein led him a miner must dig. They stuck their candles in gobs of fire-clay and set them on the rock walls, while with pick and shovel they kept heaps of ore ready for the wheelbarrow and bucket. The streets were full of these "Cousin Jacks" when Dick and Freeman rode in at sundown. As they came pouring up from their diggings they blinked at the light with eyes almost universally blue and heavily fringed. The saying went that a blue-eyed Cornishman could make his fortune in a hole some other man had abandoned.

Ox-carts made a creaking procession as they took the day's last load uphill to the smelters. Edging past the wide racks with their spilling loads of ore, past the spreading horns of the oxen, Dick and Freeman made their way upward to the school. Bradford Academy had an air of aloofness, not so much because it was set on the hill, apart from the rest of the town, but because of its architecture, so different in appearance, and so classically spacious. The three buildings were of red brick with spreading white verandas, pillared porticos and tall windows. They flanked three sides of a square. In the center of the campus was a well with tin dipper, an iron flagpole with the stars-and-stripes, and some wooden benches. The newcomers dismounted and tied Betsey and Duke to the hitching-rail.

"You're welcome," Dr. Busch greeted them, "though you've come at an unusual time."

Dick stared at the man, thinking how perfectly Freeman's description fitted him. Disembodied he certainly seemed. The clothes he wore barely suggested that there was flesh beneath them; his features looked to be carved from some pure, transparent material. Silvery hair fell back from his magnificent forehead. He might have been either sixty or eighty, but his eyes were young.

"We've been having a little trouble," he said. "Our president left us just this morning and you'll find the boys over-stimulated. For the time being I've had to take charge of the school . . . Well! You must be tired and hungry. Freeman, make yourself at home. You and your friend may use my room and join me in half an hour at supper."

They had eaten in the saddle and while Dick had wanted to be rid of his life only that morning, he had

begun to think starvation a poor way to die. Even so
fastidious an appetite as Freeman's was roused at the
mention of food. Dr. Busch brought them soap and
towels. Strange as it seemed, he owned a basin and
pitcher too, though no one would have thought he ever
need wash. Stranger still, to Dick, was the sight of a
half-filled pipe on his desk, a collection of coins and
arrow-heads under the glass top of his center table, the
signs of a lively human interest everywhere. Busts of
Homer and Hesiod served as book-ends on his table
beside a chess-board with a game half-finished.

"We saw a dummy of your president in the woods I
think," Freeman said. "Wasn't his name Jonas? They
hung him in effigy. Very lifelike. I might have been
startled if I hadn't thought to investigate."

"Is that so? Well, we must cut him down," the Greek
professor replied, smoothly. "His successor will have to
ride in by that road, and it wouldn't do for him to see
what happened to Dr. Jonas."

Freeman's eyes opened very wide at the cold-blooded
tone of this remark. Dick could see him beginning to
scent a mystery. His nostrils dilated, his glance began
to dart about the room. As soon as they were alone he
noiselessly opened the closet door, the drawers of the
wash-stand and desk, the medicine cabinet. He turned
over the papers on the desk and examined them.

"Behave yourself!" Dick said sternly, but he could
hardly keep from laughing at the openness of Freeman's
vices.

"One moment, please." Freeman tried out several rubber-stamps on a piece of paper, crumpled it and put it in his pocket. He lifted the pictures away from the wall and looked behind them.

"What in the world . . . ?"

"You never can tell, my friend. A bit of information accidentally acquired is sometimes priceless. Improve each shining hour. I know that I know not, but I know not that I know."

They were late coming into the dining hall, but seats had been reserved for them at the table with the teachers. Dick's faced the room. He looked down the rows of tables where two hundred boys were eating by early candle-light. They looked like any other school-boys—the youngest in long trousers, pleated at the waist and button-trimmed jackets, the older ones in frock coats and gay "weskits." Most of the older boys were proud owners of silky beards above which their eyes looked amazingly innocent. All were in extreme high spirits, shouting, leaning across the tables, banging knives and forks and otherwise making a terrific hubbub which none of the teachers tried to suppress, though they had great difficulty to hear each other speak.

"Quite a little excitement," Dr. Busch said, benevolently. "They've just finished an educational experience, a revolution, you know. So fortunate no one was badly hurt. You like young people, don't you, Mr. Wentworth?"

"I must, or I wouldn't be enjoying myself."

"A rare trait. You wouldn't say these boys looked vicious?"

"Surely not. A trifle hysterical, perhaps."

"Just so. A man would do well not to put much pressure on them. New wine in old bottles, you know. Let them effervesce and after a bit nature will be on our side. Tell him about our boys, Mr. Humphrey."

"Which ones interest you?" asked the mathematics teacher.

"The handsome chap with a horseshoe in his cravat."

"Cass Jones from Wiota. His father cleaned up one fortune, sold out to Hamilton and hit the gold trail. Left four sons here in school, but three followed him. Skipped out in the night. I don't know why Cass stays."

"He has an adventurer's face."

"He's certainly no student. Anyone else?"

"The thin lad with the scowl—opposite him."

"George Lennox. His father was at Hardscrabble in the first year. Struck a four-o-clock vein and took out three-hundred-thousand. His mother died when George was born and his father married a Chippewa, so George has nine half-Chippewa brothers and sisters."

"I suppose I can teach the Latin classes for a while," Dr. Busch was saying to someone across the table.

"My friend is a Latin scholar," Freeman remarked innocently.

Dick had begun a protest, but Dr. Busch fixed him

with a look of intense attention. "How much have you read? Catullus? Ovid?"

"Yes, sir. I studied with Whitford Rush."

"Oh, excellent! You're just the man."

"But I . . ."

"Nonsense, my boy. Any student of Whitford's . . . I know his standards."

Dick looked at Freeman and met his too-casual smile as if in a trance. What was happening? The unexpected again. The solid oak table, the substantial men around it seemed unreal enough to vanish in a puff of smoke. The boys' voices murmured on his ear like waves in a cockle-shell.

"I've never taught. I don't feel capable."

"You have the first essential. You like young people. Dr. Jonas was unfortunate in that respect."

"What happened to Dr. Jonas? Where is he now?"

"Now?" Dr. Busch took out his watch and consulted it. "At the rate he was going, he must be just about in New Glarus."

"Sorry to throw you to the dogs, Dick," Freeman said. They were preparing to sleep in a bare dormitory room.

"Oh, don't apologize. Don't even bother to explain yourself."

"I heard strange rumors about this school yesterday. Today we passed an ox-cart loaded with lumber, coming out of Bradford. Now, there's no lumber native here. They import it from Arena, so I took another look. A box was under the boards and it had a hinged end, just big enough to let a man into it. Then we find the school in some sort of turmoil and the president gone . . . what do you make of it?"

"Nothing to reconcile me to teaching Latin."

"Give me a few weeks, Dick."

"Why don't *you* teach and let me go on to Galena?"

"Unfortunately Dr. Busch knows my Latin."

"I'd rather hang myself to that oak tree than face a class of boys. What do you expect of this famous investigation of yours? You wouldn't call in the sheriff no matter what you found."

"Of course not," said Freeman, but his eyes flickered away. Dick looked at him doubtfully, sighed and got into bed.

In the morning the tall chimneys of the ridge furnaces began to smoke at five o'clock, the water-wheels began creaking in the rapid current of the creek, the bellows of the Drummond furnace groaned in the power of the wheel and sparks shot from the chimney tops. Dick got up and went out into the town. Everywhere miners were pouring through the streets, disappearing like gophers into holes and crevices under the pavement, under the houses, in the sides of the hills. Dull blows of pick and gad sounded out of the hollow ground. Dick walked above these sounds, reading the swinging signs of tallow chandler, saddler, gunsmith and baker, and the announcement to Freemasons that Mr. Rountree of Platteville would speak in the village hall.

He had left Freeman asleep and was not sorry. Alone, and without cynical comments, he could enjoy his senses. The twisted streets and cobbled courtyards, crammed tightly together in a country where space had no value, showed the character of the people who had built the town. They huddled timidly like sheep, afraid of being alone. How few men can bear to stand alone, to face the open prairie of life and death without a companion! So, in Holmesfield, Dick's mother had told him, four families sometimes lived in a small cottage together. The poorer they were, the more ailing and wretched, the closer they packed themselves in.

Apple trees were blooming strangely on the edge of slag-heaps. The Wesleyan church had a small cemetery around it. Even under the graves the noise of mining could be heard, but the immortelle and yew went on growing as if their roots were not reaching down toward nothing. The tombstones and markers trembled. On either side of the churchyard were the saloons. Bradford village had six. Candle-light shone from the grogshops in spite of the rising sun and hairy men came out, wiping their mouths on the backs of their hands.

The swift creek turned the water-wheels on the ridge and tumbling downhill, ran beneath the main street into a mill-pond. In the breezeless hush of five o'clock, the pond was mirror-smooth, skimmed by dragon-flies and swallows. A boy stood looking at the water. Dick walked down the bank and paused beside him, recognizing George Lennox who claimed a Chippewa step-mother. The young Welshman had both hands in his pockets. His face was lifted to the sunrise, his expression rapturous. He seemed unconscious of Dick's presence.

> "For 'twas the morn; Apollo's upward fire
> Made every eastern cloud a silvery pyre."

he said.

"Do you like *Endymion?*" Dick asked.

The boy blushed furiously, scowled and walked away.

When he found himself alone, facing four Latin classes, Dick was seized with an unfamiliar malady. His knees quivered, he perspired and the room swam. He had no idea what to say.

The atmosphere was distinctly hostile. In the rear rows a conspiracy was taking shape with whispers and snickering. Dick smelled rum and Virginia Plug; he saw something round being passed secretly from hand to hand behind the benches. He cleared his throat.

"I am glad to be here, though I regret the accident that makes it necessary . . ."

Catcalls from the rear. The round objects looked like potatoes. Was he about to be bombarded? Dick looked to right and left and seeing no escape, began again:

"Latin is a useful subject. In almost every profession . . ."

The ringleader let fly his potato. Dick reached out an expert hand and plucked it from the air. There was an awed hush. Evidently the boys had thought their plot securely hidden. Dick's stage-fright left him and he laughed.

"Your shot went wide," he said. "Watch me and I'll plant your potato for you."

He took aim at an open stove-pipe hole in the wall. The students turned to look. By almost miraculous good luck the potato went neatly into the opening, and the boys rose to their feet, stamping, whistling and cheering. Cass Jones brought up the bag of potatoes and put it on the floor at Dick's feet.

"Try it again, professor?" he asked respectfully.

Freeman had dug himself in by securing a job as clerk in the president's office. He wrote letters and kept books, but whenever he was not so occupied he was tapping at walls, peering behind cupboards and trying locked doors. Dick thought this tiresome and childish, especially as he was beginning to like the Academy. His boys treated him as no other Latin teacher was ever treated. They told him their most naïve thoughts and offered him candy, liquor and cigars with equal innocence. They called him by his new nickname, "Potatoes," whenever no other teacher was near. Before the month of June was past, he knew two hundred names and the young faces they belonged to.

Meanwhile he had explored most of the surrounding country on foot or in the saddle. He had ridden north to the military road that followed the ridge just south of the Wisconsin River and had watched the great stage-coaches with their four or six-horse teams carrying passengers to Portage and Green Bay from the Mississippi towns. From the Ridge near English Prairie he had counted the many streams that flowed into the Wisconsin at almost regular intervals, denting the line of bluffs with deep chasms: Helena Creek, Mill Creek, Otter Creek . . . they were different from the wide-branching Pecatonica on the southern slope. They rushed downhill more rapidly, wore deeper ravines, made more noise as they flowed over stony beds. And the river itself had a continuous procession of little steamboats plying to St. Louis with lead from Pedlar's Creek and the Muscoda smelter.

At English Prairie, miners from Derbyshire lived, separated by several hundred miles from their farming neighbors at Hampstead Prairie. Many names were the same—the accents could not have been told apart by a stranger, but Dick could hear the Yorkshire influence in the miners' speech, making it less musical than the country-folk's talk. He could hardly remember Holmesfield, but he had somehow carried a part of it with him through the years as a butterfly carries the pattern of its chrysalis. So, when he met Englishmen or heard the familiar Wesleyan hymns rolling out of a church in broad Derbyshire style, he felt a kinship he had almost disowned. Outside a white clapboarded church in a tiny ridge village he sat his horse hesitantly, half inclined to dismount and go inside, while the reed organ notes mingled with the well-memorized words:

> By cool Siloam's shady rill
> How fair the lily grows!
> How sweet the breath beneath the hill
> Of Sharon's dewy rose....

Dick bent his head, holding the reins against Betsey's withers. He was not bowing out of the usual reverence for any God who might be present among these worshippers. He was trying to hold the nostalgic mood of the tune and the aroma of more innocent and trusting days. He saw a wagon in the freezing Milwaukee wilderness, boxes covered with sheepskins, himself, a round-faced child, gazing into the sunset. If only that red finger of light would point once more to the zenith, telling him that the master of the universe sat there, serene and all-knowing!

> Lo! such the child whose early feet
> The paths of peace have trod....

Those paths were closed to him now. He could never walk in them again. He sighed, brushing his right hand back over his forehead in a habitual gesture that threw his luxuriant hair into confusion. Oh for that simple acceptance that once made the world so beautiful to live in, its people so good to know! It seemed to him now that no one was pure in heart as he once believed. Not his father. Not Harry, whose duplicity he had first understood because he had been a partner in too many schemes. Not Lucy, who had demonstrated her love for the good things of life. His mother, perhaps, but her mind was content and incurious, while Dick's was restless, explorative and alert. He could never hope for his mother's sort of peace. He must go on, even at the price of lost faith.

In the hush after the hymn, he heard his sigh echoed and saw that he had a neighbor. An old man was sitting in the long grass and daisies of the cemetery just beyond the fence. He supported himself against a marble slab and spread out on its base a variety of small stones, but his attention was wandering, his eyes fixed on distance. The tombstone, the urn of flowers, the man in his black coat, high-buttoned and long-skirted, his white hair and beard framing a melancholy face, made a consistent picture. Dick felt that a steel engraving had come to life. He tied Betsey to the fence and leaned against the top rail.

"Good morning," he said. "We both seem content to listen outside the gates."

The stranger raised deep-set, burning eyes. He was not really old, but only painfully thin, with a transparency of skin that suggested illness.

"Heaven's gates are wide," he said in accents of precise beauty. "They enclose much more than the church.

I feel sure that these bits of ore belong to Him, and I may enter Paradise by the side door reserved for geologists."

Dick hastily decided he must pursue this acquaintance. It might be that this man could show him a new sort of faith. He swung one leg over the fence, then the other and sat down by a stone dedicated to Theobald Fitzarthur.

"Let me worship with you," he said. "Tell me about the ores."

"This nugget is almost pure copper. It is not native to these countries, but was planted at Swindler's Ridge by a man who wanted to sell his worn-out diggings. Probably the Ojibwas brought it down. Their runners come as far as Fort Winnebago. This you must know . . . galenite. The whole territory lives on it. Here is 'black-jack' and this is 'dry-bone.' These last two are likely to fulfill the Bible prophecy about the stone the builder rejected. For years they have been thrown out as worthless, used as foundations for buildings, for road-grades and pavements. The miners had their hearts set on lead. Now, as they reach the water-level they will find it expensive to go on. Perhaps they will begin to smelt these for the zinc that is in them. They will have to find new markets, though."

"We hear all sorts of rumors around the Academy," Dick said. "Some think the whole lead region is done for, and others say if they dig deep enough they will find the main supply. I hear Mr. Percival, the state geologist, thinks the lead has boiled up from below. That encourages the miners to go on digging."

"Mr. Percival is not omniscient," the geologist said, smiling. "Haven't you heard the other theory, that the lead drifted here in some solvent form on great ocean currents in the past? If it has all been mined, where shall we turn to find the treasure-house of that dead sea?"

"Most of my colleagues consider Mr. Percival omniscient. But perhaps you know him."

"Rather well. I often think he should have stuck to writing poetry, but of course there's no revenue in verse. Even less than in geology. Do you know his poems?"

"I seem to remember . . ."

"Let me recite one of them," the stranger said, before Dick could finish his sentence, and began in an affected voice:

> Music and dances
> Smiles and bright glances
> Love's happy chances
> All are at play.
> Youths with gay sashes,
> Girls with calashes. . . .

"What in the world is a 'calash'?" Dick thought, looking uneasily at his feet. It was evident that the geologist admired this poem, but Dick thought James Gates Percival should by all means stick to geology.

"I'll tell you a touching incident that happened to Mr. Percival. He was resting in a miner's home, a very poor place, at Hardscrabble a number of years ago. The name was Lennox. In the midst of great squalor a young boy sat reading poetry. Mr. Percival looked over his shoulder and saw that the poem was his own work. It was *The Coral Grove*. Do you know that poem, Sir? Well, no matter. At any rate, here sat the boy, oblivious to the dirt around him and to his half-Indian brothers and sisters who seemed very numerous. He was deep in the land of poesy. He had memorized that poem. It was touching. He thought poor Mr. Percival a great writer. You say you don't know *The Coral Grove?*"

"Very slightly. I know the lad, though, George Lennox. He's in my class at the Academy. You know that his father made a fortune?"

"Ah! I hadn't heard that. I'm very happy to learn of it. Now, unless we are thrown into a war with the South, the young man will have the advantages he deserves. Ask him if . . . if he still remembers the poet whom the world has forgotten."

Dick promised and made an uncomfortable departure. He had guessed some time since that he was talking to the state geologist but he did not intend to betray his knowledge. Poor fellow! Master of a dozen languages, learned in medicine, chemistry and several other sciences, owner of the most coveted library in the West, he cared only for the thing he could never have, a worldwide fame for his poems. The stubborn gods refused him that, though they carelessly dropped it in other laps, like that of George Lennox, perhaps. Some boy, who wanted nothing from the public and hugged poetry to his bosom like a secret love . . . he would be the one to get the laurels.

Back at Bradford, Dick encountered Dr. Busch, who asked him to his rooms for a bite of brook trout. The immaculate Greek professor had been out with rod and line. He had hot corn-bread too, and a pot of tea.

"Take the leather chair, my boy, and you'll think you're still in the saddle," he said, getting out his own worn slippers and putting the stem of his incongruous pipe into the marble chastity of his lips. "Where have you been today? I saw you setting out."

Dick told him of his encounter with Mr. Percival.

"Yes," Dr. Busch said, after a few moments of silent contemplation. "Your judgment on his poetry is correct. He's not so eager for fame, however, as you seem to think. Mr. Percival's trouble is a strange one. He has a passion for overcoming difficulties by sheer logic and in the case of poetry it won't work. Once before he had the same experience, but that was more serious. He was a young doctor and he thought that by angry and violent effort he could save human lives where other doctors failed. His patients died; it was an epidemic. I suppose he has found that human lives and poetry are both mysteriously managed from somewhere outside. Science is his natural field; it yields, though too slowly. Do you see this chess-game?"

Dick looked at the chess-board, on which the ivory

pieces still stood in the same position as when he had first arrived at Bradford.

"I began this game with Mr. Percival. You'll see by the positions of the rooks and King's Bishop that I was employing Petroff's defense. Mr. Percival maintained that his next move could be so made as to win the game in advance. I don't know what he had in mind. I told him to take as much time as he thought necessary before he made the move, and he's taken a year. Perhaps I'm too hopeful, but I still believe he'll come back and win."

"Unless he dies first. He doesn't look very well, I'm afraid."

"That, too, seems beyond his control," Dr. Busch said, placidly puffing at his pipe.

By this time Dick cared not at all what had happened to his predecessor or why. Cass Jones knew the answer. He felt sure of that. Cass knew a great many other things of doubtful value. Miners complained that he molested their daughters and threatened to set their dogs on him, and he had been the promoter of every school riot for two years. Between him and Dr. Busch, however, some sort of secret understanding seemed to exist. Freeman had spoken of it and Dick had noticed how easily Cass got absolutions for his sins.

"We can leave in two weeks," Freeman announced one day, rubbing his hands together and walking lightly about the room on his toes. "I intercepted a letter."

"Suppose I don't want to leave. Listen to this, Freem." Dick spread out a composition book and read:

How steep Soracte stands in gleaming snow,
No more the trees their glistening burden bear.
The rivers with the frost are sealed and slow...

"Why he's written his whole translation in rhyme!"

"What of it?"

"Nothing." But Dick was thinking of his first encounter with young Lennox, that angry look as he turned away. The rhymed lesson was an offer of friendship.

"You don't ask, so I'll force the information upon you."

"Oh, yes. You intercepted a letter. Go on."

"Knox College is sending up two runaway slaves. Bradford is to pass them on up the Wisconsin River."

"And what's our part in this drama?"

"As a law-abiding citizen I'm bound to throw a monkey-wrench into the cog-wheels."

"And collect the reward, I suppose."

"That might be a minor incident in the plot."

"Don't forget Dr. Jonas. He probably had the same idea." All at once the whole affair was clear to Dick, and his own intentions resolved themselves. "Your sense of duty blinds you to consequences, Freem. For one thing the poor devils will be horsewhipped, and for another, Dr. Busch will go to jail."

"And for a third, you intend to bind and gag me."

"It won't be necessary, I hope."

On June evenings the boys played ball in the square. The sun was still high at seven o'clock and the hours after supper were spent out of doors. Mail was distributed at the supper table and read afterwards, either in the dining-hall or on the benches in the square. Usually Dick's letters were opened with a table-knife and hastily scanned before they went into his pocket. Freeman wrote constantly to newspapers and magazines, to advertisers of patent medicines, to famous actors, congressmen, reformers. Letters were his hobby and his mail was correspondingly plentiful. Dick paid no attention to these missives, but he was surprised to see that Freeman read them with as keen an interest as though they were from friends. On an evening, late in June, he had opened only one letter from a pack of five when he rose abruptly and left the table. Dick glanced up from his own mail.

"I wonder what upset him."

"His sister's letter, apparently. At least the handwriting looked like hers," said Dr. Busch, who sat next to Freeman at table. "Do you know them well?"

"Fairly so."

"An odd relationship."

Dick dropped his eyes, but not before he had seen the gleam of curiosity on the faces of the teachers of rhetorics, gymnastics and history, three young men who looked on Freeman as a museum specimen. Whatever his own feelings about his roommate might be, Dick did not intend to share them, so he opened his disquieting

259

mail, Lucy's first note from the Bermudas. He could have shared the *letter* at least. It was all about the admission of Kansas. Should the new state be slave or free?

"The devil take Kansas!" he muttered.

"The devil is trying to," Mr. Humphrey said.

Later, as he crossed the square he was surrounded by students.

"Come on, Potatoes. Have a go at the bat."

"Did you see the papers? They're talking war between the states."

"If we had war, would you have to go, Potatoes?"

"We'd all have to go and I'd be glad," Cass Jones announced. "Bullets talk. Blow some sense into those southerners."

"Blow Georgia and Carolina right off the map!" a shrill-voiced child from Beetown cried. Dick looked about him and shrank from the thought that these slender bodies and smooth faces might be shattered by gun-fire and slashed under frantic hooves.

"No, no! War isn't the way. Violence never settles anything," he said. "War is like lopping off the hydra's head, lads. One hundred more troubles grow where we cut off one."

At the far edge of the square another group were kicking at the grass, prying up bits of sod. "There's lead under here," one of them said.

"How do you know?"

"Mason-weed. It always runs down to a vein."

Dick tried to pull up one of the yellowing stalks which ran in a straight line across the grass.

"You caint pull it. Caint even dig it out unless you mine for lead," a second generation Kentuckian explained. "When my Paw hit mineral at Stump Grove thar was mason-roots hangin' fifty-six feet down."

"You look above any old mine," another youngster agreed. "The mason-weed's always dead after the first level's mined out. Has to have lead to live."

The door of his room in the dormitory was locked. This was so unusual that Dick tried the latch for several minutes, thinking he was mistaken. Then he went around outside, found a box and climbed on it to look through the window. Freeman was in the room, lying face down on the bed. He had not thought to fasten the window, so Dick pried up the sash and climbed in over the sill.

The smell of laudanum was heavy in the air. Dick was used to the odor, though he had often tried to talk Freeman out of the habit. Something in his friend's nature refused to face the simple fact of physical pain. At the first onslaught of migraine he got out the drug and tried to dose himself insensible. This time he had succeeded. He was in a deep slumber and snoring, his face flushed and swollen where it lay, sidewise on the pillow. Dick surveyed him with great disapproval. Casual contacts with Freeman had been stimulating, but living with him was another thing, in fact it was growing disagreeable. Probably he had felt the pain coming on at dinner, but that was no excuse for rushing to his room, locking himself in and taking too much opiate. Dick sighed as he often found himself sighing of late, and sat down to correct translations.

"Tell me, fair Lydia, why wouldst thou slay poor Sybaris with love. No more does he bear the combat and heat of battle . . ." Twenty-five readings of this lament made an aching heart seem much less serious than migraine and much more common. What good was it to teach such stuff to the sons of lead-miners? Unless, like George Lennox, they enjoyed learning it.

George had written in verse again. His facility with rhyme and meter did not interest Dick half so much as his personality. At fifteen few boys can make their friendship worth seeking. Young Lennox gave out approval as a sort of reward for merit, not grudgingly, but with discrimination and integrity. He was often alone, but never lonely. His thoughts flourished whether or not they were discovered, like a patch of mandrakes in a deep wood. His capacity for silence was astonishing. Dick had walked beside him often, either by accident or intention. Sometimes George expressed himself clearly and intelligently and sometimes he said nothing at all until they separated, but in either case he appeared to have enjoyed the contact.

Freeman was breathing queerly. Dick went over to the bed and tried to turn him on the pillow. His face had a purple cast. One of his arms was bent under him and when Dick managed to lift him and lay him on his back, he saw Josephine's letter in the depression of the mattress. After a moment's hesitation he opened the torn envelope and began to read. His features went through varying stages of astonishment and disgust. Josephine was announcing her marriage to Whitford Rush. She gave one page to this and four pages to abuse and accusation. Dick put the letter between the mattress and bed-ropes and ran out into the square, colliding with a lounging student.

"Oh, Cass!" he said, with a feeling of relief he had no time to analyze, "Can you get me some whiskey?"

"Why, sure!" said the youngster, taking a flask from his hip-pocket. "Keep it, Potatoes. I've plenty in my room."

"I'll want a doctor, Cass."

"No, you won't. Just sleep it off."

"It's for Mr. Wills. He's taken too much laudanum."

"Oh! I'll send someone." Cass moved off rapidly toward the town. Dick went back and tried to force whiskey into Freeman's half-open mouth. It ran down and soaked the pillow. He gave up the effort and began pacing the room.

Whatever this letter of Josephine's meant—and it seemed to suggest the brother-and-sister relations of a Greek tragedy—Dick was sure it had been the cause of attempted suicide. He could not reconcile the chaotic, jumbled words with Freeman's character. She mentioned tortures . . . "hideous tortures." Dick looked at the unconscious features of the sleeper. Even in their swollen condition they appeared fastidious, but forceful too, with that queer misdirected energy his friend displayed.

What a whirlwind Josephine would make in the quiet Rush household! Whitford must have had his heart set on her happiness, but this letter had no happiness in it. She seemed to blame Freeman for her marriage. It was a mystery, but hardly one Dick cared to solve. The unhealthy affair reminded him of mushrooms growing in a deserted cellar.

The doctor had gone, the floor was littered with bottles and sodden towels, and Freeman was rolled in the only blanket. It was two o'clock in the morning. Dick yawned at the window, where he half lay with his head on the sill. The candles flickered, casting a light over the bed, and he looked up and saw that his roommate's eyes were wide open.

"So I go on living," Freeman said, with a feeble return of cynicism.

Nine hours later Dick came back from his classes to find the room in the process of being searched. Freeman had emptied the desk drawers on the bed.

"I had a letter . . ." he said, and when Dick lifted the mattress and handed him the letter, "I suppose you read it."

"Yes. I'm sorry."

"Then you know all about me."

"Do I?" Dick would have given a great deal to avoid the coming discussion, but he saw Freeman's distress too plainly. He must listen; even give sympathy if possible.

"I suppose it seems horrible to you, but it began when I was a child. We were alone a great deal and I got hold of some old books on the subject. Even then I had a great deal of power over her, but I found that every time I exercised my will it grew stronger. She would do anything I suggested. It never occurred to me that I was injuring her. I was drunk, really drunk with my discovery. I thought about it all the time. Did you ever have a day-dream as a child, so fascinating you wanted to be alone and dream it over and over again?"

"Yes. I had one for years." Dick remembered Marie Gagnier.

"This was my dream. In school I was ignored or laughed at. I was small for my age and different from the others. At home I was powerful. It wasn't until years later that I tried my power on others. I kept it for Jo.

"All at once she began to change. She was growing into a woman. I doubled my efforts but I couldn't hold her back and she began to hate me. I was like a king who is losing his kingdom. But I decided to let her go . . .

"It was like trying to unfasten your hands from a pair of electric batteries. When I expected it least some suggestion of mine would control her again. She did things she would never have done alone. Some of them

265

were good enough in themselves. I told her she could skate without falling and from the first she never fell. Then you came and without thinking I threw her into your arms."

"*You* threw her?"

"I suggested it. I was teasing her, of course, but it took hold and I couldn't stop it. When I saw how badly it worked out, I knew I must get away and never see her again, so I came with you."

"Freem, this is nonsense. It sounds to me like an attack of imagination. This mysterious power is as much mine as yours. Didn't I talk you into coming with me?"

"No. I did it of my own free will."

"I suppose you think you could influence *me* if you tried."

"Of course. Why did you leave the State House? Why did you start west? Why are you teaching Latin?"

Dick stared at him, got up and went to the open window, where he drew a long breath of outdoor air.

"If I were you," he said slowly, without turning around, "I'd go to some large city and use the power of suggestion to get an excellent position. With such a secret you could go far."

"Not on twenty dollars. That's all I have."

Dick took his wallet from his pocket and pressed it into Freeman's hands. At the moment it seemed to him a cheap price to pay. Then he saw the saddle-bags by the door. They were already packed.

Like the first cold wind, the premonition of a panic began to be felt before October. Some of the eastern banks failed. Forty boys dropped out of school. The market was fluttering in Buffalo and the price of lead went down. Just as Mr. Percival had predicted, zinc began to be talked about as a possible salvation, but it was mined at the water level and required expensive pumping machinery.

Bradford Academy began to feel the pinch, though for nearly a year funds came in from a mysterious source. Dr. Busch went about with a grave expression and the students, having less money to spend, spent it more wisely.

Coming into his classroom one evening in late September, Dick saw Cass Jones sitting at the desk. He had locked the door as usual before going to supper, and had just now unlocked it again as he entered.

"What are you doing here, Cass?" he said sternly, "and how'd you get in?"

Cass laid his finger against his mouth and sat listening to the sound of voices and footsteps in the lower hall. Men were going from room to room.

"Better lock the door, Potatoes."

"If you're in mischief again, I won't help you. You're twenty this year. That's a man's age, Cass."

"All right. Don't lock it then. They've got a warrant, I guess."

Dick sat down on a bench and looked sorrowfully

at his pupil. Cass wore a blue cape overcoat the color of his eyes, and his cravat matched the coat. His hard, handsome face was beginning to show signs of dissipation. Why he stayed in the school had been a puzzle to Dick for some time. His Latin papers came in perfectly blank, or adorned with pen-sketches of pretty girls. Probably some furious father had called out the law.

"Where did you get a key, Cass?"

"I didn't have one. I said *hocus-pocus* and passed myself right through the door."

"What do you expect me to do?"

"Nothing. Just wait."

The men were at the door. One, as Dick had foreseen, was the sheriff. Dr. Busch was with him, milder and more apologetic than usual, and there were two others—fat men, chewing tobacco and spitting on the class-room floor. Dick was used to the spitting. He did not mind the oaths which accompanied every remark, but he thought that if either of these men got Cass for a son-in-law, the poor lad would pay for his wild oats.

"Look for yourselves, gentlemen," Dr. Busch said in tones of weary refinement. "You can see the whole room plainly. No fugitive is hidden here." He took out his handkerchief and mopped his forehead. "These things are exhausting and I am an old man."

Above the dark thatch of Cass Jones' hair the blackboard bore words in Dick's handwriting: "Integer vitae, scelerisque purus." The wrong label, alas, for the boy who sat beneath them. But something more important

268

ailed the quotation; it was trembling. The blackboard shook with an infinitesimal tremor. Suddenly it seemed essential that the visitors should not look in that direction.

"If you'll excuse Dr. Busch, I'll take you through the rest of the building," he said, stepping forward.

The men refused this suggestion with scorn and profanity.

"This is a Christian school and I find your language offensive," Dick said, moving to turn their eyes from the board. Cass and Dr. Busch looked as surprised as the strangers.

"I won't change my talk for any pap-sucking son of Jesus," the nearest man said. Dick shot out a fist and hit him on the chin. His eyes appeared to cross; he swayed in a semi-circle and fell while the other man lunged across him. Dick threw up his right arm and got a paralyzing blow on his elbow. He was about to return it with his left hand when Cass Jones aimed a well directed kick at the under side of the fat man's knees. They buckled and the floor seemed to swarm with objectionable strangers.

"Pshaw!" the sheriff exclaimed. He had been standing well out of danger with a look of pleasure not too carefully concealed. "You gentlemen hadn't ought to stir up trouble in an academy. Move along now and we'll finish up the job."

A few minutes later Dr. Busch came back alone. He tapped on the blackboard. "Come out, Custis," he said softly. The blackboard swung around like a revolving door and a young negro came out. He was still trembling.

"He'll have to go up river tonight, Cass. You've got it fixed?"

"All fixed."

"Going to be cold tomorrow. He ought to have a coat."

"He can have mine." Cass draped the resplendent blue overcoat about the shrinking runaway. They left the room, not through the door into the hall, but through the revolving blackboard. As he disappeared, Cass looked back.

"Violence never settles anything, Potatoes," he said.

Part Three

I

By NOVEMBER the country was in the grip of panic.
All the banks of America were closed. Great mer-
cantile houses in New York, established fifty years before, crashed over night never to open again. Million-
aires faced starvation. It was widely believed that the
democracy had failed because of pride and profligacy,
that God had turned his face against the new world.
The weak jumped off the Brooklyn ferry or blew out
their brains on expensive Brussels carpets; the strong,
and among them Simeon Drake, organized labor guilds
and laymen's prayer-meetings or went about with
baskets of food trying to create momentary comfort in
a great tide of hunger and misery.

"We are faced," said the newspapers, "with the col-
lapse of that republic for which our fathers fought. No
country can rally from such disaster without the inter-
vention of a miracle."

A few more thoughtful men began to understand
that rich and poor are a part of the same structure,
two heads on one body. Employers carried hundreds of
laborers down with them in their fall; New York carried

down Philadelphia, Chicago, and Prairietown. Because the eastern banks could not meet their demands, the farmers of Hampstead Prairie could not sell wheat or pork or meet their taxes. They turned away their Norwegian hands, and the hands, who had thriftily banked their money, found the banks closed and their savings gone. And after a while, almost the last to feel the pinch, the miners began to take their sons out of Bradford Academy.

For several months the teachers worked without pay. The students swept churches, chopped wood, built fires, raked leaves and demonstrated that the sons of rich folk could live very much like the sons of poor. Then the black cloud settled lower. Ministers swept their own churches. Old men and sick men raked their own leaves and chopped their own wood. Cass Jones divided his clothes and money among less fortunate boys. George Lennox disappeared overnight and was not heard from until he had a job in a Chicago printing-house. At length, with only ten students left, the Academy closed its doors.

When Dick came home in December to his father's farm, he saw how the long arm of depression had reached into the isolated prairie. The Great Ocean to Ocean Tea Company had ceased to pay dividends. His father's stock was almost worthless, and into that stock all his savings had gone. He looked broken and dismayed. No doubt he wished he had been more liberal with that money, that he had helped his sons to an education and bought pretty clothes and household comforts for his wife, whose hair was almost white now. She could have had the bonnets and dresses she loved before she lost interest in clothes and his boys could have shared their success with him. Too late. And the money was gone.

He put the certificates away in a steamer trunk in the attic. Those gilt edges had seemed so precious to him, but they were worth no more than waste-paper. He had been cheated again in the new country. He attacked his last acres of woodland, chopping, chopping grimly into the dark, splitting tree-trunks with wooden wedges, sawing the split trunks into cordwood for which he had no sale.

No sale for his milk either, yet the forty cows must be milked. Dick could not be idle. He found himself becoming a farmer once more. Like the one hired hand, he worked for his keep and no wages.

Now the customs of his childhood closed around him. Nothing had been forgotten. Straining the foaming milk by lantern light through the wide-rimmed pewter strainer he could have fancied that he was fifteen instead of twenty-three. The physical weariness, the plunge into cool homespun sheets scented with lavender, the unbroken sleep were all as pleasant as they were familiar, and he could have been happy, but for the sore spot in his heart where his love for Lucy was trying to die. Lucy wrote him occasional letters, chill and perfunctory. She said no more about coming home.

In Milwaukee, Harry's business seemed one that did not suffer with the rest. His first child had been born and named for her grandmother, but in deference to her proud French ancestry they intended to call her Annette.

"The child is not defective in any way," Harry wrote. "Agnes suffered the usual discomfort of which she has been making capital ever since. She will be a devoted mother, and I'll not be sorry to share her attentions."

Dick laughed at this letter, but Ann Wentworth looked distressed.

"He's brewing himself a pot of trouble, is Harry."

"Oh well. 'Tis just one of old Harry's jokes."

"Women need coddling at such a time, Dicky."

"A lot you've ever had!"

"Thy father were tender as an angel to me. But mind thee, Dick, don't do as thy brother does. When thy own firstborn comes, be loving with Lucy."

He shrank from this remark as if it had been the point of a knife. What future could he expect? His one suit was almost threadbare. His savings amounted to one hundred and fifty dollars. But he put his pride from him and wrote a long, almost desperate letter. He would mail it from Lebanon Center that afternoon.

He was prevented from making the trip by Wisconsin's worst blizzard in twenty years. The snow fell so thickly that Gunnar was lost between barn and house and had to be rescued by Tommy Wentworth's stentorian shouts. Sheep, nibbling at frozen grass in the pasture, found themselves buried in a huddle; they thawed a room under the snow with their breath and lived until they were dug out again. Drifts of snow blocked the last light from the kitchen windows. Lisbeth, who had been helping in the kitchen, could not go home to the mill.

A fire blazed in the hearth. Dick had rummaged in the book-shelves and was re-reading *The Faery Queen,* when a folded paper fell out of the book. It was a list of proposed territorial roads, written in Roger Morton's fine hand.

> From the house of Seymour Wilcox to the beaver dam.
> From the shot tower at Helena to Cross Plains.
> From Boatyard Hollow to the white-oak springs.
> From Outlet Koshkonong to Catfish Mills.

"Whatever are you looking at, Dick?" Lisbeth asked over his shoulder.

He handed her the yellowed paper. "I'm thinking, Liss, what lazybones we are compared to the men who settled this country. All those roads had to be hewed out of virgin forest. What hopes they must have had, to risk their lives that way, and how are we repaying them? It seems to me they meant this land to be a good one, where life could be free and happy, but it's overrun already with money-grabbers and selfish politicians."

"I often think about my father, Dick. How he made

277

the mill out of hickory wood with his own hands and waited so long for my mother to come and marry him. Oh, Dick, do you think he's living?"

"If he were, it seems he'd have let us know, somehow. Your father wouldn't desert his family."

"Sammy shouldn't have gone. He's too young, Dick. He can't do anything worth while. I'll tell you a secret. I've got twenty dollars saved to go to California myself."

"Twenty dollars wouldn't take you to Kansas. Besides, a girl can't travel alone."

"I'm sick of being a girl. I'll wear trousers and travel with a family of schooner-folk like Sammy did. You don't know what it's like at our house now. Uncle Ben's always after mother to marry him. I hear them through the walls!"

She began to cry, and Dick put his arm around her and comforted her. The world was too full of trouble. Only his mother seemed happy. She wanted nothing for herself, but was content in serving others.

As the panic progressed, the trail delivered up the waifs of fortune, men broken, hungry and sick. Back from the gold rush, no richer, but infinitely wiser, back from the lead-country they drifted, the dregs of a race of adventurers. Farmhands, set adrift by impoverished farmers, or families who had lost their land. Ann Wentworth sheltered them. Bustling about her kitchen she served them hearty meals. Lantern in hand she went to the "sod house," carrying clean sheets, tallow candles and a Bible for the reading-stand. She filled the tin bucket from the spring, swept out the litter of dust and leaves and made everything ready for her ravaged guests. If she found the Bible untouched the next morning, the sheets spotted by vermin, the floor covered with whiskey bottles and mud, she did not lose heart. She pitied, but never condemned.

The blizzard left the roads blocked. By the time they were clear, Dick had lost the impulse to mail his wild letter. He tore it up slowly, and wrote another, colder, more rational. Then he set out on horseback to Leeds postoffice. At the creamery he stopped to chat with Caspar Fletcher, who brought out his State Journals tied with twine.

"Here you are, Dick. What did I tell you? Buchanan's ruined the country, but it won't last, boy."

Dick took the newspapers and rode on his way. At the postoffice the window was closed. He stood by the stove and opened the roll of Journals. Comments on the "financial revulsion" occupied the front pages, but set in a box in the upper left-hand corner he saw an item called "Wedding-bells."

"One of Madison's fairest daughters will be united with the scion of a wealthy New York family . . . rumor fully substantiated by the young lady's mother. . . ."

The paper was already two weeks old. Dick went to the stove and put everything he was holding on the fire. Lucy was marrying Charley Drake.

He was surprised at his lack of feeling. It seemed that

something heavy and unresilient jolted up and down
inside him as he rode home. He was bent low over his
pommel, a deep scowl between his eyes. Neighbors who
passed him were offended because he did not speak.

February thawed, cleared, and froze again. The
world was sheeted with ice. Dick tried to find a skating
companion but gave up. His friends had all grown stolid
and muscle-bound and thought it rather silly to skate
at their age. He decided to go by himself, and struck
off alone with his new skates over his shoulder. In the
frozen marshes the projecting reeds kept his feet from
slipping on the ice. At the end of Crabapple Point,
the cakes of ice were piled on the shore. He sat down
on them and began to screw the runners to the soles of
his boots.

He was near the site of White Crow's old camp.
Nothing was left to tell that Indians had lived there
but the old corn-hills and grassed-over winter food-
cellars. The barren grove was not cut, the land had
not been plowed, but the white men owned it at last.
No Winnebagos would come back to claim it. Then
Dick remembered White Crow's grandson, Joe Sobish,
and wondered whether he might still be living in Thebault's cabin across the lake. He needed a destination.
Thebault's Point was as good as any. He set out on
his four mile run.

At first the half-circling shores kept off the full force
of the wind. When he came to the real center—the

river channel, the northeast gale nearly swept him from his feet. He was grateful for his sheepskin coat and wool underwear, all from his father's Cotswolds. Many times he had cursed that home-made underwear for its scratchiness, but when it was called on to keep out a thirty-mile gale it did its work. Skating partly against the wind, he turned from side to side, giving shelter first to his left cheek, then his right.

"My nose gets it, either way," he thought.

The familiar geography of the lake encircled him. Carcajou Point, looming starkly on his left, gave way to a vista of the upper river-mouth, the scattered docks and boat-houses, the stripped masts of ice-boats. From the center, the long lake looked almost round. The beach where Whirling Thunder's village had once been a landmark was now the frontage of a dairy-farm. The Mormon settlement was gone too. The latter-day saints had followed their leaders westward, leaving behind them a legend of thievery and loose-living which the Methodists loved to roll upon their tongues. The Winnebagos were supposed to have leagued with the Mormons in their raids on the settlers' horses, passing them from one hiding-place to another until they reached the sanctuary of the wild unnamed point north of Carcajou. From that station they vanished, taken by the Lord, the Mormons said when they were finally brought to justice. But Ezra Watt had found his sorrels there, not yet delivered to Jehovah.

Three miles away, on his right, Dick could see the

stone tavern on Taylor's bluff, rising above its fringe of wintry trees. There too, stories of wickedness centered. The "Forty Thieves" who preyed on the Wisconsin legislature had sometimes adjourned from their famous "Monk's Hall" meeting-place in Madison, to hold parties at Taylor's. Midnight orgies had kept its windows blazing with light when honest folk were abed. Now the smoke rose from its four chimneys into the wind and streaked across the sky and one could imagine that the long table in its dining-room was being set for the usual mixed assembly of guests. Skating parties from Milton or Janesville, the ladies richly befurred and bonneted, lumbermen in rough clothing and boots, naturalists, professors and politicians—they sat down to drink their midday coffee at that table like members of one family.

While he was still a mile from shore he began to feel the protection of Thebault Point. The wind died; his stinging face grew warmer. From the chimney of the cabin he could see a spiral of smoke, weaving into the air.

Joe Sobish's white wife was sitting on a bench at the end of the house, rubbing two ears of field corn together to shell them into a pot which she held between her knees. When she saw Dick, she stood up, shaking a few stray kernels from her lap.

"Joe isn't here," she said. "He went to town." She looked remote and somewhat hostile.

"I didn't come to see him," Dick answered her defensive attitude with friendliness and moved a few feet toward the open door of the cabin. He thought he had forgotten his one encounter with this woman, but she had been in his mind all the while—her voice, soft and slurring with the intonations of Indian voices, her heavy yellow braids, drawn forward over her shoulders.

"Do you want to get warm?" she asked, and stood aside from the doorway to let him go in first.

Dick looked around the interior of the cabin at the rolled blankets and scattered skins, the tripod and kettle in the fire, and other signs of Indian occupation. The woman stood by the door, waiting for him to sit down. Her ankles were wound with soiled strips of white cloth above her rough shoes. Remembering the snowy buckskin leggings of Indian girls he had seen in childhood, Dick looked at the pathetic imitation and was sorry for it. Under the cloth were slender curves like those of the wrists and hands crossed on her breast. She was fingering something. A crucifix, hanging between the braids of her hair. Dick started and put up his hand to the pipestone cross on his watch-chain.

"I didn't thank you that time you brought Joe home," she said, and he realized that she remembered him, that perhaps her feeling was like his own. "After you were gone, I wanted to thank you."

"It wasn't because of Joe. I did it for White Crow, I suppose. I knew him when I was a small boy."

The woman gave him a sudden, searching glance and seemed to retreat behind an invisible barrier. Her eyes grew enigmatic. She crossed the room to the hearth, passing behind him, and put a piece of wood on the fire. He recognized the wigwam courtesy which prevented women from shutting off the heat and light from their men-folk or guests. As she stooped, her full breasts swung beneath the man's shirt she wore. Her waist, slender and pliant, bent and righted itself like the trunk of a sapling, and he was surprised to notice the whiteness of her hands against the bark of the wood. She appeared to have that velvety but tough texture of skin that is not harmed by work or weather. It lay smoothly over her flesh, like cream-colored vellum, contrasting with the sloe-blackness of her somewhat oblique eyes which she now turned toward him again.

"White Crow was a good man," she said, simply.

A breathless excitement began to mount in Dick's veins. He devoured with an avid interest every detail of Joe Sobish's wife, meanwhile holding himself as still as possible as if he feared a movement might frighten her away. Indeed, she suggested the wild creatures of the forest but it was not her physical presence he was afraid of losing. He wanted to hold her spirit in a mesmeric grip for fear it might dart away from him again like a chipmunk in a rock-pile. As he had often tamed little wood-animals by immobility, so now he tried to deceive her by folding his arms across his breast, but there again he felt the pipestone cross, hanging free.

"What's your name?" he asked with unintentional roughness.

"Mary. Joe's Mary, they call me."

"I know that, but wasn't it Marie?"

"Yes," she said, after a moment. "It was Marie."

Dick laid down his skates and opened his coat. He took the pipestone cross from his watch-chain and laid it in her hand.

"Where did you find it?" Her fingers closed on it.

"You lost it in White Crow's camp. I have your prayer-book too."

She stared at him with darkening eyes. "Why didn't you come back?"

"I was sick, but my father came with some other men. You were gone."

"Dog Head saw you running away. We went far into the woods."

He was trembling slightly with cold and excitement. He moved closer to the fire, and then realized that Marie was still standing because he had not given her the right to sit down. He dropped cross-legged in front of the smoking fire and she sat modestly some distance from him.

"You better take this," she said, laying the stone cross on the hearth-rug. "I have the one the sisters gave me."

"The sisters?"

"At Saint Clara. I was at school there five years."

Dick looked his question and she explained. "They shot Dog Head in the Sugar River country and the priest took me."

He put the small cross on his watch-chain again. She nodded approval.

"That's right. It isn't good to be without one."

"Shall I bring you the prayer-book?"

Marie looked around the cabin as if she saw no place to keep a book. Then she appeared to deliberate.

"I want to see it again. My mother wrote in it."

In answer to questions she told him a little more about her rescue. By the priest, he supposed she meant Father Mazzuchelli, whose labors among the Indians of the Sugar River country were famous. Certainly Marie, the child, had fallen into good hands, and he wondered why she should have left the peace of Saint Clara's School for the hardships she must later have endured. Even if the Dominican sisters were stern, they were known to be merciful and sometimes over-fond of the children they instructed and there had been more than one tale in Bradford Academy, of children taken by disease for whom the sisters of Saint Clara had risked their lives. The father-founder, too, had been able to inspire in the English Methodists of the region a grudging admiration for his zeal, as well as acknowledgment of his saintliness.

"Why did you leave Saint Clara?" he asked.

"I was always wanting to go back to the woods. When I was with the Indians it wasn't always good.

Sometimes we were hungry and cold. Afterward I didn't remember the bad times. You know how they live. They make everything out of the earth. When the sisters gave me linen to sew, and said I must make my own clothes, I didn't know what they meant. I remembered scraping a deerskin for my dress and chewing the thread out of the deer's muscles. I wasn't making the linen. I didn't understand them."

The real meaning of this escaped Dick at first. An hour later, as he skated homeward its inferences gradually grew in his mind and astonished him. Poverty as the white man knows it has little charm. As the Indians knew it—that was different. Even starvation had dignity. It was a matter between man and his maker. Marie, the child, having learned that sort of poverty, was bewildered by the artificial privations of the nunnery. She had fled from it.

His own feelings were too mixed to be easily analyzed. While he sat near Joe's Mary he had been full of passion, tempered by the purest pity, by nostalgia for his early dreams and by an emotion he could not recognize but which resembled foreboding. As soon as he left her, all but the pity vanished. She was married to an Indian, sullied and destroyed by that fact. Even as he said this to himself, bracing his bent head and shoulder against the cold wind, he began to plan how he might help her, this odd human being with whose life he had collided twice. He would take the prayer-book to her. That might be some comfort, some link with her lost identity.

Perhaps she might even find the family she had lost. She could certainly find Belle Fontaine.

As if he had skated out of one world and into another the thought of Lucy in her new lover's arms came down around him like a cloud. He felt his skating stroke grow weaker and a vise-like compression around his heart. What sort of shuttlecock must he be to allow the hand of fate to toss him back and forth so willfully? Two years of his life were already lost because of a misplaced love. He said to himself reasonably that neither he nor Lucy was to blame. It had been a mistake, and she had been the first to correct it. Yet this sickness that would not leave him—he must root it out somehow, replace it with another interest if he wanted to live.

Perhaps he could find another love and by pretending more than he felt, learn to forget. Even so, Joe's Mary had no part in such a program. She might not be consciously good, but she had the simple integrity of primitive people, and Dick longed to aid, not seduce her. Not there. Not in Hampstead Prairie, nor in Madison he was sure, would he find anyone to erase Lucy's image from his heart. Yet he must try.

Before the ice broke, Dick had crossed to the fur-trader's cabin several times. His first excitement at finding Marie was soon gone, replaced by the chilling discovery that his childhood's most romantic dream had been woven about an ordinary human being. For years he had been haunted by a disembodied spirit of the woods, now he found it had been a robust young woman, ignorant, ragged, but with a baffling degree of self-respect. Joe Sobish's wife held him at arms' length. Dick's curiosity was aroused and he asked many questions, some of which Marie declined to answer by retreating into a dignified silence which might have seemed rude if it had not been so precisely the Indian manner. Often, Dick had seen the Winnebagos assume just such an attitude of folded arms and sealed lips when pressed too far by well-meaning white men. Begging at his mother's door, destitute or degraded, the natives still kept their treasured right of solitude and silence.

When Marie had identified her name in the prayer-book, he asked how she knew it for her mother's handwriting.

"I saw her write it there."

"How old were you?"

"Six years. I lost count of my age after the Indians took me. No one told me."

"But you knew your name and the town you came from. White Crow would have taken you home, wouldn't he?"

"I was always begging him to take me home, but he knew my people were dead. He didn't tell me till he gave me to Dog Head."

"That day, when I saw you . . . were you asking me to take you home?"

"Yes. But even then, I wasn't sure. I remembered my

mother . . . she had hair like mine and I remembered. . . ." She stopped. Dick realized much later that her mother had been scalped.

The little French girl in the woods by the creek had been voluble and friendly. That outgoing nature had been turned in upon itself, partly by the Winnebagos and partly by the calm sisters at St. Clara's. Loneliness, too, had done its work. Marie kept her own counsel because she had learned by hard experience that few persons could be trusted. Her speech was strangely confused. The grammar she had learned at school was perfect but she had an intonation half-French, half-Indian. Nothing seemed native to her. Even her beliefs were a patchwork of superstitions and she cautioned Dick against losing his crucifix as if it were a magic amulet.

How she happened to marry the grandson of White Crow remained a mystery. That period of three years after she left the school and until she was married was one she never talked about. Dick found that the least approach to it met a barrier of reserve. Some bitter or humiliating experience was being concealed, and he carefully avoided asking questions about it, but the idea of rescue took strong hold of his imagination as it had in childhood, and hopelessly as then. The child lost in the hundred-mile forest was no more inaccessible than this woman who did not want help or pity. Such free-flowing sympathy as Dick's mother gave other refugees would have frozen Marie permanently behind her defenses.

Gunnar Larson was still a member of the Wentworth household, though there was little work to do. Dick was somewhat puzzled that his father, usually quick to turn away unwanted help, kept the young Norwegian with him. Gunnar slept in the kitchen now. When work was slack he went to the country school where he was learning to read English. Twenty-three years old and six feet tall, he wedged his knees under a child's desk and took his place with the Third Reader boys to recite. The children's laughter did not bother Gunnar. He was trying to be an American. He spent long hours at the kitchen table copying Dick's script. In return he was teaching Dick a great deal about perseverance.

One afternoon in February he was lounging outside the stable door, chewing a wheat-straw when Dick came by. He seemed less cheerful than usual. Dick paused and looked at him inquiringly.

"Who did you kill, Gunnar, and where did you hide the body?"

"I aint kill him yet, Dick, but I'm going to, maybe."

"Someone I know?"

"Ja. His name's Gunnar."

Dick was astonished. He knew of nothing that could have happened to make the young Norwegian think of suicide, and was much relieved when the explanation followed:

"Dis Gunnar you been seeing wasn't the real Gunnar, Dick. In Hardanger I'm a great man for dancing and drinking and sometime with the girls. Now I got good chance to be that way again, but I don't know. First I got to kill the new Gunnar, because he's all the time got his mind on work, make money, get ahead. I like to go to this dance up by Stoughton. You know about that, Dick?"

Dick did not, so Gunnar continued:

"A newcomer girl name Alma Eriksdatter is getting married with Ivar Holberg who works for your aunt by the mill, yet. She's Hardanger too, and I know her people before I come to America. After vedding they'll have big dance in big new hayloft they got. Lot of beer and whiskey, Dick, and plenty girls. I like to go, but dis new Gunnar won't let me."

"I think you ought to go. You don't get enough pleasure. Why, Gunnar, I didn't even know you had friends."

"I tell you, Dick. You come with me. Then I won't go too far, maybe."

2

THE WEDDING WAS OVER and the bride-money taken up on a large platter before they arrived. Gunnar had prudently come late and held Dick back in the cold entry while the girl friends of the bride passed the platter around.

"I thank you dearly," Alma Eriksdatter said, bowing to left and right as the pile of nickels, quarters and dimes was set before her.

She was plump as a peach, and though her fresh complexion was her only beauty she looked pretty in her native costume, brightly embroidered blouse of white linen, full black skirt and laced girdle. An apron of Hardanger needlework covered the front of her skirt. She wore white stockings and black slippers.

The groom seemed troubled by his clothes. His yellow hair, parted in the middle, stuck out in a bush around his raw, red face. Above the heavy suit of black broadcloth he looked too highly colored. He would wear that suit all his life, to church, to funerals and other weddings, but this was the first time and he found it difficult. He twisted his brick-colored neck and ran his finger round the inside of his high collar before he bowed, adding his thanks to those of his bride.

Now the guests struck boldly into a song, linking arms and swaying back and forth as they sang.

"That is to wish them happiness," Gunnar whispered. He led the way into the lamplit room and Dick found himself mingling with the crowd. In front of him four old women stood, their aprons tied about their waists. They were full of mischief and giggled like girls. Another woman, still older, came up to them.

"Holla, Mother Dagmar!" they said.

Dagmar's face was criss-crossed with a thousand wrinkles; her gums were toothless, her fingers warped into claws. Dick thought he had never seen so old a woman. Yet, as she greeted her friends, she caught up her skirts in skinny hands and bowed playfully. Her eyes, set in wrinkles, were bright.

He turned to speak to Gunnar but found his friend had disappeared. In his place a young lady was standing, quietly taking in the scene. Her oval face was tanned a golden color like coffee with plenty of cream, her brown hair was looped in braids at the back of her smooth head. Her eyes were childlike, innocent and merry.

"Greetings, Eva, kjaereste," Old Dagmar said to her.

"Greetings, Moder Dagmar," she answered.

They began to chatter to one another in Norwegian and Dick gathered from their glances that they might be discussing him. He wondered how they knew he was not a Norwegian like themselves, and wished for Gunnar to be interpreter. Perhaps the girl could understand English and he could talk to her. Otherwise the evening bade fair to be a lonely one.

In the kitchen, lamps were lit and Dick could see that tables had been made from planks and saw-horses and loaded with food of all sorts. The smell of strong coffee filled the house. He had heard a great deal about Norwegian feasts at weddings and funerals, but this was the first he had seen and smelled. Two or three women were working in the kitchen, piling up the flat-bread that looked like folded cardboard and cutting cheese in wedges. Dick had ridden twenty miles in the sharp air. He was hungry and wondered how soon the food would be passed. He looked at Eva. She smiled.

"Komme," she said, and held out her hand to him simply as a child. He took it as simply and followed her from the room.

"Moder," she said to a woman who was putting sugar-lumps in a saucer, "this one is hungry." She spoke in Norwegian, but so much Dick could understand from his association with his father's help.

"Ak!" said her mother, "of course he is hungry. He is a man."

Dick burst out laughing at this and they both laughed with him, looking at him meanwhile with the kindest of expressions. Eva put a large slice of buttered bread in his hand and poured him a cup of black coffee. Two

295

other women came up and stood staring at him while he ate.

"Engelsk," one said, and the other replied, "Ja, I think he is from Hampstead."

"He understands you," Eva warned them, and turned to Dick. "Can you talk Norsk?"

"No," he answered her in almost the only Norwegian sentence he knew, "I can understand it a little but I cannot speak it. Can you talk English?"

"Yes," she said, surprisingly. "I can talk it pretty good. I go to school two year up by La Crosse. My fader got a farm there. I'm Alma's cousin."

In the new hayloft, the dance had begun. One by one the couples straggled out from the house, some of them still munching on lefse and lutfisk. Dick saw Gunnar standing in the moonlit snow, his feet wide apart. He seemed to be looking about him in search of someone, so Dick went up to him. Gunnar was already fairly drunk.

"Where is he?" he kept saying, "Where is that hedgehog, that rabbit, that shoat?" He was full of fight. Dick had been amusing himself by talking with Eva while he ate supper and now he regretted it. He should have been looking after Gunnar. That was what he came for, not to play with a strange golden wood-creature like Eva Oesterdahl. The girl was only fifteen, she had told him.

"Who are you looking for, Gunnar?" he asked in mollifying tones.

"That ski-jumper, that *usling,* that *musehöge.* . . ."

"Come on, Gunnar. They're going to dance now."

From the barn came the sound of fiddles tuning up. Dick took Gunnar's arm but the man remained rooted, only turning bloodshot eyes toward the music.

"Come on!" Dick said, more peremptorily.

At that moment a group of men passed by and Gunnar appeared to bristle. He bent forward, peering at their faces in the dusk. One of the three thumbed his nose with a scornful laugh. Gunnar leaped at him. Before he knew what was happening, Dick was knocked flat in the snow by the clinching fighters and as he picked himself up he knew he could never separate them. They were both full of whiskey and six feet tall.

The nose-thumber's two companions were unconcerned at first, but gradually the vicious nature of the fight alarmed them. They held a colloquy in Norwegian and then shouldered in vigorously. Dick got Gunnar by the back of his collar. Neither man would let go and it appeared that Gunnar intended murder. He closed his arms about his foe in a rib-crushing vise. A small group gathered, watching with anxiety.

"It's Peder. No it's not. It's Olaf. Tell who the other is if you know."

"Gunnar Larson, by the look of him."

"Ak! That's a bad thing. Two weeks now they aint spoke."

"At a vedding, too. Fie!"

"Fie upon you Olaf Tromsel for a trouble-maker!"

"And on you, Gunnar!"

Now the women had finished washing the dishes and were coming out of the kitchen. Eva Oesterdahl glanced toward the wrestling knot of men. Her mother tried to drag her past.

"Tys, Eva. Tys, for shame! Don't look, nu."

She broke away and ran to Dick's side. He was bearing all his weight against Gunnar and finding him immovable as a granite cliff. The girl looked, hesitated a moment, and then slapped the drunken man resoundingly on his cheek. He loosed his grip and was promptly pulled away.

In the hayloft the music was at its gayest when Dick came in with Eva. Jens Jensen, master of ceremonies was making the rounds.

"Two more couple for the quadrille!" He stopped in front of the newcomers. Eva looked at Dick expectantly.

"I'm sorry. I'm a Methodist and don't know how to dance," he said.

"Metho-deest, Metho-deest!" jolly Jens exclaimed, puffing out his cheeks. "Two peoples don't dance. Metho-deest peoples and dead peoples."

"You watch a little. Maybe you learn," Eva said hopefully, leading him to a bench.

Along the wall of the hayloft, kerosene lamps were

hung. The center of the floor was cleared for dancing and sprinkled with cornmeal. At one end the hay had been shoved aside and was used as a lounging place for the younger couples. The older ones sat stiffly on a long pine bench that ran the length of the barn, and the three fiddlers had a platform opposite the hay. As they fiddled they shouted out occasional lines of the songs they were playing:

My grandfather tells me, go slowly, go slowly,
Tra-la, the fine yellow-haired lady.

She came to my window. Go slowly, go slowly,
Tra-la, the fine yellow-haired lady.

Dick looked intently at the changing figures of the quadrille. They seemed easy enough, but it was plain to see that one blunder upset the whole pattern and he did not care to be the one who made the mistake. Eva would have to find another partner.

"Why you not dancing, Eva?" Old Dagmar said, coming along the bench. "Vile you been young you must dance. Too soon you be old."

As she said this she wrinkled her face like a naughty elf and indicated by pirouetting that she was not too old. An ancient man seized her about the waist and twirled her around.

"Lars Knutson, du gamling! Fie!" she cackled merrily. The two danced off together.

Alma, the bride, passed them in Gunnar's arms. He was sobering now and danced well, swinging Alma about till her full skirts and petticoats stood straight out from her waist, showing plump calves and garters. Alma looked curiously at her cousin as she went by. Gunnar's cheek still bore the mark of Eva's palm.

"Why did you slap him?" Dick asked.

"Lots of times I slap drunk men, Deek. Drunk men wake up when you slap them."

The sound of the fiddles and shuffling feet filled the barn to bursting. The pile of hay at the dimly-lit end of the loft rustled with the movements of laughing couples who half-lay in one another's arms or rested heads on shoulders. Dick looked at them and felt he was not living, that he was a starved outsider looking in on happiness. The figure changed, the fiddles swung into the music of a reel:

> You Olé o'er the meadow
> How happy you must be
> To own the pretty maiden
> Who once belonged to me. . . .

"I can dance a reel. Come, Eva," he said, and took her in his arms. She moved as lightly as a child at play, her looped braids swinging. Her full skirts swirled as she turned, looking back to meet his eyes with a glance warm, honest and admiring. They joined the long double line of dancers who were stamping their feet and waiting for Jens to call out his instructions.

"One more gentleman!" Jens held up the hand of a lone lady. "Gus Christianson!"

"He aint here, nu."

300

"Peder Berg!"

Faint murmurs of laughter from the hay, where Peder reclined in a girl's arms.

"Peder Berg! Come on, nu. Stand up and be a man!"

Peder got up with his hair full of hay and joined the reel, grinning sheepishly. The fiddles began again:

> You Olé o'er the meadow
> How happy you must be. . . .

Eva and Gunnar, crossing from opposite corners of the reel, clasped hands high in the air, bowed and backed to their places again. Dick, crossing, bowed to the bride, returned and twirled Eva. Over his shoulder she gave Gunnar a long look, full of invitation.

When he came back to his room at two o'clock in the morning it seemed lonely, cold, and chaste. His brain was still revolving with the dance music, his blood racing from the rhythmic movement and the warmth of Eva's arms. As he passed his hand over the bed in the dark, preparatory to turning back the quilts, he encountered a small square package on his pillow. He lit the candle. Before he opened the package he knew what would be inside it and for a few minutes he stood still while the familiar pain rose in him, engulfed him and subsided. He set himself angrily against the pain as a man bites on an aching tooth. His name in Lucy's handwriting was straight and firm and the knots had been neatly tied. He put the sapphire ring in his wash-stand drawer.

3

ETHAN HODGE had seen Dick crossing the lake to the fur-trader's cabin and promptly accused him of succeeding with Joe's Mary where other men had failed. Dick denied it vigorously without convincing Ethan. A poor woman who lived with an Indian had only one status with the Methodists of Hampstead Prairie; she was the strange woman against whom the Old Testament warned them. Their attitude toward Marie was a queer mixture of secret excitement, sly pleasure and hatred.

"'Tis a plague-spot that 'ouse. Murder were done in it."

"An abode of evil-doers."

"Aye. Drunkenness and worse."

"A snare to our young men."

Their grumbling conversation with its undercurrent of frustration told Dick a great deal about the elders of his father's church, and something too about Marie. He resolved to see her again and perhaps make one more attempt to help her. A sense of danger threatening her was strong in his mind as he set out across the lake in the last week of March.

Where the river current entered at the head of the lake, ice was breaking. Flocks of birds flew high above the center, however, settling again as they reached the small area of open water. Dick judged from this that the center of the lake was still frozen over. The surface was too rough for skating, so he set out to walk, feeling that all the eyes of the settlement were on his back, concealed in duck-blinds or fishing-shelters. After a while the misty air seemed to shut down behind him like a curtain and he was walking alone, seeing only forty feet of ice ahead of him at a time. It was four o'clock on a dark afternoon.

As he neared the point smoke blew around him in the heavy air. He thought at first it was the smoke from the cabin chimney, but soon he heard the crackling of flames and men's voices. Perhaps someone had made a fire on the beach. He came out of the mist and saw that the cabin was burning.

Marie stood alone in the center of a ring of heavily-bearded men. Her arms were folded on her breast, her face pale, bruised, and smeared with blood. She gave Dick a blank stare with no recognition and he realized that she was trying to protect him. On the ground, not far from her feet, lay Joe Sobish, his mouth welling blood. He appeared to have been shot in the forehead and chest. Dick strode into the circle and saw that several of the men were his neighbors and members of his father's church.

"What's happened here?" he asked roughly.

"The man were a 'orse-thief," Silas Hodge muttered defensively. "Took two of Jason Fowler's animals and a sack o' meal."

The others muttered too, and shuffled. A farmer kicked the body so that fresh blood flowed.

"Get help, someone," Dick said angrily. "The poor fellow's dying." He tried to interpose himself between Marie and the gruesome sight, but she was staring straight ahead, her pale features immobile and calm.

"He's dead." Nathan Goldthorpe rumbled. "He came oot with a gun and 'Ennery Piper shot 'im." Henry had obviously gone off, leaving the other men to face the outcome, and they were not in a happy mood about it. Apparently they had thought to burn the cabin with the dead man in it, but decided not to. Now they lacked leadership. Dick took charge.

"Get the poor fellow into your wagon, Mr. Hodge, and take him to the tavern at the bridge."

" 'Tis not my wagon yonder."

" 'Tis mine, but I'll not lend it," another man said sullenly.

"If you don't want to be accused of murder, you'll do your part. Carry him down there to the wagon," Dick insisted sternly.

" 'Tis Tommy Wentworth's lad," he heard Silas

304

Hodge explain to the other, who promptly became obedient.

"Now, Marie," he said, turning toward her and ignoring the knowing look on the mens' bearded faces. "Will you go with them?"

"I'll 'ave no 'eathen 'ussy in my cart," the owner barked, turning around. The two men guarding Marie fell back and left her facing Dick. On her cheek-bone, just below the eye, the red bruise was swelling.

"She be a wildcat, sure enough," said Silas Hodge. "Fair clawed our eyes out."

"I'll be responsible for her. My mother'll take you in, Marie. Better come home with me."

She lifted her eyes to his dumbly, but with a momentary look of passionate gratitude. It vanished, leaving her as impassive as before. She wrapped her blanket closely around her.

"Is there anything you want to bring?"

"My little book. But it's too late." She was right. The heat from the dry timber was intense and flames were licking through the doorway.

Silas Hodge lingered. "I don't doubt thy father'll have a word to say of this. Tell 'im I'd no hand in it."

Privately Dick doubted that his father or anyone else would be much concerned over the death of Joe Sobish. Even Marie seemed easily resigned, or perhaps she was concealing emotion beneath the waxen mask of her face.

"Better stay a while and see the trees don't catch fire," he suggested to Silas as he moved away. Marie followed him like a squaw, hugging her blanket around her.

Several times as they crossed the first half-mile of ice, Dick turned to look at her. He wondered how far she could walk in those clumsy shoes that clattered along over the frozen ridges. They were evidently much too large for her and once or twice he thought her face twisted with pain. Again, he saw her look sadly toward the burning cabin, now far behind them.

"I had soup in the kettle," she explained.

"Are you hungry?"

"Yes. It was a duck."

"Never mind. It's burned up by now. I'll give you food when we get home."

She plodded on with no more words until, toward the center of the lake she stopped and sniffed.

"Ice breaking. I smell water," she said.

Dick smelled it too, the wild, rainy smell of the first open water in a thaw. He heard a familiar booming sound, far up the lake. A crack was forming and racing toward them. If it should yawn at their feet they might stumble in. He hoped it would be behind them, otherwise they must retrace their steps. Marie spoke surely,

"Run. Run ahead, fast!"

They ran. The crack opened behind them. "Good!" said Marie in the soft, nasal voice of a squaw.

This was his dream, fulfilled. He was leading Marie

Gagnier home at last. And what was he to do with her, now she was saved? Hampstead farmers and their wives could make her life unbearable if he tried to find a place for her on the prairie. There would be nothing she could do. Like the Indian women, she would be useless as a kitchen drudge because she had been brought up to look on dirt leniently by a race who moved away when refuse accumulated. The English could not assimilate Marie. His mother would be kind but bewildered.

Never mind. Let the future take care of itself. At least she could not have been left behind on the desolate point with her burned cabin and dead husband. He tried to speak to her, but she persisted in keeping several paces behind him and the wind was strong. He shouted from one corner of his mouth:

"Was it true, what they said? That he had a gun?"

"Yes. It was true."

"Did he steal the horses?"

"No. He never stole horses."

Marie said this calmly and with a certain wifely pride. Apparently she identified herself with the man who had been killed, even while she was indifferent to his death. He threw another question into the wind.

"Will you go there tomorrow? The tavern?"

"No. I don't want to see him."

"They'll come and get you for the trial."

"There won't be a trial. Nobody cares what happened."

Her voice held a dreadful wisdom of mankind's ways.

He turned and faced her, and saw in the half-twilight how dark her eyes seemed in her white face. The blanket, held under her chin, framed her cheeks and made her look like a ragged madonna.

"I'll take care of you," Dick said. "You mustn't be afraid."

"All right."

His father's house was deserted, and he remembered that this was the night they were all to have had supper at the mill. It was late; they had given him up and his mother had left a cold meal for him on the kitchen table. His father would come home first with Gunnar to start the evening chores. His mother would stay to chat for another hour. The situation could hardly be worse, but until someone came the house was warm and quiet and there was food.

"Sit down, Marie," he said. He had fallen already into the habit of commanding, and she obeyed.

"My feet are bleeding," she remarked uncomplainingly. The tea kettle was boiling. He poured her a pan of hot water and gave her a towel. Marie took off her shoes and unwound the strips of cloth from which her ankles emerged, white and slim. Dick began to make tea, to slice bread and cold ham. He had rolled his shirt-sleeves above the elbow and hung his coat on a chair, and was deeply involved in the task when his father came in. Thomas Wentworth stood in the doorway, fixing his son with his piercing eyes. A few years

308

earlier, Dick would have shrunk from this look, but now he thought only that he would have to make Marie wait for her food, and felt only irritation at the unnecessary dramatics.

"Father, this is Marie Sobish," he said.

"Ah!"

"They shot her husband and burned down the cabin yonder."

"Ah!"

"So I brought her home. She's nowhere to go."

"What is this woman to thee?"

"To me?" Dick was about to say "nothing," but it would not have been true. Marie had a place in his life he could not explain. She was hardly a friend, but she had come into an existence unbearably empty and made it endurable by being unfortunate and brave. Dick would have pitied himself if he had not met Marie. He had learned a great deal from her humble pride. How tell this to his father?

"What is this brazen Jezebel doing in the house of virtue?" Thomas boomed. "I have not been blind. Thy comings and goings have been reported to me."

"Oh for Heaven's sake, Father. Don't be . . ." Dick stopped. In another moment he would have told his parent not to be an old fool. He handed Marie a cup of tea, which she gulped gratefully.

"I will give thee one minute to take this shameless woman from my 'ouse."

Dick brought Marie the bread and meat. She ate it in ravenous bites. Color came back into her face.

"One minute!" Thomas roared. Marie glanced questioningly at Dick, put on her shoes and stood up. She faced the furious older man with a look of patience and pride, then as he moved back and held the door wide, she walked through it. Savage anger seized Dick. He snatched a quilt from Hugh Henderson's bed and rolled it with shaking hands. Inside the roll he put the last of the supper, wrapped in a tea towel. He got into his coat.

"Dick!" his father protested. He walked past without a glance and out into the night. A few moments later he found Marie.

In the morning she said, "We have done wrong. You must go back to your father. He loves you."

They had spent the night together in the vacant "help-house," the door of which Dick had kicked from its hinges because he found it locked. Marie was lying under her red blanket, her yellow hair tossed about her on the blue straw-tick. The colors were vivid in the morning sunlight, and Dick felt an unreasonable happiness as he looked at them. His life should be in ruins, but at least he was living and another human being was in his care. He was making very bad coffee in a battered pot. The last Norwegians had left sulphur matches and kindling. He put out the remnants of bread and ham on the old puncheon table.

"We have been wicked," Marie said, staring at the roof. "You must go back to your father and mother."

"Back there? No, Marie. Get up and eat."

"They don't know where you are."

It seemed strange to him that she should be concerned for his father, who had insulted her. Then he understood. She was thinking of her own parents, of her own childhood.

"I'm a grown man, Marie. I haven't lived at home for two years—nearly three."

"Dick, I must run away and leave you. I am very bad luck. When my mother had me, they killed her. 'Woman who talks with owls'—my Winnebago mother—fell and broke her neck. And they shot Dog Head when he was raising me for a wife. The sister I liked best, she died too. That's why I left Saint Clara's. And now Joe. I must run away."

"I won't let you. Put it out of your head, Marie. Be a good girl and get up, now. We must go away together."

She sat silent, considering this remark. Her dark lashes lay against her cheek, emphasizing its peculiar pallor, a paleness that was not unhealthy, but rather like mother-of-pearl, radiant with underlying life. Dick had marvelled before at the fine texture of her skin. Now, having touched it, he still wondered that it could be so fresh and resilient. Wind and weather and the smoke of a fireplace had not injured even her hands. As she fingered her rosary he thought of how those hands must have grubbed for roots, built fires. He had seen them scour iron pots and shell field-corn. Yet they had the look of idleness.

"How do you know nothing bad will happen to you?" she asked.

"Well, Marie, I have your crucifix, haven't I?" he said, laughing.

"If we do wrong it won't defend us. That's what the sisters told me."

"Then we won't do wrong."

"Do you want me for your wife?"

Dick pushed aside his empty cup and laid his head on his folded arms on the table. Outside, the song of an early robin dripped into the morning air. Happy birds, returning always to the same mate! They had what human beings lacked, the certainty of faithful love. Hunger and cold and the hardships of migration were nothing to them, because of that faith. In the rigorous business of keeping alive, finding food and shelter and reproducing the race, mankind suffers most because he is tortured by doubt, torn by jealousy, drained of his strength by lack of faith. Why not make sure of loyalty by taking a mate more humble than himself? Marie would be grateful, dependent, adoring. He raised his head. She was sitting with clasped hands and immobile face. Her mouth quivered, so slightly only Dick's sharp eyes could have seen it.

"Yes," he said. "I want you for my wife."

4

S NOR BERGSTROM was bending over his table. He had
tacked down some large sheets of brown paper on
which delicate leaves of pressed ferns had been glued.
Above the leaves he was writing with a goose-quill in
Norwegian script the word *Pteridophyta* and a para-
graph of description. Along the edge of the table he had
spread ten broken limestone concretions with fossil
ferns exposed. Snor was trying to relate the fronds of
Paleozoic ages with those of 1857.

In everything but science, Snor's mind was a blessed
blank. It had become so when his wife and child died of
diphtheria two years before. Sometimes when the cradle
rocked as he brushed against it, he would look at it and
wonder why it stood there. His wife's aprons hung on
wooden pegs, taking the lines of their hanging permanently into their shapes. He plucked at them with
puzzled fingers.

Grass and mushrooms had sprouted from the dirt
floor. The fireplace was packed with ashes that spilled
out over the hearth. Snor's hair hung long on his shoul-

ders and his clothing looked slept-in. But he trimmed the delicate fronds and fitted them into the page with exquisite precision. He made no errors in his work.

His neighbors brought him food. Sometimes he ate it; sometimes he forgot. When he heard Dick and Marie at the door he hid a loaf of bread because he had forgotten to eat it and thought Jane Weymouth might see it and be hurt. The act was instinctive. He had no idea why he hid the bread.

Dick seemed familiar, but Snor could not think of his name, and he looked vaguely at the stranger. He thought Marie was a man.

"Snor," Dick said, speaking distinctly, as if his old friend were deaf, "we want some shoes."

"Hm? Vad? You vant shooss?"

He started to take off his own boots, but Dick stopped him and pointed to Marie's feet.

"Oh, ja!" Snor still failed to understand. Marie laid back her blanket and he saw her yellow braids. "Oh!" he said. Light broke momentarily in his foggy mind. He began to climb the ladder. The floor of the loft, swaying as he stepped on it, let down a shower of dust on paper and fern-leaves. Dried snakes, mummified bats and seed-pods shook where they hung from the ceiling below.

"You vant dress tu?" Snor called down, amid a great banging of cupboard drawers.

"Yes, please, Snor."

"You vant hat?"

Marie nodded at Dick in feminine excitement. "Yes, Snor," he said.

Snor came down with bonnet, dress and shoes, and Dick enticed him outside while Marie dressed in Helga's clothes. Ben Weymouth was coming along the trail in a farm wagon. He reined up as he saw Dick.

"I never thought to set eyes on thee again. Thy father called down God's wrath, thy mother wept, and the devil was to pay."

"I'm sorry for that. Where are you bound for, Ben?"

"The tavern at the bridge. They'll bury 'im today, but not till John Hall's had 'is say on the law of it."

Marie came out and stood beside Dick. Ben Weymouth looked at her admiringly and winked broadly at Dick. He slapped up his horses.

"Better travel in the other direction, lad. Hampstead's buzzing," he said.

At Weymouth's Crossing, his aunt was standing on the porch. When she saw them, Jane Weymouth went in and shut the door. Dick followed her and knocked loudly. She opened, with a face like granite.

"I'll ask you inside," she said, "but as for her, she can wait on the stoop."

"Then I'll talk to you out here," Dick replied pleasantly. He leaned his bedding roll against the rail. "I left my savings at home, Aunt Jane, and I need them. Will you let me have some money now and ask my father to pay you back from mine?"

"Is that all you have to say?"

"Not quite all. Tell my father I kicked in the help-house door and broke the lock. He'll want it repaired. And tell my mother I'm doing what I have to do. She'll understand."

"Very well. But not one cent will you get from me, Dick. You're breaking your mother's heart. Give up this woman and all I have is yours, gift or loan, it doesn't matter. Not one cent for folly!"

"Good-bye, Aunt Jane," Dick said. He started off toward the trail and Marie followed. At the corduroy road they heard running feet. Lisbeth caught up with them.

"Here!" she gasped. "Here's my money, Dicky." She thrust a pocket-book into his hands.

"Oh, Liss! We shouldn't take it. My father'll pay you back, my dear."

"I'll tell them all what I think of them. Pigs!" She kissed Dick, and went to Marie and took her hand. "I hope you'll be happy," she said, and gave her a frightened peck on the cheek before she ran away. Marie's lashes fell. Two tears slipped from beneath them.

"Where shall we be married?" Dick asked to divert her.

"You know the place in my prayer-book. Belle Fontaine."

"It must be two days' ride, Marie."

"I wore a white dress there, and knelt by my mother and grandmother in church."

"All right. We'll get to Belle Fontaine."

316

After all, it was the one place in the world where Marie had not been a waif.

Like the rest of Dick's dream, Belle Fontaine, when he found it, was commonplace. The clapboard houses, with turned-back eaves and shuttered windows, the muddy streets and blacksmith shop might have belonged anywhere. The church was new, replacing the one where Marie had knelt as a child. That church had been destroyed by a tornado, and many of the tombstones and crosses in the churchyard had been blown down by the same storm. They were leaned against the fence now, for fear of marking the wrong graves. The priest was not the one who had known Marie as a child. No one in Belle Fontaine was French now, except one man, Paul Girard, the blacksmith. The town had petitioned to be called Bell Fountain.

The wedding service was intoned, the prayer said, and Dick put a cheap gold band on Marie's finger. Paul Girard, the one man who recalled the Gagnier family, had been a witness. After the wedding he stayed in the village square to chat. He was somewhat excited to see the child who had been kidnapped so long ago, but there was no one to marvel with him. Even his wife was a stranger in Bell Fountain.

"My father's name was Jules." Marie said. "I remember his name, but nothing else about him."

"He was always in the woods. A lumberman. Yes, Jules Gagnier. That's right."

"Why isn't his tombstone with the others?"

"Poor man. There wasn't much to bury. The wolves ate him."

"Who was Aimee? I remember my grandmother calling that name."

"Aimee was your mother."

The two French women had gone with the child Marie into the woods to boil maple sap. While they made sugar the Fox had come upon them. In the morning the loggers had found the women scalped and dead, but the child was never seen again. Rumors drifted back. Some said she was with the Winnebagos, that they had taken her in a battle.

"Yes," Marie said. "The Winnebagos took me."

If no roof covered them, there was still the sky, Marie said. She slept uncomplainingly on the ground, rolled in her blanket. If the sky was unkind and it rained, then it was time enough to look for shelter. If they ate, they ate. If they were hungry they were like the animals of the woods who were always hungry except when they were eating. Poverty was natural to Marie. It was the condition ordained for all living things and she could not understand why her new husband was anxious.

She sat in the grassy hollow between the roots of two trees fingering her rosary. One after another she pushed the beads aside, saying fragments of Latin and with them words that sounded like the noises of wind and water.

"What is that you say when you count your beads?"
he asked.

"Those are the names I gave them when I was a
child, after I forgot my prayers. Do you want to know
the names of my beads?"

"Yes. Tell me their names."

"The deer, the spotted fawn, the bear, the beaver,
the wolf. The otter, the turtle, the duck, the frog, the
snake, the muskrat. The loon, the yellowhammer, the
kingfisher, the crane. Daylight, dusk, darkness, rainwater, springwater and wind."

"That's very beautiful, Marie."

"They are only the names of common things."

She had one anxiety. She was afraid something would
happen to Helga Bergstrom's faded velvet bonnet. At
the first sign of rain Marie hid her bonnet under her
blanket. Dick had more worries than he cared to count.
He had tried to find work in every lumber camp they
had come near, and had found instead that lumbermen
were drifting away because the market was slack. Depression had reached the very heart of the pine and oak
forests.

"I ought to give you back to the Winnebagos," he
said. "At least they knew how to get along without
money."

"So can we. It's only half a mile to the Dalles. There
we can sleep in a cave."

"How do you know? Have you been here before?"

"Oh, yes."

"You know this country, these roads?"

"Yes, but we stayed in the woods. We didn't walk on the roads."

As she spoke the look of despair and loneliness deepened her eyes. She moved toward him as if to reassure herself and stood close, but not touching him. That was as near to a caress as Marie ever came in the daytime. Intimacy at night was like part of a ritual in which she had a share, but in the daytime she held herself inviolate, wrapped in her blanket and her dignity.

"You were unhappy here," he said. "We'll leave tomorrow, but it's going to rain now, I think."

"Then we should go now, and find shelter before the storm."

They came soon to the Dalles of the Wisconsin River. Even before they reached the rocky gorge, the air grew cooler, sometimes coming up with a rush from secret caverns, and the top of Chimney Rock could be seen, rising above the underbrush. The river itself was invisible, flowing far down between its precipitous banks so that they did not see the water until they were standing upon the palisades one hundred feet above its surface. Dick stared in astonishment at the rugged beauty of the scene. Like a man who has read about the sea but never sailed, he could hardly believe the Dalles, though he had heard of them many times. Marie's knowledge of the cliffs and her casual acceptance of their magnificence were almost irritating to him.

"The Manido made this deep place," she said.

"He made everything," Dick replied, smiling, as if he were talking to a child.

"But when he made this, he was a snake."

"Wasn't that the devil?"

"No. It was the Great Spirit. He wiggled on his belly and wherever he went the water followed him. When he lashed his tail it made all the lakes. Down there is the place where he had a hard time to get through. He was very angry. You can see where he tore the earth."

"Do you really believe that, Marie?"

She gave him no answer but a faint reflection of his own smile.

The sound of men's voices could be heard, echoing from the high walls, and approaching from upstream. The conversation appeared to be first near at hand, then far off, with a ventriloquist's magic. Finally a raft of sawed logs approached, rebounding like the voices against the tortuous channel, while lumbermen in bright greens, reds and blues, leaped about with their poles trying to keep their long platform from being shattered. They looked small and unreal on the water below, like the painted lead soldiers in toy-shops. Their struggles and even their curses were in miniature like the efforts of ants to carry a dead beetle. Dick looked down on them, a Jupiter from Olympus, and wondered whether his own difficulties were not just as unimportant.

"No wonder they are working! If the raft breaks up they will drown, Marie."

"No. They will ride on a log. Once I saw a Frenchman in a red cap riding a log down through the Jaws all the way to the tavern. He looked like a woodpecker —the one they call 'hard-to-kill.' "

The lumbermen, maneuvering and sweating below, barely prevented their raft from crashing against a projecting parapet and then, relaxing, allowed it to drift out of sight around a curve. They were nearing the Dalles House and a brief rest with a swig of whiskey before they went on to the Arena sawmills. As they disappeared, thousands of swallows boiled out of their holes in the sandstone wall on the west bank and scolded them shrilly.

"I wonder how those round holes came there, just the right size for a bird's home, and so many of them," Dick said.

"The swallows make them. Every time they come back, they make the hole a little deeper. An old bird is one whose bill is worn out."

"Well, we'd better find a hole of our own. At any minute we'll have a downpour."

The clouds hovered low, casting shadows into the deep gorge, so that the somber reflection from the water disappeared altogether. They turned back from the river's edge, passing through a natural arch of woodbine into a grotto of limestone set with pillars and fantastic chairs. It looked like a rude chapel, especially when one fancied that the raised rock at the far end was a pulpit. However it lacked a roof, so they could not linger but climbed the opposite bank and came out

in a quiet pasture-like acre. Marie looked about her
with an air of recognition.

"Over there," she said, pointing to a clump of silver-
leaf maples. "That is the cave I mean."

It was more like an animal's den. As they went down
into the ground between walls of dark brown sandstone,
Dick saw the opening to a larger room below. Marie
was ahead of him, supporting herself with a hand
against either wall and steadily descending.

"Don't go any farther," he said. "This is too cold."
A gravelike chill was rising into his bones from the
cavern. Marie turned her face upward and it swam iri-
descent and unreal in the nimbus of light from above.

"When our eyes are used to the dark we can see," she
told him.

"How still it is! And a minute ago the wind was so
loud!"

"If you listen down there you can hear the roots of
the trees. They cry when the wind blows." She went
down a little farther.

"Please come back," Dick said. It seemed to him she
was about to vanish into the earth like Proserpine.

"I want to find my name."

"Your name?"

"I cut it in the rock here, a long time ago. The Winnebagos were sitting in the cave, hiding from the Fox.
I climbed up and cut my name."

Dick followed her for a few more steps, thinking
of that little girl who had seized his hand with passion-

ate entreaties and how she had once stood here cutting letters on the rock. Marie was that child, but what had they to prove it? Only her own memory, a slender thread to bind past and future together and reassure them of her identity. No other living soul could bear witness that the child who had asked him for help was the woman he had rescued.

"Here it is," she exclaimed, running her finger-tips along the stone. Staring painfully, he made out the crude capitals.

"Let's make a fire in the cave and sleep there," she suggested.

"No, Marie. I don't like it at all. You're much too pale down here, almost like a ghost. Sleep above ground tonight."

They lay in an upper room of the tavern at La Farge, looking idly out at one of the summer thunderstorms that sweep so suddenly across the hills and change small streams to raging rivers in the space of an hour or so. The day was just breaking and they had been waked by the thunder. Against a flaming sky one tree stood out, tall and fierce. Marie looked at it quickly.

"That is the Tooth," she said.

"What? The tree?"

"Yes. That's what we called it."

"So you know this place, too. Did they name all the trees?"

"I don't remember."

"Why do you remember the Tooth, then?"

"That's where they buried my mother . . . I mean . . ."

"Didn't the Winnebagos bury in the earth?"

"Not when there were wolves."

In late August they came to a country so wild there seemed no reason to go on. Forbidding bluffs stood in their way, heavily forested with birch, beech, scrub-oak and pine. Even the gentler slopes were hard to climb because of shale that slipped underfoot, and the more difficult ones were an endless confusion of fallen blocks of limestone, rolled down in a hopeless chaos with tree-trunks and brush and tall dead grass. For more than a day they had seen no houses but the most inhospitable kind, huts and dugouts with starved, yelping dogs and frightened children. No farmer could make his living here. No use to go farther. This was the government land Gunnar Larson had talked of finding, a place where one could have acres for almost nothing, the bluffs of Buffalo County. The road had dwindled to a path and Dick looked up it, wondering where such a path could lead. Certainly no one lived above them. Some hunter, perhaps.

"We'll have to go back," he said. "You can't climb now."

Marie was waxy white, glistening with sweat. Helma's dress stretched taut over her swollen figure. She was six months with child.

"There's nothing here. Nothing ahead," he went on,

his voice dragging with weariness. Dick had the beaten look of a man who has asked too often for work and been too often refused. His face was dark with beard, his eyes haggard. He rested their pack of belongings against a tree and could not meet his wife's questioning eyes.

"Listen!" she said.

Faintly, the sound of a singing voice came down to them as if it floated on the stream that flowed beside the path. With the song the lowing of cattle blended like bass.

"There can't be a farm up there!" Marie exclaimed, but the sounds continued.

"Come on, then," Dick sighed, picking up his blanket-roll.

To both the song seemed an omen of better times. They began to climb again, Marie following behind as always, but sometimes signifying by a wordless murmur that she wanted help up a steep bank. As they ascended, the stream came down past them and the sound of the girl's singing grew clearer.

"I don't know those words," Marie said.

"They must be Norwegian. Yes. They are." The chorus came to them clearly.

> The thread in the needle,
> The seed in the apple,
> The cork in the bottle,
> The love in my heart.

Dick had heard the song from wandering farm-hands who knew many vulgar verses. He had never heard it sung by a woman before. After a few minutes they came over the edge of the cliff into a small haymeadow, bathed in breezes, and could see a sort of table-land of tilled fields and pastures with a large white house and long limestone barns. Beyond the farm the cliffs rose again, frowning with scrub-oak and evergreens.

> They call me poor Peter.
> My coat is in tatters.
> I sing for my betters,
> And this is my song. . . .

In the hayfield a girl was raking. She wore blue overalls and a headkerchief and her feet were bare. It was Eva Oesterdahl.

For a moment she stared at Dick with no recognition and he gradually realized how low his fortunes had fallen. Then she called him "Deek," blushed, and dropped her eyes to her bare feet. Marie took in the scene with enigmatic eyes.

"Ak! How good you could find us! My moder will be glad to have you for guests." Eva leaned her rake against a horse-chestnut tree and adjusted her kerchief. "Come in with me. It's dinner-time now and you can sit to table with us."

5

OLE OESTERDAHL had built his own home from the
limestone of the cliff that towered above it. He
had not been content with the natural light-brown color
of the stone. That was all right for the barns and out-
houses, but his dwelling must be white, so he had burned
the limestone in a home-made kiln and produced white-
wash enough to give the house an uneven coat of sugary
paint. Surrounded by bright hollyhocks it was dazzling
against the birch and pine trees. Its three chimneys of
red brick added a pleasing decoration.

Eva paused outside the kitchen door to slip her bare
feet into embroidered cotton shoes. The floor was of
white pine, sanded and swept. Dick remembered that
Norwegian housewives were supposed to be able to roll
out their "flat-bread" on the kitchen floor. He could
believe this of Signe Oesterdahl, who came hesitantly
to the door, but beamed with welcome when Eva's introduction recalled Dick to her mind.

"Oh ja! Oh ja! At Alma's wedding!"

Her husband, a burly fellow with the pink cheeks and
blue eyes of a baby, remembered further that he and

his family had spent a night in the Wentworth's "sod house" when they were traveling west from Milwaukee. He was so pleased to be able to repay this hospitality that he wrung Dick's hand several times and thanked the dear God aloud. More cotton shoes were produced and Signe proudly led the travelers to the stream of running water that flowed into the side of her kitchen through a wooden pipe from the spring on the hillside. Falling constantly into a barrel, and then outdoors again through another pipe, this water created an impression of coolness and cleanliness merely by its sound. Marie's hot hands and arms were held under the stream. They washed, drank and were refreshed.

Chris, Eva's twelve-year-old brother was sitting at the long table, patiently waiting for dinner to be served. He had an open book before him and was tracing the lines with one finger as he read. Dick's quick glance took in the shape and color of the book. Even from across the large room he guessed it to be Irving's *Alhambra,* a strange bit of reading-matter to find in these hills.

The walls were covered with red-and-brown prints of the sort sent out to prospective immigrants by promoters. America, the land of plenty! Farmers' wives, in rich drapery, led fat children to look at the harvest. Farmers in clothes more reminiscent of mediaeval Europe than of Wisconsin, piled baskets with impossibly large peaches, melons and grapes. The early Presidents were there too, Washington, Jefferson and Monroe, and in their midst, looking legendary and lost, Gustavus Adolphus drew his lithographed sword.

A corner-cupboard held a few relics of Norway; the starched cap of a grandmother, the horn-handled cane and broken steel spectacles of a grandsire, a fiddlebow and penciled score of music. And in another corner, inspiring wonder as to how it had ever been transported over the ocean and up the Great River from New Orleans, a porcelain stove reached almost to the ceiling. It was cold and white. On the black iron stove near the door a pot of coffee was boiling, filling the air with its powerful aroma.

"Dinner ready," Signe said, carrying the coffee-pot to the long table.

At the base of the great cliff was an area of rubble and fallen stone and a grove of birch-trees. An old road wound among the trees. It had been made in the 'forties by loggers and was not used enough now to wear down the fallen leaves in its ruts, but at the far end of the road, half a mile from the farm-house, the loggers' cabin still stood, its door barred and its one window boarded shut. Ole had lived in the cabin while he built the larger house. Now he offered it to Dick.

There was a box-bed into which Ole put some clean straw, a bench and chairs made of hand-hewn lumber with the bark still on it, a table with hinged leaves. The mud fireplace was cracked and there was no floor but the earth. Bats had gotten into the cabin in spite of the boards and bars, and mice had littered the table and hearth. Marie regarded the place with a satisfied smile.

"It's a very good house," she said, and then changed her tone at the sight of Dick's face. "Why don't you like it?"

"I do like it," he said.

"It's as fine as the one that burned. You know—that one."

"Yes. And there's a stove."

"I can use a stove. I learned at Saint Clara."

"That's good. You'll keep warm when I'm away."

He had some vague notion of leaving her here and setting out again, but she took alarm.

"Where? If you go, I want to go too."

"Nowhere. I just meant . . ." he began confusedly. For the first time he realized that he could not go home and that his adventures were over. He felt imprisoned.

"If you could work for *him*, he'd let us live in this nice house and we could have food. There was a bee-tree by the road. I can get some honey."

Marie sat by the rusty stove and in her eyes was the look of home-seeking women throughout the ages. She viewed the cobwebbed beams between narrowed lids, brooding.

"When the cold days come and the bees can't fly—that's when I'll get it. You can pick them up and throw them out of the hole."

She was no longer a roaming Winnebago. She was a French peasant woman—thrifty and possessive. Remembering how she had lain beside him under the stars, he smiled.

"In the Dalles you didn't want a roof over you."

"I want it for the child."

Signe knocked at the door. She was bringing rag rugs and quilts. She looked angrily at the cobwebs.

"Ak! So slusky it got in here!" she said and began to ply a wrathful broom. The dust flew, the bats circled and escaped through the open door. Marie watched, fascinated, and learned more about the ways of housekeeping than the careful nuns at Saint Clara had taught her in five years. Thereafter she spent an hour with the broom every morning until the dirt floor was almost swept away. She even swept the ground about the doorstep and the path to the spring. As for the rugs and quilts she never thought of them as her own and for two weeks refused to use them at all.

One morning after Dick had been lying awake for some time, he realized that the sounds he was hearing came from the grove near by and were made by an axe. He wondered why Ole went so far from home to cut up fallen logs. It would be pleasant to get up while Marie was still sleeping and go out for a chat with the big Norwegian, whose pink cheeks would be even pinker in the morning wind and whose silvery hair and beard would be blowing. He slipped cautiously from the box bed, pulled his trousers on over his nightshirt and went out barefoot.

Eva was in the grove, swinging her axe with strong brown arms, cutting huge wedges from a fallen log. Dick paused a moment to admire her. She swirled her lithe young body back and forth and her aim was so accurate that the axe-blade never missed its mark, but bit cleanly into the log each time in exactly the same place. The chips flew. A bevy of tiny nuthatches hovered near. They might have been looking for insects in the bark, but they seemed to Dick to be watching Eva as he was, with astonishment and pleasure.

"Good morning, little woodchopper," he said.

Eva stopped and drew her arm over her sweating forehead. She turned a laughing glance toward him.

"I'm cutting your wood for you so you don't freeze in winter."

"Cutting *my* wood? You mustn't do that."

"Ja. Chris and I will cut your wood. Then you not got to work so hard."

Her simple friendliness left him at a loss. He realized that the large pile of split sticks represented several days of work and that either Chris or Eva had been here in the grove before, thinking of his welfare and making no claims on his attention.

"Let me do my own work, child. You don't owe me anything."

Eva's smile faded. She looked bewildered.

"We want to help you, *fordi* we like you so good."

"You might hurt yourself," Dick said, merely for something to say.

She laughed. "I never hurt myself. When I was only a *pattebarn* I could chop, yet. Once it was a big, big snowstorm and Chris and me were all alone. Moder and fader went to Freedom in the sleigh. It got darker and they didn't come home and the fire was going out. That time I'm only eight years old. I went outdoors and I couldn't see to the woodpile, even, but we got a big log by the door to sit on when we take off our shoes. I cut it up with a little handaxe and kept Chris and me warm all night."

"Freedom? Where's that?"

"Twelve miles away, only. But the snowstorm was too big and they couldn't find the road."

"Don't you want to live in a town, Eva? Aren't you ever lonely?"

"Ja, sometimes I'd like to know a lot of people. I meant to ask you, Deek, are there more men like you that aint married, yet? I got to get married some time, I know, and I aint seen anyone I liked, only you."

"The world's full of better men," Dick murmured, turning away.

Marie was sitting up in bed when he came back. Her thick braids were ruffled from sleep, her eyes strange and rather wild.

"You knew her before," she said, tensely. "Where did you know her?" She had heard their voices.

"Eva? I met her at a dance."

"What dance? Was it the corn dance?"

"No. At a wedding."

334

She seemed satisfied. Marie had some idea of ritual in her mind. A dance at a wedding was a ceremonial in which men and women joined. Dick thought it just as well that she remain ignorant of the barn dance, the couples in the hay and the pagan reel. She got rather ponderously out of bed and began to make his coffee. He left the cabin every morning at five to milk Ole's cows.

"In the spring we'll have maple-sugar," she said, putting a spoonful of dark honey into his cup.

"Do you know how to make it?"

"Yes. I can make sugar. I helped my mother when we were in the Ojibwa country. We went out to the sugar lodge while there was still much snow, to put the new bark on the roof. Then we took the dishes, the 'makuk,' from under the piles of bark and got them ready...."

"Do you mean your *Indian* mother, Marie?"

She looked confused. "Yes. I mean 'Woman-who-talks-with-owls.' My real mother made sugar too, but that was before I knew how."

"Go on, then. How did 'Woman-who-talks-with-owls' make her sugar?"

"First we had to put the bark on the roof."

"Of course," Dick said, suppressing a smile. It was always the same, when Marie told a story. Each step had to be given due importance as if time were nothing, just as the Indians sometimes prolonged a tale for two weeks without reaching a conclusion.

"For that we must take out the ladder. Under the ladder were rabbits and the little brown mice. They were very sleepy. We put new steps on the ladder where it was broken. Then the women took the ladder out of the door and set it up against the lodge. Then I took the roll of bark. Then my Winnebago mother went up on the roof to find the holes. My little sister, whose name was Cloudy Sky, stood halfway up the ladder and helped me with the bark. That is the way the women and girls put a new roof on the sugar house."

"End of Chapter One. Now, when I come back at noon you can tell me how you made the sugar."

"First, we had to make the troughs out of logs. They looked like boats."

"All right. You can tell me that when I come home for dinner."

The hills north of La Crosse were populated by people of many races. There were the fringe from the lead-mines, men who had prospected so far into the forest that they had left the galena deposits behind and taken to farming instead. For the most part they barely kept themselves alive, scratching the stony earth every spring to plant a few potatoes, some corn and less wheat. Kentuckians and Virginians were most numerous and best able to endure the mountainous conditions, and not far from Ole's farm was the village of Little Chimney, settled by Cumberland mountaineers. To reach Little Chimney, though it was only three miles away, one had to climb a precipice. Three miles may be a short distance or a very long one. When much of it is straight up, it is long. Eva had gone to school at Little Chimney by climbing up over the cliff and now Chris began the autumn by doing the same thing. The schoolmaster's name was Mr. Shakespere, the schoolhouse a log cabin. Chris left at half past seven, his "tornister" or knapsack strapped to his shoulders so that his hands were free for climbing. For another half hour his sturdy figure in its red shirt and blue trousers would be visible against the face of the escarpment, slowly worming itself higher. Then it would disappear triumphantly over the upper edge to reappear toward supper-time.

The English and Cornish element cared less for rugged uplands. They had clustered together about the town of Freedom in a valley beyond the ridge. Freedom had its "foreigners," mostly Bohemians, Poles and Russians. The Germans and Norwegians were considered hardly foreign because they learned American ways and speech so rapidly. They built good houses as soon as they were able, saved money, bought American clothing. "Those others" lived in dugouts and gave all their money to the priest, Ole said.

The tumbling stream was called "Carrot Creek" by the Kentuckians and English, but the Oesterdahls called it "Evasvand" after their daughter. It flowed out of the side-hill on their farm, so they had a right to name it, they thought. Chris came back one day with the disquieting news that "Eva's Creek" did not begin on their property, but sprang from a little lake some distance beyond the top of the cliffs. It merely disappeared for a time and came out again in their upper pasture. They continued to call it for Eva, but with less pride of ownership. At any rate no other family had been able to confine it, pipe it through house and barns or direct a part of its stream across a square of lawn to keep it green.

Two miles downhill along the course of the stream, was the home of the Yanceys. No one knew where these people had come from. There were three families who went by the same name, though the fathers were not brothers. The children mingled indiscriminately, eating and sleeping at whatever house they happened to be playing in when mealtime or bedtime arrived. There were twenty of these children and of the whole number not one had escaped a hereditary taint. Three were albinos, three were tongue-tied, four were deaf-mutes. Two were still infants at six years of age. They sat on the floor, drooling and crying. Odd little creatures of various ages greeted the visitor with idiot smiles. Signe Oesterdahl gently admonished her children to come home from Yanceys' before dark, but Eva knew the names of all twenty, and sometimes nursed the smallest nightmarish baby in her arms.

High on another hill, visible from the farmhouse door, was the cabin of Old Dagmar. Sometimes the old woman came scrambling down her path to the logging-road and walked to Ole's house in time for afternoon coffee. Sometimes the entire Oesterdahl family went up to Dagmar's. At all times they kept a close watch over the treetops for signals. Dagmar had been Eva's nurse in the old country.

"What you think Dagmar got for food today?" Signe would say, peering up the hill toward the faint column of smoke that rose from the little cabin. "Run, nu, Eva. Take the tornister and fill it with the warm bread." Eva or Chris went up to Dagmar's with a part of every baking. It would have been easier, Dick thought, for Dagmar to live with Ole's family, but Ole explained:

"Signe keeps too clean a house for Dagmar Ruysdal. In the old country the Ruysdals got to have five hens and a dog in the kitchen or they get lonesome."

The first snow fell for three long, dark days and buried rail fences and boulders, brush-heaps, stumps and other landmarks under a white blanket. Snowshoes were brought down from Ole's attic.

"I wore those when I was a child," Marie said, watching Dick fasten the thongs. "Mine were made out of deerskin and I ran very fast on them."

He looked at her and his heart contracted with pity for her misshapen body and ragged clothes. He remembered the fair, clean little girl in the Indian camp, her embroidered blouse and snowy leggings.

"The Winnebagos took better care of you than I," he said.

In the afternoon as he stood by the farmhouse door,

Ole came out and peered beneath his palm at the snow-laden roof of Dagmar's cabin.

"Two days now there's no smoke," he muttered, while Signe, Eva and Chris gathered silently behind him, all staring at the hillside.

"Let me go up," Chris begged.

"Nei," Signe moaned, shaking her head. "It might be death, Chris. Ak, poor Dagmar!"

Ole looked disconsolately at his bandaged ankle. He had sprained it the day before, jumping out of the hay-loft.

"I'll go," Dick offered. It would be dark before he returned though Dagmar's roof seemed so close to the Oesterdahl's door. He took the bag of food Signe hastily packed. Ole limped to the stable and came back with a squawking rooster, its legs tied together with twine.

"Dagmar Ruysdal like to bleed her own fowl," he said, fastening the bird upside down to Dick's belt.

The sun was still high as Dick set out across the treacherous snow. All the tangle of fallen logs, rocks and underbrush was so covered that he could walk lightly over it, but now and then a jagged corner of limestone or forked oak-branch reached up from below and tripped him. The road could be followed only by noticing the distance between tree trunks. The rock called Little Chimney rose high on his right, and beyond it was a desolate chasm of dead and falling trees. He passed the entrance to this chasm and began to climb toward Dagmar's. Soon he had risen so far he could see the town of Little Chimney at the foot of the high rock. He looked back at Ole Oesterdahl's farm. It was small and trim on its white shelf.

Up on the clean, crisp top of the world life seemed very simple. No wonder Old Dagmar had liked to live here by herself! She owned the whole hill by squatter's rights, and though there was only a small patch of fertile ground it was enough to raise her potatoes and pasture her cow. That was exactly as she had lived in the old country, Ole said, and this hill was much like the hill at Hammerfest where she had taken her father's cows to pasture half a century ago.

Dagmar's cow lowed from its cold stable and the rooster at Dick's belt croaked an answer. He took pity on the poor fowl and held it right side up with his left arm. He came into the small houseyard and saw that no footprints led from the door. The old woman had not been outside since the snow.

She was lying in bed and the room was bitterly cold. She had dragged the feather bed on top of her for warmth; her face and one gnarled hand protruded from the side of a mountain of covers. The remains of her last meal lay on the table. Dick had released his rooster, who now hopped to the table, stretched, crowed and began pecking at the crumbs. Dagmar was sleeping soundly.

Dick raised the griddles of the stove and stuffed it with chips from the woodbox. Where was the tinder and flint? He began a search of the room and could not find it. Finally he came to the bed. He had looked everywhere else. Could it be that the tinder-box was in bed with Old Dagmar? If she had found her tinder damp, she might have taken that way to dry it. In gingerly fashion he peeled back the quilts and feather bed. There was the box, clasped against her breast.

As he took it from her he knew at once that she was dead. Her clutching hand remained stiffly in the air. Had she frozen to death because her flint would not strike a flame in the wet shavings? He hardly thought that possible. She had lived through too many winters to be frozen so easily. Dagmar must have come at last to the halfway place where life and death almost balance and a hair can turn the scales. The fire would not start, so she had found it easier to die. Before her bodily warmth left her she had dried the tinder. Dick lit a fire.

His fingers were like stone. As the fire roared up the chimney he wrung his hands together and felt, as living people sometimes do in the presence of death, an overwhelming gratitude for life. The blood would flow back again into his stiff fingers and warm them. They would bend and flex themselves and go on serving his will. The sun streamed in through the dirty little window, the flames crackled, the rooster crowed beside the teapot. Dick drew a deep breath as if he were greedy for air. He looked again at Dagmar's face. Only the cold had preserved it. With the first warmth it had begun to sink, to fall away from its semblance of sleep. He pulled off the feather-bed and rolled her tightly in quilts, covering her face and the skinny claw.

The cow was lowing in the little log barn. He went out and gave her food and water. She was about to calve and had no milk. He left the bucket full of well-water where she could reach it and came back into the house, looking about him for some sort of sledge and seeing nothing that would do. He knew he must bring Dagmar's body away with him. That was what Ole would wish.

Should he tear the house-door from its hinges? It seemed a pity to let the biting cold into the house. He went outside again and saw the outhouse door hanging loose. In a few minutes he had it off. It was a little longer than Dagmar. He laid it on the snow.

By the time he had torn a sheet into strips and tied her securely in her quilt the sun was going down. He hurried feverishly. The rooster crowed a good-bye as he went out again, carrying his stiff burden. He had fastened a rope through the little round window in the top of the door and he started down the steep hill, pulling his sled. Sometimes it stuck fast, sometimes it slid down too fast and almost tripped him, at which he started away, shuddering. At the bottom of the hill he came into forest and it began to grow dark. He wished he had brought the lantern.

Far off at first, and then nearer, he heard the cry of a wolf. There was an echo or answer from the ravine

343

and another from the cliff above the Oesterdahl farm, then an ominous silence and he could imagine the pack gathering.

Dick was not afraid of wolves but he had a shepherd's hatred for their slinking ways. How could they smell death so far? He had seen them sit back in the underbrush waiting for a sheep to die, and now it seemed that they had been watching from the cliffs until he was too far from Dagmar's cabin to go back. He tried to run, and struck the sled sidewise against a tree. The blanket fell away from the dead woman's face. He covered it again and moved forward more carefully.

What were those dark shadows, moving among the birches? They looked almost like a part of the dappled shade on the snow, but as he watched them they circled furtively, pursuing a course like that of a tacking sailboat, always coming nearer. Just as they had sometimes circled a stray sheep in his father's woods, now they circled Dick. He looked about him for an accessible tree and found one with branches lower than the rest. If the worst came, he could abandon his sledge, but it would have to be the worst. Even when dead a human being is too good for wolves, he said to himself grimly. He detached the rope of the sledge and knotted it around his wrist, swirling it like a lash. Under the snow there must be rocks for hurling and bludgeon-shaped pieces of wood, but he had no time to find them. With his back against the chosen tree and the sled pushed

344

aside, he stood his ground and the wolves circled nearer. He could see the leader's phosphorescent eyes, shining in the twilight. Soon he heard their panting breath on all sides of him. There were five wolves within hearing distance and perhaps others farther away.

Then he remembered that this wild cousin of the dog fears the human voice. He shouted "A-a-a-ah!" They cringed. Their heads down, their backs bristling, they faded momentarily into the darkness. They reminded him of Bije, his collie, shrinking from a scolding, but what had been endearing humility in Bije was loathsome cowardice in these creatures. A brief respite and they were back again, stealthy, inexorable.

Dick shouted again, waved his arms and made wordless sounds. His own voice sounded ridiculous to him, ringing out so raucously in the chaste air. "Booh!" he said to the wolves. "Back there! Lie down!" As long as he shouted they gave him a truce.

With so much lung power to be spent, it seemed to Dick he must spend it wisely. He began to recite the psalms. Into the cold, white woods he threw out the beautiful lines, thunderously as his father had thrown them from the pulpit.

"The heavens declare the glory of God and the
    firmament sheweth his handiwork,
Day unto day uttereth speech and night unto
    night proclaimeth knowledge."

The wolves drew back whining from this good magic. They sat on their haunches in a semicircle like Indians

345

before a missionary. Dick went on sonorously. Not in vain had Thomas Wentworth exacted a weekly psalm from the memory of his younger son. They flowed spontaneously from his lips—words he had not thought of for years:

"Yea though I walk in the valley of the shadow
    of death
I shall fear no evil . . ."

Half an hour went slowly by. The wolves stirred restlessly and the bitter cold struck through his motionless body. He stamped and swung his arms to keep warm and wondered whether, after all, his vainglorious pleasure in being alive had been premature. He could not keep on shouting all night. If he climbed the tree he might be dead of cold before morning.

"The earth is the Lord's and the fullness thereof," he was crying hoarsely, when he saw a lantern among the trees, bobbing up and down, a miraculous, golden light, though it was only the horn lantern from Ole's stable. He could not see the bearer until she was beside him and then as he turned, the leader of the wolves closed in, snarling, on the sledge. Eva snatched a hatchet from her belt, leaned forward and cleft the wolf squarely between his eyes.

"Good girl!" Dick said, fervently as the great gray fellow reared, fell sidewise and stained the snow with his blood. "Oh, good girl, Eva!" The pack crept off into the forest with a tremolo baying.

"We could see you up on the hill when you start down with the sled. Ak, poor Dagmar! So she's gone, then." As if the dead wolf could understand, she turned toward him with curling lip. *"Du slet-hund!* Sleep well," she said.

When Dagmar lay in the upstairs best bedroom of Ole's house and Signe had already begun to sew her shroud, Dick went home. Marie was sitting alone by the fire. She hid something hastily under her full skirt.

"What have you there, Marie?"

"Nothing."

"Yes, you have. Let me see it."

She slowly took out a corn-husk doll, dressed like a Winnebago in clothes of rags and bark. He thought she might be making it for the child, so he took it up and pretended to admire it.

"What name shall we give it? It must be the corn spirit's daughter."

"It has a name. I call it Eva."

Her tone was very strange. Dick said, with an unnatural smile:

"I thought you didn't like Eva."

Marie picked up the clasp-knife which lay opened on the table and dangled the doll in front of him with the knife-point at its throat.

"This doll is no good," she said. "This doll is a thief. She has taken something that belongs to me." She stabbed the knife through the corn-husk body.

"What sort of bad medicine is that?" Dick exclaimed angrily. "I thought even Winnebagos would be ashamed of such foolishness."

Marie's lips quivered. She turned away with tear-filled eyes.

"Besides," he added gently, "what you said was not true."

"It was not true?"

"No. Have I ever lied to you?"

She took his hands and held them palms upward a moment and then released them. The next day at noon she brought him two dolls instead of one. They were man and woman tied firmly together with twine.

"This is much better," he said.

6

I N THE WINTER, Marie bore a son. In one corner of
the room she had fashioned a sort of shelter after
some memory of the "birth-lodge." It was made of
quilts and rugs hung from the rafters and inside it she
had collected a few treasures. The blue bonnet hung
above the bed. It was bitter cold outside but the fire
in the hearth was roaring and the stove-fire was burning too, with a kettle of water steaming on the griddle.

"It begins," Marie said. "Keep the fires going." She
went simply to the screen of quilts and disappeared.

"I'll go for Signe," Dick said.

"Not yet. I'll tell you when to go."

He walked about the room nervously, consulted his
watch several times and threw unneeded wood on the
fire.

"I'd better go, Marie."

"All right." She put one hand through an opening
and he held it. It was warmer than his own and quite
steady. He got into his outdoor clothing and set out
for the farmhouse. A light was burning in the window

and when he knocked, Signe answered at once. She was warmly dressed and wore boots.

"How did you know?" Dick asked.

"Oh, inside me I know. I say to Ole, 'It will be to-night.'"

When they reached the cabin Signe threw off her wraps at once and dove behind the screen. Dick heard Marie's labored sighing and felt wretchedly helpless. He sat down on the bench by the fire. As far as any part in the birth was concerned, he might have been a stranger, he thought. What queer fate decides a child's inheritance! Blood of Derbyshire peasants and French trappers was about to flow, mingled, in the veins of a living creature, and toward that event the matings of all the centuries before had pointed. What is a father? Only one more link in the endless chain. A vision of the value of human life came clearly before Dick's mind as he sat on the rough bench with his head in his hands. Into every new life come the converging lines of the thousands who have died; out of it go the diverging lines of the thousands to be born. He made a humble resolution that this child should not be born in vain. With his utmost effort he would cherish and protect it.

Out of the heavy stillness he heard a strange sound. It was like the mewing of a hungry kitten.

"She's sleeping now," Signe said, her kindly face seamed and tired. "You got a fine boy. It aint snowing any more. I can get home now."

He thanked her and let her go. Tiptoeing to the blankets he looked in. Beside Marie, a candle was burning on an upturned bucket. She lay exhausted, her head thrown back on the pillow, her hair dank with sweat. In the curve of one arm she held a tiny bundle, the swaddled baby, its head coal-black in the candle-light, its crumpled face fiery red. Dick stood looking at it a long while, disturbed at the lack of fatherly love in his heart. At last he blew out the candle and went back to his place by the fire. There he fell asleep too, fully dressed and sitting upright, his head against the stones of the fireplace, his hands hanging between his knees.

When he woke, cramped and cold, the light was beginning to break. He built the fire again and went back to the bed. Marie was lying wide awake; she had smoothed the covers and braided her hair. He sat down beside her. In the half-dark he could barely see her face with its calm, smiling lips. More than ever he felt the barrier between them, the veil through which he could not intrude.

"How do you feel?" he asked awkwardly.

"All right. I slept."

"I know. You were brave, Marie."

"Brave?" she said, as if she hardly knew what the word meant. "Did you look at him?"

"Yes. While you were asleep."

"Take him to the window. It's too dark here. Tell me how he looks."

Dick saw that she wanted him to hold his child, so he

351

put unaccustomed hands under the small body which barely filled his two palms.

The morning light from the window fell full on the tiny face. He felt a reeling shock as if he had been struck with a club. Beady eyes, high cheek-bones, straight, thick hair, the child bore the strongest possible resemblance to Joe Sobish. There could be no mistake. Later the likeness might be softened, but now only one parent seemed represented—the father. The baby might have been a full-blood papoose. Dick stood, turned to stone, barely able to refrain from dashing his burden to the dirt floor.

"What is it?" Marie asked, weakly.

For answer he returned, and speechless, laid the child on the bed. She rose on one elbow and gazed down at it.

"Ah!" she hissed as if she had touched a snake. She fell back on her pillow. "Kill him," she said.

"No, Marie! No!" The impulse seized him to leave them both and dash out into the world he had lost. Unjustly, he blamed the woman beside him for everything, the poverty, the exile, the unwanted child. Lucy! Once he had been in love with Lucy. The clean streets and orderly houses of Madison flashed before his memory and he winced. Here he stood, dressed in rags a beggar would scorn. Here was his house, with its dirt floor and crude furnishings, here his wife, with her half-breed child. Why not go, walk away, never come back?

Who could hold him now? They would live somehow.
Ole would take care of them.

A sound escaped Marie's pale lips. He turned un-
willingly and looked at her and in a moment everything was changed. Whatever his suffering might be,
hers was greater. He stroked her hand.

"Are you hungry? Can you eat some porridge?"

"I don't want to eat. Let me die."

"Nonsense." He went to the stove and began to stir
oatmeal into a pot of water. Later he would take up his
unhappiness. Now he must lay it down. They must eat,
be warmed, even sleep. Life must go on.

In front of the cabin, the hill sloped away to the
creek's steep valley. Little patches of Indian paint-
brush, skunk cabbage, wild phlox and purple asters
colored the gray shale and limestone, but there was a
tiny green lawn at the door where the wash water had
encouraged grass to grow. Marie often sat on this green
square as summer came and passed, holding the swarthy
child in her arms. Several weeks after his birth she had
asked Dick, timidly,

"May I call him Jules?"

"I don't care."

"Jules Gagnier. That's for my father."

"All right."

It was nothing to Dick what she called her child. He
had enough to do to keep from rushing out of the house
when she nursed the dark-skinned creature at her white

breast. His heart beat sickeningly at the sight. He would turn his head and pretend indifference, but what he felt was the most violent emotion he had ever known. He supposed it to be jealousy and was properly ashamed when it left him. Surely he had known her past when he took her. Nothing had changed since then. She was blameless, innocent, more a victim than he. Yet he had the impulse to murder, and wrestled with it, silent and remorseful.

Nature had come to the rescue of Marie and Jules. She loved her child. In his first months of life she tried to hide her love, playing with him only when Dick was away, but as the baby began to talk with meaningless words, to follow her about with his eyes, she found it harder and harder not to respond.

"You needn't do that," Dick said.

"Do what? I don't understand."

"Yes, you do. Pick him up. Talk to him. I don't care."

Obediently she took Jules out on the slope where Dick heard her singing a Winnebago song. He set himself the bitter task of making a bed-rail for the child's cot. Soon Jules would be trying to crawl out of bed. Dick whittled the rails with his pocket-knife and smoothed them with a piece of rough sandstone, doing penance for his hatred by making every part perfect.

Physical labor was like an anodyne. If he let himself be idle he began to suffer, to drift too far on a black tide of unhappiness. He seldom looked in a mirror in these days, but when he did he was face to face with a stranger. Stern and haggard, heavily bearded, he could have walked unrecognized across Hampstead Prairie.

Sometimes he remembered his final conversation with Ben Weymouth. "Thy father called down the wrath of God . . ." How often he had heard his father's pet curse:

"Thou shalt build a house and shalt not dwell therein; thou shalt plant a vineyard and shalt not gather the grapes thereof."

The curse had come upon him, and he could bear witness to its harshness.

And this exile into which he had rushed so hastily was not a temporary thing. It was forever, even unto death. When Marie appeared in the farmyard, carrying Jules pick-a-back, the look on Ole's face told Dick what he might expect in the outside world. If the simple Norwegians pitied him, what would less kindly people think? He could imagine what Ole's family were saying in the evenings, nodding in their kindly fashion:

"Ja, these things happen. Ak, what a pity!"

As for Eva, she looked more than ever like a brown fawn, hovering in the background always, uncertain and sad, afraid to meet his eyes. She seemed to be puzzling, trying to decide what had gone wrong and who was to blame. Chris was the only comfort. He noticed nothing amiss.

355

The saying goes that time softens all hurts. It is not time alone that comes to our aid, but the events which pass almost unnoticed, like ripples in a great sea, each one doing its part to knock the sharp stones together and make them into smoothly rounded pebbles or silken sand. Something occurs, something quite unexpected and irrelevant, and when it is over, the pain, re-examined, has lost its former power.

In April Dick saw a woman, standing by the cattle-yard. She looked like a scarecrow, with her matted hair, her long nose and almost toothless smile.

"Hallo!" Dick said. She stirred, twitched her skirts so that the rags fluttered, and pointed up at the hill where Dagmar's empty cabin stood. Ole came up to her.

"Holla! What you want?" She shook her head and pointed.

Signe was baking in the outdoor oven. She took out a loaf of brown bread, wrapped it in a towel and gave it to the tattered stranger, who bowed repeatedly, still pointing at the hill. They looked again, and saw a thread of smoke rising from Dagmar's chimney.

"Nuvel!" Ole exclaimed. "Somebody got into that house already. I like to know who."

"Chris, Eva!" his wife called, *"Komme her!* People in Dagmar's house."

The scarecrow woman danced about, delighted that they understood.

"Don't you know her, moder?" Eva asked. "She's

356

that Katerina, who lived in a hole in the hill. We used to see her when we went to Little Chimney."

"Somebody got to go up to Dagmar's with her, then. She's got in the box and got Dagmar's things all out by now, I bet."

Ole drew Dick to one side.

"That's the one got mixed up with the Yanceys down hill. That's terrible thing for happen, Deek. Long time those Yanceys got to have children all by themselves so other people don't get no bad blood into them. Up at Little Chimney they drove her out with sticks and stones and now she got into Dagmar's and had her baby, it look like."

Dick, Chris and Eva were sent up the hill to sort and bring back Dagmar's possessions.

"I know all about her," Chris said as they went along. "They smoked her out like a gopher."

"Why, then?"

"She's got a baby coming and no man."

"Fie, for shame!" Eva looked at Dick and blushed furiously. "You know a lot that aint so," she told her brother with crushing scorn.

The tattered woman ran nimbly on ahead and the walk to Dagmar's was shorter than usual. Someone had pried the hinges off the kitchen door, leaving the lock intact and setting the door ajar from the wrong side. Katerina slipped through and they followed.

Above Dagmar's four-poster hung a great red-and-

357

blue picture of the sorrowing Christ, his hands pierced with nails, his head heavy with thorns, his blood falling in drops as large as cherries. It was the only possession Katerina had brought with her, that and the twin babies who lay in the bed.

"Ak! Look at the *twillinger!*" Eva cried, clasping her hands. "Oh, Deek! Aint they lovely?"

The twins were hardly a week old. They lay, swathed in rags, their tiny fists curled above their heads. They were sound asleep. Their mother looked at them and laughed, an excited cackle. She had not wanted help or even food. She had felt the universal need of a mother— someone to admire her children. She turned her ruined face to first one, then another of her guests, wanting more admiration, unable to get enough.

"It's all right for you, Eva, but how about me?" Chris lamented. "Now I got to bring back Dagmar's cow. They got to have milk, aint they? Three hours it took to get that dumb *esel* down the hill. Now I got to get her up."

"Maybe she didn't want to leave home. Back up will be easier."

Dick observed that Katerina was to be given house, cow and land with no question of ownership. Her twins were her triumph. Eva bent above the bed examining them. The Yancey taint was not apparent. Katerina had broken the spell, perhaps.

"That's a fine thing that happened to poor Katerina," Eva sighed enviously on the way home. "Maybe she aint

got so much else. But she got good luck to have twins,
all right."

When Dick came home to his cabin he felt a little
less bitter.

The crib was finished. Now he began to make other
things for Jules . . . a wooden teething-ring, a bird with
a whistle in its tail. It gave him something to do. While
he whittled he need not look up and see Marie tending
her child. Months slipped away. Jules was trying to sit
up, but Dick had never spoken to him or touched him.
He began to make a high chair, working evenings, tight-
lipped and grim. Marie watched him always, but seldom
spoke.

Finally the chair was done. He set it in the middle of
the room and went to the barn. When he came back
at noon Jules was in the chair, his fat legs straight out
in front of him, his fat fists pounding on the shelf. Dick
glanced at him from lowered lids, hating him still, but
less than before. After a few minutes he went to the
chair and pretended to examine it. The baby seized his
finger and squealed with pleasure.

Dick's impulse was to pull away, but he did not, and
a warmth began to creep through him from the contact
with the child's soft hand. He felt as if his heart had
been frozen and was thawing, painfully, but hopefully
too. Poor little Jules, so small, so helpless! Why blame
him for being born? And he thought of an unwanted
puppy he had seen thrown in a pond, swimming gal-

lantly toward shore. Was Jules of less value than a mongrel puppy?

In the Indian camps there had been children of doubtful parentage, wearing the look of their French, Irish or Scotch fathers and the copper skin of their mothers. They had been known as Chippewa, Potawotami, Menominee or Winnebago and lovingly reared. All life belonged to the Earthmaker, the Indians said. They proudly cared for His children. White men usually ignored such offspring, or half acknowledged them.

This was the child of Joe Sobish, but it was also the great grandson of White Crow, an honored friend. Dick looked down at Jules and saw how the joints of his brown body were lost in the deep creases of fat, how his knuckles, elbows and knees were dimples, his eyes almond-shaped and black, his mouth and nose as round as buttons. The baby was trying to put Dick's finger into his mouth. Dick smiled and resisted. When he glanced up again he met Marie's adoring gaze. She stood with clasped hands, her pearly face uplifted to the entering sunlight, like a statue of Saint Anne before the Holy Child. He was stirred and troubled. How could he take a love so complete?

"Well," he said cheerfully, "I think I'll make high chairs for a living. This one isn't half bad."

That night the moon was full. It shone across the slope in front of the cabin, softening the rock's outlines, making everything more beautiful after the strange fashion of moonlight. Dick sat at the window, looking out, remembering the years when he had hoped to marry Lucy. How long ago it seemed! Profoundly happy he had been, that night in his father's kitchen when he had looked out at the moon. That dream was illusory like the moonlight, lovely, but unreal. It had never been meant to come true, any more than the iron pot outside on the slope had been meant to have a rim of charcoal and silver and a subtle, shadowy form. In daylight the big rusty kettle might not be beautiful, but at least it was real. It could be swung over the fire with a mess of beans in it. If only it need not be ugly!

What is reality? Perhaps daylight is no more truthful than the light of the moon and man might play a trick on his misfortunes by seeing them always in a light that makes them lovely.

"Marie," he said, "did you know that some colors show in the moonlight?"

She came and sat beside him, near, but always apart.

"Yes. I know that. Sometimes I've seen the leaves when they were changing. Even at night some were yellow and some green."

"The red blanket, out there on the line, isn't red to-night, though."

"Oh, yes. It's red."

"But it doesn't look red."

"Our eyes can't see it."

"Well, suppose we were always in moonlight. Would the blanket be red?"

"Someone would know it was red."

"You mean God, I suppose. Do you believe in a God who knows everything, who sits outside the world and looks in at us?"

She fingered her rosary with downcast eyes.

"No, I don't think he knows everything. The sisters thought so, but the Winnebagos didn't. Sometimes he made mistakes, just like men."

"At least they seemed to be mistakes."

"Well, you know, he might be a rain or he might be sunshine. Sometimes he was a little squirrel. What was good for the Winnebago was bad for the Fox and how was Earthmaker to tell?"

"If God doesn't know the blanket is red, how can we be sure, Marie?"

"The truth is somewhere."

"You were hunting for the truth, weren't you, when you ran away from Saint Clara? Where did you go?"

Marie's eyes veiled themselves and her features became immobile.

"Never mind. You needn't tell me."

She seemed to struggle with herself. At last she said in a low voice: "Joe was my brother in White Crow's camp. I thought it would be like that."

"Why didn't you leave him?"

"He was my husband. I promised the priest not to leave him."

"When men are drunk and cruel, their wives should break their promises."

"I never heard of a woman doing that," she said, scornfully.

Dick thought that any priest who would marry an innocent girl to Joe Sobish should be defrocked. It was another instance of the French complaisance toward mixed marriage, born of the fur-trading days. A Frenchman with an Indian wife had been able to drive a sharper bargain for furs and so one overlooked the frequent tragic mistakes, the half-breed children, the desertions. The Hudson Bay Company with its million-dollar investment was all-important, even to the priesthood.

"I didn't stay until he was buried," Marie said, as if speaking to herself.

"My father would see to that."

"Yes. Your father is a great man, Dick."

He thought that of all the women he had known, Marie had the least vanity. The way his father had treated her had no effect on her estimate of his character. Dick looked at her pale face with its purity of outline and wondered from what mediaeval ancestor she inherited her features, which might have set men to duelling in the Renaissance. Again his heart was wrenched with pity.

"I wish I could take you back with me—give you something better," he muttered.

"I have everything I want."

"Don't you want new gowns, a nicer house?"

"This house is all right. Don't you remember? We were warm all winter."

"But the hard times must be over out there. I could get work."

"I want your child to be born in this house."

The lake on the hilltop was called Summit Pool by the people of Little Chimney. It drained out through a crevice in the cliff to form the rapid-flowing Evasvand, but its own surface was as still as if it had no outlet. Birch leaves floated to rest on its clear water and flies left a feathered wake as they skimmed over. Here Dick and Marie sat on an October day, surrounded by the leathery yellow leaves, holding home-made fishing poles. Jules had ridden up the cliff on Dick's back and lay asleep in the shade.

Here was a universe tiny and complete. The autumn haze gave a look of enchantment to everything. It might have been the country at the top of Jack's beanstalk, Dick said, and Marie asked,

"Was that the same as the Manido land?"

"I don't know. Tell me your story."

"In the old days there was a little boy who had a dream. In the dream the Manido came to him and told him to hunt out the tallest tree in the forest and climb it. When he woke he did as he had been told, but he climbed for three days and did not reach the top. He had taken a little bag of pemmican and it was almost gone and he was afraid. Then he smelled the deer-meat they were cooking in the sky-country and pretty soon he was in the Manido land at the top of the tree. There were cruel spirits in the Manido country. Some of them looked like men, but they were very tall. They had small heads and long arms. When the little boy saw them he knew he must hide or they would eat him. He hid under the kettle of deer-meat, but the fire did not harm him because he was obeying a dream. The tall men looked for him everywhere but they never thought to look in the fire, so when they had given up he climbed down the tree and went back to his mother."

Before Dick could tell the beanstalk tale, Jules began to cry. Marie got up and went to comfort him, and while she was away the sound of falling stone and slipping shoe-soles called Dick's attention to the other side of the lake. A wizened man had clambered down the bank there, and was impaling a frog on his hook. He threw out a line in a manner which betokened long practice and gradually worked his way around the little pool to Dick's side. Passing near the trees where Marie was tending her child, he paused, stared, took off his knitted cap and scratched his head.

"Aint thet Joe's Mary?" he whispered, peering into Dick's face a moment later.

"That's my wife," Dick answered, shortly.

"Lord help ye," the old fellow said and moved away. Soon he came back.

"So ye married her, eh? Well ye've picked up something hot."

His face, withered and weathered to the complexion of a dried plum, had yet something familiar.

"Lem Shotwell!" Dick said aloud, but uncertainly. Lem rubbed his eyes as if to clear a clouded vision.

"I be a ring-tail bob-cat if it aint little Dicky Wentworth! Lord, ye've changed, boy. But I know ye."

"You've changed too, Lem."

"I've been in a institootion, thet's where I've been. Sick in the head. I'm right as rain now, though."

Dick doubted it. Afterward, when he thought over the old fellow's words, he realized that he had been warned.

7

EVERYTHING WAS READY for another winter. The hams hung in the log smokehouse, turning in the hickory smoke. The sausage was in a bucket, far down in the well. Side-pork in barrels of brine filled a dark corner of the cellar. The cider, fermenting in its kegs, smelt of hops. The corn-crib was bulging with yellow ears, the hay in three gently rounded mows had already felt the first fall rain. Frost had blackened the pumpkin vines, but now, when it was least expected, a week of summer weather arrived. It made Dick restless, knowing that it could not last. He walked away from the barns in mid-morning and instead of taking the usual path home, he turned off where the road branched toward Freedom, following a natural cleft in the cliff.

Freedom! The name of the town seemed symbolic. Outside the hills there was liberty, life, adventure. What spell was on him that he no longer wanted these things? Once he had felt hemmed in by the hills; now they seemed like a mother's arms, enfolding him, pro-

tecting him against intolerable injustice and pain. Once
he had longed for the companionship of other men.
Human beings had seemed all that made the world
worth living in. Now he saw, or thought he saw, that
nature is good but men are essentially cruel. To struggle
with darkness, cold, hunger and thirst was wholesome
even when one lost. To be buffeted by one's fellows was
another thing. Dick was content to stay in the hills; he
was satisfied with his diet of locusts and wild honey.

From the rocky gateway he could see the road on
a series of summits until it melted into the horizon five
miles away. A short five miles, because half of it was in
the deep valleys out of sight. On one of the farthest
hills a moving dark speck appeared to be a horseman,
riding toward the farm. Dick was not sure, and while
he waited for the speck to appear again out of the valley
into which it had descended, he had an odd premonition
of something personal about to occur, that the horseman, the moving dot, or whatever it was, had something to do with his own life. He counted four hundred,
and the speck appeared on a nearer hill, disappeared
into a nearer valley. The next time he could distinguish
the rider from the steed. The man was tall and rode
bareheaded; at least his head seemed to shine in the
sunlight.

Like a bobbing cork on a wave, the horse and rider
kept disappearing and coming up again. Dick's hand
went to his forehead, shutting out the sun. He stared
from beneath his hand at the man, whose purposeful

forward slant in the saddle reminded him of someone as close to him as his own childhood. Who rode that way? Only Harry! Tall, blond, dynamic as an arrow against a bowstring, it must be his brother. It could be no one else.

Dick walked into the middle of the road with wildly beating heart. At the first touch of his past his contentment had crumbled. His brother came up over the final rise, saw him, reined up, doubtfully. Then he jumped down and seized Dick by the elbows.

"I thought I'd never find you."

"Harry, old lad."

They stood looking at one another. Harry's hair was prematurely silvered, his jaw prematurely stern. His clothing spoke of success. The very way he grasped his crop in a strong, clean hand, suggested the surgeon. Through narrowed blue eyes he scrutinized his brother, who drooped before him in his worn overalls.

"Some of the Norwegians got word of you down there. Gunnar Larson came up with me as far as Freedom. From then on I've inquired of everyone I passed."

(Eva or Signe had written their cousins. Of course! How could he have thought himself hidden?)

"Well, you've found me. I don't know what good it'll do you," he said, bitterly.

"I'm to bring you home."

"Tie your horse and sit down. I can't go home and you know it."

"We'll come to that later, then. I have some news for

you. It might make a difference. Dick, they tell me you have a child here that isn't your own."

Anger surged through Dick. Someone had betrayed him, indeed. He said with motionless lips:

"That's true enough."

"What possessed you, Dick?"

Dick made no answer. He was seeing himself now with another man's eyes and wondering with another man's wonder at all he had done.

"One thing's obvious. You must pull yourself out before it's too late. Nothing's happened that can't be undone. A few more years might ruin you, lad, but come out of it now and you'll forget."

"Forget! Harry, I'm married to Marie. There's no forgetting a wife."

"No, my poor lad. You're not married to her, and that's what I came to tell you. The Indian didn't die. One bullet went through below the collar-bone, they say—probably nicked the left subclavian artery but didn't sever it, the other stunned him by grazing the skull. I'm sorry, Dick. They ought to have told you this a long time ago, but you'd disappeared."

"It doesn't matter," Dick muttered, but the news had struck him with terrific force, nevertheless. "It doesn't make any difference. I have to take care of her."

"Buy her off."

"Don't talk nonsense!"

"Look here, Dick. The child belongs to that fellow.

You can't hold it. And the mother won't abandon it. What can you do? Legally, you've no rights."

"Then she must get a divorce."

Harry looked at his brother as if he thought him deranged.

"Lad," he said, gently and reasonably, "there's nothing to keep you here. You ought to see yourself. You've lost fifteen pounds. You look ten years older. I wouldn't have known you if I hadn't been looking for you. Come! Take hold of your life and save yourself."

"I'm all right. Until you came I was happy enough."

"So's a drunkard till he's sober. Look, Dick. This is no life for you. Think what you were. You could have had anything. If you go back you'll think of this time as a sort of sickness. You can begin all over again. You never appreciated yourself, lad, but you've got rare gifts. Will you throw life away for this woman, this child that's not your own?"

"The next child will be."

"My God! I believe you *are* crazy."

"Leave me alone," Dick groaned. He thought with anguish of the life he had left, though he had renounced it so easily an hour before. Youth, hope, all the good things of the world! Harry had brought their flavor into the bare hill country and shattered his peace.

"I can't leave her," he said, more steadily. "Go back and forget me, Harry. I've made my choice."

His brother took a letter from his pocket and silently

371

pressed it into Dick's hand. It was a square envelope, sealed with the initial L. It had been lying at Hampstead Prairie undelivered for a year.

"By this time," Lucy wrote, "you must know of our tragedy. Such an overthrow of all my ideals makes vanity disappear, and it is only pride, Dick, that has come between us. Probably you have adjusted yourself and no longer think of me, but it will relieve my mind to tell you what course my reasoning took. Then forgive me, even if you must forget me.

"At first I thought it could do no harm if I planned our meetings and tried in every way to force an engagement. You were inexperienced and I was a woman, or so I believed. Then I found out what every woman should know, that the man should be the hunter. I tried to change. You know what happened better than I. When I retreated, so did you.

"Perhaps I am doing wrong to write you now, but bear with me, Dick. My life, which started so happily, is in ruins. I have always loved you. No other marriage is possible for me, even now."

Dick sat so long without moving that his brother stirred uneasily and turned toward him.

"I don't know whether you heard about the Colonel?"

"No. What. . . ."

"He shot a woman, and then himself. Double suicide, the papers called it, sparing the family. She was prominent in Washington and the affair had been going on for years. His widow and daughter came home to Madison."

He saw with clear eyes the squalor of the cabin, the simple ignorance of this woman who was not his wife. He saw the little half-breed in his soiled dress crawling on the dirt floor, the unwashed kettles, the bucket of peelings and coffee grounds, Marie, with her fair braids in disorder, trying to clean the house, heavy with his unborn child. He found a mirror and shaved off his beard, hoping to read in the gaunt face beneath the answer to his problem. His dark eyes looked back at him from the glass, steadfast and sad. There was no way out. He must not even tell Marie that Joe still lived, but stay in the hills and keep his secret. Her vows had been sacred to her. "I never knew a woman who left her husband," she had said with scorn.

He spent the evening in making a wooden water-wheel for Jules. It ran in a bit of lead rain-trough, whirling when the trough was tipped back and forth. Jules sat on his fat little haunches, enchanted by the new toy.

How could he have been so blind? Now that he had learned from Marie what a woman's pride could be, he wondered at himself for not seeing that all Lucy's pretended indifference had been caused by suffering. She talked about abolition because she could not talk about love. She did not urge him to come to Washington because she feared she had already been too forward. She was only giving him a chance to prove his love and he, poor fool, had let her go!

"Go, go!" Little Jules said, edging nearer on the floor and pointing to the water wheel. He seemed to be echoing Dick's thoughts.

The whole affair of the Drake yacht might have been nothing but a ruse to allow him his freedom if he wanted it. Yes, and then her mother had tried to force it to a conclusion by letting it get into the papers. And Lucy, with that gentle strength he knew so well, had resisted, even though she had nothing to put in the place of such a marriage, though her first love had failed her. He remembered vividly that day when he had come back to Madison, burning with eagerness, and found her cold, distant, planning to go away. Even then it had been a sham, her coldness. She had been hurt because he had stayed away all summer, uncertain whether she had forced an engagement he was not ready to make. How quickly she had melted in those last days—the last they had ever known together!

"Go, please!" Jules said, taking his thumb out of his mouth and seizing Dick's hand in a wet little paw.

Slowly Dick began to tip the trough back and forth and the wheel spun around. Jules squealed with pleasure. Marie looked up, smiling, from some garments she was making for the second child.

When Amy was born, a foretaste of spring was already in the air. The months of waiting, shut in by winter, had seemed interminably long. Now the cliff swallows were loud in the birch grove and a few robins had appeared. In the disheveled bed, Marie lay wanly with blue eyelids and fluttering pulse while Signe bent over her applying hot cloths to break her chill. Dick seemed almost oblivious of her weakness. He stood at the window, holding his daughter, turning her gently to look at her face. Something of his mother was there, in the tiny features, the broad forehead and black hair. How small she was! Yet she changed his whole life. Amy! *To be loved*. Marie had wanted to call her for her own mother and it suited his feeling exactly. To be loved, to be cherished. At last he had something of his own.

"She aint so gude," Signe sighed, straightening. Marie was asleep.

"Shall I get a doctor from Freedom?"

"Nei, it's too far. Doctors, pfui! What do they know? I sit here myself."

He went to the barns for his morning chores, and though he should have been anxious, his heart persisted in rejoicing because his child was born. The gap between the old life and the present was less wide, now that by his own act he had given a new immortality to his father's line. Mysterious and sweet revenge! The woman his father had thrown out into the night was now the mother of Amy Wentworth, whose eyes would be like Ann's. And yet there was no room in Dick's mind for thoughts of revenge, but only that his father was Amy's grandfather . . . and hope, and resolutions toward a better future. The milk, drumming in the pail kept up a triumphant rhythm. Yes, now he must go back. He must break the situation to his will. Amy must have a chance to live and advantages he had never known.

"It isn't a son," Marie said, weakly. "I'm sorry about that."

"I don't care. I wanted a girl."

"She looks like you, I think."

"A little. Too bad she hasn't your hair."

"No." Marie's eyes deepened in protest. "I wouldn't want that."

The absorbing new interest swept spring into summer. Amy began to make cooing sounds, to sit up in her crib. She seemed to her father to be a most remarkable child in every way. He forgot Marie, forgot Jules, who leaned stolidly against his knee, comforting himself with his thumb. He could not believe his good fortune.

"This gown isn't clean," he said, critically. "We must always keep Amy clean."

"You didn't care about Jules."

"Jules is a boy." (And a little Winnebago boy at that. Lovable and patient, to be sure, but not to be thought of as in the same class as Amy.)

376

"Marie, I think we should have the baby christened."

"I thought you didn't believe in church."

"Well, it's a custom, you know. Maybe it would be better."

"Shall we go in to Freedom . . . to the church in there? We can't climb the cliff to Little Chimney."

"We could borrow Ole's cart and go around the other way. There's a road to Little Chimney from out-side."

"All right."

On the following Sunday when he came back from milking he found that Marie had remembered. Amy was dressed in the christening gown that had been Eva's. Beside her crib, in a suit made from Marie's red blanket, was Jules. Marie shone with pride in her children.

"Jules can be christened too! It will save us another trip. Don't they look nice together?"

Dick's heart turned over with a sick thump. He stood gazing down at his beautiful pink and white daughter, who reached one hand through the bars of her crib-rail to hold the dark fingers of her half-brother, Joe Sobish's son.

"Marie, I think. . . ."

"What is it? Don't you like his coat? It's too warm, but we can be back before noon."

"Do you care if we don't go? I think Ole needs the horses. Anyway, I've rather changed my mind."

Marie folded her arms on her breast. For a moment

the illusion was strong in him that she was actually turning to a marble statue, mild, impassive, with no thoughts or emotions, yet he knew she had read repugnance in his face and he was desperately ashamed and sorry. He had dealt her another wound, and she so little deserved to be hurt. He took savage hold of his unworthy pride.

"Shall we christen them ourselves? Jules is a Winnebago. What would White Crow have liked us to do?"

"Sometimes they gave an old man tobacco, and he named the child after a dream."

Marie's voice, soft, slurring and casual, gave no evidence of the fact that she was trembling. She went on:

"When the Winnebagos took me, my sister, Cloudy Sky, was just born. They laid the baby on the old man's knees and put some tobacco in his hand."

"Well, we haven't either an old man or tobacco. Come here, Marie."

She stood beside him and he held her tapering fingers in one hand and laid the other on the black crown of Little Jules' head.

"Great Spirit, who made us French, Winnebago and English, we promise to cherish and rear your child, Jules Gagnier Wentworth."

On his own surname his voice faltered. He had remembered what had been thrust into the back of his mind for nearly a year. Marie was not his wife. The real father of Jules lived somewhere, and while he lived no one could safely promise to cherish and rear his son. Marie, knowing neither of these things, was happy. She lifted Amy from her bed.

"Amy too."

". . . And your child, Amy Wentworth, to give them both healthy bodies and minds if we are able to do so."

Marie, clasping the little girl to her bosom, devoured him with worshipful eyes. It was evident that the simple ritual satisfied her—that her husband had taken on certain attributes of priesthood in her thoughts. Dick, himself, felt content to have addressed his ceremony directly to Earthmaker without the intercession of Catholic or Methodist medicine men. Moreover a subtle change came into his feeling for Jules, now that he had voluntarily given him his name. The use of ritual became clear in his mind. It served a purpose, but only because of man's weakness. The marriage vows, for instance, cast their weight in the balance against wantonness, and the "dust to dust" of the funeral service laid the ghost of sorrow. So, because his vow had been made aloud, he truly meant to cherish the son of Joe Sobish.

"I got something to ask you, Deek," Eva said a few weeks later. The barrier of shyness which had come between them at Jules' birth seemed to have lifted again with Amy's advent. "I want you to tell me, is that *Gunnar* here? The one I danced with at Alma's wedding?"

"Yes. I heard he was in Freedom, but I don't know how we can find him."

He had told no one of Harry's visit. He saw the puzzled look in Eva's eyes, as if she wondered how he could have gotten news from the world outside, but he ignored it and went on:

"Maybe your cousin would know how to find him for you."

"I don't tell Alma everything."

"Oh. I thought you did."

Eva attempted to meet his accusing eyes, gave up the struggle and looked down at her feet.

"I'm sorry about that, Deek. I been sorry a long time I told Alma that."

"It's no matter. Some day I must go back anyway, and then everyone will know."

"I thought *she* played a trick on you. I thought, if I told where you was, someone would come and get you and take you away from *her*. I like you so good, Deek, and she aint nice enough." The girl's breast heaved in half-sobbing sighs. Her face was fiery with blushes.

"If I find Gunnar, what shall I tell him?" Dick asked quickly.

"Tell him if he wants to get a farm he could look at Dagmar's. Katerina, she took her *twillinger* and went to Yancey's."

"Why did she do that?"

"You know, those poor babies aint right. They can't make any sound with their mouths only a croak like a

380

frog and they don't hear, not even when a gun goes
off. They'll be dumbies, it look like."

He promised to keep his eyes open for Gunnar on
the streets of the frontier town. He had made other
promises. Ole wanted to know the name of the best
candidate for President of the United States.

"You ask questions, Deek. I like to know who to
vote for in November. We don't want a foreigner like
last time."

"I'll do my best, Ole." Dick had said.

The yellow pine buildings of Freedom included a
printing office where a crude weekly news sheet was pub-
lished. A group of farmers were standing outside the
shop, holding freshly printed papers and struggling with
the blurred type and their own lack of learning. They
stopped Dick, accepting him as one of their own sort.

"Can you make sense of these here pothooks?"

He took the page and read aloud: "The choice of
the Republican Party is Abraham Lincoln of Illinois."

Was it only yesterday he had heard Lucy's clear voice
discussing the Springfield lawyer?

"He seems sincere, Dick, but he's weak. His attitude
on abolition is only a compromise. My father says he's
an able orator, though. He heard him talk in Peoria
and was much moved."

He pulled himself back to the present by a supreme
effort. The men around him had been impressed by his
ability to read. They were waiting. He handed back the
Freedom Press to the man who had given it to him.

"Well," he said, "Abraham Lincoln's a moderate man, not a wild one. He's been poor and ragged like you and me. I think we'd be safe with him."

He left a note in the post office, addressed to Gunnar in care of general delivery. As he did so he was conscious of an unanalyzed wretchedness, a strong wish that Gunnar should never call for his mail, that Dagmar's house and farm should remain empty rather than house the man who had lived in his father's kitchen. But he released the envelope, nevertheless. It dropped irretrievably through the slot. A farm for Gunnar. A possible husband for Eva. These were fundamental needs, more important than any abstract considerations of pride.

As he rode homeward he faced the sunset. The October wind was chilly, the birch leaves falling about him made the road yellow. Another year was passing. On a nearby hill he heard the howling of wolves and saw the trees of a Sioux burial-ground bent sidewise in the gale, spilling their burdens of ragged blankets, crumbling bones and burial offerings to the ground beneath. Against the red sky the branches with their dreadful bundles stood out in silhouette and it seemed to Dick that another dead man had been added to the eerie village. Yes, that would account for the wolves. Some of the Sioux had come back to leave an old man with his people on the hill. Because he had once climbed to

382

the top of that hill, Dick knew how time would do its work. The bright blanket, tightly trussed around the body, would slowly weather and fade. The ropes would burst, the head or hands emerge. In five years, or at the most ten, the bones would begin to fall. The skull, framework of the beloved face, would roll down the slope and lodge against the underbrush. What is pride?

In the cabin door, Marie held Amy up to the last rays of the sun.

"South Wind," she said, in the effortless, nasal voice she used for her children, "South Wind, come back. Your child is getting cold."

In November, Abraham Lincoln was chosen by the people of the United States as their sixteenth president. Ole would not go in to vote.

"I tell you, Dick, I don't know enough about him. Maybe the country get into trouble, and then I've voted wrong and I don't have no peace. Next time I find out more about who to vote for."

Dick drove twelve miles and made his cross on the ballot. He counted five of the Yanceys at the polls—the two aged half-wits among them. It seemed to him that his vote, uninformed though it might be, was as good as theirs.

As he came out of the polling-place, he felt a touch on his arm and turned to look into the smiling gray eyes of Gunnar Larson.

"Well, Gunnar!" he exclaimed, and realized that he had been quite mistaken about his feelings. He was glad to see the tall, cheerful fellow. Very glad.

"Holla, Dick. I got your letter all right, but you must have put down the road wrong. I been trying two weeks and aint found it yet. You say there's a farm nobody want up there?"

"Not much of a farm, but there's a house and some fields. Maybe eight acres of plowing—on a high hill."

"That's a fine thing. I don't want no plowing anyhow. I'm going to raise sheep."

"Too many wolves," said Dick.

"Oh, so? Then I raise some these long-horned cows."

Dick counseled him on the road problem and started back. No use taking a farm until spring, Gunnar said. He had a snug room over a stable in Freedom. Meanwhile he sent his greetings to Eva Oesterdahl, whose memory still made his cheek tingle.

The wind had changed into the north and was full of a driving rain, half-frozen into sleet. Dick pulled his hat low over his ears and wrapped himself in the laprobe. Around him the dead oak leaves blew in the rain, settling into the cart on top of the sack of flour, box of nails and barrel of sugar. The wind was becoming a gale, colder and colder, and ice was forming on the tree-trunks. Dick got down behind the dash-board but the whirling gusts of sleet attacked him from the rear. He thought with real longing of the warm cabin and his supper of corn-meal mush and milk. Would Marie be able to keep the fires up on the small amount of wood he had carried in that morning? His mind leaped ahead to the evening with his strange family . . . Jules, Amy, who should be asleep by now, but would wake for her milk later.

His horse shied violently away from something moving in the road. People passing in the dark, in the sleet. A man. A woman, carrying a child. Poor souls, to be abroad on foot on such a night! But perhaps they were only bound for the nearest farm-house, where a light showed yellow among the bare trees.

His hair was matted with ice, his clothing frozen stiff. Ahead was the cliff, supporting on its crest the village of Little Chimney, dividing at its base where the road passed through its natural gateway. He would soon be at home.

When he had stabled the horse and was approaching the cabin on foot, he heard Amy crying. He hurried, smiling a little as he recognized her "hungry cry," wheedling, cajoling, with a slight catch in the voice. Marie would be warming the milk. He could see just how the baby would take it from the cup, so greedily that her face would show a red crescent at the corners of her mouth when the cup came away empty. He could see her nodding with sleep afterward, like a flower.

A few minutes later he opened the door. His first

thought was for the fire. It had burned out and the room was cold. Amy lay tangled in her covers, wet, chilled and unhappy. He made a new fire, took the child in his arms and sat down with her, close to the hearth, changing her diaper with the skill of long practice.

"Mama," she said.

"Where did Mama go?" he asked the baby as if she could understand and answer. Where on earth could Marie have gone, and why should she take Jules? But of course she couldn't leave the little boy. He would fall into the hearth. Perhaps she went after milk, when Dick failed to arrive as soon as she expected him. She might have done that. But then she would have seen him stabling the horse. She would have come out to the barn and walked home with him. How foolish to leave the baby in such weather, to let the fire go out. He began to be angry and anxious.

The milk was on the table in the pail. He had overlooked it. She must have brought it in and then gone out again. Perhaps after wood. But there was the fresh pile of wood. She had gotten that too.

He put Amy in her crib and went for the pan to warm her milk. On the table, pinned to the wood with his knife, lay a sheet of paper with Marie's wavering handwriting running uphill and down.

"Joe came back. I have to go with him. I will leave Amy and take Jules. I don't want to go."

She had signed her name carefully, *Marie Gagnier,* as the sisters had taught her.

There are caves in the hills of Buffalo County where
no white man has ever been. The Indians know about
them. They have handed the secret of their location
down from one generation to another and it has spread
from tribe to tribe, so that Ojibwa, Sioux, Fox, Winnebago and many other clans have used them through the
centuries. In some such place, Dick thought, Marie
must be living, poor Marie, in her shabby clothing, her
shoes he had cobbled himself, her thin shawl and old
blue bonnet. Where, where? And little fat Jules, bewildered and patient. Where was he?

Dick gave Amy to the care of the Oesterdahls and
hunted day and night. His horse gave out; he went on
foot until the soles of his boots let the stones through.
He climbed the butte-like hills and looked out over the
desolate November world. For days at a time there
was no fire in his cabin. He slept where he found himself when pitch darkness set in, and began again the
next day from that point.

Farmers shook their heads after he left them, indi-
cating their belief that he was "touched." Sheriffs refused him aid, either from the same suspicion, or from
a realization of the hopelessness of his search.

"What, Sir? Trace an Indian in this country?"

He tried to draw a net around them by riding from
town to town until he had described them to villagers
wherever they might pass. Misha Mokwa, Mondovi,
Gilmanton, every tiny hill town knew him in the months
that ran into winter, the ragged, worn, bearded man

who asked for an Indian and a woman with yellow hair. At last the day came when he could go no farther, when he fell and could not get up. A farmer took him back to the Oesterdahls.

As he lay in a clean bed, the tick of corn-husks rustling when he moved, he babbled deliriously, sliding in and out of reality like a swimmer in waves. He called for his mother, for Lucy, and more than once he held long chaotic conversations with Freeman Wills. All the time he was more or less sure that it was neither his mother nor Lucy who bent above him, but someone else. He had forgotten Eva. One day he came out into full consciousness, feeling pure, empty and weak. He was in an upstairs room of the farm-house. A little stove was glowing hot in a corner of the tiny bedroom. Along the wall, opposite the bed, Eva's dresses were hanging and on the lowboy were a girl's hand-mirror, brush and comb. He was in her bed; the hangings were of pink mull.

He raised himself on one elbow, but had not strength to hold himself so. He had been able to see the chair at the head of the bed. Eva's warm wrapper and slippers were on the chair. She had been sitting with him through the nights, those nights when his life had seemed so lightly tethered to his body that the least movement might let it drift away. The tears that fell upon his hand had been Eva's. This moved him, that anyone should care enough about him to weep over him.

He drifted to sleep and woke again to hear a child's voice in the rooms below. Whose child could it be? Slowly he remembered that he had a daughter. But that was the voice of an older child, not Amy's baby cooing and gurgling. Too weak to ponder, he slept again. The waves of unconsciousness were still coming over him at regular intervals, but now they brought sleep, not delirium. Deep, healing sleep, with not even a dream to mar it.

When he woke again, Eva was sitting beside him, holding a plate of food. He tried to smile at her, but she could not see the faint change in the position of his lips, so he gave up the smile and closed his eyes again.

"Come," she said, "open the eyes, nu, and have the nice food."

What she put into his feebly opened mouth was the end of a piece of flat-bread, rolled like a cigar about a section of jelly-like lutfisk.

Dick squirmed away from the plate and held the morsel in his mouth without swallowing it.

"It don't taste so gude, then?" Eva asked, anxiously. She seemed enormous to him, solid of flesh, almost unbearably healthy.

"No," he replied.

"Nuvel! We go back to the soup. We thought maybe you like a change, but you got fond of that soup, ei?"

He tried to understand this remark and gave it up. Outside the window a bright sunlight shone through a constant dripping of water from the eaves. He could see this without turning his head.

"Thaw?" he asked.

"It's the spring. You been sick all winter, Deek."

Dick thought this over in silence, while she put several spoonfuls of soup into his mouth. Out of the muddle of delirious memories, one clear fact presented itself. Marie had not been found. The child began to cry in the downstairs room and he heard Signe's voice hushing it.

"Who?" he said with great effort.

"Amy. Don't you know Amy? It looks like she fell down again. She's pretty smart at walking, though."

When he was well enough to sit in the kitchen, with his bony knees covered by a shawl, he renewed his acquaintance with his child. She had grown amazingly. Her hair, that had been downy and straight, now curled tightly all over her head. She had learned a great many words, but she had forgotten one, too. She never said "Mama." Her looks were like his own, Dick realized, but her hands, even at one year of age, were shapely and graceful, with tapering fingers.

Gunnar Larson had been at the farm twice during the winter and was now repairing Dagmar's house and barn. Dick felt a twinge of jealousy at Eva's interest in him. She had talked her mother into opening Dagmar's chest and taking out enough quilts and sheets to make up the bed in which the old woman had died. All Dagmar's linen was damp with the winter; Eva had gone up on the hill to dry it. She was showing toward Gunnar the same unselfish friendliness she had shown toward Dick, but with a difference, a coquettishness she had never used before. Perhaps she was only growing up, but Dick suspected there was another reason. Eva had been too honest and it had not worked. This time she would be more chary with her affection. Nor did she swing the axe in Gunnar's presence, but contented herself with smoothing and airing the linen.

In April, Signe handed Dick a letter. She made no comment on the fact that it had arrived months earlier, and he said nothing of his surmise when he saw the Trempealeau postmark. It was from a priest who had performed the final absolution for Marie Gagnier who had died "with the wafer between her lips." She was buried at Trempealeau on holy ground, having contracted lung fever from exposure. Her husband and the child Jules had gone on into the Minnesota forest.

He had not seen Marie's dust consigned to dust. For a long time her ghost walked, a reticent ghost that asked little of the living. Mostly he saw her descending into the cave at the Dalles, retreating underground until nothing was left but her pallid face, swimming in the dark.

"My name. I wrote it here. I'm looking for my name."

"Come back, Marie. Sleep above ground, tonight."

"But I wrote my name down there. Down there the wind doesn't blow. You can hear the roots of the trees crying."

8

WHEN DICK CAME HOME to Hampstead Prairie, the roads were full of marching men. Some were the last of the volunteers in the blue uniforms of the Army of the Republic, some were the first of the conscripts in home-made country clothing. They marched southward, often bearing banners with the names of the towns they were leaving behind—Merrilan, Sparta, Black River Falls, Baraboo. Wisconsin was building her contingent of ninety-one thousand men to fight the confederates. The faces and accents were strangely mixed—Swiss, German, Norwegian, Irish, Scotch, English—but they were all Americans now. Dick reined in his horse by the New Glarus Tavern and looked down from the high tavern-yard at the passing ranks in the road below. Young faces, achingly familiar. It seemed to him that he saw in them a composite of his schoolboy friends at Bradford Academy, and he almost cried out as one slender youngster turned in his direction. He had thought for a moment that it was George Lennox, the poet. Then he remembered that George must have aged a little since Academy days. This was only another lad. Seventeen, perhaps, and with those far-seeing eyes of youth.

The ranks were suddenly halted. They marked time, waiting while, from a crossroad, another company poured out into the turnpike. Volunteers, these, resplendent in their new equipment. They brushed shoulders with the boys of the first draft, wheeling around the turn.

"What's your outfit, brother?" a lean young German called to the soldier who had almost knocked him down.

"Stevens Guard. Captain Hamilton commanding."

Strange how they kept cropping up, these sons of Alexander Hamilton's seven sons. In the lead mines, in editor's offices, in politics. This was Roswell, of Richland Center, of whom Dick had heard during Academy days. His men passed by and vanished, drums rolling. The conscripts stopped marking time and began to file past again.

On the pommel of Dick's saddle, Amy sat in a little basket chair he had made. She was nearly three years old now. She twisted her curly head to look up at him and pointed into the ranks below.

"Man, man, man. Sojer. Baby hungry."

"All right," her father said, dismounting, and un-buckling the straps that held her chair, "Baby eat."

He had been called in the first conscription, brought out of hiding like a badger from its hole. A lonely man from the hills finds the light of open country a little

394

hard to bear and Dick felt naked, as if the cliffs had been a cloak and were now stripped away. He was conscious of this feeling, but he was not thinking about himself. It was chiefly of his child he must think now. Suppose he fell in battle. Would she remember him? Would she be glad he had taken her back to his own people, or might she have been happier with the Oesterdahls? He had given her a great deal of freedom there, running about with the geese and chickens, clinging sometimes to Eva's hand, but for the most part untended, rolling and tumbling in the haycocks like a wild thing. Would she suffer from the stricter discipline to which he must take her?

He had written to his parents with no hint of apology for his years of silence, a proud, stiff note. Within two days he had the answer.

"Bring thy little lass and come home."

Ole had given him a horse and saddle. The cabin was closed forever, shuttered again. Nothing he could use there—only a crib, a high chair, a little heap of handmade toys. As he passed through the limestone gateway and looked back at the hill-farm for the last time, he had said to himself:

"Never again. I'll never see this place again." But still he could not believe it.

Mushrooms and grass would sprout from the dirt floor, the fireplace would crumble and the logs decay. What had happened in that cabin might never have happened at all, yet here was Amy to prove it had all been true, and on his watch-chain the pipestone crucifix still hung.

Here was Amy, indeed. She bounced in her wicker chair, she turned and twisted, warm, hungry and alive. Dick took her into the tavern. Amy thought the tavern a fine place like all the rest of the world. The more she saw of life the better it looked to her.

"Good," she said, nodding vigorously as she crammed her mouth with bread and milk. "Good. Baby have more."

No one could resist her. The tavern-keeper broke into chuckles as he wreathed his finger in one of her curls. Women from the other tables gathered around her, admiring her, looking curiously at her father. They were following the troops. They were not the sort of women who love children, but for Amy they became soft, motherly and full of advice. Dick smiled in his beard. No one could tell him how to care for a child, especially his own. Hadn't he washed her clothes, tended her through childish upsets, bathed her, fed her? Dick was sure he could hire out as a nursemaid. He was proud of his accomplishments. What would they say, these solicitous busybodies, if they knew he was having qualms about turning Amy over to his own mother?

For some time he had been wondering uneasily if Ann's baby-tending days were not too long past. She might have forgotten what a three-year-old needs; she might spoil Amy with her kindness, feed her too much

rich food. Then there was the question of obedience.
Dick had trained his daughter to understand "yes" and
"no," and thought he had discovered this remarkable
feat himself. His method of punishment was very effec-
tive. He simply stared at her for a few minutes without
smiling. She would be puzzled, then coaxing, then angry.
In the end she obeyed. He thought his mother ought to
be told about this new method of training a child. And
then he remembered that she had done something of the
sort with him when he was small.

"I suppose no one's indispensable," he said, looking
thoughtfully at the little girl, "Perhaps I'll be the only
one to suffer."

"Sleep," she said. "Baby sleep now."

At noon of the next day they rode into Leeds. The
town had been growing. Beside the tracks of the new
railroad, a row of long warehouses stood from which
a queer, rank odor exuded, filling the streets. From the
open door of one of these buildings men were carrying
packing-cases and loading them into a box-car on a
siding. Dick paused to watch them. Everything about
the operation was unfamiliar to him, but the odor was
tobacco. Riding around the end of the warehouse, he
saw with astonishment the name above the front door:
Thomas Wentworth; Leaf Tobacco.

Though neither Harry nor Gunnar had said a word
about this new venture of his father's, Dick realized
that he himself had seen it beginning when he was still

at home. Tobacco buyers had been coming into the
prairie, trying to interest the farmers in raising the new
crop and Thomas had not turned them away, had listened to them in silence with only an occasional "Aye."
That should have told anyone he was partially convinced. Here, after nearly five years, was the result.
Thomas was on his way to another fortune. Dick felt
an unexpected thrill of pride. A born gambler was
Tommy Wentworth, a man not easily downed.

New stores had been built in Leeds. They stood above
the mud of the street, two stories high. The board sidewalk ran on pilings close to their doors and under the
sidewalk were basement windows where an occasional
opened sash or sound of hammering showed that all
available space was occupied. On bulletin-boards Help
Wanted notices were mingled with the military an-
nouncements of meeting-places for officers, entrainment
points for conscripts and the latest news of victory or
defeat.

Dick rode past the creamery. It was unchanged. Caspar Fletcher looked at him quickly as he passed, decided
he had been mistaken and looked away. Outside the
town the wheel-ruts bent unexpectedly toward the south.
The new road had gone through at last; the trail was
abandoned. It had not yet been fenced off, however,
and only a little grass had grown in its deeply scarred
surface. Dick decided to ride home by the trail. He felt
sore and sensitive still, disinclined to meet friends.

Some of the houses had been moved away from the

trail, leaving yawning cellars and scattered outbuildings. Through thinning trees he could see these houses, half a mile to the south, fronting the state road. The forsaken yards, surrounded by broken picket-fences looked dismal, reminiscent of the irreclaimable past. Compostheaps, grassed over, wells with sweeps high in the air and dangling ropes from which the buckets had been removed, flagstone walks littered with leaves and the silt of rains—they were like his childhood memories, slowly being buried. Then he saw his father's church and the cemetery with its sprinkling of white markers.

The stone church looked almost new. The porch and doors had been freshly painted; the grass clipped. A row of whitewashed stalls had been added to the stables in the rear and a garden walk of English posies led to the graveyard. On the rose window the sunlight gleamed.

He came up the lane toward his father's house and smelled the wood-smoke from the kitchen chimney. The noon dinner must now be finished. Perhaps they were at prayer. Clean, decent, English ways of living seemed to surround him and welcome him home. Ivy, turning red on the limestone walls, white shutters, trimmed hedge; everything was the same until one looked past the barns and saw the two great tobacco-sheds and the acres of newly-harvested fields beyond, ridged with their brown stubble. Proof of the new prosperity, a team of Clydesdales had been added to the farm's supply of horses.

Here was the life against which Dick had cast off the dust of his feet. Well, he had eaten husks, he thought with a last small flicker of bitterness. He told himself that he would not be humble. He had nothing to ask pardon for. The child he was bringing home must be accepted as a priceless treasure, without reservations, or he would snatch her away again, even though he deserted his company to do so. His heart quailed before the thought that Amy might be pitied and shunned. "Born out of wedlock," a good old English phrase. Would they say that about Amy? One person could prevent it. On Hampstead Prairie, Thomas Wentworth could stand like a bulwark between his grandchild and any whispering foe. Dick dismounted and lifted down his sleeping daughter.

In the moment before his parents started up to greet him he had a revelation. Two lonely souls—an aging couple, deserted by their sons. His father had changed the most. The marks of suffering were on his stern face.

"Ah, Dick! The blessed, blessed baby!" Ann Wentworth cried, quite in her old cheerful voice. "Coom, lad, let me 'old her. Her's a little beauty, sure enough."

Thomas took his free hand and wrung it, gravely, saying nothing. He gazed with reverent wonder at Amy, while she was being transferred to his wife's hungry arms.

"Get me the shawl from yon hook, Tommy. 'Tis a mite chilly. We'll e'en put her on the pallet in the window, Dick, till a better bed can be fixed, for we didn't

400

think to see thee till dusk, and so thou's caught us nap-
ping. I had a cousin, Amy, in Dromfield Wodehouse,
lad, though I never told thee, like enough. Her's got the
Bland eyes, I wouldn't wonder, and I can't 'ardly wait
till her opens them. God forgive me for my vanity, Dick,
but I fancy her looks a bit like me, the lamb."

Most of the men had gone to war. Young Sammy
Weymouth had come home from the West, but he
would not stay long. He must go, like the others.
Women milked, harvested, drove the wagons. Thomas,
for all his recovered fortunes, could not hire enough
help and had to work seventeen hours a day. Dick
would have spent his last two weeks in eating and sleeping if nature had been consulted. He was tired to the
very marrow of his bones. He had forgotten the excel-
lence of his mother's cooking and the soft comfort of
his old bed. Yet, when he heard the roosters crowing
and the clatter of breakfast things, his father getting
the milk-pails and lantern ready for the morning milking, he had to bestir himself. Habit was too strong. He
came down at five o'clock on the first morning of his
return and took the pail from his father's hand. They
went out to the barns together.

With a mixture of jealousy and relief he saw that his
mother had not forgotten the least small thing about
caring for a child. In fact she knew a great deal that he
had never learned. His old toys came out of their hiding
places, the building-blocks and tops, the hen on its nest,

the pig-and-trough, the whistles, balls and linen scrap-books that had been forgotten so long. One day he found his mother and daughter playing the game of run-sheep-run, but this time it was Amy whose fat neck was nipped by the wolf. Oh, well! Let the child forget him. He might never come back.

That afternoon his father laid a hand on his arm.

"T' Goldthorpe lad's been and gone, Dick. He's a cast in 'is left eye and thought to keep oot of the draft by that, but 'twas no use."

"They'll be less particular from now on."

"He tried to hire Frank Piper to go in 'is place, but the Piper lad's price were too 'igh."

"You can't blame him for that."

"Five 'undred dollar, it were."

"I suppose a man's life is worth that to him."

Thomas took from his pocket the well-remembered roll of bills. Silently he peeled off ten fifty-dollar notes and held them out with shaking hand.

"No, father, no! I won't buy my way out," Dick said. "Don't fear for me. I'll come back safe and sound. You'll see."

"Aye, well!" his father said, sighing, and putting back the bills.

In Koshkonong Creek his Aunt Jane's mill-wheel still turned, but the old wooden machinery had been replaced by metal until, bit by bit, the whole was new. The house and mill no longer shrieked and lamented while the grain went into the hopper and the stones revolved. The place looked rather forbidding to Dick, partly because he remembered how he had been turned from its door, and partly because his Aunt Jane had forgotten to keep her flower-gardens alive. His cousin Sammy was on the platform, unloading grain, tossing sacks of corn to one side and sacks of wheat to the other, his legs wide apart, his stocky, strong young body balanced against the weight. With one of those flashes of memory Dick sometimes had, he saw a picture from his early childhood, Sam's father standing in front of the congregation at John Hall's house, holding by the hand a young, slim girl, who must have been Aunt Jane.

"Hush!" Harry had said. "Her's getting wedded."

Sammy looked now exactly as his father had looked then.

"Lay off work when you get through unloading, Sam. Give me a half hour."

"Can't do it, Dick. Got a grist to grind."

"No hurry," the farmer said. "I can call back after sundown."

In a short time Sam dusted his hands on his apron, took it off and came down from the platform.

"Place the same, Dick?"

"Pretty much. I can remember when I used to tend you and Lisbeth over yonder in the woods. You were a handful, then."

"That wasn't me. That was my brother who died, I guess. He had my name."

"So he did. Yes, of course. By the time you came, I was too big for baby-tending."

"All the Weymouths look alike and I guess he must have been like me, too. Gives me a queer feeling."

"Yes. A moment ago I remembered your father at your age. He must have been your double."

"He is."

Even as he said it, Sammy tried to catch himself, failed, and gave his cousin a desperate look. His frank, snub-nosed face was not made to conceal a secret.

"Better tell me about it, Sam," Dick said softly. "You found him?"

"God! I thought I'd die before I told."

"It can't hurt anyone to tell *me*. I've got to go in a day or so. You'll feel easier to have shared it."

"I told Ben. That's why he left. He was only staying because he thought he'd get the mill. Lisbeth mustn't know, though. I wouldn't want to do that to her. She worshipped him. Nor Mother."

"You know I won't tell."

"Sometimes I hope they'll take me in the draft as soon as this fall's grain is ground. Sometimes I want to die and let what I know die with me. You don't know what it's like, Dick, to have your own father hate you —want to be rid of you. I saw him before he saw me, and even with another name I knew him. It was like looking in a mirror. Mr. Waters. That's what they called him.

"I walked into a store and there he was, eating a

cracker, sitting on the cracker barrel. That was the
second year out there. I must've been seventeen. He got
white as flour and the freckles all showed, just like on
me.

"I knew, but I didn't know. You can't just walk up to
a stranger with another name and say 'Aint you my
father?' But I knew. I followed him when he went out
the back door. He started to run. Then I was sure. I
went back and asked the store-keeper where he lived
and he told me. Said Mr. Waters had a wife and two
young ones. First I was so sick I thought I'd give up.
You know how it is when you're seventeen. You aint
got hard yet. I'd spent all that money, though, and come
so far from home and been away almost two years. I had
to talk to him. Next day I went to his house and he was
packing up to move. I saw his wife. She wasn't any
older than Lisbeth and they had two babies.

"Well, he saw me, and made some excuse and came
out of the house. 'Let's get away from here,' he said.
'You're Sammy, I suppose.' He still talked like Derbyshire folk, but not much. Just an accent.

"We went off up a hill and sat down. This was outside Sacramento. I'd been in other places too, 'Frisco
and Feather River, trying to find him, and now he was
moving to get away from me. I started to cry but he
didn't do anything nice like take my hand. He just acted
cold and afraid. Said he'd give me some money to go
back home. I said all right, and took the money. I was
mad clear through. I didn't come home. It seemed if I

did, I'd have to tell. I stayed there two more years and every time I got short of money I showed up again and he had to give me more. All that time I was telling Mother I couldn't find him.

"He moved around, but he couldn't leave Sacramento because he had a stake there. Wasn't making much, I guess, but he kept thinking he'd hit it rich. They're all like that out there. Crazy, thinking they'll be rich next week. I just kept bothering him. We hated each other, but we had to talk sometimes and I found out all about him. He ran away with the water and left Hugh Henderson to die. There wasn't enough for two. He didn't dare come home.

"I told him no one would blame him for that. A man wants to live. But after a while it got like a poison in me. I looked too much like him. It seemed I'd be like him in every way if I stayed there, so I tied up with some folks who were going back East. Not many people want to try the mountains again. Most of them go on ships around the Horn or by Panama before they'll take the same trail home. I found a family who knew a better way than the old one by Humboldt Sink and the South Pass. When I went to say goodbye to my father I told him what way I was going and he said 'Fine!' but I could tell by the look in his eyes he didn't mean it. He thought I'd never get back and he almost hoped I wouldn't. I did, though."

Sammy's voice trailed away. He locked his freckled hands about his knee and stared into the woods.

On the last day, Dick put on his uniform and made ready to join his company at Leeds. The blue coat, the flat cap with vizor pulled down, the wide belt, buckled tightly around his waist. He stood by the kitchen window, holding Amy on his left arm. She played with his metal buttons, leaning her head lovingly against the blue drill of his coat. Nothing he wanted to say had been said, as is usual at such times. He could only hope that his parents guessed what was in his mind. All the instructions for Amy's future were unspoken; it seemed futile to plan ahead for a time when he might not be living. He had taken the crucifix from his watch chain and hung it about the baby's neck on a ribbon.

There came a rattle of pebbles in the drive, a sharp "Whoa!" in a stranger's voice. A carriage had driven up outside, the coachman leaped down and opened the door and from it emerged a lady in deepest mourning, black plumes nodding from her bonnet, a black-bordered handkerchief in her hand.

"Let me introduce myself, for I see I have found the proper house, though for the greater part of our journey I was quite uncertain as to the direction, owing to the local brogue which I found almost impossible to . . ."

"Mother . . . Mrs. Hammond," said Dick.

His mother began to bob a curtsey, caught herself in time, dusted a chair with her apron and set it out for the guest. Mrs. Hammond seated herself, took out a small black fan and plied it to and fro.

"I have a message for you Dick, if I may still call

you so, though you have changed so greatly and so much has happened which might have been avoided if we had been granted more wisdom. But who is wise in times of prosperity?"

Dick gazed at her steadily and waited, while Amy tugged at his buttons. Through the window behind her chair, the scattered headstones and the steeple of his father's church made a backdrop for the Colonel's widow.

"I . . . I heard you were free. I knew you had been drafted. I came to tell you . . ." Breaking down suddenly Mrs. Hammond began to sob, to remove her glasses and wipe the bridge of her eagle nose. "Oh, oh, I have ruined my child's life. She is all I have left."

"There, there," Ann Wentworth soothed her, bringing forward a larger handkerchief, but the tears still flowed.

Dick took out his watch and held it in his palm while the last minutes of his hour ticked away. Beyond the darkness of war he saw a light, mellow and peaceful. It was not happiness—not yet—but rather a lantern showing the way to the place where happiness might be found.

"I have so little time . . ." he said. "Tell Lucy I'll come back to her. Nothing has changed me. Nothing can keep me away."

THE END